The
DOG
PARK
Detectives

Blake Mara is a pseudonym of Mara Timon, author of Second World War thrillers *City of Spies* and *Resistance*. She started writing as a child; mostly short stories, but when an idea caught her imagination, she followed one 'what if' after another until her first (and second, and third . . .) novel emerged.

Mara is a native New Yorker who moved to the UK about twenty years ago. When Covid hit, she went cliché and got a pandemic puppy – a miniature dachshund with a massive personality. This opened her eyes to the canine-loving community that blossomed around the local dog park and who became the inspiration for *The Dog Park Detectives*. But while her dog park pack have tackled some local crimes, they haven't found a dead body in the park . . . yet.

For more information, follow Mara at her website or on social media:

www.blakemara.com
X @TheBlakeMara
BlakeMaraAuthor
@mara.timon

Writing as Mara Timon:

City of Spies
Resistance

The
DOG
PARK
Detectives

Blake Mara

**SIMON &
SCHUSTER**

London · New York · Sydney · Toronto · New Delhi

First published in Great Britain by Simon & Schuster UK Ltd, 2024

Copyright © Blake Mara, 2024

The right of Blake Mara to be identified as author
of this work has been asserted in accordance with the
Copyright, Designs and Patents Act, 1988.

1 3 5 7 9 10 8 6 4 2

Simon & Schuster UK Ltd
1st Floor
222 Gray's Inn Road
London WC1X 8HB

Simon & Schuster: Celebrating 100 Years of Publishing in 2024

Simon & Schuster Australia, Sydney
Simon & Schuster India, New Delhi

www.simonandschuster.co.uk
www.simonandschuster.com.au
www.simonandschuster.co.in

A CIP catalogue record for this book
is available from the British Library

Paperback ISBN: 978-1-3985-2423-1
eBook ISBN: 978-1-3985-2424-8
Audio ISBN: 978-1-3985-2425-5

Typeset in Sabon by M Rules

Printed and Bound in the UK using 100% Renewable
Electricity at CPI Group (UK) Ltd

For the Dude, my beloved, stumpy-legged partner in crime. How is it possible that such a small hound can fill my world with so much laughter, love and adventures? You make me smile every day, and you teach me so much about myself. You are far more than my inspiration – you are part of my soul.

Meet THE PACK

Louise Mallory and her dachshund **Niklaus** (**Klaus**) moved to the neighbourhood after her divorce. Klaus is a pandemic puppy, and Louise's introduction to the dog park community. Klaus doesn't think he's a miniature doxie – he thinks he's a slightly short Rottweiler. Louise used to be called the same in the office, but she's now stepping back from the company she founded and looking around for the next challenge.

Irina Ivanova moved into the building next door to Louise about a year ago. Her accent reads like a map of Eastern Europe, but since the Ukrainian War began she plays down the fact that she's from Moscow. She is having an on-off affair with Tim Aziz, referring to him as 'As Is' when they're on, 'As Was' when they're off. She thinks no one knows but everyone does. Despite working in law, her superpower is internet stalking. Her Scottish terrier, **Hamish**, is Klaus's best friend and a canine trash compactor who will eat anything (and then get sick). Irina gets irked when people mistake Hammy for a schnauzer.

Ex-convict **Gav MacAdams** looks older than he is, thanks to a dozen years in prison for GBH. He has a wonky hip but can still handle himself in a fight. He once told his daughter he wanted a Dobermann pinscher but she (mistakenly?) bought him an Affenpinscher, **Violet**. On a good day, Violet looks like a demented Pomeranian; on a bad day, she resembles Gru's dog from the Minions movies. Gav and Violet are usually inseparable, though Gav doesn't like to take her to the pub (she gets ugly when no one gives her beer, and uglier when they do). While part of the dog community, Gav is more comfortable drinking with his East End mates at the George and Dragon pub.

Jake Hathaway just moved in across the canal from Louise with his grey-and-white Staffordshire terrier, **Luther**. Jake is a dark horse, with no online presence. Louise is attracted to him, but can't seem to find out much about him. He's even defied Irina's stalking skills, making them wonder who he really is and what he's doing in the neighbourhood.

Ejiro is a soft-spoken gentle giant from Birmingham, who is often the voice of reason within the Pack. His smart-mouthed partner **Yasmin** is petite and energetic. They have a boxer, **Hercules**, who is ball-obsessed. Ejiro and Yaz live only one street from the park and have been known to take Herc there after dark, often resulting in them having to chase drug dealers out of the enclosure.

Fiona ('Fi') is a good friend of Louise's, and her cocker spaniel, **Nala**, is very fond of (and submissive to) Klaus. Fi is an attractive Australian redhead who doesn't take much seriously, including herself. She's a financial analyst with one of the City firms.

Claire is a journalist for the local rag, *The Chronicle*. She's Irish and has a French bulldog ('Frenchie') called **Tank**. They both have a tendency to brazen their way through stuff, even if Tank sometimes does randomly barf (it's a Frenchie thing).

Meg works as an IT programmer for a finance company in Canary Wharf. She has a brown dapple dachshund called **Tyrion**. Because, you know, what better name would you give a feisty and clever little fiend? All dogs love Meg; she's a goldmine for treats.

Phil Creasy was a local entrepreneur, who was murdered and dumped in Partridge Park. He and his girlfriend, **Grace O'Donnell**, used to live further up the canal, but would occasionally visit Partridge Park with their cockapoo, **Alfie**. When Alfie died of parvovirus, the couple went through a bumpy patch and split up not long afterwards. Phil got involved with dog charities. Grace now has a new cockapoo puppy, **Daphne**, and a new man, **Mike Aspall**.

Tim Aziz and his girlfriend **Sophie** have a Jack Russell called **Loki**. Tim's the local Lothario and, perhaps because of that, Sophie dabbles (a lot) with Botox, fillers and other bits of cosmetic work. She and Irina do their best to avoid each other, a situation made difficult as Hamish and Loki love each other.

Paul and his partner **Ella**, the local French ex-pats, have two black Labrador retrievers: **Bark Vader** and **Jimmy Chew**. Jimmy is notorious for stealing other dogs' toys (and breaking the squeakers). Vader likes mud puddles.

Dr Indira ('Indy') Balasubramanian has a Romanian rescue called **Banjo**. Banjo looks to be part border collie, part corgi and 100 per cent street dog. He's come a long way since he was adopted, but isn't overly interested in engaging with the other dogs.

Outside the Pack (but still of note)

Andy Thompson is a detective constable with the Met Police. He's smart, ambitious and, with his partner **DC Scott Williams**, one of the first detectives on the scene when Phil Creasy's body is found. Andy fancies Irina, despite her blowing hot and cold.

Ivy Woodhouse is known in the area for having poisoned some local animals a few years ago, in an effort to get rid of the foxes that were destroying her garden. She's old and kind of racist.

Gav's mates **Jono** and **Norma** own a café in Poplar and have a mastiff called **Rocco**. While a lot of local mastiffs are owned by neighbourhood thugs (and become part of the problem), Rocco has been trained and socialised, and is quite gentle.

Dr Caroline Aspen, Dr Chetan Singh and **Dr Ben Cooper** are vets at the local surgery, Village Vets. Dr Aspen is also the owner and practice manager. Dr Cooper has a crush on Louise. She hasn't noticed.

 **Barbara** ('**Babs**') **Lane** is Louise's very capable second-in-command at the consultancy firm she founded. **Mandy Barker** is one of the consultants working for Louise. She has a corgi called **Amelia**, who Klaus has a crush on. **Samuel Osman** is one of Louise's protégés.

Annabel works for one of the property management companies developing the area around Partridge Park. She's posh, bolshy and brooks no BS.

Sunday

1

LOUISE

Partridge Bark

Fiona (Nala's Mum)

Anyone want to bet who
was sick first after Girls'
Night last night: Tank or
Claire?

Yaz (Hercules's Mum)

A French bulldog who
has a tendency to barf,
or a journalist who
was drinking **@Irina's**
cocktails? Tough one, but
my money's on Claire.

Claire (Tank's Mum)

Yeah. Yeah, it was me.
I'm not going to make
the recovery walk this
morning. Soz.

Early morning sunlight stabbed my eyes. I adjusted my sunglasses and tightened my grip on Klaus's lead. Took a deep, steadying breath; Claire wasn't the only one hungover.

'You look like something Hamish might have dug up,' Irina Ivanova called from across the street, gesturing at the black Scottish terrier at her side. With her fair hair hanging lank around her round, pale face, in sharp contrast to her designer leggings, top and trainers, Irina looked like a well-dressed zombie.

I knew I didn't look much better, but there wasn't much point in getting dressed up for an early dog walk in Partridge Park. Particularly not after our monthly ladies' night. I pushed my sunglasses further up the bridge of my nose and ushered my dachshund, Klaus, across the street. 'Who else are we waiting for?'

'No one. Although I'm not sure why you're all blaming me, I didn't force you to drink anything,' Irina said, her voice sounding like Eastern European gravel.

As sharp as her words were, there was no malice behind the usual refrain. She smiled as Hamish bypassed Klaus to greet me. Today he wore a blue bandana that read *I'm not an effin' schnauzer.* It was a sore point with Irina, although I suspected that as far as Hamish was concerned, as long as you were a dog or a human, you were cool. Squirrels, geese and cats were a different story.

'To be fair, from a distance . . .'

'Don't start,' Irina grunted.

I fought off a wave of nausea as I leaned down too fast to greet Hamish. 'Good morning, sweetheart,' I said, ruffling his ears. Once my world stopped spinning, I straightened and accepted a travel mug of coffee from Irina. 'Do I need to worry about any "hair of the non-schnauzer dog" in there?'

'Only if Hamish snuck something in, and Scotties don't shed.'

I took a healthy gulp of coffee and winced. If Hamish had snuck something in there, it might have tasted better. I blew on the lid, pretending that the coffee was just hot, instead of hot tar. 'Jesus.'

'You know what to take for the hangover,' she said.

'Yes. A couple of paracetamol, washed down with a Berocca.' I raised the mug in a mock salute. 'Or rocket fuel.'

She shrugged. 'So make your own coffee next time, I was just trying to help.'

Hamish squatted and Irina handed me her mug, pulling a green poo bag from her pocket. 'Enterosgel is the best thing for getting toxins safely out of your body.' She carefully got down on one knee to clean up after her dog. 'Don't make that face, it doesn't taste that bad. But if you want to keep your toxins, fine with me.' While Irina had

5

been raised in Moscow (something she rarely admitted to), she'd spent a few years in the Czech Republic, with a dog that won awards for scavenging. Since then, Enterosgel had become her go-to for anything gastrointestinal, either for dogs or humans.

'I don't dispute how effective it is, just how it tastes. Kind of like the love child of chalk and charcoal.'

Irina smiled and lobbed the bag into a dog waste bin. On the front was a decal with the label 'Poo-Tin' below a picture of Vladimir Putin. The image was faded, but she still gave Mad Vlad a two-fingered salute as the bin clanged shut.

Our dog park pack – 'the Pack' – gave it equal odds that Irina was the one who put the decal there. I'd asked her once and received a lecture about the perils of defacing public property, with just enough sanctimony in her tone to more or less confirm it.

Klaus edged to the side of the path and urinated on a discarded takeaway bag. Now ready to go, he emitted a loud bark to hurry us along.

'Big voice for such a little sausage dog,' a jogger said, passing us. The guy was in his mid-thirties and up far too early on a Sunday morning to have that sort of energy.

'Don't tell him that.' I forced a smile. 'He thinks he's a slightly short Rottweiler.'

The jogger laughed and disappeared round a bend in the path. We entered the park, automatically surveying the area. The litter levels weren't too bad, and there weren't many other people around. It was even early for most of the Pack to walk their dogs. It was low risk, so when

Klaus looked up at me with liquid eyes and bounced his front paws off my shins, I gave in to his plea to be let off the lead.

'Fine,' I said, unclipping him. 'But behave.'

Klaus jumped on Hamish and in moments they were one pile of dark fur, rolling on the grass as Hamish tugged at Klaus's ear while Klaus playfully took hold of Hamish's beard. Business as usual.

My phone buzzed twice. Swiping past the low battery warning, I glanced at the screen.

Partridge Bark

Meg (Tyrion's Mum)

By the way, does anyone know what was happening in the park at 3:30 in the morning? Tyrion was going nuts at the balcony door.

Paul (Bark Vader and Jimmy Chew's Dad)

Same with Vader and Jim. I thought it was Ella, but she was only snoring on the sofa. I looked outside but couldn't see anything. It took ages for them to quiet down. I cannot believe she slept through it.

'After all the cocktails I drank last night, Klaus could have been having a rave in the living room, and *I'd* have slept through it.' I replaced the almost-flat phone in my pocket and pulled out an orange-and-blue rubber ball. I threw it into the middle of the field, watching the dogs scramble after it. Hamish was faster, snatching the ball and prancing about, but Klaus was stealthy. Seconds later, he executed a ten-point 'sausage snatch' and, with the ball in his mouth and his ears flapping in the wind, sprinted towards us.

Suddenly he stopped. Dropped the ball and cocked his head to the side. His hind legs moved, slowly rotating him until his nose pointed towards the long grass fenced off between the edge of the park and the road.

Hamish looked between the ball and the long grass a couple of times. Then he started to run.

'Not the long grass,' I warned Klaus. 'You know you're not allowed there.'

It was a canine minefield of discarded chicken bones, toxic litter and foxtails. You'd think those weeds wouldn't pose any danger, but if their seeds got stuck in an ear or a paw, it meant a painful (and expensive) trip to the vet. So far, Klaus had managed to stay off that list, and I preferred to keep it that way.

The dogs ignored us and ran towards it, their short legs

pumping. Klaus's tail pointed straight back, his back legs moving together so that from behind he almost looked like a hopping bunny, but at that moment there was nothing cute or funny about it.

I whistled for him to return, but all I could see was his black-and-tan bottom as he sprinted away.

'Hamish! *Idi syuda!* Come back here!' Irina called out. 'Three! Two! One!' She dropped a handful of treats at her feet. But as high value as the treats were, the dogs ignored us and kept on running into the grass.

Something felt off; Klaus was a mama's boy. He *always* came when I called. And I'd never seen another dog as food-obsessed as Hamish. Something was wrong.

Terrified, I started to run. 'NIKLAUS!'

Klaus passed through the gap in the wire fence enclosing the long grass.

The right thing to have done would have been to turn around and run in the opposite direction. Or have Irina try the three-two-one trick again. But instinct made me sprint faster. My breath escaped in short pants, and I grabbed a post at the entrance to the long grass, using it to catapult myself into the area where I'd last seen Klaus and Hamish. Both stood with their front paws firmly planted, barking at something that was not barking back.

I dove forward – ignoring the weeds cutting my legs – and reached for my dog. Klaus evaded me twice before I could grab him. With one hand clamped on his collar, I lunged again, capturing Hamish and pulling him close enough to trap him between my knees. I clipped on Klaus's lead and waited for Irina to arrive.

'Was that really necessary?' I wheezed at Klaus. My eyes streamed, and only now did I realise that I'd dropped my glasses somewhere along the way. 'You, my love, have lost off-lead privileges. Again.'

Klaus didn't appear to care. He was squirming and barking at a threat I still couldn't see.

Irina's shadow fell over me, and I passed Hamish back to her, watching as she yanked his mouth open and fished around the edges. 'What have you eaten now, you freaky little scavenger?' She threw whatever she'd taken from Hamish deeper into the grass. 'Yuck.'

Looking disgusted, she wiped her hands on her leggings. 'What are they barking at?'

'I don't know. Dead rat?'

Irina tilted her head from one side to the other, considering it. 'Well, they *were* bred to hunt rodents.'

I didn't dispute Klaus's prey drive – he went nuts when he saw a squirrel – but so far, he hadn't come close to catching one. Thank God.

I glared at him. 'Will you stop howling, for heaven's sake? My hangover is killing me.'

Without sympathy, he squirmed, still fixated on the long grass. I followed his gaze and felt stomach acid burn its way up my throat.

'Irina,' I choked, scrambling back and falling onto my bottom, with Klaus clutched to my chest. 'Call 999.'

'999?' She looked up and blinked. 'For a dead rat?'

In a voice two octaves higher than normal, I squeaked out, 'It's not a dead rat.'

Half hidden in the grass, amid poppies, cornflowers and

discarded crisp bags, clouded blue eyes stared at me from a grey, dead face.

Irina stood and followed my gaze. 'Oh, my—' She raised her free hand to cover her mouth as her stomach audibly rebelled.

'Don't get sick here. Forensics—'

She staggered out of the long grass – holding Hamish in one arm – and vomited into a nearby bin. 'God.'

'I'm almost out of battery,' I said once she stopped heaving. 'Pull yourself together and call 999. *Now.*'

2

LOUISE

Partridge Bark

Paul (Bark Vader and Jimmy Chew's Dad)

While **@Ella** is snoring like a chainsaw, **@Louise** and **@Irina** have found something in the long grass. Rat? Fox? Something more interesting? Hopefully nothing that needs to be sent to the labs for testing 😊 LOL

My phone buzzed, showing one last message before the screen went blank.

Paul and Ella lived in one of the new builds on the far side of the road, overlooking the park, and their balcony was easy to spot. Ella's bright red geraniums hung from planters fixed to the railings. Between Bark Vader's ball obsession and Jimmy Chew's love of anything remotely edible, Ella was in a constant state of replacing geraniums and window boxes. In the battle of woman vs Labrador retrievers, the dogs were winning.

Paul leaned through a gap in the foliage and waved. This morning he wore a red T-shirt, not caring (or noticing) that it clashed with the Hawaiian print pyjama bottoms that I knew featured photos of Vader and Jimmy. The jammies had been a gag gift last Christmas and made him pretty hard to miss.

Also hard to miss were the big black dogs beside him. Vader lay at his feet, while Jimmy stood on his hind legs, taking advantage of Paul's distraction to chomp on a geranium. Paul gestured towards his dogs, silently explaining the joke. *Send it to the labs*, he mimed. *Labrador retrievers. Get it?*

I had no idea how the couple coped with one, much less two, large and quite frankly bonkers dogs in a small flat.

'It's a miracle Ella didn't pitch Paul over the balcony the 2,000th time he made that joke,' I said.

'They're French,' Irina responded, as if that was reason enough. 'But at least he isn't accusing me of giving Ella alcohol poisoning.' Her fingers were poised over her phone screen.

'Don't say what we found in the chat. Any mention of a dead body, and it'll be a zoo here in moments. Once the police arrive, that dead man is their problem, not ours.'

'Ugh. We have to stay?' She looked at the sky and sighed. 'Of course we have to stay. Why couldn't Paul or one of the others have found him? He could probably see the dead guy from up there.' She shoved her phone into a pocket on the side of her leggings and waved away a jogger. 'Ghouls.'

Klaus's bark subsided into an unhappy whine. 'You're not going back there,' I told him and turned my back on the long grass, doing my best to keep the nausea at bay. It didn't work; every time I closed my eyes, I saw the dead man staring at me. I imagined I could even smell him, although the morning air was crisp.

Irina scraped her hair into a topknot and sighed. 'What's taking them so long? The kids'll start showing up soon for their football games.'

'Welcome to East London.' I shrugged, as if I hadn't been wondering the same.

Five minutes became ten and dragged to fifteen before the Emergency Response Team arrived, lights flashing. In short order, two men wearing police caps appeared on the sidewalk on the other side of the overgrown hedge.

'Here come the police,' Irina murmured.

They strode into the park, identically clad in dark trousers, white shirts and walkie-talkies on the left shoulder of their stab-proof vests. Probably a staple for any cop in East London.

Their eyes latched on to us in moments. 'Are you the

ones that found the body?' the first man said, flashing a warrant card but not introducing himself.

'Yes.' I pointed towards the long grass. 'In there.'

'Technically the dogs found him, not us,' Irina said, as one of the men stepped into a white paper boiler suit and booties and moved towards the area. 'I thought only the forensic people wore those.'

The officer in front of us gave her a steady look until she added, 'He's dead.'

'No one else?' his partner asked. When I stared blankly at him, he elaborated, 'Only one body?'

Panic bubbled through my veins. 'We didn't think to check,' I whispered, staring at a wide-eyed Irina. 'Oh my God, what if someone else was in there? Maybe we could have helped them—'

'You did the right thing, you called 999,' he said. 'Wait here, the detectives will want to talk to you.' He put on his PPE and moved quickly to join the other man, searching through the long grass.

'We would have messed up the crime scene,' Irina whispered to me. 'Maybe more than we already did.' Her shrug was casual, but I suspected she was every bit as upset as I was.

A few moments later, when it looked like they hadn't found anyone else, they cordoned off the area with blue-and-white police tape.

People were already gathering in small groups, like sharks sensing blood in the water. Irina's phone buzzed a few times but neither of us dared look.

A car parked on the street outside the park entrance

and two plain-clothed men emerged, one with a camera slung over his shoulder. They looked to the white-clad response team wading through the long grass, who then pointed to us.

A pair of joggers slowed down, curious, but these men – the detectives, I guessed – walked past them, waving them on.

This second pair separated; the older one stepped into a white bunnysuit of his own, snapped a few pics of us and approached the long grass, taking photographs of the scene. The younger man held up a warrant card and introduced himself. 'I'm Detective Constable Andrew Thompson.' He was tall, with blond curls, a fresh face and a surprisingly deep voice. If I had to guess, I'd say he was maybe early thirties. About Irina's age. He wore jeans, a white shirt open at the neck and a light blazer. A small rectangular device was fastened to the breast pocket, which had to be a body camera.

'That's DC Williams.' He pointed to the other man he'd arrived with, who stood with hands on hips, still trying to convince the joggers that there was nothing to see. The first team moved further out, sweeping the area.

The park was getting busier, and more people seemed to be finding new interest in this particular corner, which was mostly used by the dog people. Some of them did have dogs, but the proportion was all wrong. 'Too many people think local crime is a spectator sport,' I said to myself, aware that I was focusing on everything but what we'd already seen.

'Williams can handle it,' DC Thompson said. He

touched the device, letting us know that we would be recorded, then asked, 'Can you tell me what happened?'

I stared at him, watching his mouth move, but not registering the words.

'What time did you – and your dogs – find the deceased?'

'Twenty-four minutes ago,' I said, my eyes on the street. A third vehicle flashing blue lights had stopped. A man and a woman got out and split up. The man knocked on a nearby door, while the woman moved up the street, her eyes scanning each building. For what? Blood? Doorbell cameras? 'We called 999 as soon as we saw him. What are they doing?' I asked, pointing at the two officers moving up the street.

'Their jobs, ma'am. Did you see anything suspicious before then?'

'Before we found him? No,' Irina said.

The detective looked at me. 'And you?'

I shook my head. 'Me? No. But I understand there was a commotion around here late last night.'

Irina gave me a sideways glance, while the detective asked, 'What sort of commotion?'

'Sorry, I didn't hear it, but the others mentioned that something set the local dogs off. They all started barking around 3:30 a.m.'

He raised a brow. 'The others?'

'It was posted in our WhatsApp chat,' Irina explained.

From his expression, I realised that we weren't making sense. 'We have a WhatsApp group for the locals with dogs. The dogs that live next to the park started barking around 3:30. Can you check CCTV to find out what happened?'

Thompson held up a finger and turned away from us, speaking quietly into a radio. The man at the door glanced over and gave him a thumbs-up.

They're narrowing the timeframe, I realised.

'That's what Grant is checking for.' Thompson answered my question, gesturing to the woman.

'London is famous for its "ring of steel" CCTV cameras,' Irina was saying. 'Presumably it includes more than the doorcams that the public set up themselves? Or does even the ring of steel shy away from this part of town?'

If the detective was offended, he didn't let it show. He turned towards me and asked, 'Can you show us the messages?'

'My phone's out of battery. Irina?'

She gave an exaggerated sigh and moved closer to the detective. Tilting her head almost coquettishly, she scrolled past the messages speculating as to what we might have found. 'There, see – something happened at 3:30.'

DC Thompson took several photos of the chat. I hoped Irina hadn't scrolled too far up; there were pictures from last night's party shared in the chat that she probably wouldn't want him to see.

'Did you touch anything?'

We exchanged a glance. 'We tried not to,' I said.

'But . . . ?' DC Thompson prompted.

Irina shrugged, and the neckline of her loose jumper edged down a bit. If I hadn't known better, I'd have sworn that she was flirting with the young detective. Over the body of a dead man.

'We both grabbed the pole when we entered the long

grass,' she explained to him. 'Everyone does. If you dust that for prints, you'll end up with a more accurate list of who lives around here than the last census.'

'And . . .' I prompted.

'And I pulled something from my dog's mouth,' she added, giving me a chilly look from the corner of her eye. 'I threw it further into the grass.'

'What was it?'

'I don't know. A bit of fabric, maybe?' Irina shrugged again and her jumper eased further down. 'I fish things out of his mouth all the time.'

For a moment, DC Thompson looked at a loss. He shook his head and opted for a different line of questioning. 'Did you recognise the man? Did he look familiar?'

'No,' Irina said.

'No,' I echoed when he looked at me, adding, 'but I didn't get a good enough look.'

The detective sighed. 'Let me take your details. You'll both need to make a statement, and we might need to take fingerprints and DNA samples – to exclude you, of course.'

More cars parked on the street. Another, wider, perimeter was set up around the long grass. Inside, a couple of new arrivals unpacked a tent and set it up over the body.

Another man emerged from a battered sedan. He yawned and ran his fingers through untidy silver hair. I imagined he was here to confirm that the man in the long grass was indeed dead.

I could have saved him the trip; that guy had been dead for hours.

As intriguing as it might have been to decamp to one

of the balconies and watch how these things unfurled in real life, this wasn't a TV show, and the dead man wasn't a dummy or an actor. Whoever he was, he deserved better than to be made into a public spectacle.

I answered the remaining questions as best I could, embarrassed by how often I had to say 'I don't know'. With the dead man's eyes haunting me, all I wanted to do was go home and take a shower.

Finally, DC Thompson tucked his notebook away in a pocket. 'Thank you for your time,' he said. He gave us both his card. 'Call me if you think of anything else.' Irina held his eyes as she hung on to the tip of his card a second or two longer than necessary, prolonging what already felt like an awkward moment.

She cocked her head at him and, if it weren't for her dark glasses, I'd swear she was batting her lashes at him. 'See you tomorrow.'

I held Klaus in my arms until we were out of his earshot. 'See you tomorrow?' I repeated, staring at my friend.

'We need to give a statement, remember?' she reminded me, in a voice that held less innocence than Rasputin's.

'I thought he was videoing us.'

She brushed that aside, as if going down to the station and repeating ourselves was standard procedure. And maybe it was.

She glanced over her shoulder, where people still lingered near the tent the police had erected over the body and shook her head.

'Ghouls.' I echoed Irina's comment, half considering her part of that group.

'Do you want to stop for a coffee? The Nest should be open by now.'

The Nest, officially the Partridge Park Café, did make exceptional coffee, but all I wanted was to go home. 'You stop, if you like. I just want to get home.'

'It's not like an American to turn down a coffee,' Irina teased. I knew she was trying to lighten the mood, but just then a large van braked outside the park, unmarked save for 'Private Ambulance' written on the side in small letters. I didn't want to see the body photographed. Didn't want to see it placed on a gurney and taken away, wrapped in a bag. I didn't want to stay near the park any longer than I had to.

'I don't envy the forensics team going through the long grass,' Irina said. Her eyes lit up with an idea. 'Do you think they'll bag all the rubbish they find?'

'If they do, it'll be the one good thing to come of it.'

We left the park and walked home along the canal in silence. 'How's your hangover?' she asked as we entered the iron gates to the converted warehouse complex we lived in.

'I lost it somewhere between chasing Klaus across the field and hearing you vomit in the bin.'

'Good.' We stopped at the door to my building. 'Will you be okay?'

'Better than the guy in the park. I'm going to have a hot shower, and as soon as the sun is over the yardarm, I might well pour myself a very large G & T.'

'Sun over the ... What does that mean?'

'When it's late enough that I won't feel like an alcoholic, day-drinking after a big night out.'

Irina smiled. 'Hair of the dog.' Her face had reverted back to its usual assured expression, but I wasn't sure how unaffected she really was.

'What do you think happened to him?' I asked.

She looked into the distance for a moment or two, visibly choosing her words. Then she sighed. 'I don't know. I'll do what I can to help the police, of course. But it's not my job to solve the crime. Not yours either, Lou.'

Her stern tone carried an underlying message: *Don't get obsessed with this, Lou.*

'I know,' I said, waving at her and opening the door. I let Klaus off his lead as soon as we reached my flat, plugged in my phone, took a shower and brewed some coffee.

Taking the cafetière and a large mug onto the balcony, I set them down on the table. Instead of lying on the dog bed beside my chair, Klaus jumped, pawing at my knee until I picked him up and settled him on my lap. He licked my neck and ear, circled a couple of times, then curled up with his head on my forearm.

My phone buzzed again and again, as Paul updated the group from his own balcony. The body had been taken away, and a couple of uniforms remained at the scene, keeping everyone outside the perimeter. The rest of the police were walking around the park and streets surrounding it, looking up, looking down, checking out the rubbish bins and knocking on doors. With each buzz my nerves stretched tauter, until I shut the damned thing off.

'Sweet boy,' I murmured, dropping a kiss onto Klaus's smooth head. He snuffled some sort of assent and closed his eyes.

When my hands began to shake, I blamed it on the caffeine and switched to decaf, even though I knew that wasn't the problem. For the next hour or two, we stayed like that, watching people going about their business. I fancied that I could tell the difference between those going shopping, going to brunch and going to church, as if nothing had happened a short walk away.

My eyes locked on a man wearing dark glasses and a cap, who crossed in front of my building with a white Jack Russell Terrier on a lead. He was buzzed into the adjacent building and swaggered inside.

'Aw, nuts,' I muttered to Klaus. 'Irina and Tim are back on again.'

Moments later, Tim's Jack Russell, Loki, appeared on Irina's balcony alongside Hamish. Klaus lifted his head from the mat beside me and barked a greeting to his friends.

'Quiet, Klaus. Irina's doing her best to keep her mind off the morning's events. I get that. I just wish she'd find someone single so I don't have to avoid looking Tim's girlfriend in the eye.'

Klaus didn't seem to care, pawing my leg three times, requesting to be let down. He did a full body shake, starting at his nose and ending at his tail. Placing his front paws on the edge of a planter to get a better view, he continued barking.

If Irina thought she was keeping the affair under wraps, then she'd failed to consider that Klaus was alerting everyone to the two dogs on her balcony and that half the neighbourhood knew who owned the Jack Russell.

Her problem, not mine.

I looked at the dregs of coffee in my cup, went inside and mixed myself that gin and tonic.

Reclaiming my seat, I watched a white storage van park on the other side of the canal. The buildings on that side were part of the same complex I lived in, and I'd never seen the man or the grey-and-white Staffordshire terrier that met the van.

'Looks like we've got new neighbours, Klaus.' His ears perked up, and he barked a greeting to the Staffie. Hamish and Loki chimed in, completing the chorus.

As the driver began to unload the van, the man turned, locating the dogs. His gaze found mine and seemed to hold it for a few moments. And then, without a backwards glance, he picked up a box and, with the driver, began to ferry packing crates and furniture inside.

3

GAV

Gavin MacAdams held a hand up in farewell and pushed through the George and Dragon's door into the cool evening. He turned left and moved through the remains of the street market. During the day it bustled with stands selling fruit and veg, fish, carpets and cheap school uniforms. But now, not far off 10 p.m., only the stalls' metal skeletons remained; anything that could be stolen or broken had long since been packed up for the night.

There had been only one topic of conversation at the pub that evening: the dead man found in Partridge Park. Gav had nursed his beer and listened to his mates' theories. The consensus was that it was gang related, but Gav wasn't so sure. A gang thing, you leave the body where it drops, or pose it somewhere for effect. You don't lob it over the fence into a park, like an old McDonald's bag.

Even if the fence was only some four and a half feet high around there.

Whoever did it was an amateur. Someone who killed a guy and had to get rid of the body fast. Someone, maybe with some of their crew, fit enough to hike the stiff over a fence, in the middle of the night, and not be caught.

That was clear enough to Gav. He and his mates weren't strangers to East London, or to crime, often joking that even CCTV was afraid to be there. But this felt different, and you didn't need to be Sherlock Holmes to realise that none of them had a clue who the dead guy was, why he was killed, or why he was dumped in the park.

And *that* spoke volumes. Not much happened in the neighbourhood without Gav or one of his mates knowing about it.

The night was quiet. The cars on the high street were few and far between, and the slap of his footsteps on the pavement had a pleasing, if uneven, rhythm, the echoes bouncing off the silent buildings like a soft bass. Most people avoided the market square at night, but Gav had grown up here. Knew the area. Knew the players. And the players knew Gav, at least by reputation. The sensible ones steered clear of him.

He paused to rub his hip, briefly glancing around. The ache was a constant companion, but one that he'd learned to deal with. Prison had taught him never to show pain.

The air changed, became dense. Charged. Gav kept his shoulders loose, his pace steady. He couldn't see whoever it was, but he could *feel* them, watching him.

Walk too fast, and you're a target.

Too slow, and you're also a target.

Truth was, they already had their eye on him, he knew that. Maybe because he was asking questions in the pub about that dead body. Maybe because he looked old. Who knew?

He kept walking, didn't let them know he knew they were there. That was the trick. That way they didn't know you were expecting it, right? That way, you were ready when they came at you, and *that* gave you an edge. Sort of.

He looked around again, this time with sharper eyes. It didn't take long to blink the four of them into view. Faces covered by bleedin' hoodies. Young thugs, who thought they were the real deal, leaning against a closed shop that advertised jellied eels and faggots.

The old and the new.

Only, the old-timers, they were *hard*. These kids, they shoved crap up their noses, smoked weed that stunk like shite and clung to them, like some sort of badge that they were off their heads.

Their clothes were baggy, knock-off brands that were maybe bought from one of the stalls. That wasn't an issue, Gav was all for supporting the local entrepreneurs and all that. Why not? He knew most of them.

One of the kids moved forward. He was small and skinny. He took a swig from a bottle of cheap vodka and passed it to the guy behind him. 'Where you goin', old man?' he said.

'I don't want trouble.' Gav raised his hands, keeping his knees soft. The hip was another matter; it didn't always do as it was told.

Don't let me down now.

Skinny Boy's head tilted to one side then the other, weaving back and forth. *Like a bloody cobra*, Gav thought. *Only, a cobra would be smarter.*

'Don't matter what you want,' the lad said.

'You going anywhere nice?' another boy said, stepping forward. 'Mebbe we can come along.'

Their accents, the way they spoke wasn't Cockney. Wasn't East London. New blood to the area maybe, with something to prove. He'd seen groups of them wandering around. Getting pissed on the corner outside News-N-Booze and harassing or attacking anyone they didn't like the look of.

He calculated the odds. There were four of them and one of him. In this part of the market there was no CCTV, and even the police stayed away.

He wasn't a fool; he knew he wasn't a young man anymore. But he also knew he wasn't as old or unfit as the kids thought.

Gav glanced beyond them, to his car parked across the street. He kept a crowbar in the boot, just in case. It couldn't be more than fifty yards away, but that was fifty yards too far. He'd have to make do.

He shifted as the boys tried to circle around behind him. Gav kept his hands up, palms facing out. 'It's not worth it. Just walk away.'

Skinny Boy stomped forward, laughing.

Dumb kid, Gav thought and loosened his body. One thing he'd learned, long before he was sent inside, was that people saw what they wanted to see. Even more so when they were with their mates and showing off to each other.

Gav might look old, he might have a dodgy hip, but he wasn't feeble. He bent away from the kid's lunge and grabbed the bottle of vodka, breaking it on the side of a metal post. His eyes stayed fixed on the boys as the broken glass reflected weak light from the tired streetlamps.

Ignoring the pain in his hip, he slid to the left, coming around the big kid that stunk of skunk and cheap cologne. One muscular arm held the kid against Gav's chest while he touched the broken bottle to his throat.

Gav muttered a curse as all the warm fluffy crap he'd had to spout at his parole hearing dissipated. He looked at the remaining boys one by one, finally alighting on the leader of the pack; Skinny Boy.

His hand tightened on the neck of the bottle. 'You really shoulda picked an easier target, *mate*.'

Monday

4

LOUISE

Partridge Bark

Claire (Tank's Mum)

Careful, guys. T and I were walking yesterday and saw a bunch of kids mug a girl. They stole her phone and ripped the headphones off her head. Tank started barking so they definitely saw us. And while Tank looks like a ... tank, he's all mouth and no trousers. When they started towards us, we ran into a shop and

33

waited there until some guy offered to walk us home.

Ejiro (Hercules's Dad)

Are you OK?

Claire (Tank's Mum)

Yeah. I've been writing about that sort of thing happening around here for the paper, but didn't expect it to happen to us. At the time, I was just wondering if they chased me because they knew who I was, or because I was a single woman walking her dog. It was only when I got home that I wondered if they might have been involved in the guy getting killed.

Yaz (Hercules's Mum)

Are you OK? Herc and I had to chase drug dealers

out of the park again the other day. Maybe it was the same group of kids? I got a pic of them that I'll DM you.

Fiona (Nala's Mum)

OMG, that's horrible! BTW, I saw your article about the guy in the park this morning, @**Claire**. It didn't say if the man's death was related to those gangs.

Claire (Tank's Mum)

Coz we don't know. Yet.

Ejiro (Hercules's Dad)

And we can't jump to conclusions. We don't know the guy. Could be anything. Glad you and Tank are OK, Claire, and good reporting. But I think we all need to be more careful, at least

until we figure out what's
going on.

The estate agent had called the neighbourhood 'up and coming' when I moved here from West London, fresh after a messy divorce. What they didn't tell me was how much the area resisted change and how over the years it had become an uneasy mix of the old and the new. The professionals who'd moved there, a good percentage of whom were internationals, liked the proximity to Canary Wharf. The Cockneys would have liked things to stay the way they were back in the '60s and '70s. Add in a couple of ethnic communities and, of course, the gangs, and you had the eclectic mix that lived near Partridge Park.

Even the architecture was a cacophony of council houses, pretty new builds and the odd remaining pre-war-warehouse conversion.

On most days the neighbourhood operated under a tacit détente, with each group keeping to their own circles. The exception to the rule was the enclosed dog area at the back of Partridge Park. Here, anyone with a dog was welcome, as long as the dog was reasonably well behaved and well socialised.

Given the amount of time we spent there, the dogs had become friends. So had the humans, and the Pack made some of the dicier aspects of the neighbourhood bearable.

The day was already warm as Klaus and I joined the throng of joggers, dog walkers and a few suits heading towards the park; the scene was so *normal* that it was easy to forget that anything untoward had happened there over the weekend.

Until you noticed the police tape flapping in the breeze near the long grass, or the bored-looking PC standing next to it.

'Someone dumped a dead body there yesterday.' An elderly woman was sitting on a bench nearby. The two Yorkshire terriers at her feet yapped a greeting. As usual, all three were poured into coordinating animal-print ensembles. Today was cheetah. The old woman lit a cigarette and exhaled smoke over her shoulder. 'They moved the body right quick, but the CSI people were here until late.'

'SOCOs,' I corrected her automatically. 'Scene of Crime Officers.'

'Whatever.' She dismissed the words with a wave of her cigarette.

Klaus gave each Yorkie a gentle sniff, then weed on a discarded can.

'Foolish to dump him there,' the woman said, scooping up one of the dogs and settling him on her lap. 'If it were me, I'd have chucked him into the canal. That water'd have him down to the bone in no time.'

'Good to know.' I kept my voice even, trying not to imagine her dragging two yipping lapdogs and a dead body down to the canal.

The woman's smile revealed a few missing teeth, like an ageing alligator, and I reconsidered. In her heyday ... maybe she could have. But if she had, I didn't want to know. I bade her a swift goodbye, urging Klaus forward.

He sniffed the posts at the park's entrance, but didn't linger, pulling me towards the friends he saw playing near the red-brick café. I waved at a few familiar faces sitting at The Nest's outside tables and stepped into the queue behind a tall Black man with a brown boxer dog at his side.

'Heard you had a bit of excitement yesterday,' he said in a deep voice seasoned with a Brummie accent.

'Hey, Ejiro.' I leaned over to pat his dog. 'Hey, Herc.'

Hercules was more interested in Klaus. They started circling each other, sniffing each other's butts while Ejiro and I moved with them, keeping the leads from tangling.

'You think the police know who did it?' he asked, passing his lead under mine and looking over his shoulder to give the barista his order. Herc's lead was black and industrial strength. Klaus's was orange, with cartoon hedgehogs marching along its length. I wondered if his friends made fun of it.

'Not as far as I know.' I moved to the counter and ordered a latte.

'You found him, didn't you?' a different voice interjected. Tim Aziz was sitting by the window, sunglasses firmly in place, black hair glistening in the sunlight. He was carefully dressed to look casual, but everything on him was designer and current. Tim liked the good things in life. Which at the moment included Irina, as well as the young woman sitting across from him.

Sophie was young, pretty – no stranger either to beauticians or to the Botox needle – and officially Tim's partner, although for how much longer was anyone's guess. Her rigorously maintained exterior hid a brighter brain than her boyfriend had, and she had to know that he was cheating on her.

'Was he still warm?' Tim continued. 'Did the foxes get him?'

'Tim!' Sophie glared at him, but one manicured hand dropped below the table to pat Loki. Maybe that was it: she stayed with him because of his dog.

'Don't be an arse.' Ejiro wasn't one to mince words. He picked up his coffee and mine. Once we got outside, he unclipped Hercules and gave the signal that it was fine to have a run. I bent to unhook Klaus from his own lead. My fingers froze and I fought a wave of apprehension.

Clouded blue eyes . . .

I shook the image away and undid the clasp. Klaus bounded after Hercules, barking happily, and I took my coffee from Ejiro. 'You saw the article?'

'*The Chronicle* said that the dead man was found by two women walking their dogs,' he said. 'No name, no photo of the guy. Thought they might be playing their cards close to their chests.'

'Maybe,' I said, but I wasn't so certain.

Ejiro continued, 'They included an appeal for more information, although I imagine that's routine.'

'London has one of the best CCTV set-ups in the world.' I remembered Irina's phrase. 'A ring of steel around the capital. Even if it doesn't extend this far east, there's got to be *something*. You think they'll bother to check it?'

'Maybe.' His big shoulders lifted. 'I hope so. If it's not disabled, they might at least be able to isolate the car that dumped him.'

Disabled.

'Anything's possible,' he continued, answering the question I hadn't voiced aloud. 'You know what some of the kids are like here. I'm assuming he was dumped by car simply because no one would be stupid enough to carry him that far. Too risky.' He tilted his head to the side. 'Although I suppose he could have died in the park and maybe you found him where he fell in the grass.'

'I want to believe it was an accident,' I said. 'But . . .'

'Yeah. But.'

Another dog came near, but veered towards the bushes. In his previous life Banjo had been a street dog in Romania, and while he was friendly enough, he wasn't interested in interacting with the other dogs. His owner, Indy, gave a half-hearted wave, before cursing and going down on one knee to fish something out of his mouth.

'Well, even if they don't find the murderer's car – and I know this is terrible to say – maybe they'll catch the boy racers on CCTV and do something about them. One of these days they're going to hurt someone,' I said.

'They already have those reg plates. Yaz mails videos of them racing to the cops, the council, whoever she can, on a regular basis.'

I didn't doubt that; Ejiro's partner was usually on top of these things. I tilted my head, teasing out a thought. 'Do you think they might have hit the guy? Dumped his body afterwards?'

'The fence at the edge of the park is what, four and a half feet? Five? And then there's the hedge next to it. It'd take a bit of muscle to get a dead body over that. Did he look like he'd been hit by a car?'

'I don't know. I don't think so. At least, not from what I saw.'

'Okay. I could be wrong, but I don't think a hit-and-run would have stopped and risked getting caught.' He took a sip of coffee and seemed to consider options. 'And they wouldn't have dumped his wallet in a rubbish bin further up the street.'

'They found his wallet?'

'Just a guess, Lou. Someone saw them pull something from a bin. I'd guess a wallet or a phone. Good thing it happened on a Sunday and the council doesn't collect rubbish over the weekend, right?'

'Right . . .'

'But it really could be anything. Maybe he overdosed and whoever he was with got spooked.'

'I wouldn't know the signs of an overdose if they smacked me in the face. Vomiting, I guess? Froth around his mouth?' I'd seen that on TV or in a film. 'Truth is, the only vomit I saw was Irina's, and the guy's face looked fine.'

Dead, but fine. I shuddered.

'Bruising?'

'Not that I could see. And to Tim's point, if the foxes got to him, I didn't see any evidence of it, not that I had that close a look. Did *The Chronicle* say anything else?'

'Nope. Nothing important, at least.'

Ejiro was right, it wasn't likely to be a hit-and-run. And it wasn't likely to be self-inflicted if his – or maybe, *a* – wallet was found in a bin. People who commit suicide want to be found, don't they?

Which meant that it was likely murder. Or at the very least, manslaughter.

In front of us, Klaus chased Herc, who'd managed to find a ball. Klaus's little legs couldn't keep up, but he didn't let that stop him. Nothing did. That said, Klaus could bark for Britain, but brave and fierce as he was, he was only six and a half kilos. Herc was big enough to hold his own and defend Yaz and Ejiro, but Klaus . . .

'Don't think I haven't thought of it,' Ejiro said, guessing the way my mind was going. 'Until we find out what happened to that man, we all need to be careful. Even those of us with big dogs.'

He put his cup on a nearby table and turned to look at me. 'Yaz won't be walking Herc alone after dark. Not with the gangs. Not with the possibility of a murderer out there. You shouldn't be out alone either.'

'I won't do anything to put Klaus in danger.'

'Or to put yourself in danger, Louise. That was a man that was killed,' he reminded me. 'Not a dog.'

5

LOUISE

Irina (Hamish's Mum)

> Fancy going down to
> Lambeth together to give
> the statements?

Can't. Sorry.

I hadn't suggested a time, but it sounded like the same
sort of abrupt brush-off I sometimes got when suggesting
coordinating an after-dark dog walk and she was expecting Tim over. My money was on her being interested in
the young detective, if she wanted to go by herself. Poor
guy; he didn't stand a chance when Irina put her mind to
something.

Klaus bumped my leg. 'Don't worry, you might not get to hang out with Hammy, but let's see if one of your other chums is free.'

Meg (Tyrion's Mum)

> Hey Meg, are you able to watch Klaus for a couple of hours this morning? I need to head down to Lambeth to give the police a witness statement.

> Sure, bring him by. I'm working from home and I know Tyrion would love the company.

I took a sip of my still-hot coffee, texted my second-in-command, Barbara Lane, to let her know that I'd be offline for the next couple of hours and crossed the park to a new build on the far side. Klaus was already dancing, pulling me towards Meg's flat, barking happily.

An older man held the door open for us as he left, so I took the lift straight to the fourth floor, already hearing Meg's dachshund, Tyrion, barking from down the hall. Klaus joined in, and not for the first time, I wondered just how much Meg's neighbours hated us.

She edged the door open, half crouched to hold Tyrion

back. Klaus didn't care, brushing past her to jump on his friend. Where Klaus was a short-haired black-and-tan sausage dog, Tyrion was brown, dappled with beige, his intelligent eyes a bright, piercing blue.

Uninterested in the humans, Klaus paused only long enough to let Meg unclip his lead. 'So, you're off to see the police,' she said. 'Is Irina meeting you there?'

'Ahhh, no. Not as far as I know,' I said carefully. If anyone else had noticed the early signs of Irina's interest in the detective, that was on them. I wasn't about to be the one to put it out there. 'I don't think I'll be there very long.'

Meg wore her usual uniform of a T-shirt and flowy skirt. She'd bleached and dyed her hair grey a while back – something that I didn't really understand, having had to dye the silver from my own hair since my late twenties – and as it grew out, she often tinted it some funky colour. Today it was lilac.

She smiled, her childlike face lighting up. 'Take your time. I love having Klaus here, and I've got plenty of treats.'

The interview room DCs Williams and Thompson led me to was small, airless and painted a clinical white. In the centre was a desk with a computer screen on it. Two chairs lined it on either side. The room felt claustrophobic, and if it made me edgy, I could only imagine how it would seem to someone with something to hide.

They gestured for me to take a seat on the far side of

the desk, while Williams lowered himself onto the chair behind the computer screen. He had the smashed face and cauliflower ears of a rugby forward. He had to be nearing forty, as opposed to Thompson's early thirties, but from the unspoken conversation the two had while I took my seat, it was clear that Thompson would be the one leading the interview.

'Thank you for joining us, Miss Mallory,' he said. 'Williams will be taking down your testimony. I hope that's okay.'

How many people said they weren't okay with that? 'Sure.'

'All right. So, let's start off with the basics. Can you please state your full name and address?'

'Louise Mallory. Flat 801, Colourway House. I live in the old converted upholstery warehouse by the canal.' I realised I was babbling and gave them a weak smile.

'Occupation?'

'Entrepreneur, I suppose. I founded a consultancy specialising in business transformation a few years ago. The official address used to be Canary Wharf, but we've given up the office space and either work from home or client sites, so if you need the address, it's the same as my own.'

Stop babbling!

'You're not British, are you?' Williams asked, his tone light, as if he were trying to put me at ease.

'No,' I replied, trying to match his tone. 'Although you'd think that after more than ten years, I'd have lost my American accent by now.'

'New York?'

'Connecticut.'

'I've been to New York.'

'It's a different state, Williams,' Thompson said, giving me a slight smile.

'Right. Of course it is, but it's near, right?' Williams cleared his throat. 'So, tell me. What were you doing when you found the body?'

The next few questions were roughly the same as the ones they'd asked yesterday, until Williams asked, 'Do you know the victim?'

'No, but to be fair, I didn't get a good look.' Just those cloudy blue eyes. I shuddered.

'What did you see?'

'A man, lying in the long grass. He looked dead, I mean, he clearly was dead. We called 999. My friend called, because my battery . . .' I shrugged.

'Do you know what happened?'

'No. Whatever happened, happened before we got there. We didn't see it, didn't see anyone even near that part of the park. There were a few people around at that time, though: joggers, people with dogs, people waiting for the café to open. It opens at 8,' I added helpfully. 'Even on a Sunday.'

'What do you think happened?'

'I don't know. There are a few gangs hanging around the area. Been a few robberies, assaults. Maybe something went wrong?'

'You mentioned that your dog group heard something?'

'At around 3:30, yes. I guess that's when it happened.' I thought about my answer for a second, then clarified.

'Maybe that's when it happened, or when someone dumped him. "Dumped". What a hideous word. Like he was rubbish . . .'

Williams grunted, but Thompson nodded, continuing the questions. 'Can you give me the names of the people who saw or heard the, ah, disturbance?'

I took out my phone and checked. Gave them Meg's and Paul's details. 'But to be honest, there could have been more. Those are just the ones who mentioned it.'

The detectives exchanged a glance. 'How many people are in your group?'

'I don't know. Maybe a hundred, although you might have both pawrents – I mean dog parents – in there. And maybe some people have moved away but still stayed in the group. In any case, it's the same handful that tend to post. Want me to check?'

Williams sighed.

'And you found him at 7:30 a.m.?' Thompson asked. He checked his notes and added, 'While you were hungover?'

Ten points, for him not laughing.

'Do you have children, Detective?' I asked.

He nodded while Williams said, 'Two.'

I wasn't sure why, but I'd expected only Williams to have a kid, not Thompson as well. A reminder that just because he wasn't wearing a ring didn't mean he wasn't in a relationship, or that he didn't have family commitments. His situation didn't matter much to me, but it'd be interesting to see Irina's reaction.

'Right. Just how much do they care if you wake up with a hangover?' Williams gave me a sheepish grin and shook his head. 'Well, a dog isn't that different, really. And if they tell you they need to go outside, it's best to do it. Cleaning up a dog's accident with a hangover is worse than walking them.' I offered a wry smile. 'And we tend to go early most days anyway, so the dogs are used to it. Now that it's summer, the parks fill up quickly with kids, a good portion of whom are afraid of dogs around here, so it's best for everyone if we can avoid them.'

Williams nodded.

'Besides, it's amazing how quickly finding a dead body will make a hangover disappear.'

'I bet,' he said, with enough sympathy to make me wonder how many crime scenes he'd been to while hungover.

Thompson cleared his throat. 'Have you ever heard the name Philip Creasy?'

It rang a bell, but I couldn't place it. I took my time answering. 'Is that the man you think did it?'

'Please answer the question, Miss Mallory. Do you know the name Philip Creasy?'

'I . . . I don't know. Maybe.'

Thompson produced a photograph, something that looked like it'd been downloaded from LinkedIn or a company prospectus. The man in it was clean-cut and well groomed. He wore a dark jacket and white shirt open at the collar, and stared at the camera with an *I-can-conquer-the-world* type of expression that made me feel infinitely sad. They didn't have to tell me that this man wasn't the suspect; he was the victim. Only he hadn't looked like he did in the picture, lying in the long grass. Not really.

My brain ran through mental files of business contacts, and came up blank. Widened the search and, in that moment, something shifted. The jacket became a wind-cheater, the hair mussed up, or under a beanie. He held a lead ... it was red ...

My morning coffee burned its way back up my throat as I made the connection. 'He had a dog, called ...' the name was on the tip of my tongue, then something inside me shook it loose. 'Alfie. Jesus. How could I not have seen it?' I blinked at the officers. 'I didn't recognise him yesterday. That ... no. It can't be.'

Thompson nodded. 'What can you tell us about Mr Creasy?'

Images flitted through my memory. 'Phil was one of the first people I met after I got my dog. He told me that on Fridays, people would go into the dog park with a bottle of wine or beer and a picnic blanket – this was still during lockdown, you see. We didn't break the rules – everyone was more than two metres away from each other – but the dogs needed the exercise, and I guess we needed to see other human beings in real life, even if it was socially distanced.

'Alfie was a cockapoo. That's part cocker spaniel, part poodle. He was light, kind of caramel coloured, with a pale fringe that used to be pulled back into a ponytail and ridiculously long eyelashes. He loved chasing a ball – almost as much as he loved stealing one from another dog.' Another memory surfaced, and I couldn't quash a sad smile. 'And he wasn't neutered, so he'd try to hump anything. Girl dogs. Boy dogs. The park bench. He didn't care.'

'That's all very interesting, but what can you tell us about Mr Creasy, ma'am?'

I nodded, trying to stay focused. 'I'm getting there. Alfie died last year. I'd heard it was parvovirus, which is super contagious, so everyone was scared. Phil didn't come back to the park after that – no reason to, I guess. I messaged him once or twice, but he didn't respond, and I stopped trying.' I offered the detectives an awkward shrug. 'He was a good guy. He didn't deserve this.'

'How well did you know him?'

'Well enough to say hello at the park. We'd talk, sure, but about the same things everyone did. Collars versus harnesses. Which foods our dogs preferred and which pet insurance we used. He had a partner, but I didn't see her at the park very often. Grace something or other.'

'Anything else?'

I forced back the tears for a man I used to see most days, but now realised I barely knew. I shook my head. 'I'm sorry.'

'Do you know of anyone he didn't get along with?'

I didn't have to think about that. 'No.'

'Or any reason that someone would want to kill him?'

'So it *was* murder?' I shook my head. 'No. As I said, he was a good guy.'

'Can you think of anything else?' Thompson asked. 'Anything that could be relevant to the investigation?'

I looked from his hands to his face. 'What? No. Sorry I can't be more help.'

'Please let us know if you remember anything else.'

'You did just fine,' Williams said, his eyes kind. He hit

a key and a printer under the desk churned out page after page. He waited until it had stopped whirring, before handing me the neat stack of papers. 'Can you please read this, and if you're happy, sign each page?'

This statement is true to the best of my knowledge and belief, and I make it knowing, if it is tendered in evidence, I shall be liable to prosecution if I have wilfully stated in it anything which I know to be false or do not believe to be true ...

I took the pen that he handed over and, feeling ill, scrawled my signature.

6

LOUISE

Partridge Bark

Fiona (Nala's Mum)

Hi all, Nala has gone
off her food. Again. I've
switched her to wet food,
so if anyone wants an
almost full bag of kibble,
it's yours.
And @Claire, I see the
BBC have picked up your
story. You're gonna be
famous!

Mark (Dudley's Dad)

Fame aside, I hope they get whoever did it soon – Alex is really shaken.

Irina (Hamish's Mum)

Probably not as shaken as Louise was, haha.

'Cow,' I muttered to myself, as I paid for my third coffee of the morning. By the time I got back from Lambeth and picked up Klaus, the crowd at the café had changed from the office-goers to mums with small children and people like me, who often worked from the tables in the back.

Klaus dozed on a blanket beside my chair. It'd been a big morning for him too, between running around with Hercules, then with Tyrion. I pulled a bottle of water from my bag and poured some into his bowl, before taking a sip myself. I put the bottle away and adjusted the screen of my laptop.

Thirty new emails vied for my attention, and I muttered a low curse, knowing I'd cleared everything out before signing off on Friday. Most were status reports from the previous week. A few were from Samuel Osman, our self-appointed social secretary, arranging Friday night drinks for whoever was around Canary Wharf. A few early holiday requests (which could be actioned by Barbara) and a heads-up from her about one of our clients who might try to play chicken with us on a contract renewal.

I flicked through all of them, barely registering the words as my mind swam with half-constructed theories.

It was late enough that Irina might have already finished her interview. While the police had asked me to keep whatever was discussed to myself, I figured that she'd already know everything I did, and I found I needed to talk. I fired up WhatsApp and messaged her.

Irina (Hamish's Mum)

> Remind me: which one of us vomited into the bin?

☺

> Have you given the police your statement yet?

Yes, I just got back to the office. Strange to be on the other side of the desk, answering questions instead of asking them, but Andy was great.

> Andy? As in Detective Thompson?

Yeah, he's kind of cute, right?

Sure. He tell you about his kid?

That wasn't the way I'd expected our conversation to go.

While DC Thompson might look young, he didn't strike me as someone stupid enough to get involved with a witness. Especially if he knew Irina was a solicitor and despite how persuasive she could be when she wanted something. It just wouldn't look good if the case ever went to court.

Or made its way into the papers.

I didn't know what his situation was, but I hoped it might make Irina put on the brakes; as far as I knew she wasn't overly keen on children.

'Hey, Lou.' The barista approached with a water jug, adding about three drops into Klaus's still-full bowl. The café was dog friendly, but the barista had never stooped to dog-bowl detail before. I braced myself for the inevitable conversation and turned the phone over to hide the texts.

'I hear you were the one to find the body yesterday,' he said.

He was about thirty, slim and Spanish. I was pretty sure his name was José, but most people called him Joe. Which, I supposed, was preferable to the usual English pronunciation of 'Josey'.

Or 'Ho'.

'That was all Klaus.'

'You'll be able to dine out on the story for months.'

'Not by choice.' I couldn't think of anything worse. 'Unless that means I'll get free coffee here?'

'Dine.' He laughed. 'Not drink. Any news?'

I offered him a wan smile, unsure how much I could offer.

'Article's online,' a well-dressed older man said from behind me, in a strong Cockney accent.

Joe took out his phone. 'BBC, Gav?'

'That's what my daughter said.'

Joe located the article and read aloud, '"The body of a thirty-two-year-old man was discovered in Partridge Park, East London at around 7:30 a.m. on Sunday morning. Police and medics were called, but the man, named as local entrepreneur Philip Creasy, was confirmed dead at the scene. Mr Creasy ran a fintech company out of Canary Wharf . . ." What's that? Finance?'

'Financial technology,' I said, waving at him to continue. There was no point in mentioning that the only 'medic' I saw was likely the coroner.

'"In his spare time, he volunteered as an advocate for those without a voice."' Joe looked up. 'What does that mean? Someone who's mute?'

I shrugged.

'"No arrests have yet been made, and the police are appealing to the public for more information."'

Joe held up his phone, displaying the same photograph the detectives had shown me; Phil's confident expression pierced my heart all over again.

'He was good-looking,' Joe conceded.

'Nice guy, too,' the Cockney said. Gav was maybe late sixties, if not older, neatly dressed in a pressed blue shirt and trousers. His shoes were black, polished and good quality. He was a regular at the dog park, with his Affenpinscher, Violet. He'd always been friendly – most local dog people were, I'd found – and Violet's perennial grumpiness made me laugh. For all I knew, it was a breed thing; she was the only 'monkey terrier' I'd ever met. Small, black, with a flat face and large expressive eyes, today she looked more like a demented Pomeranian than the furry psychopath she sometimes resembled, and she seemed to be tolerating Klaus's antics as he did his 'I'm cute, you must love me' dance and flirted with her. 'Hey, Violet.'

'You knew this guy?' Joe asked him.

'Phil? Sure.' Gav stretched out his legs in his seat. He idly rubbed one of his hips. 'So did you. He was local. Spent time in the park, for a while. His dog kept humping Violet.'

The Affenpinscher's flat black gaze made it clear how offensive she considered unauthorised humping.

I didn't blame her.

'I don't get out of the café much,' Joe said.

Gav's eyes fell on me. 'What about you? You found him, didn't you?'

'I guess death changes the way a person looks. I didn't recognise him yesterday, but I was pretty freaked out by finding a dead body.' I shook my head, mentally trying to banish the cloudy eyes. 'I also hadn't expected it to be someone I knew.'

He shrugged. 'You never do.'

Something in his voice made me wonder how many dead bodies he'd found in his life so far.

Gav leaned back in his chair. 'Maybe the cops will find out what happened. Though I'll bet they take the easy route and blame it on the gangs.' He rubbed his hip again, his voice becoming pensive. 'Maybe clean up a few of them while they're at it.'

'You don't think it's the gangs?' I asked the question, but it came out as a statement.

Gav shook his head; he didn't think it was the gangs, and I wasn't sure I did either. Phil had struck me more as a beardless hipster than a gangster. Why on earth would someone kill him? Wrong time, wrong place? But, if that were the case, any of us could be at risk.

Resolve hardened in my belly and I knew I would do whatever I could to find out what had happened.

It wasn't just because I'd found him, although that was part of it. It was someone I knew. In my local park. Another entrepreneur with a dog. A decent man who deserved better.

I was doing this because I had to. Because *this* was feeling increasingly personal.

7

GAV

Gav left the café; the coffee was good, but the visit had been a waste of time. Everyone was talking about that dead man in the park, but someone thought *he* was the threat? Enough of a threat that they'd bloody pointed them dumb kids at him the other night? Why? Because he had a dog?

The high street was a few minutes' walk away. On one side of the street, the shopfronts were part of new-build apartment buildings. On the other, the Bells pub stood like an ugly brick warrior, resisting change and redevelopment. The place probably hadn't even seen a fresh lick of paint in decades.

He ambled past the hair salon, blaring its usual heavy metal fare, the Tesco Express with its windows displaying disposable BBQs and picnic chairs, the lighting shop that never had any customers and an equally empty drycleaner's. The charity shop, boasting a broad assortment of clothes and tat, had too many customers, by contrast. He craned his head, relieved that his Doris didn't appear to be shopping there at the moment.

Violet picked up her pace, marched him past Village Vets. 'Don't worry, love, we're not going in there,' he reassured her. 'Not today, at least.'

He waved to a friend behind the counter at the betting shop and slowed as he saw a group of kids loitering at the corner outside News-N-Booze. They wore the usual uniform of tracksuit bottoms and hoodies. He fixed his face into a neutral expression, cataloguing each one: their height, shape, everything. He couldn't tell for certain if they were the same kids. Hoped they weren't. He didn't want them to see him with Violet.

Anyone who knows you, knows about her.

He grunted at himself and walked past the group, past the displays of fruit and veg and into the off-licence.

The boys didn't look his way. Maybe the little sods didn't want to attack him in daylight, or maybe it wasn't them.

He pushed his sunglasses to the top of his head and nodded at the kid behind the till. Zed. That wasn't his name, of course, but someone had once joked that he was the last letter in stupidity, and it had stuck. Dumb name; *stupidity* didn't have a zed in it, but if the kid had a problem with it, he'd learned to live with it.

Gav strode down an aisle; booze on one side, crisps on the other. The booze shelves turned into a fridge, and the aisle ended at a door. Gav pushed through it, into a dimly lit room. Two men moved in the semi-darkness.

'You got lights in here, Mo?' Gav called.

'Got 'em, but gotta get 'em fixed,' came the response, as a middle-aged man waddled into sight. He put down a large box with a grunt. 'What brings you here, Gav?' He reached down to pat Violet, jerking back as she growled at him.

Violet moved towards a corner and lay down, watching Mo with opaque black eyes.

'Your dog's terrifying, you know that?'

'Yeah. Four kilos' worth of killer.'

Mo grunted again. Irony was lost on him, but to be honest, Gav wasn't sure how much he was joking. Not that he'd admit that to anyone.

He leaned against a wall of stacked ten-kilo rice sacks. 'Didn't see you at the pub last night.'

'Had deliveries, man.' Mo rubbed his shoulder. 'Usually the boys do the heavy lifting but one of 'em messaged. Wasn't feeling well.' He reached for a couple of cans of cola, passed one to Gav and gestured to a skinny kid to continue restocking.

'On a Sunday?'

'Yeah, on a Sunday. This ain't France, Gav. We can get a delivery any day. I miss anyfin' int'restin'?'

'At the pub? People wondering about the dead body in the park.'

Mo popped open his can and took a gulp. 'Terrible business that. Who you think did it?'

'Damned if I know.'

'The boys have any ideas?'

'Nothin'.'

'Huh.'

Gav opened his own can. 'A couple of kids came after me on the way home,' he said, watching Mo carefully. 'Don't suppose you heard anythin' about it?'

'Mate! You aw'right?'

'Better'n they are.'

The skinny kid sniggered.

Both older men looked at him. Under their gaze, his skin paled. 'Jus' guessin'. Someone'd be kinda dumb to piss off Mr MacAdams.'

'What d'you know about it, man?' Mo's eyes had narrowed, and his voice had taken on an edge.

'Nuffin,' the kid said, his hands held up, palms out. The poor lighting did little to hide the acne scars on his face, or the guilty flush that rose on his cheeks. 'Nuffin. Just sayin' that anyone'd be thick to go against Mr MacAdams.' His head bobbed in Gav's direction. 'Man, you're a legend.'

Makes you wonder why the kid on the till got that crap nickname, not this guy.

Gav didn't know this kid's name either, but decided that if the idiot on the till was Zed, this one was Y. Truly the last letter in 'stupidity'.

He had the feeling Y was trying to blow smoke in his direction, which in his experience meant that Y had something to hide. 'You know anyone that thick, kid?'

'No, sir.'

I got this, Mo gestured and turned to the kid, his hands on his hips. 'Spill, you fool. You hear somefing, I wanna hear it. *Now.*'

Gav nodded.

'Alls I heard was there was a tussle. Gang of kids had their arses handed to them on a plate by an old man. Not that you're old, Mr M,' he added.

'What else you know?' Mo said.

'Nuffin. Just that. No names, nuffin. But if I hear somfin', I'll tell youse.'

'Jesus,' Gav said, believing him. He waved the kid away. Less of a fool than the boy on the counter after all, he grabbed a box and backed out of the storeroom, mumbling something about stocking shelves.

'Lived here all my life,' Gav said, 'an' no one's been dumb enough to attack me before.'

'People movin' in, Gav,' Mo sighed. 'The rules, they don' know 'em.'

'Maybe. But me, I don't believe in coincidences. This happens the same day a body is found in my park? The one I walk Violet in every day? I ask questions, then these little sods attack me? You think it's *not* connected?'

'I don' know, Gav.' Mo expelled his breath with a soft whoosh. 'I don't know. But I'll keep an eye out. I hear anyfin', you'll be the first to know. I promise.'

8

LOUISE

Irina (Hamish's Mum)

How could you not recognise Phil?

> Might have been because I didn't get that close a look yesterday. And it wasn't like I was expecting to find someone I knew there. Like that.

But even when they literally showed you a picture of him?

> Big difference between the way someone looks when they're trying to impress clients, and taking their dog out for a run and a poo.

Hahaha, yeah.

> So did you recognise him?

No answer was forthcoming.

If Irina had recognised Phil, she would have said something before now. I slipped the phone into my pocket and looked at the notebook in front of me. Instead of the usual notes (and doodles) from my afternoon meetings, I'd started to jot down a few theories on his death. They were roughly broken down into three categories:

1. <u>Self-inflicted</u>
   - Overdose: drugs? Alcohol? No wound visible. No outward signs of overdose - something else?
   - Location: why the park? Sentimental? To be close to his dog's playground?
   - Why was his wallet (or phone) found binned?
   - Note: check with his girlfriend (Grace?)

2. <u>Accident</u>
   - Hit & run: why spend the time dumping the body and hiding his phone (or wallet)?
   - ??

3. <u>Murder/Homicide</u>
   - Targeted Murder: what is the motive?
   - Indirect: had Phil stumbled on something? Witnessed something he shouldn't have?
   - Crime of Opportunity: yobs looking for trouble?
   - Location: why the park? Why not the canal?
   - ???

I hadn't gotten far, and I kept feeling like I was missing something.

I drew arrows from points one and three to a new column on the opposite page.

<u>Who would know?</u> (It seemed better to put that than 'suspects')
   - Grace (Surname? Was she still with him?) - see who has her current details if she's not still in the Partridge Bark group
   - Friends
   - Work (Rivalries? Money issues?)

<u>Known Enemies/Rivals/Adversaries?</u>
   - Any exes? Who would know?
   - ??

They were the usual groups of people, from what I had learned from a lifetime of reading crime books, and as good a place to start as any.

I closed the notebook and stared at it. The coroner would run a tox screen that would presumably confirm whether Phil's death was self-inflicted or rule it out. The police would check whatever CCTV existed and speak with any witnesses they could find. Heaven only knew how long that'd take, or whether they'd be able to find someone who could tell them enough about Phil to provide a clue as to why he died.

Klaus was getting restless, so I packed up my stuff. My next meeting wasn't for another hour, so I slipped in my earbuds and phoned Babs while we walked home along the canal.

She answered on the first ring. 'Heard you had a bit of excitement in the area over the weekend.'

'The dead guy in the park?' I cringed, hoping that no one at work had realised that I was involved.

'Yeah. Found by two women walking their dogs. Utter tosh. No chance it was the women. I read somewhere that something like a hundred dead people are found each year by joggers and dog walkers, but it never is the dog *walker* is it? It's the dog. It's always the dog.'

'Dogs do have better noses than humans,' I agreed. 'Anyway, the article said he was working at a financial tech company down in the Wharf.'

'A fintech? Which one? Anyone we're doing work for?'

'Fidelio Technologies.' Thanks to Companies House, it had been easy enough to find out where Phil had worked.

'I think they were launching something with financial services automation. We spoke to them a while back, but they weren't at a point where we could start anything.'

'Ahhh, FidTech. Their motto was "FidTech for fintech", wasn't it? So, you met him then?'

'No, that day we pitched to the COO, Tabitha Halder, and a few people on her team. There were three of them who started the company: Phil Creasy was the CEO and handled the clients and investors. Probably sales too. The CTO guy was called Jim Clark. They branched out from there.'

'Okay. You have the memory of an elephant. So, where's the question in there?'

It was less the memory of an elephant and more the result of online searches, but I was starting to run into walls.

'Can you do me a favour – find out what you can about them. I want to know who the shareholders are. The dynamics between the partners. The culture. Morale of their staff. Any financial troubles they might be having.'

'Anything the internet can't dish up, you mean.'

'Yes.'

'Any reason that their chief was killed. Assuming, of course, that he was killed.'

'Exactly.'

'Okay. So you're joining the Met Police now?'

'Don't be silly.' I could almost see Babs roll her eyes. 'Look, I knew the guy. Not professionally, but from the park. I'm sure the police will be asking the same questions, but I feel like I owe it to him.'

Because I knew him, or because I found him?

Because I'd let him go when Alfie had passed away and he'd stopped coming to the park. I'd texted a couple of times. Kept meaning to call to offer condolences. But I didn't have the words, and I'd used the silence on his part as an excuse to stop trying. To my shame.

'Okay, Lou. I'll have a nose around.'

'Thanks. And if you can get me a meeting with one of them, that would be great.'

'Gotcha. Anything else? The real identity of Jack the Ripper?'

'Cute. Okay, don't worry about the meeting, they'll be up to their eyeballs on damage control anyway. And seriously, this is a personal favour. Only do it if you have the time.' I took a deep breath and redirected the conversation to one we were both more comfortable with. 'On the subject of tech firms, thanks for the heads-up about Gen. Also, the status reports are nicely worded, but I sense that the team are skating around something.'

Babs laughed. 'Not so much skating around. It's just that there's not a lot more to say from last week. The contract is agreed in principle, but we're waiting on the paperwork. If I were a betting person, I'd say that the CFO is about to start playing games.'

'What sort of games?'

I could almost hear Babs's frown. 'If it's not one thing, it's another, and we're well into the realm of pedantic here. I'll bet you dinner that they're waiting on another bid to try to renegotiate our rates.'

I'd spent enough time with Gen to know where this was coming from.

'Moany Tony.' I sighed. I hadn't been the one to coin that nickname, but it described Tony Frater quite well. Along with his other title, Gen's Chief Frugal Officer. 'What's that phrase? Penny wise, but pound foolish? If they can find a better team who're cheaper, then good on them. But if Tony thinks he can make us sweat enough to lower the rates, then he's going to be disappointed.'

'We have more work than people,' Babs agreed. 'And if our bid for the City contract comes through, we might not need him.'

'Okay. Let's see how that plays out before we burn any bridges, Babs. Have the team continue handover documentation on the assumption someone else will pick up the next stage, and if we get it, great.'

'Which leads me to another point. That documentation might take a little longer than usual; Mandy Barker called in sick today.'

Mandy was one of our best analysts and one of the few people who could work with Moany Tony. That she wasn't well could make things trickier.

'Is she all right?'

'She didn't sound herself, but I'll keep an eye on it.' Babs took a deep breath. 'Hey, Lou. Don't take this the wrong way, but people are getting killed in your 'hood. Promise me you won't take Klausi out for a walk by yourself, okay? Or poke your nose into something that could get you in trouble.'

She was the second person in two days to say that, and I was fast losing patience with people warning me off doing the right thing.

'I can handle myself, Babs.'

'I know you can, but I also know what you're like when you get the bit between your teeth. I just don't want to have to bail you out for kicking anyone's arse. It'll look bad on the quarterly reports.'

My laugh turned wry as Klaus began to bark. 'Not sure if he's agreeing with you or not,' I said, 'but I've got to run.'

I hit the red button to end the call and scowled at my hound. 'You haven't barked this much in ages. What's going on with you?'

His attention wasn't directed at me, and I followed his gaze towards a man holding the lead of a grey Staffordshire terrier with white markings on his chest. The same Staffie that had moved in the other day. The bigger dog gave Klaus an amused look, as if to say, 'I could eat you for breakfast, and *you're* barking at *me*?'

'Don't worry, he's friendly,' the man said. He was an inch or two above six feet and looked like he worked out – a bonus when you had such a muscular dog.

'So is Klaus.' I found myself staring up into a rugged face. Dark blue eyes and a strong jawline that was enhanced rather than concealed by black stubble. I felt my mouth go dry. 'Barky, but friendly.'

The man smiled and eased a little slack into the Staffie's lead so the dogs could sniff each other. 'You're local?'

'With this accent?' I laughed. 'No. Originally from Connecticut but I've lived around here for a few years.'

'Right.' His voice was low and raspy, as if he smoked two packs a day. His own accent was harder to place.

British, but without any strong regional tones. Except for the slightest growl of the Rs. 'We just moved to the area. I don't suppose you can recommend a GP practice in the area and a vet for Luther?'

We. As in, him and his partner, or him and his dog?

'Well, I use the GP over by the Tube station.' My voice warbled like a teenage boy's. I cleared my throat and pointed at a shopfront just down the street. 'Klaus is registered with Village Vets over there. Most of the locals have their pets registered with them.' I lifted a shoulder in a half-shrug. 'And you can usually get an appointment when you need one. With the vet at least, it's a bit trickier with the GP.'

He laughed. 'They're decent, then? The vets?'

'The worst thing I can say is that they do the hard sell on whatever brands they're trying to flog. Whether your dog needs them or not.'

He grunted and put a large hand on the Staffie's broad head. His smile was wry and sort of sweet. 'I can handle a hard sell.'

'I'm sure you can,' I said, hoping my voice didn't sound as bad as I feared. 'This is Klaus, by the way. And I'm Louise.'

'Nice to meet you.' One large hand reached out and enfolded mine in a warm grip. 'Jake. And this is Luther. Good to meet you, Louise. And Klaus.'

He turned and began to walk away.

'The local dog park is Partridge Park,' I called after him. 'Just down the canal from here. We have a WhatsApp group for the dogs. Mostly to share information, like who's down at the park so our dogs have friends to play with, that sort of thing.'

Oh, and it's where we discuss the dead body that my friend and I found yesterday.

Damn. Good way to scare him out of the neighbour-hood, genius.

Too late. Jake had already closed the gap between us.

'Sounds useful.' He held out his hand for my phone and entered his name and number as a contact. 'Thank you.'

With a wave he turned and left, walking past the entrance to the canal.

'Hey, Jake,' I found myself calling out.

He turned and looked at me, his expression inscrutable. 'Yeah?'

I wasn't sure what I'd intended to say until the words blurted out: 'Fancy getting an ice cream some time? There's a good shop not too far away.'

Slick, Mallory.

'Just to welcome you to the neighbourhood,' I added, feeling my face flush with embarrassment.

His eyebrows raised, but the smile was genuine. He gave me the thumbs-up and continued towards the High Street, and presumably Village Vets.

Something cracked against my ankle and I looked down. Klaus had found a fallen branch about three times longer than he was and had managed to hold it aloft.

'You're not keeping it,' I told his black-and-tan posterior as he strutted down the street with it. 'Bloody hell, Klaus, how are you even able to pick that up? And just so we're clear, you're absolutely not taking it into the flat.'

Still holding the stick, he paused, delicately balanced on three paws as he raised the fourth to wee on a littered takeaway bag. He glanced back at me, a definite challenge in his eyes.

I'd once read that if someone was looking for a cute little pet, not to get a dachshund. That sausage dogs are like little toddlers in fur coats. Sassy, smart and, above all, stubborn.

That didn't cover the half of it, but they were also – in my completely biased opinion – the best breed in the world.

Klaus put down the stick, only to readjust his grip on it. Picking it up again, he led the way home.

9

IRINA

It had been a long day. She'd been parachuted in to handle a new client after the associate who'd been working on the case dropped the ball, then had to run down to see the Met Police to give a statement, only to return to the office to find another mess to sort out. The one highlight of her day was seeing the cute detective.

She could murder a drink. Hell, she could murder that colleague, but a drink was safer. She paused at home only long enough to pick up Hamish, before heading to Louise's. She always had something in her fridge, and Hamish and Klaus loved playing together.

She tailgated into Lou's building and into the lift with a pair of stoners, trying not to breathe too deeply, even after they got off on the fifth floor. The lift opened on eight and she pushed open the unlocked door of Louise's flat. And paused, unsure how to react.

Louise was wearing ripped jeans and a cranberry-coloured cotton blouse with ruffled sleeves. Her thick chestnut hair was pulled back in a loose plait and draped over one shoulder. She wasn't the most fashionable, but that wasn't news. What was surprising was the state of her: on the floor on three out of the all fours, holding a scrap of red lace in her hand.

'Mine,' she crowed, pulling on it. On the other side, Klaus clung on with his fierce little fangs, shaking the lace as if it were a badger. He glanced up at Irina, but was more interested in his prize.

'*Mine*,' Louise repeated, pulling Klaus closer.

'And you wonder why you don't have a boyfriend?' Irina said. Hamish's legs were already moving, a whir of claws on hardwood. His lead kept him in place, and she unclipped it now, watching him race down the hallway.

He distracted the sausage just enough for Louise to free the lace from her dog's mouth and brace herself as Hamish launched himself at her. Ridiculous dog, he always greeted Lou before Klaus.

She stood up and put the material on the table. 'I don't wonder. I don't have a boyfriend because I don't want one. Not enough time in my day,' she said, but a flush started high on her cheeks, and she looked away.

'That's good. If you change your mind, you'll need to go shopping for new knickers. Those are disreputable.'

'Yeah. Wait, what?' She reached for them and held them up to the light, which revealed a new hole. She scowled at her dog. 'Those were my last good pair.'

'What a pity.'

Louise got to her feet and dusted off her knees and bottom. 'I didn't hear you knock.'

Irina opened a cabinet and pulled down two wine glasses. 'Why would I? The door was open.'

'The door automatically closes.'

'But it doesn't automatically *lock*. You really should keep your door locked. It's not a safe neighbourhood.' Irina looked in the fridge and frowned. 'No white? No rosé? What's wrong with you?'

'You drank the rosé last week and I took the last two bottles of white to Fi's on Saturday. I have to order more. You can pick up a bottle at News-N-Booze if you're desperate, or there's plenty of reds in the rack.'

Unacceptable. Irina frowned at the rack, pulling one bottle out after another, muttering to herself. 'Insipid.' Another one was 'jammy'. She didn't want jam, she wanted wine. Eventually, she settled for a nice Malbec.

'Make yourself at home,' Lou drawled.

Irina glanced at her, noting one hand placed on a hip.

'Yes, thank you,' she replied and uncorked the bottle with a satisfying pop. She poured two glasses, handing one to Louise, and stepped over Klaus on her way to the L-shaped sofa.

Louise sat opposite her, facing towards the balcony on the other side of the floor-to-ceiling window. 'You didn't recognise him either, did you?' she asked.

Irina blinked. 'Who?'

'Phil Creasy. The dead guy we found yesterday? Remember?'

'Oh yeah. I thought you meant Andy, and I was pretty sure that I hadn't met him before.'

Louise took a sip of wine and raised her eyebrow in a way that made Irina bristle. 'What? You asked me a question. I asked for clarification.'

'All right. Two questions, which you can answer in either order. One, did you recognise Phil when we found him on Sunday? And two, did you stay in touch with him after Alfie died?'

'Nope and nope.' Irina kicked off her shoes and wiggled her toes. 'But I didn't get that close. Didn't want to mess with the evidence.'

Louise's face maintained a neutral expression. So she didn't believe her; that was her choice.

'How did it go when you saw PC Andy today?'

Irina was aware that Louise was trying to wind her up; she knew perfectly well that Andy was a detective, not a regular PC. She'd have to do better.

'Technically that's a third question,' Irina corrected her friend. She held up her glass, first admiring the colour, then higher in a sort of victory toast. 'I don't think I gave him much that they didn't already know. They found Phil's wallet dumped in a bin, so they already had a name. They'll check it for prints, if they haven't already done so. From what I understand, he lives around here. Andy. He'll want to get this sorted.'

Louise stared at her with narrowed eyes. Irina held her gaze, certain that Lou couldn't know that Irina had already started researching Andy. Williams, too. But only because she couldn't understand why Williams seemed to defer to Andy. At least, not until she'd seen his background; Andy was clearly being fast-tracked.

'You didn't ask him out, did you?'

'What? No!' Irina took a sip and put the glass down. 'I'm not going to compromise the case, Lou. And before you ask what that means, I'm not going to ask him about the investigation. I'm not going to interrogate him. And I'm not going to shove my nose in things that are not my concern because I'm bored, or because I read too many crime books.' She raised a single finger. 'However, if I see him at the Hound, will I buy him a drink? Yes. Yes, I will. Because he might work harder if he has skin in the game.'

'You said he lives locally. And it's his job. He already has skin in the game,' Lou pointed out. She looked like she was going to say something else but then just shook her head. Her eyes had a wary look to them, the one that told Irina that she'd hurt her friend's feelings, but Lou had to know that it was for the best. Irina knew Lou could get obsessed when there was something she set her attention on.

She softened her tone and said, not unkindly, 'It's Andy's case, not ours. Let them work it without us muddying the water.' She couldn't resist holding up a sanctimonious finger. 'Remember, they're the professionals.'

Hamish was sniffing around the dog bed by the window, probably trying to find a hidden treat, so Irina pulled Klaus onto her lap and rubbed his belly while she let her words sink in. Once Klaus gave a contented sigh, she tilted her now-empty glass back and forth. When Louise didn't move to refill it, she put it down on a coaster. 'Pass me the bottle, will you?'

Tuesday

10

LOUISE

Partridge Bark

Fiona (Nala's Mum)

I had another look at that Beeb article. Call me thick, but does anyone know what they were referring to when they said Phil was an advocate for people without a voice? At first I thought maybe he was a lawyer but they said entrepreneur. Anything you can shine a light on, @Claire?

Claire (Tank's Mum)

> No idea. The Beeb is able to get interviews that I can't, damn them. They're not even sharing what they find out with their fellow journos at *The Chronicle* ☹ If anyone finds out, let me know, right?

It was a good question. What did it mean, and more importantly, was it what got him killed? Was he advocating for something controversial? Refugees or something?

The BBC had updated the article earlier, adding quotes from friends, colleagues and even his ex-girlfriend. Grace O'Donnell. I wasn't sure I'd ever known her surname or that they'd broken up, but now I added her full name to my Notebook of Theories.

There was no new information on Phil's death, so the article had turned into more of a human-interest story.

But the question remained: why dump him in the park, thrown away like an empty drinks can? The old lady with the Yorkies was right, there were better places to dump a body.

I kept coming back to the whys. Why was he killed? Why was he left there? Why had no one (as far as we knew) managed to come forward with any information?

Outside my window, a narrowboat moved up the canal. A couple stood at the helm, the man's arm slung over his partner's shoulders while she drove. My laptop sat open in front of me, but my attention kept straying to the notebook at my elbow. At the top of the page was Phil's name and the list of possible causes of death. Under the 'Murder/Homicide' heading, I'd added 'advocate for people without a voice', underlined it and circled it twice.

Klaus, who had been sunbathing on his bed beside me, stood up and barked.

'What?' I asked. I looked around, confirming that there were no people in the courtyard, no dogs on the canal path and no leaves falling. It was almost noon, and he was ready for his lunchtime walk. The morning had disappeared in a swamp of inactivity, but an idea popped into my mind. I might not know what the BBC was referring to, but I knew someone who would.

I glanced at my watch, realising that if I left now, I was in with a chance of finding them. 'Come on, Klaus. We're going for a walk.'

On the days that I wasn't working from The Nest, or from a client site, Klaus and I would walk along the canal to Partridge Park at lunchtime. It gave both of us a bit of fresh air and a chance to stretch our legs.

Today, instead of heading south along the canal, we headed north. It was a pretty walk, with wildflowers growing on either side of the towpath. The tide wasn't low enough to make the canal look like a mudflat, but nor was it high enough to flood the path. I waved at acquaintances as we approached the small park where I'd first met Phil and Alfie.

It was far smaller than Partridge Park; more of a wide green area, with trees planted on raised false barrows, built up to separate it from an industrial estate on one side and council houses on another two. While the barrows provided a clear demarcation, they also turned the park into a pond when it rained.

An ice cream van was parked near the entrance, and we paused to get a cone.

The pack that gathered here aimed to meet as close to noon as possible, to finish by 12:30, when a local school let out and the children took over the park.

The lunchtime pack began to arrive with their dogs and Klaus yipped until I unclipped his lead. He ran at a beagle, bouncing a few times before he tackled the larger dog.

'Hey, we have not seen Klausi in a while,' the beagle's owner said. He was a chubby German man. Damned if I could remember his name, but I was fairly sure the beagle was called Charlie. 'We have not seen you either. You are looking well.'

I grinned and sat beside him on the bench. 'Keeping too busy to get into any mischief.'

He laughed and raised a finger at me. 'That is too bad. A little mischief is good for the soul.' He tilted his head to the side. 'Maybe not too much, though. Terrible thing about Phil. You heard?'

'Yeah, it's all anyone's talking about,' I said, keeping

my role in finding him quiet. 'I thought I'd come this way and offer condolences to Grace. Does anyone still keep in contact with her? I mean, since Alfie died?'

'*Ja*, of course. She comes here most days.'

Which meant only one thing. 'She got another dog?'

'Another cockapoo. And another man,' he said. 'This one is called Daphne. Brown like chocolate. The cockapoo, that is.'

A new man; that was interesting. I tried not to sound too eager to find out more. 'So that she doesn't remind Grace too much of Alfie?' I asked, licking my ice cream.

'I suppose so.'

'You think she'll be here today?'

He shrugged. 'Maybe, maybe not. Stick around, though. You know Charlie always likes to play with Klaus.'

I glanced over. Klaus had stolen Charlie's ball and was running, ears flapping, like a six-and-a-half-kilo demon. Every time Charlie got close, Klaus would stop short, swerve and head in another direction.

'How possessive is Charlie over that ball?' I asked, although I wasn't overly worried. Klaus liked to be chased, and if he wanted to slow things down, he'd run between someone's legs, where a bigger dog couldn't follow. And if he was frightened, it'd be my legs he'd run between.

'He's a beagle, he likes his ball.' The German smiled. 'But he also likes to run after other dogs.'

More dogs appeared with their owners, and I knew my time to question Charlie's dad was coming to a close. 'So have you met Grace's new man?'

'Mike.' The German stretched back and lifted his

arms over his head. I kept my eyes on his, if for no other reason than to avoid seeing the few inches of pale belly the stretch exposed. '*Ja*. You know what Grace is like? Smart? Elegant, even when walking her dog?'

'Yes?'

'Well, what is the phrase? Opposites attract?' He giggled. He leaned close, as if he were about to share a secret. Then, eyes widening, he straightened and waved at an enormous man. Tall, muscular, with a heavy brow, shaven head and tattoo sleeves. Although the man's fingers were the size of gun barrels, they closed lightly over a cockapoo's lead. 'As if by magic.'

'Holy crap,' I muttered to myself. 'She's really gone for a bit of rough, hasn't she?'

'Nothing like Phil,' the chubby German acknowledged.

No, he was nothing like Phil. This man looked like he could hold his own against a small army. Or at least against a solitary man.

Maybe a solitary man who had once been involved with Grace O'Donnell?

11

YAZ

Partridge Bark

Paul (Bark Vader and Jimmy Chew's Dad)

Can anyone recommend a good GPS tracker for the dogs? I want to take Vader and Jim to Wanstead Flats, but all it'll take is a duck in flight and the boys'll be off to the races.

Emma (Flash's Mum)

We got one with a video before we took Flash to

Greenwich. We played it back when we got home and Pete turned green. Had to turn it off. FYI, running with a greyhound is not for the faint hearted!

Don't forget to bring towels and enough water to wash the boys before heading back. Ella'll kill you if you splatter mud all over the flat.

Paul (Bark Vader and Jimmy Chew's Dad)

Kill me? The woman can't keep her hands off me! Hahaha

An image of Paul's hairy knuckles flashed through her mind and Yaz had to laugh. 'Keep telling yourself that, sunshine.' She shook her head. 'Better Ella than me.'

She used her hip to open the gate to the dog park. She held her phone in her teeth and was about to let Hercules off the lead when she heard a low rumble, deep in his chest. She followed his stare over to two men at the far end of the park. A quick glance confirmed that Herc was the only dog in sight.

That always made her nervous. People rarely came into the dog area without a dog, unless they were looking for trouble. And, without fail, they always left their rubbish in there too, without caring that some of it was dangerous to animals.

The men were young, maybe late teens, maybe early twenties. Both were wearing hoodies, despite the warm afternoon sun. One of them sat on the backrest of the bench while the other stood beside him, fingers dug deep into low-riding baggy jeans. Empty cans of strong cider were discarded at their feet, an open takeaway container containing wings and chips on the seat between them.

Yaz took a deep breath, then cringed as the strong smell of weed assaulted her nostrils.

Hercules began to bark. Yaz snapped a quick pic of the men then dropped her phone into her bag, needing both hands to restrain him.

'Hey, guys,' she called out. 'This is the dog park.'

'Yeah?' one of them said. 'So?'

The other pretended to bark.

'Clever,' Yaz said. 'If you want to have a conversation with my dog, that's your call. But in case you can't read, the sign on the gate says this is the dogs' exercise area. And my dog needs to exercise.'

Both men brayed. 'The little girl has SASS!'

'Yeah?' Yaz said. 'Well, the *little girl* has a 35-kilo dog that doesn't like the smell of skunk. Think you can outrun him?' She made a show of reaching for the lead's clasp, her eyes never leaving the men.

The man on the bench cursed, but his friend took a couple of swaggering steps towards Yaz.

Don't let them see any fear, she told herself. *They'd be stupid to come close when Herc is here.*

Unless they had a knife.

Jesus.

She maintained a stony expression, her eyes locked on the man approaching her until he cursed again and jerked his head at his friend. 'We were leaving anyway.' The man on the bench leaned forward, tipping the container and sending chicken bones and soggy chips tumbling to the ground. 'Whoops!'

Anger fuelled her frustration, and Yaz unclasped Hercules when the men were still a few metres from the gate, regretting it instantly. What if Herc caught them? Bit them? She didn't think he would, but what if he did? What if they reported Herc to the police and the dog warden took him away?

Herc was already running, his muscular body surging forward, racing towards the intruders. The men moved fast, and Yaz counted it a small victory when they slammed the metal gate behind them.

'Morons,' she said, her voice shaking.

While Herc stood with his front paws on the top of the gate, barking at the retreating men, she collected the chicken bones and empty cider cans in a spare poo bag then lobbed it into a rubbish bin. 'You'd hope they'd at least clean up after themselves.' She smiled at Herc. 'Do you think they would have, if we'd given them more time? No, probably not.'

She took a ball from her rucksack and threw it for him. He chased after it and she eased herself onto the recently vacated bench. She dropped the pic of the men into the Partridge Bark chat with a description of what had happened and put the phone away before the usual wave of outraged comments could appear.

Herc returned and dropped the ball at her feet, tail wagging. She picked it up and threw it again. It bounced and landed in the bushes. The little dogs had chewed off the lower branches, but while there was enough clearance to see the ball on the ground beneath, there was no way a big dog like Hercules would be able to fit without getting stuck. And Herc wasn't a fan of small spaces.

'Should have got a smaller hound,' Yaz said, but patted Herc's head as she passed him. 'Just kidding.'

She got down on one knee and looked around. Next to the ball she could see a phone, its screen cracked. She looked at Herc's ball but, hard as it was, she couldn't see any way it would cause the sort of damage the phone had taken.

'Huh,' she said. No one in the chat had mentioned losing a phone, which meant there was a good chance it belonged to one of the kids that hung out there, drinking and smoking. She took the ball and backed out of the bushes. Threw it as hard as she could in the opposite direction and grabbed the roll of poo bags.

'Gotcha,' she muttered, crawling back under the shrubs. 'Bad enough you morons come here and pollute my park. But this time I'm gonna have your prints.' She ripped off a bag and slid her hand in with the confidence of someone who did it two or three times a day, every day. Branches pulled at her hair as she shimmied through the undergrowth until she could grab the phone. The case was a little further away.

'Preserve the evidence,' she giggled to herself, scooping up the phone. She shimmied along and grabbed the case in a second bag. On a whim, she turned it over. 'Oh hell.'

She closed the bag, tying it loosely. Backed out of the bush and cursed again.

Her hopes of fingerprints linking the phone to the drug dealers who operated in the dog park morphed into righteous anger.

'You might not be a drug dealer's phone,' Yaz said, carefully wrapping it in its bag and tying it off. 'But maybe someone is just dumb enough to leave their prints on you. And if so, you might just play a big part in putting the bastards behind bars.'

Evidence secure, she pulled out her own phone and sent a message.

12

LOUISE

Yaz (Hercules's Mum)

Hey Lou, are you taking
Klaus down to the park
this afternoon?

Wasn't planning on it, we
already walked up the
canal and he had a good
run with the hounds there.
What's up?

Could you swing past?
I found something that I
want to show you.

We continued past the turn-off for home, and Klaus dug in his paws. To be fair, he had walked a lot, but I was intrigued by Yaz's message. I picked his protesting body up and, with my little sausage comfortably slung over my shoulder, carried on down the canal.

Klaus got a second wind when he saw the iron gates to the dog park and wriggled until I put him down. That was a Klaus thing; he didn't mind being carried if no one was around, but he didn't like his friends to see him looking like a parrot dog.

I opened the gates, and he sprinted over to Herc, dancing between the bigger dog's legs. Yaz was sitting on a bench, her face tilted towards the sky. Her sun-streaked dark hair had escaped its usual ponytail and fell loose around her shoulders. I didn't think I'd ever seen it down before.

'You're here late,' I said, joining my friend on the bench. Her eyes were hidden behind enormous sunglasses that would have made anyone else so petite look like a bug, but on Yaz they looked trendy.

'We usually do lunch late. Some of the little dogs are afraid of Herc.'

We both looked over to where Klaus was trying to keep up with Hercules and she added, 'Not Klaus. Obviously.'

'Obviously. What's up?'

'Found these under a bush over there,' she said and picked up a pair of poo bags.

I flinched. 'Chuck it out yourself.'

'It's not poo. It's a phone.' She pushed her sunglasses down her nose, her black eyes holding mine with laser-like intensity. 'I think it's Phil Creasy's.'

I felt light-headed, and for a second I saw again his clouded blue eyes.

'Why?'

'On the back of the case is a picture of a cockapoo. One of the personalised ones, not some generic dog pic that you find online.' She untied one of the bags and jiggled the contents until the picture on the back of the case was visible.

She was right.

Each dog was unique, and I could always immediately spot Klaus in a sea of dachshunds (proven on a monthly basis at the sausage dog walks). He was a sleek, smooth-haired, black-and-tan little hound; his eyes didn't protrude, and his nose wasn't pointed like Tyrion's. There were the tan markings on his chest that reminded me of two hearts touching. But it was more than those easy descriptions; there was the intelligence that shone through his eyes and his vivid expressions, which could vary between soft and loving, mischievous and bark apocalypse.

It wasn't too unlike humans; different colours, sizes, shapes and faces.

Alfie was caramel coloured, with large, friendly eyes and a fringe that turned white-blond in summer. Although he visited the groomer's regularly, that fringe was kept crazy-long; Phil had said that Grace wouldn't let him cut it.

The image in my hand was of a cockapoo on a beach. He was playing in the water, a bandana around his neck. His fringe was pulled back into a topknot.

Surfer dog's rocking the man bun in Devon. Phil had

included the laughing emoji when he'd posted the image in the chat and on Alfie's Insta page.

'Oh hell,' I said, and looked up at Yaz. 'What do you want me to do with it?'

'Get it to the police, Lou. We both know it's connected to the case. Maybe they can get fingerprints off it. I saw a couple of local yobs in here earlier. I'll bet you anything that they had something to do with it.'

'Why don't you call the cops yourself? The BBC article gave out a number for anyone with information on the—'

She shook her head. 'That'd go to a call centre. Maybe it'd get to the right team eventually. You know who to give it to, Lou. I picked it up in the bags to preserve any prints, so even the East London cops should be able to find something. Maybe prove who killed Phil.'

I stared at the dogs for a few moments, trying to collect my thoughts. 'Have you texted Irina?'

'The Tsarina? No, just you.'

I paused and looked at her over my glasses. Yaz wasn't the only one to call Irina that; I knew it had less to do with her being Russian and more to do with her being prickly. Irina was usually her own worst enemy. 'Yaz. Be nice.'

She rolled her eyes. 'I *am* nice. I just find her hard work. Good on you for making the effort.'

'She's always there for me when I need her,' I said, although it wasn't really an explanation. 'And Klaus, who's an excellent judge of character, loves her. Although granted, she doesn't like to show her softer side.'

'Except, maybe, to Loki's dad,' Yaz added as I fumbled in my bag.

I looked away to hide my smile. 'We're not supposed to know about that,' I said, pulling DC Thompson's card from my pocket.

'Then she should consider being a tad more discreet.'

I didn't disagree with her, but she didn't expect a response anyway. I typed in a quick message to the detective.

DC Andrew Thompson

> Good afternoon, Detective. This is Louise Mallory, we spoke on Sunday when my friend and I found the dead man in Partridge Park, and I gave a statement at the station yesterday. Someone here just found a phone that we think is Phil Creasy's. Maybe you can get fingerprints from it?

OK, where are you?

> The dog enclosure in Partridge Park.

Stay there. I'll be there in 20.

'He's on his way,' I told Yaz. I typed a quick update to Babs to let her know that I was out of commission for the next hour or two. She rang seconds later.

'Hey, Babs, what's up?'

'Afternoon, lovely. Just a quick heads-up: the team just confirmed that the Chief Frugal Officer is meeting with some of the big names about bidding for the next stage.'

I would have liked to have been able to at least pretend to be surprised.

'Look, Lou, you're the boss and it's your call of course, but we've got enough work coming in that we don't need Gen Tech. Do we really need to put up with Moany Tony's antics for the next stage?'

'Careful, Babs. One of these days, we're going to slip and call him that to his face,' I said, though without heat. 'The bid for the work in the City still looks good, so we might not need them, but let's confirm that first before we tackle him.'

I could feel Babs's reluctant shrug over the phone. 'Okay.'

'Anything else?'

'Yeah. I spoke to Mandy earlier. You might want to have a conversation with her.'

Sitting beside me, Yaz raised her brows, her intelligent eyes scrutinising me. I gave her an awkward half-shrug and turned away. 'Why? Is she still ill? Is it serious?'

'I don't know.'

'But?'

'I called her earlier, and she sounded awful. She said she needs the rest of the week off for "personal reasons".'

'Of course the answer will be yes. Did she give you any more information?'

I didn't need to imagine Babs's eyeroll. 'No, Lou. I got my Tarot cards out.' She let out an exasperated sigh. '*Of course* I asked her!'

I issued my own eyeroll. 'And?'

'Look, I know HR wouldn't approve, but she's a mate, right? So I pressed a bit. She mentioned something about a boyfriend.'

I eased up. 'I didn't know Mandy had a boyfriend.'

'No one did.'

'So Mandy is more of a dark horse than we knew, but it's not a crime to shield your love life from the office gossips. Look, she's asked for the time off, so let's give her some space. If we don't hear from her in a couple of days, I'll call her and see if she needs anything.'

'Okay.'

'Thanks, Babs.'

I rang off.

'Problem?' Yaz asked. 'In addition to the one we already have?'

'Someone on my team is having man troubles,' I said, putting my phone away.

'Huh,' Yaz said and leaned back, smirking.

'Yaz?'

'Hmm?' She hummed the response without looking in my direction.

'What have you done?'

'Me?' She peered over the rims of her glasses at me. Again. 'Why do you ask?'

'Yaz?'

The smug smile widened a bit. 'All I did was text the Tsarina. Let her know what was going on. Like you asked.'

I hadn't asked.

I also hadn't told her about Irina's interest in the detective, although I wouldn't have put it past Yaz to have found out anyway.

She pushed the glasses back up her nose and settled back on the bench. Maybe to wait for the cavalry to arrive. Maybe to wait for the show.

Whichever came first.

DC Andy Thompson arrived, with DC Williams trudging behind him.

'Bit young, isn't he?' Yaz said as he paused outside the gate, running his fingers through his unruly blond curls.

'To be honest, I don't care if he's Doogie Howser, DC, as long as he finds out who killed Phil.'

DC Andy scanned the dog park.

'Only us,' Yaz drawled, grinning as Herc thrust his face into DC Andy's groin, then DC Williams's, making the latter jump. 'Don't worry, he won't bite anything off. I hope,' she added with a wicked grin.

'Afternoon, ma'am,' DC Andy said to Yaz, not noticing her bristle. 'Afternoon, Ms Mallory.' He reached down to pat Klaus's head then Hercules's. 'Good boys. What did you find?'

'It wasn't Hercules that found it,' Yaz said, slowly

standing up. She grabbed one of the poo bags from the bench and held it out to DC Williams, who cringed. 'Not much of a dog person, are you?' she said, although I'd had the same reaction. But seeing a burly rugby player-type cop be squeamish about a poo bag was kind of funny.

She handed it to DC Andy instead. 'Don't worry, it's only the phone. Thought I'd preserve evidence.'

'You're sure it's Mr Creasy's?'

'Phil's? Well, I guess someone else could have put a picture of his dog on the back of their phone case.' Careful to keep it within the bag, she turned it over to show the detectives. 'But it's not very likely.'

'So you're certain that's his dog?' DC Williams said. 'Not some other . . . um . . .'

Still sitting on the bench, I answered. 'It's his dog.'

'Can you show us where you found it, ma'am?'

'Don't call me "ma'am",' Yaz demanded. 'I'm not old, and I'm not the Queen.'

She didn't wait for Williams's response, walking over to the long bushes and pointing under the brush. 'The phone was there – I put my scrunchie in the same place to mark the spot. The case was a little further back and to the right.'

'Why didn't you leave it there?'

'Because I didn't want my dog to eat it.' She gave him a tight smile. 'Or wee on it.'

'Ah.'

'And, you know, there are other dogs that come here, so even if I can keep Herc away, I can't vouch for the others.'

'Ah,' Williams repeated, looking nervously over his shoulder.

'And because the police usually take their time coming to this part of London, I couldn't guarantee what state it'd be in if I left it there.' Yaz's voice was bland enough, but her wink told me just how much she was enjoying herself.

DC Andy waved at his partner to get down on all fours. Williams started inching towards the red scrunchie, but within seconds he was howling, backing out of the bushes, staring at his hand.

Yaz sighed and looked up at the sky. 'You're really not familiar with dog parks, are you?'

I struggled to maintain a straight face. 'We all try to clean up after our dogs, but you can't always see what they do in the bushes.'

Yaz handed him a fresh poo bag. 'Would you mind cleaning it up while you're in there, Officer?'

DC Williams glared up at her from under his heavy brow. To defuse the stand-off, I handed him a tissue and asked if he needed a splash of antibac.

DC Andy took the spare bag from Yaz and crawled in himself. 'It was already dry, Scott.'

He was shuffling further into the brush when the gate clanged open.

'My oh my,' Yaz chortled. 'Look what the dog dragged in.'

Irina must have come straight from the office. Her hair was neatly twisted on the top of her head, and while perspiration beaded her forehead, her lipstick was freshly applied. She wore a smart blazer over a simple black skirt, stockings and six-inch heels. Which was strange; she'd taken the time to pick up Hamish and instead of changing into trainers she put on sky-high stilettos?

'I thought Hamish was in doggy day care today,' I said cheerfully.

'Nice shoes,' Yaz drawled. 'Louboutins? Didn't realise we had a new dress code here. Lou, you and me are gonna have to up our game.'

Irina gave us a dark look before her attention was drawn by the 'oof' that came from within the bush. It was quickly followed by a muttered curse.

'There was a fresh one in there too,' Yaz whispered to me.

DC Andy backed out. He stood slowly, fumbling with his left hand for a handkerchief and wiping his right hand before turning to greet Irina. He absently stuffed the handkerchief back in his pocket and rubbed the back of his head.

'He's gonna have a nasty surprise when he takes that out to blow his nose,' Yaz whispered again.

'And he's going to start to smell pretty soon,' I agreed. 'We don't have a water tap in here.'

'I suppose the Tsarina can take him home and clean him up?'

Irina couldn't have heard us, but gave us a filthy look anyway before returning her attention to the blond DC.

'Ms Ivanova,' he said, tilting his head at her.

'Irina,' she corrected, looking at him from the corner of her eye. With the heels on, they were about the same height. I was willing to bet she'd never wear those shoes around him again.

'Oh jeez,' Yaz muttered, then clapped her hands and raised her voice. 'Come on, people. Leave the flirting for later. We have a crime to solve. Who killed Phil Creasy? Who left his phone in here? I had to chase off another couple of yobs who were smoking weed just over there. Anyone want to bet they're somehow involved in all this?'

Williams and Thompson exchanged a glance. 'Madam,' Williams began, 'if you have any more information on who you think might have committed the crime, we'd be happy to follow up.'

From his expression, 'happy' might have been stretching the truth, but Yaz took him at his word. 'My name is Yaz – Yasmin – Dogan. I've sent a shedload of videos to the council – you can check with them – but don't worry, Officer. I'm more than happy to send them to you too.' Her smile widened and she pulled out her phone. 'It's always good to have a contact on the force. In this neighbourhood, you never know when you might need one.'

13

IRINA

Partridge Bark

Yaz (Hercules's Mum)

Herc found Phil's phone.
We gave that — and
@**Irina** — to the cops.

Claire (Tank's Mum)

Irina????

Yaz (Hercules's Mum)

Showing up at the dog
park in 6-inch stilettos
is more than a wardrobe

malfunction. We were worried about her sanity. Good thing the nice detective was willing (and able??) to see to her. I didn't see him cuff her, but who knows? That might be on the cards ...

Louise (Klaus's Mum)

Unless she cuffs him first.

Irina responded with a rude emoji and increased her pace. She'd lingered only a few minutes after Yaz and Lou had left – long enough to fuel their speculation, it seemed, but not long enough to grab any time alone with Andy.

She went home and changed into jeans and a cute top, then did a couple more hours of work. Once satisfied she'd wrapped up everything urgent, she prepared to head out again, slipping into white Gucci trainers and donning a cross-body bag barely large enough to hold her phone, brush, lipstick and keys. When Hamish slowed to sniff every bloody blade of grass along the canal path, she hurried him along.

'No guarantees, *Mischka*, that he'll be there at all, but you're not helping.'

Hamish looked up at her, one ear standing tall, the other curling over. It was his inquisitive look that never failed to melt her heart. And although she knew he couldn't, really, understand her, she answered anyway. 'I did my homework. All above board, you'll be glad to know, my little bear. It was all in the public space, thanks to social media. He and Williams sometimes go for a drink after work: he has a couple of public profiles and some of them have pics of him at the Grapes. It's a great pub and as good a bet as any that they might end up there today.'

Irina didn't mention aloud the other pieces of Andy's life that she'd discovered. The woman he'd married a couple of years out of school. The son they'd had. And the divorce that had swiftly followed. At least it didn't look like the kid lived with Andy. From what Irina could tell, there'd been girlfriends since his marriage had broken up, but nothing that had lasted more than a handful of months.

Hamish dug in his paws, and she elaborated. 'No. I don't know for sure. It's Tuesday, and not everyone drinks on a Tuesday. And no, I don't know what time he finishes either. But if he's not there, who cares? I'll have a glass of wine, and you might get a few bites of whitebait. Deal? Come on, you know you love the Grapes.'

She chivvied him along until she lost patience. Then she picked him up, at least until she reached Narrow Street, where she set him down, ran the brush through her hair, reapplied her lipstick and encouraged him down the street. 'Bloody hell, Hamish. When we come here with Lou and Klaus, you're happy enough to drag me in. What's wrong with you?'

She pushed through the door, scanning the bar. No sign of Andy or Williams, but there was a table that looked like it was coming free at the back. She knew from experience that the Grapes didn't serve a New Zealand Sauvignon Blanc, so she ordered a glass of the South African and some food before easing onto a chair facing the entrance. The pub was old, like 1580-something old. Long and thin enough that even in the back she had a good view of the entire place. Not including upstairs, but that was more for dinner, right?

She took a sip of wine and looked at her phone, belatedly realising she should have brought a book. Something trendy, maybe.

An hour and another glass of wine passed. Twice people came, asking to share her table. Both times she replied she was waiting for someone.

A second hour brought a third glass of wine and the whitebait she'd promised Hamish. As both disappeared, the door swung open and Williams and Andy walked through.

Irina eased back down in her seat. Squinted at her phone, as if she was reading something vitally important.

Hamish sighed and lay down, as far under her chair as he could manage.

Looking up, Irina pretended to spot the detectives. She stood and waved.

Williams saw her first, muttering something that might have been an expletive.

Andy scanned the pub until he found her, but his smile reached his eyes when he waved back.

Irina sat back down, her own smile fading when they found a different table. Convinced it was Williams's doing, she waited a bit before wandering past. 'Hey detectives,' she said. 'Mind if I join you?'

'Yes,' Williams said, his voice as blunt as his features.

'Great,' she said, offering her most charming smile and taking the free seat beside Williams and opposite Andy. 'I promise not to grill you on the case.'

'That's good; we can't talk about it,' Williams said.

It would have been delightful if the squat detective would leave. She leaned back and tried for a casual look. 'Hey, I'm really sorry if my friends were awkward earlier. You just need to understand how upsetting this is for everyone.'

'Even more for you,' Williams said. 'You were one of the people to find him.'

'Yes, of course. And I hope you know I – we all – will do everything to help you find the murderer.'

The detectives exchanged a look, Williams's expression veering between disgust and caution. 'Sure you will. Look, I'm gonna go outside for a bit. Need some fresh air.' Standing, he held up a small vape, without irony, and walked up the couple of steps to the small balcony above the Thames.

'He doesn't like me, does he?'

Andy took a sip of his pint. 'He's got into trouble before, talking to someone he shouldn't have.' He raised one shoulder. 'In his case, it was an undercover reporter. I understand his caution.'

'I'm not a reporter.'

'No, but you're a lawyer. And to be honest, even if you weren't, I don't have anything I can share with you.'

'Wrong,' Irina said. 'You're good company, and I'm happy to share that if you are. As friends, of course.'

When he looked taken aback, she added, 'I promised I wouldn't ask about the case, and I won't.' She reached down to put her hand on Hamish's head, pivoting slightly towards the detective. 'So, tell me about yourself, Andy Thompson.'

The evening didn't last as long as she would have liked, but she enjoyed Andy's company, as long as she had it, even under the watchful gaze of his chaperone, Williams.

They both walked her home along the canal, Andy's hand occasionally holding her elbow when she stumbled. A jolt travelled up Irina's arm every time he touched her, and she knew she would play a long game if she had to. She slanted a look at him. With his ridiculous blond curls and blue-grey eyes, he certainly wasn't unattractive. He didn't have Tim's wicked good looks, but he also wasn't encumbered with a wife or girlfriend ... at least as far as she could tell. It was easier getting him to talk about his son, who – blessedly – lived in Chester with his mum and stepfather.

'Are you sure you know where you're going?' Williams asked her.

She blinked at him. 'Of course.'

He grunted and reached for Hamish's lead, muttering, 'At least the dog is sober enough to find his way home.'

Watching Hamish shrink back against her leg, a cold,

hard fury scattered the fizzy feeling the wine and Andy's company had brought. Hamish was *her* dog. *Her* responsibility. And she was letting him down.

'No,' she said, keeping hold of the lead. Both men stopped and looked at her. Their faces were expressionless, but she knew they were judging her. Usually she wouldn't care, but this wasn't about her, it was about Hamish. Her little bear; her *Mischka*. They were a team; she would never be so drunk that she couldn't take care of him. Ever.

She pointed to the ramp from the canal path up to the street. 'I've got this. It's not like we have far to go.'

'You sure?' Andy asked.

She nodded, seeing the gleam of a silver lining. 'Yeah, no problem. Look, if you give me your number, I'm happy to text you when I'm safe at home.'

14

LOUISE

Partridge Bark

Fiona (Nala's Mum)

I see the BBC has updated the article on Phil. No mention of the phone Yaz found.

Yaz (Hercules's Mum)

Cops are probably still testing it. Or they don't want that released to the public. Or both.

Paul (Bark Vader and Jimmy Chew's Dad)

Or they're giving the scoop to *The Chronicle*?

Claire (Tank's Mum)

Sadly not. I don't know if the BBC knows, but I've already been contacted by the detectives and told to leave it out. Guess someone figured out I'm in this group.

LOCAL ENTREPRENEUR FOUND DEAD IN PARTRIDGE PARK

Met Police are seeking information following the death of local entrepreneur Philip Creasy.

Mr Creasy, who founded fintech company Fidelio Technologies, was found dead in Partridge Park on Sunday morning. Family and friends are 'shocked' and 'devastated', and he was regarded locally as 'a pillar of the community' who 'always had time and a ready smile' for those he knew. Colleagues described him as 'the type of boss everyone wants to have but so few people do'.

Police are treating his death as suspicious. A number has been set up for anyone with information . . .

Going solely by books and TV, in which crimes are solved in 300 pages or an hour (not accounting for ads) respectively, a person could be lulled into thinking that things always moved quickly, with breaks in the case coming thick and fast. In real life, it was a much slower pace. Assuming, of course, that the cops hadn't deprioritised Phil.

I put Klaus on the lead and wandered south towards Canary Wharf. It was only Tuesday, not the most social day of the week, but the area still maintained a good after-work vibe, and I needed a change of scene.

We drifted from Canada Square to Cabot Square, stopping for a coffee in one place and then a glass of wine in another, finding a table outside. Klaus sat curled on my lap, his intelligent eyes watching people beginning their commute home, barking at anyone he deemed suspicious. Or a potential friend. Sometimes it was hard to tell.

It was already six o'clock. The mass exodus of people leaving their offices to catch a Tube or train home was in full swing. A few years ago, most would still have been wearing suits, but now it was a mix of traditional office wear and smart casual.

A petite young woman passed by us, her dark curls

bouncing. She wore grey trousers and a lavender cotton blouse with cap sleeves. A black leather bag was slung over her shoulder, an antibac case in the shape of a mermaid hanging off a strap.

Klaus barked and lunged, on alert but with his tail wagging. The woman turned and smiled. 'Hey, Klaus. Hey, Lou.'

It took a moment for me to recognise the woman with the smart look. Usually Meg wore T-shirts with dragons or wizards on them, long, flowy skirts and combat boots.

'Meg! I didn't know you worked down here. When did you dye your hair back to black?'

'I didn't. I temporarily sprayed it dark, so as not to offend the too-conservative client I had to meet today.' She grinned, reaching down to greet Klaus and allowing him to put his paws on her trousers to kiss her face. 'Tyrion will be so sorry to have missed you,' she told him. Glancing at me, she added, 'He's staying with my neighbour, who'll probably be teaching him a new trick. Last time, she taught him how to high-five. I laughed so hard I almost fell over.'

She fished about in her handbag, bringing out a small drawstring bag. 'Aren't you the lucky one, Klaus.'

'Meg . . .'

'It's okay.' She broke the treat into two pieces.

'Be careful, he's like a shark with treats.'

'I know,' she said, but she carefully fed Klaus the treat from the centre of her palms. 'So, why are you here?' she asked, taking the seat beside me. 'I'm guessing not for a meeting.'

'Dressed in shorts, T-shirt and muddy trainers?' I laughed. 'No. I just needed a change of scene.'

'The Phil thing?' It was phrased as a question, but it wasn't really. She picked Klaus up and settled him on her lap. 'I can't imagine what it was like for you and Irina to find him.'

'Not good,' I admitted. 'Hey, Meg, did you stay in touch with him after his dog died?'

She was already shaking her head. 'I sent a condolence card and made a donation to one of the local shelters in Alfie's name. I called him a couple of times to see how he was doing, but I think it was too much for him, seeing us with our dogs, when his heart was broken.'

I nodded. 'He left the chat.'

'It must have been hard. If you bring a dog – or any animal, I guess – into your home, they become part of your family. So when they die, it's not "just a dog", like they're a cup you can easily replace. They're the furry person who's 100 per cent reliant on you, but loves you 1,000 per cent. They share more than your home; they share your life.'

'You're preaching to the choir, Meg.'

'Of course *you* get it. But not everyone does.'

A waiter came over. Meg ordered a glass of wine and a top-up for me.

I waited for him to leave before asking, 'Do you think he kept in touch with anyone?'

She shrugged. 'I don't think so. Just Grace. And after they broke up? I don't know, but I can ask around. I get the sense that he kind of retreated into himself.'

'God, that's so sad.'

Meg waved at two people walking from the DLR towards the Jubilee line. One was an older woman, the other an Asian man. It took me a few seconds to realise that they were two of our local vets, Caroline Aspen and Chetan Singh. I waved as well. 'Haven't seen Dr Caroline in ages, I thought she stopped practising.'

'No, she's still around, but she leaves most of the client stuff to Dr Ben and Dr Chetan. I hear she's thinking of early retirement. But about Phil, yeah. I think we all became painful memories.'

I was amazed that I hadn't thought to ask Meg all of this before. She was always at the centre of our group, in her own quiet, sweet way. She genuinely cared about people. Of course, if anyone would have stayed in touch with Phil, it would have been Meg.

Klaus must have sensed my upset. Despite him being perfectly comfortable on Meg's lap, he leapt to mine, landing neatly in my arms. I burrowed my face into his soft fur, breathing in the smells of baby powder-scented shampoo, grass and the underlying scent that was Klaus himself.

Fidelio.

'The Faithful One'. It was a good name for a fintech company, but I had a strange suspicion that rather than Phil naming his company after Beethoven's opera, he'd named it after his dog.

Fidelio.

The company wasn't large and, from what I read online, had a small office nearby but used shared meeting spaces for larger meetings and company-wide events.

'Meg, did you ever *see* Phil after Alfie died?'

She blinked at me. 'See him? Sure, hard not to. His office is in the same building as mine. But I knew he didn't want to engage, so when we passed each other, it was always a "Hi, how are things?" sort of conversation. He might have asked about Tyrion, but only to be polite. He didn't linger. I didn't push.'

Meg's emotional IQ was off the charts, but something she said stuck like a barb in my mind. 'Same building?'

'Same floor, actually.'

'Huh. I don't suppose you know any of his team?'

She paused while the waiter returned with our drinks, then took a sip of her wine and gave me a long look from the corner of her eye. 'What are you up to?'

Wednesday

15

ANDY

DCS Grieves stood at the front of the room. The aircon had gone off again, and it was sweltering; a concrete cell, painted sickly-white, with a florid DCS at the front of it. You could usually tell how angry Grieves was from the colour of his skin. In a good moment, it was ruddy. As he got angry, it went through the Pantone shades from red to purple.

At the moment, he was verging on apoplectic, but his voice was still calm; a good sign.

'Next case,' he slashed his hand. 'Tell me about the Creasy murder, Partridge Park. Where are we?' Grieves's gaze passed over Andy as if he didn't exist. 'Williams?'

'As you know, sir, Phil Creasy was found dead at approximately 7:30 a.m. on Sunday. Pathology estimates the time of death to be between 7 and 10 Saturday evening. The body was then dumped in the park, probably around

3:30 a.m. when witnesses heard a disturbance. No leads yet as to where he was killed.'

Someone at the back of the room barked. Then giggled.

Grieves's face went a shade darker, but he otherwise ignored the interruption.

'We've interviewed the women who found the body, those who noticed the disturbance, the ex-girlfriend and other people we identified who might have been out and about at that time.'

Grieves took a deep breath; he knew who would be 'out and about' at that hour and that they didn't make reliable witnesses, even if they were willing to speak to the police. 'CCTV?'

The CCTV officer, Jen Finn, piped up, 'None around the park, sir, but we've got hold of some from the surrounding streets.'

'Anything?'

'Not yet, sir. Just the usual idiots racing about in their Fords and Kias.' She blushed almost as dark as Grieves. 'I mean . . .'

'I know what you mean, Finn. Anything stand out?'

'Not yet, sir.'

'FLO Jo?'

The other woman in the room, the family liaison officer, whose Christian name was Nicole, looked up. She'd stopped rolling her eyes at the nickname years ago. 'Spoke with the family – both parents and a sister – and the ex. Even the ex said he was a good guy. Not the sort of person to piss someone off enough to be murdered.'

Grieves nodded. 'Post-mortem?'

'Not scheduled until this afternoon, sir,' Williams said.

'Any suspects?'

Andy looked around at the sea of detectives shaking their heads. Although he knew this wasn't uncommon at this early stage of the investigation, it was still frustrating. 'Not yet,' he said.

Grieves grunted. 'You all know your roles? Priorities on this case?'

They all nodded.

'Good. Next case – the shooting on Violet Road. Go.'

Andy let his breath out as they finished the morning summary of open cases. As he was about to follow Williams out the door, Grieves called his name.

'Sir?'

The DCS remained silent until the rest of the team had left the room, the last person closing the door behind them.

Grieves gave them a few moments to turn the corner before exploding. 'What in almighty hell do you think you're playing at?' His fleshy double chin wobbled as he shouted.

'Sir?'

'Out for drinks with a witness? We don't have enough problems at the Met, you think it's a good idea to compromise the case and flirt with a witness? *A lawyer* at that?'

How the hell had Grieves found out about that? He'd bet almost anything that Williams wouldn't have shopped him on it. Had someone seen them walk her home? It had been getting dark, and she'd drunk a fair bit. It had only been the responsible thing to do . . .

'Her statement was already taken, sir. She's not a suspect

in the case – her alibi checks out. She's not even technically a witness. And Williams was there the whole time. He can confirm that there was no talk about the case and that we were never alone together.'

He left out the bit about the bollocking Scott Williams had given him after she'd left them.

'I don't think the *Mail* will care if they get wind of it, do you?' His boss was all but wheezing with the effort of sustained fury.

Andy shook his head.

Grieves took a few steadying breaths, and his complexion gradually calmed from heart-attack purple to just-ate-vindaloo red. 'I expected better of you, Andy. Don't let me down again.'

Understanding that he was being dismissed from the meeting, but not the case, Andy nodded and lied. 'Don't worry, I won't see her again, sir.'

16

LOUISE

Partridge Bark

**Ella (Bark Vader and
Jimmy Chew's Mum)**

People are such stinking
animals. As soon as
the sun comes out the
picnickers come out and
leave the park full of their
rubbish. I had to pull two
chicken bones out of
Jimmy's mouth and let's
not even think about what
Vader got hold of!

Fiona (Nala's Mum)

Hopefully not another
body!
Speaking of which ...
@Irina has gone all quiet.
Don't tell me ... she's still
tied up?

Klaus had walked a lot the day before, so we spent the
morning close to home. I kept an eye on my phone, expecting a snarky reply from Irina, but there was nothing.
Either she was at the office, in court or giving the Pack
the cold shoulder.

Klaus tootled over and dropped a ball at my feet. He
nosed it towards me until I picked it up and threw it for
him. Once, I wouldn't have dreamed of bouncing a ball
around my flat, much less grinning as it ricocheted off
the walls.

By the third throw, I got the message: he wanted to go
outside. I checked my diary and, free for a bit, clipped on
his lead. Heeding Ella's message, we avoided Partridge
Park and headed back up the canal. There was someone
I wanted to see.

There was a spring in Klaus's step as we reached the
path, which turned into a bounce and then a pounce as
he saw half a dozen pigeons hanging out under a bridge.
I trotted after him as he burst onto the scene, scattering
the birds. He'd never caught one and wasn't likely to;

a bigger fear should have been that he'd try to follow a pigeon or a duck over the water and I'd have to fish him out of the canal, but so far, he'd never gone that close to the edge.

We arrived at the small park shortly after noon, just as a slim Black woman walked towards us. Her hair was done in thin braids, pulled back in a twist to emphasise her high cheekbones and strong jaw. While most of us wore ratty jeans to the park, knowing that anything was likely to get muddy, Grace never had. Which was extraordinary – all the cockapoos I knew had the vertical lift of a basketball player.

Today she wore a navy-blue linen sheath dress that fell to mid-calf and a pair of gladiator-style sandals. Walking beside her, off-lead, was the same chocolate cockapoo that we'd seen yesterday. While she was smaller and darker than Alfie, there were still far too many similarities. I wasn't so sure I'd make the same decision.

'Hey, Grace,' I said, leaning in to kiss her cheek. 'Sorry we missed you yesterday. Just wanted to tell you how sorry we were to hear about Phil. How are you doing?'

She gave me an arch look. 'You know we broke up over Christmas?' The tone of her voice made me wonder how many people – not just the police – had approached her.

I leaned into the flush that suffused my face. 'Getting a lot of questions, are you?'

'Yeah. The police, friends ...' She swept her hand across the park. 'Random people I don't know, looking for gossip.'

Realising I probably fell somewhere between two of

those categories, I smiled awkwardly. 'You were together for a while; I just wanted to check in.' I reached down to pat the cockapoo. 'Beautiful puppy. How old is she?'

'Eight months,' she said with a fond smile. 'Her name's Daphne.'

Assuming Grace had got Daphne as a puppy when she was about two months, that would have been right around Christmas.

'For a pup that young, she's really well trained.'

'A lot of work went into that.' Grace smiled and ruffled Daphne's long fringe. The pup looked up at me and for a heart-stopping moment, I almost imagined it was Alfie sitting at my feet. Their expressions were nearly identical.

Grace must have noticed. She gave Daphne a soft command and watched while she loped into a small scrum of dogs. 'She's a good girl. Not a replacement for Alfie, of course, but special in her own way.'

'I'm sorry, Grace. About Alfie. And about Phil.'

She nodded. 'He was a good man. Alfie was 100 per cent his, you know. He raised him from a puppy, well before we got together. Bloody man loved that dog more than he loved me. And I was okay with that – I loved Alfie too. When he died, that broke Phil. Broke us.' She kept her eyes on her dog as she spoke, a focus I sensed had less to do with making sure Daphne was out of trouble and more with maintaining her composure.

'I get that. I don't know how I'll cope when it's Klaus's time.'

My eyes strayed to the green expanse, where my little sausage dog was racing after a ball with the bigger hounds. He fell behind and lay down, his focus 100 per cent on the pack. Waiting. As they returned with the ball, he ran at the first dog, a black-and-white border collie, leaping and knocking the ball from her mouth. He grabbed it and ran as if the hound of the Baskervilles was chasing him down.

Cheeky little thing, executing a 'sausage snatch' from a collie.

'You got Daphne then? After Alfie died?'

'A little while after.' She stared at her dog running after Klaus, as my sausage executed a couple of quick turns to throw off the pack. 'The flat was empty, like it almost echoed, you know? And I was walking on egg-shells. Anything could upset Phil. I needed to get away to breathe. So, I went skiing with the girls, and when I came back I figured we needed something fresh in our lives, and I bought another dog.'

'Hence, Daphne.' I smiled.

She nodded. 'Look, I was perfectly aware that bringing a new life into our home wouldn't necessarily bring us together, but I was desperate. I tried it anyway. Daphne might be the same breed as Alfie, but she's totally different. Sure, she's as high-energy as Alf was, but she has her own personality. Phil just didn't want to know, wouldn't engage with her. He'd become obsessed with Alfie's death. He started volunteering with all the local dog charities. Wanted to raise awareness, make sure that people vaccinated their dogs against parvo, but also kennel cough, you know?'

Advocate for those without a voice.

It wasn't people. It was *dogs*.

Grace leaned forward, her eyes on Daphne. 'He had a massive list of things he wanted to raise awareness about. Cooked bones that can shatter in a dog's belly. Chocolate and grapes which could poison them. Those damned travel regulations that mean you can take a small dog out of the UK in a plane cabin with you, but you can't bring them back into the country unless you put them in cargo.' She rolled her eyes and glanced at me. 'Cargo. As if they're no more than a piece of luggage. Can you imagine putting Klaus in the hold while you're flying?'

'Nope. Never.' The few holidays I'd had outside of the UK, Klaus had stayed with Irina and Hamish. 'I've become the queen of staycations since getting Klaus. But I never knew such a law even existed.'

'Oh, it isn't a law. It's a *regulation*. Big difference.'

Phil had once mentioned that Grace was a barrister. Was it possible that he hadn't been killed because of his advocacy, but because of a case Grace was working on? A warning for her to back off? But that didn't make sense if they'd already broken up.

'Do you have any idea why he would turn up dead in the park?'

'Murdered in the park, you mean.'

'You think it was intentional?' I asked self-consciously, knowing how bad that sounded. 'I mean, that he was the target, as opposed to it being a crime of opportunity?'

Or passion.

Grace arched a brow at me, an expression no doubt designed to intimidate lesser mortals in a courtroom. 'Don't you?'

I did, but I couldn't justify why. 'It ... he wasn't into anything dodgy, was he? Drugs?'

'Phil? Drugs?' Grace laughed. 'Hell no. He couldn't understand why anyone would throw their money – and their life – away on that. He even turned down a mild sedative the doctor wanted him to take after Alf died. No, Lou. He'd be the last person involved in anything like that.'

She paused then and seemed to think about something for a few seconds. Her expression fell. 'But for the life of me, Lou, I have no clue who would want to hurt him, or why. All I can hope is that karma finds whoever it is and kicks their arse. He didn't deserve that. Phil Creasy was a good man and a good friend.'

17

IRINA

Louise (Klaus's Mum)

How was your date with PC Andy? 😊

Wasn't a date. And stop calling him that — you know he's a detective.

Sure, sure.
Look, I just spoke with Phil's ex, Grace. Did you know that you can take a small dog out of the UK in a plane cabin with you — as long as they're

under, like, 8 kilos – but regardless of weight you need to put them in the hold when you re-enter?

8 kilos, including the carry bag. UK regulation. Last time I took Hamish home for Christmas it took me 56 hours to come back.

56 hrs? Seriously?

2 flights and a ferry from Amsterdam – with a cabin so Hamish could stay with me rather than the 'dog hotel'. Of course it was storming. Of course we both got seasick. And of course there were engineering works which meant that I got a tour of the southeast.

Grace said Phil was working to raise awareness for dog issues. I can't imagine him getting killed for that. Do you think it's possible that he got killed for something Grace is working on? Maybe involved in?

Anything's possible. What did Grace say?

She said she doesn't know why he was killed.

Maybe she doesn't.

Maybe. But her 'new' boyfriend, Mike, is a big guy, a hard man. I'd bet she had him on the sidelines while finishing up with Phil. You think there was a love triangle?

Even if she did, why would he kill Phil now? Look, I've got to go.
I'll see what I can find out about Grace and her man later.

Irina put down her phone and stared at her screen. She didn't know how Lou had heard about her drink with Andy last night, but it was a small community; someone had probably seen them.

She checked the Pack chat, but no one had put anything in there. Maybe it was a lucky guess? 'Bloody place is becoming an East London spin-off of *Love Island*,' she muttered aloud. 'At least now there's something better to discuss than who I'm shagging. Not that I am shagging him.' Her reflection gave her a nonplussed look and she added, 'Yet'.

While she had the phone in her hand, she sent off another message to the newest contact on her list, unsure whether she'd get a response or not.

18

LOUISE

Jake (Luther's Dad)

We're at Village Vets.

Registering Luther? Good.

No. He was fine this morning. We went to the park at lunchtime. Projectile vomiting & diarrhoea all afternoon. Lucky to get an appointment.

Oh no! I'm sorry — let me know how he gets on.

I think he ate something dodgy at the park. Be careful.

Thank heavens I'd taken Ella's advice and avoided the park, otherwise I'd be the one wrestling something out of Klaus's mouth. 'I guess he missed Ella's comment in the chat,' I murmured to him.

I opened a browser and absently typed in "Jake Hathaway".

The results included an actor, a few people on social media sites and a shedload of photos, none of which looked like my new neighbour across the canal.

'Huh,' I grunted to myself, scrolling through. Tried "Jacob Hathaway" and several other permutations. None had a photo that looked anything like him either. None were even in the right age category.

I was by no means as good at the internet stalk as Irina, but I wasn't so inept that I couldn't even *find* him. Facebook, X, Insta, Snapchat, LinkedIn. I even checked to see if Luther had his own Insta page. Everything came back blank. I couldn't have gotten his name wrong; he'd entered it into my phone.

Who, in the 2020s, has no online presence?

I had more luck with Grace, who apparently had a number of truly gruesome cases under her belt.

Seeing what she did every day, I didn't know how Grace was able to maintain a decent home life, much less a relationship. Assuming that's what she had with Macho Mike.

Her list of cases, or at least the ones I could find (Irina could probably do better), was worrying: drug dealers, extortionists, pimps and rapists. Pretty much the scum of the earth. Maybe someone who could have taken umbrage and come after her? Maybe missed the fact that she and Phil had broken up and got him instead? As a warning to her?

I didn't know the names, didn't know the personalities well enough to know which ones came with a red flashing light. But I knew someone who might.

I turned in my chair and allowed myself a moment to stare at the canal outside my window. Realised I was about to poke a cobra's nest and was willing to do it anyway.

I checked my phone, hoping that Jake would message with an update on Luther, but there were no new notifications. But while I had the phone out, I sent off a different message instead, not expecting a response.

And yet, one came back.

We met at the dog park, despite my misgivings, Violet sitting imperiously at her master's feet. That master stared resolutely into the distance, scowling.

'Gav?'

'Yeah?' He looked up, unruffled. 'So, what'cha want?'

Straight to the chase.

'Thanks for seeing me.'

His dark sunglasses sat firmly in place, making it hard to read his expression. Unsure how to begin, I sat down beside him. 'I was thinking about Phil, the dead guy. Wondering if . . .'

'If?'

'If you might be able to help.'

'Why would you think I could?' He produced a ball and threw it for Violet, who watched it bounce a few times. Klaus was less reticent, happily sprinting after it.

'Because you've lived here a long time. Because maybe you know things, people, that I don't.' I shook my head self-consciously. 'I don't know. People around here defer to you.' I corrected myself, hoping he'd appreciate the honesty. 'Actually, most people around here, for whatever reason, are scared witless of you. I figure you must be pretty well plugged-in to warrant that.'

'Plugged-in?'

I shrugged, not wanting to say 'local crime', or 'mafia', or whatever it was called around here. After a pause, he seemed to relent slightly.

'Fine. So, what do you want?'

'Well, I did a bit of research. Phil's partner, ex-partner, whatever . . . '

'Grace.'

'Yes. She's a lawyer. A barrister. I was wondering, do you think it's possible that one of the people she's prosecuting might have put out a hit on her?'

He guffawed, whether about my jargon or about the idea, I wasn't sure.

'Would you mind looking at the list?'

'Sure, why not.' He held out a bored hand for my phone.

'These are all her current cases.'

'Jackass . . . Wuss . . . Tw—' he cleared his throat, and I guessed he was softening his language for my benefit. 'Coward . . . Ha, that one's a stitch-up . . . Nah . . . Nah . . . Nope.'

Once or twice, he grunted as he scrolled. Once his finger tapped the screen. Then he handed my phone back to me.

'Any ideas?'

He gave me a long look. 'You got balls, girl,' he said.

'But?'

'But nothing. You got balls, an' I mean that in a good way.' He paused. 'You sure you want to do this? What'cha hoping to prove?'

'Prove? Nothing. But I do hope to get a guy that deserved better a bit of justice.'

'You don't have anything better to do with your time?'

'Gav, if anything happened to me, I'd hope someone would care enough to want to find out why. If you have an idea, I'm keen to hear it. You want to pay them a visit, I'm happy to tag along.'

He laughed.

'I'm serious, Gav. I really want to go with you.'

'These people are dangerous, Louise.'

'Yeah,' I said, fighting down a blush. 'I know. And I know it's a bit of a stretch, but it's all I have and I kind of feel that I need to do this.'

'Huh,' he grunted.

'So you're okay with me going with you?' It seemed too easy, almost as though there was a catch. 'Do I need to drop Klausi off at home?'

'He okay with big dogs?'

It was best to be honest. 'Ish? I mean, it depends on the dog, right?'

'Should be all right, but if you want to drop him somewhere, I'll wait here.'

Gav promised to remain on the park bench while I dropped Klaus off with Fi, who usually worked from home on Wednesdays. She was on a call when I arrived, her auburn hair twisted into a topknot, her glasses on top of her head. She gestured to the earbuds nestled in her ears and rolled her eyes.

'Shouldn't be long,' I whispered.

No problem, she mouthed and hit a mute button. 'Where are you off to?'

'Checking out a few leads with Gav.' I let Klaus off his own lead and he ran past Fi towards Nala, who obligingly rolled onto her back. 'People who might have an issue with Grace, Phil's ex.'

She raised an eyebrow. 'What, like a hit gone wrong? So, where's he taking you? Prison?'

I didn't think so. Realised I should have asked.

'Right. You know you're wading in over your head, Lou? If someone ordered a hit on Grace but got it wrong and you're sniffing around, then you might as well paint a target on your own back.' She placed her glasses on the bridge of her nose and stared at me over the rims. 'And I'd really rather not find your dead body somewhere. Clear?'

'Crystal.'

'Good. Get out of here, and be careful, will you?' She unmuted the call and waved me out. Before I'd made it more than a handful of steps, she leaned around her front door and called after me, 'Message me when you're back so that I know you're safe.'

'You have Klaus,' I reminded her. 'I'll let you know as soon as I'm on my way over.'

She gave a thumbs-up and disappeared back into her flat, her words hanging in the air between us.

It's not about you, I reminded myself, forcing myself to move. *This is bigger than you.*

And it's the right thing to do.

I met Gav back at the park. 'Where are we going?'

He didn't answer, just started walking. I followed. 'We're not going to prison, are we?'

'What?' He stopped, startled. 'Why do you say that?'

'I just assumed that the people who might have an issue with Grace would be locked up.'

'Huh.' He started walking again. 'Some are, some aren't. Some of the more dangerous ones aren't locked up. Or if they are, they have people on the outside. But no, we're not going to see them.'

'Then who are we going to see?'

Just then my phone pinged. 'Sorry, I need to check this. A friend of mine – well, a new neighbour. His dog ate something and got sick.'

Jake (Luther's Dad)

> They're gonna purge Luther.

>> Good luck – to you and the big guy.

> Thx. We get through this and I will make sure he never eats anything off the ground again.

>> Lots of luck with that – Irina's been trying to stop Hamish from scavenging for years ...

> A trip to the vet is a good incentive.

He wasn't wrong. I replied that I hoped all went well and to keep me updated.

'He okay?'

'Fingers crossed,' I answered Gav. 'Damn horrible welcome to the neighbourhood when this happens within days of him moving in.'

Gav grunted by way of an answer. He led me out of the park and down winding streets to a café in Poplar. It looked like most greasy spoons on this side of town, and its only customer appeared to be a bespectacled man sitting at a table behind a laptop. Like Gav, he looked north of sixty. He was dressed in the sort of sweatshirts that were sold at the street market, but wore a heavy gold chain around his neck and chunky rings that looked real.

The woman in the kitchen behind him was of a similar age, with grey hair fastened at the nape of her neck. She nodded a greeting as we entered.

Gav took off his sunglasses. 'Jono. Norma. Y'awright?'

The man looked up and smiled. 'Gav. What'cha doin' here?'

A corner of Gav's mouth quirked. 'Social call.'

The man – Jono – glanced at me, then back to Gav. 'That so?'

Violet strutted through the café as if she owned it. She yapped a brief greeting to a massive lump of furred muscle lying under the table. It raised its blunt head and looked at me, as if determining whether I was any danger. Luther was big for a Staffie, around three times Klaus's size. This dog lying on the floor looked like him, that same sort of muscular breed, but where Luther was pushing twenty kilos, this creature had to be over sixty.

Glad I'd left Klaus at home – he'd have been terrified – I

patted my pockets, pulling out a scrunched-up bag. I held it up to the man. 'Lovely dog,' I managed to squeak out. 'Can I give him a treat?'

'Yeah, sure. Rocco'll love that,' Jono said, dismissing me; his attention was firmly on Gav.

'My friend Louise.' Gav introduced me as he sat down across from Jono. 'She's the one what found the body last weekend.'

'Ah hell. Bad news that.'

'Any idea who would've done it?'

I shook a few treats into my palm, holding my hand flat as I proffered them to Rocco. Klaus was a baby shark when it came to treats, and if Rocco ate the same way, he'd take off half my hand.

Jono had clearly taken the time to train and socialise Rocco, though. He took the treats gently and licked my wrist in thanks.

'Nah. Been asking around. Some think it was a drug hit. Some think the gangs.'

'It wasn't drugs,' I said, palming a few more treats. As massive as Rocco was, he was growing on me. 'Phil didn't do them.'

'You sure, girl?' Jono looked at me. 'Most people say that after they turn a blind eye to the signs.'

'Yeah, pretty sure,' I said, although I wasn't. He was right, people saw what they wanted to. I wouldn't have thought Phil the type, but that didn't mean he wasn't. Maybe Grace had either chosen not to see the signs, or had genuinely missed them. 'I think.'

Rocco rolled onto his back, allowing me to rub his belly.

Jono nodded and closed his laptop. 'I haven't heard anything about anyone who would have bumped him off.'

'Mind keeping an ear out?'

'Anyone in particular?'

Gav recited a few names from my list. Jono nodded, non-committal.

'Heard you had a spot of bother the other day, Gav,' the woman said from the kitchen. 'You okay?'

'You heard about that?'

'Mo mentioned.' She came round from the back and placed a cup of milky tea in front of him, asking me what I'd like. 'Stupid kids,' she added.

'Any idea who might've sent them after me?'

'Mate, you've been out of the game for years. No point in offin' you now. Twenty, thirty years ago, sure. Now? No point.' Jono thrust a heavy, beringed finger at Gav. 'Now you're old, man. Ir-rel-ee-vant.'

'Ta.' Gav's voice was deadpan, but Jono still grinned.

'Maybe they just saw ya as an easy target?'

The woman fixing my tea snorted. 'As if.'

'Thanks, Norma.'

She winked at him and walked around the counter to place the steaming cup in front of me. 'There's a baby gang around here. Stupid kids holding other kids up at knifepoint. Nicking bikes from the delivery guys. Stealing phones, the like. Can't see them going after you, though, Gav. You ain't their type of mug.'

There was a compliment in there somewhere, surely. Gav gave her a half nod, finished his tea and stood up.

I took a hurried sip out of courtesy and followed. Violet trotted over, looking up at her master.

'Thanks for your time, Jono,' Gav said. 'Have a good day, Norma.'

'And you.'

We left the café and crossed the street, beginning to weave our way back towards Partridge Park. 'That's it?' I asked.

'Uh-huh.'

'We didn't learn anything.' I didn't like the plaintive note in my voice.

'Learnt plenty.'

Had he been in a different place to me? 'How so?'

'It wasn't what he said, Louise. It was what he didn't say. If there was news, Jono would know it. Might not have said who was coming after me, but would've said something about Phil, if he could have.'

'What if he couldn't? And what was that about kids coming after you?'

He brushed off both questions. Continued walking, brows lowered. 'Nuthin' I can't handle.' His face softened as he turned to me. 'But Jono will start asking questions, and when he does, people – more people – will start looking at us. Watch your back.'

19

LOUISE

Irina (Hamish's Mum)

Fi told me that you had another field trip today. Everything go well?

More questions than answers, tbh. If I send you a list of Grace's clients — which I found legally — would you be able to see if any of them seem likely to put a hit out on her?

Send it over, but you
know it'll still just be our
speculation, right?

It's better than nothing –
I'll take it. Thx!

The walk home from Fiona's was tense. I was on high
alert, scanning the area, and not just for the usual chicken
bones or dangerous litter. Klaus, sensing my stress, barked
at anyone who came near.

My nerves were frayed and I could murder a glass of
wine, but my delivery wasn't set to arrive for another day
or two.

'Ups,' I said to Klaus, going down on one knee and
catching him as he leapt onto my shoulder. With one
hand on his back and the other on his bottom, I nodded
to a few youths, passing them as I stepped into News-N-
Booze. The shop might not be dog-friendly, but it wasn't
dog-unfriendly either, allowing me to take Klaus in as long
as I carried him.

'Hey Zed,' I said to the kid at the till, moving sideways
past a freezer of ice cream to get to the wine. I shifted
Klaus so that I could hold him with one arm and grabbed
a bottle of Sauvignon Blanc with my free hand. There
wasn't a lot of room to manoeuvre, so I backed out along
the aisle to the till. Klaus began to bark only seconds
before I crashed into a warm but solid wall.

'Oh my God, I'm so sorry,' I said, turning. My

voice trailed away as I found myself staring at a chest barely constrained by a black T-shirt. My gaze moved upwards, towards broad shoulders. Five o'clock shadow didn't detract from the chiselled jawline or hooded dark blue eyes.

My fingers clutched the neck of the bottle. 'Hi.'

Jake Hathaway grunted at me. Glancing at Klaus, he said, 'Didn't know dogs were allowed in here.' His accent had broadened to a light Scottish burr.

'Hers is,' Zed said from the till. In a fake German accent he added, 'Klaus is cool.'

Zed wouldn't say that if he'd seen Klaus wee on the pyramid of two-litre water bottles arranged outside, but I figured that was something he didn't need to know. With Klaus's low clearance, there was no chance of him weeing high enough to reach the caps anyway.

'Thanks, Zed.' I offered a tentative smile to my neighbour. 'How's Luther?'

'Stoned.'

'Anything else?' Zed asked, ringing up Jake's beer. 'Maybe some crisps for your stoned friend?'

I bit my lip to stop myself from laughing. Daring a glance at Jake broke my resolve. Maybe it was the stress of the day, but both of us began to laugh.

'Just trying to help,' Zed said cheerfully.

'Luther'd love crisps,' Jake told him. 'But then, he'd eat crap off the street. Which already landed him in the vet's once today. Luther's my dog.'

'Ah,' Zed said, a dusky flush rising on his cheeks. 'Sorry, man. I didn't know.'

'It's okay.' Jake pried the bottle from my fingers and put it on the counter next to his beer. 'I got this too.'

'Thank you,' I said surprised. 'Why?'

'Because I don't want to drink alone.'

Alone? He was *single*?

Jake picked up the wine and beer. 'You have other plans?'

I didn't.

'Come on. Unless you want crisps too?'

I shook my head, bemused. Still half in shock, I put Klaus down and followed Jake out of the newsagents and down the street.

The complex we lived in was once a warehouse, its red-brick buildings occupying both sides of the canal. On my side, the former administrative buildings had full balconies; on the other side, the buildings facing the canal had large windows for light and ventilation, some with Juliet balconies that had been added on a couple of decades ago for safety. The photograph in my lobby had been taken some time in the 1800s and showed a small pedestrian bridge connecting both sides. That private bridge was long gone, but further along was a rail bridge and another one for cars and pedestrians.

Jake flashed his fob at the eastern entrance and pushed the heavy metal gate open. He led the way past a garden blooming with red and white flowers and into the foyer.

Like mine, Jake's building had high ceilings and long

windows. Unlike mine, it didn't have a lift. With Klaus riding my shoulder again, I followed Jake up three flights of stairs, unsure what to expect.

Jake unlocked his door and gestured for me to precede him into the flat. I was half expecting Luther to be waiting in the hallway – Klaus always was when I dared leave home without him – but instead he was sitting on a mat in the living room, his head on the floor, his dark eyes watchful. I put Klaus down, keeping him on his lead, just in case.

He was less worried, strutting over to the far bigger dog and having a good sniff. I got down on one knee and held out my hand to Luther, so that he could get my scent. 'Sorry you're not feeling well, sweetheart,' I said. He breathed a soft whoof of air over my hand, accepting me. I sat beside him, stroking his head. Klaus crawled into my lap and the three of us sat in companionable silence while Jake poured the drinks from behind a breakfast bar.

His flat was large, with floor-to-ceiling windows on the west and south sides. A few boxes were stacked around the edge of the living room. I'd expected a black leather sofa on the back wall, against the exposed brick, but his was dark blue – the exact colour of his eyes – and comfortable-looking. Above it, four black-and-white photographs hung in simple black frames. All were scenes shot through doorways. The one on the left was the view from a ruined castle, looking down on a village. The second showed Edinburgh Castle, framed by pillars. The third was the New York skyline, as seen through a balcony door and the last, a view of Tower Bridge, taken from behind a window in the Tower of London.

'Beautiful photographs,' I said.

'Thanks.'

'Places you've lived?' I guessed. 'I mean, at least the cities or towns? Not saying you've lived in a tower or a castle . . .' I allowed my voice to trail off, aware that I was babbling.

His half-smile acknowledged the point without giving anything away.

A TV was set up on the far side of the room, atop a wood-and-metal table. Large enough to do a Super Bowl or World Cup party proud. Even though it was the sort of size that said man den, I tried not to make assumptions. Especially as it was currently playing a wildlife programme at low volume.

'Something to keep Luther entertained,' Jake said unselfconsciously. 'I can change the channel if you'd like?'

'I don't mind. You've done a pretty good job unpacking; it took me a couple of months before I even opened the last box after my move,' I said, also noting that there wasn't a plant in sight. The only personal items seemed to be the photographs on the wall and a paperback novel lying open, face down. I recognised it from the window of the Waterstones in the Wharf, but I hadn't read it. 'Good book?'

'Predictable,' he answered. 'The guy who's trying to get close to the police investigation is the serial killer.'

A silly image ran through my head. 'Well, the only one – that I know of – who's trying to insert themselves into the *Who Killed Phil Creasy?* police investigation is Irina Ivanova. And I'm pretty sure it wasn't her.'

He offered me a strange look and I changed the subject. 'Did the vet say how long Luther will be like this?'

Jake shrugged and set the drinks down on a glass coffee table. He sat on the sofa and took a couple of gulps before answering. 'The drugs should wear off by tomorrow. Vet said we were lucky to get to him in time.'

He pushed the wine glass towards me and waited for me to shuffle closer before raising his pint. 'Thanks for letting me know where the vet was. I don't think they would have seen him if Luther hadn't already been registered with them.'

'Did they say what it was?'

Jake's expression was tired, and he shrugged a shoulder.

'Chicken bone or grapes?' I guessed. 'No, wait. Chocolate?'

He shook his head.

'He was poisoned.'

'Oh no . . . Poisoned? Like, intentionally? I mean, there's always stuff left in the park. Are you sure?'

'I'm not sure of anything.'

'Would you mind if I let the Pack know? Just so they're aware and can keep an eye out.'

'Go ahead. I don't want this to happen to anyone else's dog.'

I sent off the message and put my phone on the table. Across the room, Klaus had curled up next to Luther. Whereas dachshunds looked more or less like land otters, especially when lying on their backs, Staffies reminded me of happy baby hippos. From this angle, it almost looked like they were spooning.

'Did they say what sort of poison it was?'

'No. They just purged him to get it out of his system.'

My phone buzzed.

'Go ahead,' Jake said. When I raised my brow, he added, 'Check your message.'

'That's okay, it's probably just someone responding to my warning.' I pushed the phone further away but drew my legs close to my chest. 'Which vet did you see?'

'Dr Cooper. Young guy, seemed to know what he was doing. He's going to run tests to assess whether the poison hit any of Luther's vital organs.'

'For what it's worth, Luther looks fine. Stoned, yeah, but fine.'

Jake nodded, looking miserable. I sidled over, wishing I knew him well enough to give him a hug. 'He'll be fine, Jake,' I said, hoping I wasn't lying.

He shrugged off the sympathy and picked up the TV remote. 'You okay with watching something? You can choose, as long as it isn't a crap romcom.'

'I like thrillers,' I said, realising that with the way the week was going, I might well be living one. Still, I took hold of the remote. 'Will that work for you?'

20

IRINA

Partridge Bark

Claire (Tank's Mum)

Really sorry to hear about your neighbour's dog @**Louise** – I did a bit of poking around. It seems that there were three other dogs whose owners contacted the paper about possible dog poisonings.

Indy (Banjo's Mum)

How many dogs were poisoned?

Claire (Tank's Mum)

Including this latest one, four, although not all at Partridge. Earliest one was last autumn.

Louise (Klaus's Mum)

Do we think they're connected?

Claire (Tank's Mum)

To each other? IDK. Maybe.

Irina rolled her eyes. That wasn't what Louise was asking; she wanted to know if the poisonings were connected to the bloody murder. She knew this would happen. Lou was bored; her company was doing well and she was taking a step back. She needed a new crusade, and Irina was afraid this would be it: Lou would become obsessed, not just with solving Phil's murder, but now every crime in the neighbourhood. This was East London. There was a lot of it. Some were opportunistic, others were incidental. Some were about race or religion or which group of pals you had. This wasn't a crime novel, though. Not everything was connected.

Irina wanted to tell Lou to get a life, but she couldn't be bothered. She'd worked hard to keep her life simple, uncluttered. She had no interest in becoming a modern-day Miss Marple. Not for a dead man she barely knew. And anyway, Andy had asked her to steer clear of it.

Andy. The silver lining to an otherwise bad day.

As far as she could tell, he was a decent sort of guy. Went to Leeds University, got a good degree. Did IT for a year or so before chucking that job in and joining the Met Police. *He must really love it*, Irina thought. Because that move had to have hit his wallet pretty badly.

She'd found more photographs of him online, some by himself, but mostly with friends and a few lady friends. Irina would have been more concerned if there hadn't been any of the latter – she didn't want to deal with someone else's mummy issues, or worse, someone who wasn't keen on commitment.

Keep it light. See where things go. That was the plan. Something with no demands; no expectations.

She sighed and pinged him a message, relaying Louise's concerns about the poisonings, more because she didn't want to catch grief from Lou than for any excuse to contact him.

His response was immediate:

DC Andrew Thompson

Irina, whatever you and your friends are doing, stop it now. A man is dead.

> Your meddling will either
> get you in trouble with
> whoever murdered Phil, or
> muddy our investigation.

Irina blinked, not sure what he was thinking when she was only trying to help. 'Meddling?' she said aloud. 'I don't *meddle*.'

She wrote a reply, but deleted it before hitting Send. Same with the second and third.

On some level, he was probably right. She was no crusader, with a bloody horse and flaming sword. She knew that people who asked too many questions often ended up in as much trouble as the people they tried to help.

But Irina didn't like being told what to do. Especially by someone she'd only just met.

Even more so, when every fibre of her being told her that what she was being told not to do was in fact the *right* thing to do.

God *damn* Louise Mallory for getting her into this. 'Meddle this,' Irina muttered to herself, tapping out a message.

Partridge Bark

> One man dead, three
> dogs (that we know of)
> poisoned. The police want
> us off the case.

This is our neighbourhood and our park. Phil Creasy was our friend. I do not want Hamish or any of our pups to be poisoned. I think it's time we work together.

Meg (Tyrion's Mum)

What do you have in mind?

We are the ones that people see but don't SEE. I say we set up patrols. We check in, more than usual, with anything out of the ordinary. I don't care if it's a branch where you don't expect it. Anything that looks off, we put it in the chat.
I can set up a different group if people don't want to be involved, or don't want this here.

Meg (Tyrion's Mum)

I'm in.

Yaz (Hercules's Mum)

Not sure what got into you (ahem) to precipitate this crime-fighting spree, but Ejiro, Herc and I are in.

As Is

Soph and I are in – Loki's always happy for more walks with friends.

Louise (Klaus's Mum)

Thanks @Irina. Klaus and I are in.

The messages cascaded through, one after another. Feeling satisfied, Irina opened her laptop, brought up a browser window and began her own investigations.

21

THE PACK

Partridge Bark

Paul (Bark Vader and Jimmy Chew's Dad)

Those damn street kids just stole my neighbour's bike! I can see them, but too far to get a good pic. Ella's phoning the police now.

Yaz (Hercules's Mum)

Which way are they heading?

Indy (Banjo's Mum)

I see three guys in hoodies pushing a motorcycle towards the park. Can't see the reg number, but it looks grey.

Indy (Banjo's Mum)

They're in the park, behind The Nest. I can see them! Banjo is going mad on the balcony, I'm sure they see us!

Ejiro (Hercules's Dad)

What are they doing?

Indy (Banjo's Mum)

I don't know. Fiddling with it. I guess they're trying to jump-start it? Can you jump-start a motorcycle?

Ella (Bark Vader and Jimmy Chew's Mum)

OK. Let me know if they move, I'm waiting to be connected to the police.

Irina (Hamish's Mum)

They're already on their way.

Yaz (Hercules's Mum)

Ooooh, @Irina – you got the bat light, baby!

Irina (Hamish's Mum)

WTF?

Indy (Banjo's Mum)

I hear sirens! They're running away!

Paul (Bark Vader and Jimmy Chew's Dad)

The bike?

Indy (Banjo's Mum)

They threw it into the bushes behind the café.

Ejiro (Hercules's Dad)

Indy, can you go down there and show the police?

Sophie (Loki's Mum)

Unless **@Irina** wants that role?

Irina (Hamish's Mum)

No, that's OK.

Yaz (Hercules's Mum)

Well done with the bat light **@Irina**! I don't want to know what sort of favours you had to call in, but we never get that sort of response from the police around here!

Irina (Hamish's Mum)

Bat light. Baby.

Indy (Banjo's Mum)

The police have the bike. There's another car chasing the kids towards the high street. I can't see any more from here.

Thursday

22

GAV

That was fast, Gav thought, closing *The Chronicle*'s news app. At least they hadn't mentioned the dogs. No point in painting a target on anyone walking a hound. Still, not bad going for a patrol that had formed less than twenty-four hours ago. He wasn't so certain how much he enjoyed being on the side of the police, or – as Louise would put it – 'using his contacts for good', but he disliked the new gangs more.

He pushed open the gate and allowed Violet to lead the way into the dog park. It was already close to 9 a.m. and most of the professional crowd had already left for the office or Teams meetings, leaving it largely empty. A honey-coloured cocker spaniel was chasing a ball, and a white Jack Russell was chasing the spaniel. Both seemed happy enough with the situation, and Violet, not one for too much exercise, was content to watch them, only growling when they came too close.

The cocker's mum, an attractive redhead of about thirty or so, waved at Gav and gestured that she was on a call. Maybe she was, but he'd seen her do that before to avoid speaking to the pretty boy on the bench. Stupid kid had a pretty girl of his own but thought he was some sort of Casanova. Gav knew how he'd take that damned dog for a 'walk' and visit one of heaven knew how many women. Sooner or later, he'd end up contracting something nasty and infecting half the neighbourhood.

He sat beside the kid, only because he didn't think his hip would allow him to walk to the bench on the far side of the enclosure. Pulling a bottle of water from his satchel, he poured some into a metal bowl for Violet.

'Nice bruises,' the kid said, greeting him. 'Hurt much?'

Manners are dead, Gav thought. He looked at Casanova and asked, 'What are you talking about?'

'Bruises on your knuckles, man. Those aren't from walking your dog, those are from serious impact. You working out at the gym or something?'

'I look like I work out at the gym?' Gav didn't have to feign incredulity. The bruises were days old, the skin a yellowish-purple. Of all the people to notice, he wouldn't have thought it would be Casanova. Or that the kid would be dumb enough to say something about it. He flexed his fingers and tried to joke. 'You should see the other guys.'

'Guys? As in more than one?' The kid's eyebrows raised a good half-inch, and he took off his sunglasses. 'Look, man. If you're in trouble, maybe I can help.'

Gav blinked. What help could the pretty boy give him? A comb? 'Appreciate that, but I don't need any help.'

Casanova shrugged. 'If you do, let me know. Though, I heard a couple of kids tried to beat up an old guy the other day. Turns out he was some sort of Clint Eastwood. Knocked the piss out of them. Wouldn't be surprised if they're looking to get even. Not sure who that old guy was, but good on him.' He leaned back against the bench, rising a fraction in Gav's estimation.

'Where did you hear crap like that?'

'Didn't really hear it.' Casanova grinned. 'Saw it from my window. I live in one of the flats overlooking the market.' He looked over at his dog, watching the terrier lose out to the cocker again. 'I heard a commotion. Looked out my window and saw those kids that hang out at the wings place. Me, they leave alone, but my girl, Soph, doesn't feel comfortable around them. I tried to call the cops, but the kids and the old guy were gone before I could get through.'

'Ahhh,' Gav said. The market was dark at night; if the pretty boy had seen anything, he had good eyesight. Or a damned good imagination; Gav wasn't stupid enough to confirm anything.

173

He shrugged. 'Well, if you saw that, you should probably tell the cops about it. Give them a description of the little shits before they hurt someone.' He shrugged again. 'Not that the cops'll do anything, mind.'

'I'll do that,' the kid said, looking Gav in the eye. 'I'll try to get a better description of them first, of course.'

Gav nodded, realising that the pretty-boy exterior might just camouflage a brain. 'You do that, son. You do that.' He reached into his bag and pulled out a can of cola, popping it open and pointing it at Casanova. 'Why do you wanna get involved? You've got an easy life. You make a target of yourself, that might stop.'

The pretty boy laughed. 'My girl's got her brothers visiting. Let's say it'll give me a good excuse to stay away from the house.'

As if everyone in the neighbourhood didn't know just how he did that.

'Yeah? From what I hear, those kids can be nasty.'

'I can take care of myself,' the kid said.

Gav nodded as if he believed him. 'Then you know to be careful. You poke that nest an' they may come back an' find you when you're not expecting it.' When Gav felt the boy's eyes on him, he raised his cola in a half-salute. 'Just sayin'.'

23

LOUISE

Meg (Tyrion's Mum)

You ask, I deliver. Despite a tight deadline, Fidelio mgmt gave the team a few days off to process what happened to Phil. They're meeting this evening to do drinks in his honour at the office, which is pretty decent. Wouldn't be surprised if they head to a bar afterwards ...

Between the teamwork that had resulted in last night's success and Meg's information, I was feeling quietly confident that together, we'd be able to figure out who'd murdered Phil.

I finished my morning call and pulled out my earbuds. The research I'd done on Fidelio was shining a mirror on my own situation. Like Phil, I'd started my company about five years ago with friends. But while mine had begun to step away to 'pursue other interests', allowing me to buy them out, Phil had managed to go another route, balancing his job against the egos of the other founders.

My challenge was different. While we were a consultancy, deploying a methodology based on best practice, I'd learned enough to keep the company small to maintain the culture and to always look at succession planning. That last bit I might have done too well. As a second-in-command, I couldn't ask for better than Babs, but the result was that my role was now more about showing my face and removing obstacles. And there weren't a lot of obstacles at the moment. One day – and probably sooner rather than later – I'd step back fully. And then what?

Klaus got up from his bed by the window and stretched his long body. Picked up a ball and dropped it on my foot.

'Subtlety isn't in your nature, is it?' I asked, but I obliged him, throwing the ball into the hallway. He bolted after it, his nails pattering on the wooden floor as it ricocheted off walls and doors. 'I'm going to need to get this place repainted one of these days.'

I closed my laptop and put on my trainers. It was early

for the park, but while Klaus had been well behaved, we both needed fresh air.

'Let's go, Klaus,' I called, holding up his lead.

He dropped the ball and ran over, the lure of being outside greater even than that of the toy, especially as he then watched me put it in my pocket.

My confidence was misplaced. The moment we stepped into the June sunshine, Klaus dug in his paws. *Nope. Not moving.*

'Come on,' I said, trying to ignore the amused looks from passers-by. I dangled the ball in front of his nose. 'Let's go.'

For such a small dog, those paws were like brakes. The ball didn't spur him on. Neither did the treats. I muttered a curse and resorted to picking him up and draping him over my left shoulder.

A nearby church bell rang eleven o'clock as we reached the park, and I breathed a sigh of relief. The dog enclosure was empty save for a familiar old man reading a news-paper on one of the benches. As usual, Violet lay by his feet. 'Morning, Violet. Morning, Gav.'

Gav grunted but didn't look up.

I didn't let that deter me. I took Klaus off his lead and set him down. Throwing the ball for him to chase, I stepped over Violet and sat down.

'Louise.'

'Thanks again for your help yesterday.'

Gav nodded, with a wary look, as if he knew I was about to ask for another favour. 'He didn't have anything else.'

'What? Who?'

'Jono. And if he doesn't know who put a hit out on Phil, assumin' that's what it was, then no one around here does.'

'Okay. I believe you. Him. But remember how I said yesterday that a friend of mine's dog got sick? Something he ate at the park?'

'Yeah, read that in the chat too. How's he now?'

'All right, we think. Jake isn't saying it, but I get the feeling he thinks that someone left something there intentionally. Some kind of poison, to hurt the dogs.'

'And you want to know if it's happened before? Or if I know who might've done it?' His mouth twitched into a wry smile.

'It sounds kind of silly when spoken aloud. Sorry. And sorry for bugging you.' And yet ... no harm, no foul. I gave Gav an arch look. 'But I don't suppose you do have any insight?'

'No.'

'No? Are you sure?'

'No.' He snorted a small laugh. 'We had one, a few years ago. An old woman who was trying to get rid of the foxes that kept raiding her garden. Terrorising her cats. One of the lads, he caught her at it. Poisoned dog biscuits, 'cos foxes are dogs in her book. But the lad, he had a quiet word with her.'

I didn't want to ask who the lad was or what that 'quiet word' had entailed.

'No problem from her since?'

'None.'

'You don't think she'd be up to her old tricks?'

He was already shaking his head. 'Don't reckon so.'

It was my turn to frown. 'So, you don't know who could be doing it?'

'No.' He raised his sunglasses and looked at me with shrewd eyes. 'Do you?'

I blinked, taken aback. 'Should I?'

He replaced the glasses and looked beyond me. 'Couldn't say. But you seem pretty committed to solving every crime that happens in Tower Hamlets. First the dead man. Now the poisonings.'

It was more than the boredom and love of detective stories that Irina had accused me of. More – and yet, more simple. 'I found Phil; I owe him. And I don't want someone else's dog to get poisoned. I mean, what if it had been Klaus, or Violet?'

'Violet knows better than to eat crap off the ground, or from strangers,' Gav growled. 'But if you're trying to connect this to what happened to Phil, you should know that most people who poison dogs don't tend to kill humans,' he pointed out. 'You get that, right?'

'I know.'

A strange silence passed between us. Finally, he relented. 'Fine. I think you're wasting your time, but if you want, I can pay the woman a visit. Ask if she's still got a problem with them foxes.'

'I wouldn't want you to get into any trouble with her.'

His smile widened and I realised that he was enjoying himself. 'That would be a good outcome. I suppose you'll want to come along?'

I didn't miss a beat. 'Of course. I've got your back. Again!'

'Yeah, fine. But we'll need to drop both dogs off this time. Old Ivy, as I said, she ain't a big fan.' One side of his mouth twitched and he stood up. 'You comin'? Or you wanna wait until Christmas?'

We stopped by News-N-Booze. I waved to Zed at the till and followed Gav down the alcohol aisle to a door at the back of the shop. He pushed it open without knocking. 'Mo? You in here?'

'Yeah. Whatcha wan', Gav?' A fat man waddled into the dim light, holding a paperback. I'd seen him a few times behind the till, but hadn't realised he was the manager here.

'Mind watching Violet and Klaus for half an hour?' Gav pointed to my dog, in case Mo was in any doubt as to who Klaus was.

Violet planted her paws in front of Gav, challenging Mo to agree. Violet and Mo clearly had a rocky relationship. Klaus, on my shoulder, seemed equally unsure about the arrangements.

As did Mo. Gav's friend looked like he'd rather invite a lion into his storeroom. Still, he forced a smile. 'Sure, Gav. For half an hour, you say?'

'Yeah. Gotta go see Ivy.'

'Woodhouse?' Mo blinked, then saluted Gav. 'Good luck to ya, mate.'

Gav grunted and turned around. I put Klaus on the floor. 'Thank you.'

Mo flicked his wrist in a gesture that could have meant 'it's nothing' or 'just get out of here'. I backed out and sprinted down the aisle to catch up to Gav.

'So ... Ivy Woodhouse. That's her name?'

He nodded. 'Brace yourself.'

He led the way down a side street, past a church, to a terraced row on the other side of the dog park. Ivy Woodhouse's home was pebbledashed, with a neat front garden that exploded with colours. Azaleas, rhododendrons, roses. A garden centre's worth of flowers, interspersed between two bird baths and most of the cast of *Gnomeo and Juliet*.

'Jesus,' I muttered.

Gav, hobbling in front of me, stopped and paused. 'You think this is bad, wait until you see inside.'

The woman who greeted us at the door must have been a decade or two older than Gav. Her steel-grey hair was styled in what might have been intended as a pixie cut, but better resembled a medieval knight's helmet. A warrior, draped in a flowered kaftan. Presumably with a horde of ferocious cats as her army.

'Gav.' She patted her hair and stepped back to make way for him. 'What brings you here?'

'Wanted to have a quick word, Ivy.'

A tentative smile lit her features. She took off her over-sized glasses and, tucking them into a pocket, batted her eyelashes at him.

Feeling like a third wheel, I cleared my throat.

Mrs Woodhouse looked at me, eyes narrowing in a way that had little to do with myopia.

'I'm Louise Mallory,' I introduced myself.

She grunted and led the way into the front room, shooing a fat tabby off the settee. 'Tea, Gav?'.

'No thanks, Ivy. Look, we won't waste your time. A dog's fell ill. Looks like he was poisoned. Wanted to know if you knew anything about that?'

The old woman deflated a bit. 'Yeah, well, it ain't me. I'll go fix that tea.'

Although Gav had turned down the offer of a drink, she waved him to sit down and went to put the kettle on anyway. I perched on an orange ottoman and looked around. There were the requisite net curtains, crocheted doilies on every flat surface and fox-themed cat toys scattered all over the floor.

Gav caught my eye and sighed.

'Can I give you a hand, Mrs Woodhouse?' I asked.

The only sound emerging from the kitchen was the shriek of the boiling kettle. Ivy reappeared a few moments later, carrying a tray bearing a red-and-blue crocheted tea cosy and a couple of cups. She set it down, and I realised that the design, the theme, was the Union Jack.

Ivy poured tea into the two cups, handing one to Gav and offering him a plate of biscuits. When he turned them down, she poured milk into the second cup of tea.

I pulled a bottle of water from my bag, wishing I'd brought popcorn as well. She was clearly flirting with him. So, was she a geriatric cougar or did she just look a heck of a lot older than she was?

'I don't like foxes, Gav,' she said, stirring her tea. 'You know I don't like foxes.'

'I know that, Ivy.'

'But I don't have a problem with dogs, Gav. You know I like dogs. Even your little dog. Victoria.'

'Violet.'

'Violet, yeah. That's what I said. But no. No. I learnt my lesson last time. No more poisoning the foxes.'

I believed her, mostly because I didn't think she'd lie to Gav, but also because I figured she probably wouldn't want to risk her cats getting at whatever poison she might leave out.

Gav nodded his head. His expression hovered somewhere between interested and empathetic. A lot of effort must have been going into it. 'Any idea who might be involved, Ivy?' he asked.

She leaned back in her armchair, lower lip thrust out as she considered the question. Somewhere in the cluttered house a carriage clock chimed.

'Have you checked out them boys what hang around outside News-N-Booze?'

I leaned forward. 'What do you know about them, Mrs Woodhouse?'

'I know they're trouble. Harass good people goin' about their business. Prob'ly truants from school. Trouble, I tell you,' she said, waggling her finger at me, as if I was responsible for the yobs.

I took a sip from my water bottle, not taking her silent accusation personally. 'Do you think they'd be poisoning dogs?'

'They don't like dogs, I tell you. Don't like anyone, s'far as I can tell. Ev'ry time I walk in, they're leering. Making nasty comments. Ain't Christian, I tell you.' With each word, her finger stabbed towards my chest. Ivy Woodhouse might be old, but to me she was far more terrifying than the teenagers that hung around outside the News-N-Booze.

'Okaaay.' I stretched the word out for a few seconds, trying for a neutral tone, even though what she'd said wasn't strictly true. I'd seen the kids with a big American bulldog once or twice. Treading carefully, I continued, 'I get that they don't like dogs, but there's a big difference between not liking dogs and poisoning them, Mrs Woodhouse.'

She drew a deep breath. When she spoke, her voice was low and vicious. 'How dare you come into my house and accuse me of all sorts?'

I wasn't aware that I'd accused her of anything other than over-dramatisation of the situation, but she wasn't in the mood for an explanation.

'I won't stand for it!' In a voice that came straight from *EastEnders*, she howled, 'Get outta my house!'

Things went downhill from there, and in short order, the old woman frog-marched us both out of the front door and along the path, as the garden gnomes watched with wide eyes.

The gate had clanged shut behind us before Gav dared turn towards me. '"They might be creeps, but that doesn't make them poisoners",' he chuckled, before sobering up. 'T'be fair, those kids are little bastards. They're dangerous, but I don't think they are the ones poisoning the dogs.'

'Why not?' I asked, more from a devil's advocate perspective.

'Nothing to get out of it. They poison a dog, so what? They get nothing. Braggin' rights? No chance. Not for poison. An' some of 'em have dogs of their own. Not that they bother to clean up after 'em.' Gav rubbed his hip and led the way back to News-N-Booze. 'No, for the poisonings, same as for Phil Creasy, we need to look at who gains.'

Had he also sensed a connection? I let my question slide for now. 'Who could possibly gain from hurting a dog?'

'I don't know,' he said, his eyes forward. 'Not yet. But trust me when I tell you: I'll find out. And when I do, they'll regret it.'

24

GAV

Gav ignored the pain in his hip as he strode down the street. He didn't like Ivy; never had. Didn't like her xenophobia, her views. But he didn't disagree with her that the kids outside News-N-Booze could be dangerous.

There were four of them today. A tall Asian bloke with a hoodie covering half his face. A smaller guy, his face also hidden but for eyes set too close together. A white kid with pockmarked skin and a girl with long blonde hair and soulless eyes.

Gav was certain they weren't the kids who'd attacked him, but he couldn't be as sure that they hadn't been up to some sort of mischief elsewhere.

'Do you think Ivy pointed us at the kids because some of them are Asian?' Louise whispered as they walked through the off-licence.

'Wouldn't put it past her,' Gav grunted.

From the other side of the door at the back of the shop, they heard the chorus of Klaus's and Violet's barking. 'It's us,' Gav called. The door opened, and the two dogs bounded into the bright light. Louise dropped to one knee as Klaus launched himself at her, licking her face. Violet, on the other hand, stopped short a yard away from Gav and gave him a dark look.

'Thanks for letting me come with you,' Louise said over her shoulder, holding Klaus's lead as the little dog pulled her out of the shop. She would have noticed the stand-off between him and Violet, but hadn't said anything.

'Fine,' he muttered to his dog. 'Stay here then.' He turned his back on her and walked to the front of the off-licence, watching as Louise and Klaus stepped onto the zebra crossing.

A tell-tale bang echoed from down the street. People new to the neighbourhood would think it was a gun, but this risk was worse, at least to the average person. Gav shouted a warning as the car backfired again, this time close enough for Louise to hear the revving engine.

She froze, turning in its direction. Her mouth gaped and she picked up Klaus and sprinted across the road as the 2003 blue Ford screamed towards her. When she wanted to move, the girl could *move*.

Gav held his breath until she made it to the kerb. The car swerved, as if the idiot driver was trying to actually hit her. Louise raised her free hand and shouted something that was lost in the noise as the blue Ford careered past.

Gav shook his head. It was one thing if a Ferrari made that sound; it was supposed to. But not a car that was older than the stupid kid driving it. The fool should take it in for servicing, although he didn't disagree with the other choice advice Louise was still shouting after it.

He winced at a particularly colourful suggestion, then turned to re-enter the shop, almost tripping over Violet. 'Sorry, love.'

He didn't understand Louise; didn't understand why a nice girl like her would want to get involved in someone else's mess. But she was sharp, perceptive. He was willing to bet she hadn't missed anything at old Ivy's place. And she had the bit between her teeth on the Phil thing too.

Gav knew people like that. Most of them acted all holier-than-thou, but Louise didn't appear to, and this was a cause he could sign up to.

Ignoring the pain in his hip, he turned to see Zed standing in the doorway, frowning after the Ford.

'What?' Gav demanded.

The kid shook his head. 'Wrong tyres for racing.'

'Wrong road for racing,' Gav growled and brushed past Zed, striding down the aisle towards the room in the back. Mo sat in a chair, leaning back against a wall padded with sacks of rice. A magazine was open on his lap.

'You back again, mate?'

'Looks like a World War Two bunker in here,' Gav said. 'You know that, right?'

'Yeah, well.' Mo lifted a shoulder in a shrug. 'It was neater before your little demon got the hump on.'

Gav ignored him and slowly hunkered down on one knee. He ruffled Violet's already fluffed fur and slipped her a couple of treats.

'How'd your meeting wi' Ivy go?'

'Old Ivy reckons that them kids are poisoning the hounds,' he said without preamble, jerking his head towards the entrance.

'Old Ivy's cracked in the head. The kids smoke weed, drink a bit. Shoplift a bit.' Mo pursed his lips. 'They're shits, but why poison a dog?'

'Because they can? Jesus, if they try to harm Violet.'

'Then that devil spawn will rip their faces off,' Mo said, standing up. He clapped Gav on the shoulder and moved quickly out of range. 'No one would dare mess with your dog. She don't let anyone close. They'd need one of them poisoned umbrellas to get her.'

Gav grunted, unamused. 'Keep your ear to the ground, mate. You hear anythin', and I mean anythin', you call me.'

Mo's usually cheerful smile faded, and he nodded. 'Yeah, Gav. I hear anyfin', you'll be the first to know.'

25

LOUISE

Irina (Hamish's Mum)

Macho Mike's real name is Michael Anthony Aspall. Born Nottingham, 7 Feb 1981. Arrested for GBH in August 2021.

What happened?

Waited outside a club. Beat a guy up. Turns out the guy was the ex of the woman he was seeing. Pleaded not guilty, although there were plenty of witnesses.

> You think Grace knows?

> It was easy enough to find out. I'd be surprised if she didn't.

I leaned against the bollard, still breathing heavily from my sprint across the street, feeling winded. Fi's words bubbled through my mind; had I painted a target on my back? Was someone trying to kill me? My heart raced, and a cold sweat trickled down my spine.

Get a grip, Lou, I told myself. *The boy racers speed through every bloody day. Fi was almost clipped last week, and Yaz has the council on speed dial over them. You were just distracted . . .*

I forced my breathing to slow and sat on a low wall until my vision cleared enough to reread Irina's message. And immediately felt my heart rate increase again. Macho Mike had beaten up his then-girlfriend's ex-boyfriend. Seemed better than average odds that he'd done it again, but how the devil was I going to find out where he was the night Phil died? Ask Grace?

No, she'd only tell me that Mike couldn't have done it. People rarely believed bad things about people they cared for. And if it came to it, Grace was a barrister; she'd know how to protect him.

If she chose to.

Irina (Hamish's Mum)

> Nothing on your new neighbour. You sure you got his name right?

> Yeah.

> Maybe Witness Protection? 😊

> Well, at least we can rule him out; he only moved into the neighbourhood on Sunday.

> Yeah? From where? Who's to say he didn't have a dispute with Phil?

It was a fair point.

'Louise?'

I started and looked around, blinking in the bright sunlight.

The man walking towards me was waving, but I was damned if I could place him. He was well dressed; far better than the average person on the street in this part of East London. Burnished hair and a round face that looked incongruous above a toned physique. I raised my hand in a half-hearted wave. 'Hey.'

The man pushed a pair of black Prada sunglasses to the top of his head. His blue eyes were friendly, jogging my memory.

'Don't worry, it took me a second too, Louise, but Klaus was a giveaway.' He leaned forward to stroke him, but Klaus moved back, making a low guttural sound. And for me, *that* was the giveaway.

'Afternoon, Dr Cooper. Not sure I've ever seen you outside Village Vets, let alone wearing civvies.'

'Call me Ben,' he corrected me, laughing. 'I've got to say, you had some form, moving across the street like that. Glad you're okay. People drive their cars way too fast along this stretch.'

'Hadn't noticed.'

'Yeah. And I'm also sure you hadn't noticed the way they use the zebra crossings to see how close they can get without drawing blood.' Dr Cooper shook his head. 'Sooner or later, they will, too. I don't suppose you got a good enough description to tell the police?'

I thought about it for a moment. 'All I saw was a blue car. Couldn't even tell you what type. Did you see anything?'

He shook his head. 'Too far away. Did you see the driver?'

Tapping into my memory only brought on the panic of seeing the car coming straight at me. Had the driver been young? Old? Dark or fair? Wearing a hat? 'I don't know.'

He nodded sympathetically. 'They're a terror, but I'm glad you and Klaus are all right.'

Klaus might have had other thoughts; being in

proximity to the vet, even though Dr Cooper wasn't in scrubs, was unacceptable. Another low growl vibrated through his body, a precursor to a full-on bark-fest. I handed him a treat to head it off.

'Sounds like you could do with a drink,' Dr Cooper said. 'It's almost five. I've been at work since eight and missed lunch. I'm starving. Fancy a trip down to the Wharf? Pergola? The Parlour? The Ivy? All of them are dog-friendly.' He winked. 'And I can drive if being a pedestrian is too daunting at the moment.'

'You have a car? Where do you travel in from?'

'Canary Wharf.' He leaned in and whispered as if we were in an al fresco confessional. 'I usually take the DLR, but it's convenient to park the car here.'

Convenient equals cheap. A parking spot in the Wharf probably cost as much as a bedsit in Poplar.

'Thanks, but I'm okay to walk.'

'You sure?' He gave me a conspiratorial smile. 'It's a beautiful evening and the new Merc's a convertible. Come on, Louise, it just arrived. Give me a chance to show it off.'

'As tempting as that sounds, I really can't go too far. I'm meeting a friend at six.' Actually, my plan was to go to the Wharf and gatecrash Fidelio's drinks, but Ben Cooper didn't need to know that, and Meg hadn't yet texted the location. 'Happy to do a quick drink at the Hound, though.'

He nodded, 'As the lady wishes.'

Good.

We walked a few feet in companionable silence, a question preying on my mind. It might be opportunistic to ask him, but it couldn't hurt to try. 'I hear there've been a number of poisonings in the neighbourhood. My new neighbour's dog being one of them.'

He nodded, running fingers through his hair. 'Who's your neighbour?'

'Jake Hathaway. His dog is a Staffie. Luther.'

He nodded again. 'Grey with white, right? I remember him. Your neighbour was lucky he acted quickly. We have some people who wait for hours before bringing in a sick dog and then blame us when we can't save them.'

'That happens a lot?'

He shrugged. 'Sometimes. Usually if the cat or dog ate something they shouldn't have, and the owners are too embarrassed to admit what happened. Or sometimes they just wait until they have the time to bring their pets to us.'

'Why be embarrassed?'

'Some of the things the dogs eat shouldn't be within their reach. Same as with kids.'

'But that wasn't the case with Luther. I heard he ate something outside.'

Dr Cooper shrugged again. 'That's what we were told. Truth is, I'm not one to judge, and I'm not sure it matters. What matters is that he got Luther to us in time, and we were able to get the poison out of Luther's body.'

'True.'

We reached the Hound, and Dr Cooper leaned around me to open the door. The sun reflected off gold cufflinks, making it hard to miss their neat monograms.

'Well, be careful,' he said. 'I wouldn't want anything to happen to Klaus.'

Dr Cooper waved me to a table by the front windows

and, without asking what I wanted, went to the bar to get some drinks.

From the far corner, Tim Aziz's girlfriend, Sophie, spotted me and waved. She was sitting with three hulking men and gave me as much of an enquiring look as her Botox would allow, glancing in Dr Cooper's direction.

I shook my head, *no*. Jerked my chin towards her, silently asking who she was with.

My brothers, she mouthed, with an apologetic shrug.

While I waited for Dr Cooper, I studied them. Tried to imagine, based on their features, what Sophie would have looked like before all the work she'd had done to her face. It was truly hard to tell.

Dr Cooper returned, not with a glass, but with a bottle of rosé. 'French,' he said, pouring the wine. 'I can't say no to a good rosé from Provence. And I ordered some nibbles. I hope you don't mind.'

He pushed one glass in front of me, leaning forward a bit more than he needed to. 'So, tell me about yourself, Louise. All I know about you is that you have a healthy miniature dachshund called Klaus. Who's trying to stay as far away from me as he can.'

I didn't blame him, but tried to laugh it off. 'Don't take it personally. He'd be trying to get away from Dr Aspen and Dr Singh too.'

'Well, hopefully neither will ask you for a drink.' His smile was just this side of smarmy.

'Oh my God, I hope not.' Realising how aghast I sounded, I offered an apologetic, 'Sorry, Dr Cooper.'

'Nothing to be sorry about. But please, do call me Ben.'

I wasn't sure how comfortable I was with that. 'Errr . . . right. Regardless, I still need to leave in less than an hour.'

'That's fine, let's see how far we can get in that time.' He topped up the three drops I'd sipped from my glass.

Fighting off a wave of ick, I forced a smile. 'Not much to know, really.' I took a sip of wine and blurted out the best thing I could think of to kill any buzz he might be entertaining. 'Other than the fact that I found that dead body in the park.'

For a moment Dr Cooper froze, but his expression quickly turned to empathy. 'I'd heard someone walking their dog found that poor man, but I hadn't realised it was you. I'm so sorry, that must have been awful. Are you all right?'

'It wasn't the highlight of my week, to be honest. Finding a man that it turns out you know . . .' My shudder was all too real. 'But you knew him too, didn't you?'

Dr Cooper shook his head. ''Fraid not, first time I heard his name was when I read the article about his death. Tragic.'

'Really? But you're one of the local vets – you didn't treat his dog? Alfie?'

He shrugged. 'I'm a locum. I do shifts at several surgeries. Which means that some people, who might be regulars at one in particular, I might know well, or not at all. I don't recall Mr Creasy, or his dog. Sorry.'

He refilled my glass and placed his hand on mine. 'But it must be awful to lose someone you know, and to find them that way.' He shook his head and squeezed my fingers. 'As I said, tragic. I am so sorry for your loss . . .'

I slid my hand out from under his, raising it as I saw a slim woman enter the pub. Her skin was tanned, and she had a blazer slung over one forearm. She pushed her sunglasses to the top of her head, revealing bright green eyes and freckles. She gave me a tired smile and walked towards us. I pushed an empty chair out with my foot. 'Pull up a pew, Annabel,' I said, not looking at Dr Cooper. 'You look knackered.'

'The bloody Bells,' she said, her cut-glass accent at odds with her greeting. 'The idiot landlord is driving me round the bend.'

'Annabel, this is Ben Cooper, one of the local vets. And Dr Coop— I mean Ben, this is Annabel, who – for her sins – works for one of the property developers trying to regenerate an area that isn't always amenable.'

'You can say that again,' she said. She hooked her beige Ferragamo bag over the back of her chair and held out an immaculately manicured hand to Ben.

'How do you know each other?' he asked, his gaze moving from Annabel to me and back again.

'We both drink here,' I said.

'And her dog's cute,' Annabel added. 'Do you have a pet, Ben?'

'No,' he said. 'I love animals, work with them every day. But I know I probably wouldn't be the best dog dad.'

Interesting.

Before I could find out more, Ben gestured to the bartender for a glass.

'What's happened now, Annabel?' I asked her, settling into the conversation.

'Same old. We're trying to get them to sell off that damned pub to us.'

'You want to run a pub?' Ben asked, amused.

Annabel spluttered. 'Hell no. It's not bad enough that the Bells is an eyesore. It has more vermin than punters, even on a good day, but the council can't be bothered to do anything about it, so we're trying to.' She tucked a strand of hair behind her ear and leaned back. 'We'd knock it down before it falls. Replace it with something better.' Another glass arrived, and Ben poured her some wine. She thanked him with a sigh and an apologetic smile. 'My father warned me that working for a property developer was hard work. He wasn't joking.'

Ben smiled.

'Have you even been in there?' she asked.

He shook his head. It'd be hard to imagine the fastidious Dr Cooper, with his monogrammed cufflinks, drinking a pint at the Bells. Then again, it was hard to imagine Annabel, with her designer outfits, drinking there either.

'You're not missing anything.' She cast a quick glance over his smart clothes. 'Fleapit, on a good day. So where do you like to go?'

Ben leaned forward, waxing lyrical about a bar in the City that I'd never heard of. The two seemed intent on each other and I felt a glimmer of hope that I could make a clean escape. I sneaked a look down at my phone.

Meg (Tyrion's Mum)

Sounds like they're almost done in the office. I hear they'll be continuing over

199

at one of the bars over by West India Quay.

Which one?

Not sure – I don't think they've decided yet. But you're going to have to fly on your own on this one. I have a class this evening ... and I sort of need a bit of distance from the guy I know at Fidelio. Too clingy. Don't worry – you'll have no problems finding them – I promise!

Why?

Trust me on this one – you wouldn't believe me if I told you!

I glanced up from my phone, feeling less guilty about sneaking off a quick text while Annabel and Ben were keeping each other occupied. And to be fair, they would make a handsome couple ...

Meg's text was intriguing. Why did she think I'd

recognise the group? Because I'd met the two other founders a few years ago? How would she even know that?

Or had she just assumed (correctly) that I'd done a LinkedIn search for any past and present employees of Fidelio?

In any case, her message was the excuse I was waiting for. I smiled at Ben and Annabel. 'Really sorry, but that's the friend I'm meeting. I need to shoot off now, but you two stay.' I placed Klaus back on the floor and dusted off my jeans. 'Have fun!' I called over my shoulder, reasonably certain they'd both be fine without me. And if a bit of romance brewed between them, they could thank me later.

I hurried Klaus out of the door and picked up my pace, almost sprinting to the DLR. The train came quickly. I took a seat and settled Klaus in my lap, trying to figure out a plan as we approached the Wharf.

Most people hadn't yet begun the evening migration homewards from the Wharf's offices, and I had no problems finding a table at one of the bars on West India Quay. I took a table facing the small bridge connecting the Wharf to the Quay, where I could keep an eye out for familiar faces, ordered a lime and soda in a G & T glass and accepted the hostess's offer of a dog bed for Klaus (even though it was more likely he'd remain on my lap).

'Cute dog.' A couple of young women hovered nearby. 'Is he friendly? Can we pet him?' They swooped in before I could answer.

'He'd like that,' I said, figuring that being part of a group made me look less like I was waiting for someone and was much more social than the book I would have brought in my pre-dog days.

The girls cooed over Klaus until the lure of a post-work drink was too great and they headed to a nearby table, signalling to the waiter.

I checked my phone, but there was no update from Meg, Irina, or anyone else in the Pack. Just one from my brother checking in on me.

I paid my bill after the second lime and soda, then looked over the bridge and smiled. A group of about twenty-five or thirty people were crossing, accompanied by seven dogs, ranging from a Chihuahua to a chilled-looking mastiff that was the size of a small horse. My money was on the Chihuahua bossing the mastiff.

'Holy crap,' I breathed, certain these people were from Fidelio. Klaus began to bark. His tail was wagging – a good sign – and he pawed at my leg, his cue to be let down. I allowed him to pull me towards the newcomers.

'He's barky, but friendly,' I called ahead. 'Can I introduce him?'

The first guy, ridiculously tall and solid, but with a full strawberry-blond beard and head of hair that made him look strangely similar to the Chihuahua in his arms, waved us over. He put the Chihuahua down and stood back while Klaus and the Fidelio dogs circled and sniffed each other, barking happily.

I laughed as a whippet rolled onto her back for Klaus. 'I love your pack. Are you usually based around here?'

The whippet's owner, a woman with green hair the exact colour of her dog's lead and collar, shook her head.

'Not really. First time we've got them all together at the same time, actually.'

'Dog-friendly office?' I guessed.

'Since before it was fashionable. We usually have a couple in on any given day, but, like I said, this is the first time . . .' her voice trailed off.

'For a good occasion, I hope?' I tried to sound casual.

The mastiff's owner, a short bald man, shook his head. 'Not really.'

'Our boss died,' Green Hair explained. 'The dog-friendly office was his idea, so we thought, first day back in after it happened, we'd bring the dogs and go out for a drink. Toast him goin' over the rainbow bridge.' She lifted her free hand in an arc.

'I'm so sorry.' I looked down at Klaus, who was getting far too friendly with the prone whippet. 'I really am sorry! Klaus!'

She laughed it off. 'She likes it.' Clearing her throat, she added, 'Not sure where we're going, but you're a dog person. You're welcome to join us.'

I smiled and leaned into it.

'Always happy to have a drink with other dog people, as long as you don't mind me gatecrashing your event.' I paused and looked at her pack over my shoulder. 'But just so I know, who are we drinking to?'

'Philip R. Creasy,' she said. 'Our chief exec.'

'The guy that was killed last Sunday,' Chihuahua's owner added.

'Alfie's dad,' I said, taking a chance that they wouldn't think I was some sort of ghoul.

Green Hair blinked. 'You knew Alfie?'

Chihuahua Man took a half-step back. 'You knew Phil?'

The others looked at me with suspicion that bordered on incredulity. 'The news didn't mention his dog . . .'

'You're not another reporter, are you?'

They began to regroup, pulling back on their dogs' leads and closing ranks against an outsider.

But once I'd started, I couldn't go back. 'I'm local,' I explained. 'So was Phil. Our dogs played together at the same park. When Alfie wasn't trying to hump Klaus, that is.'

Chihuahua Man pursed his lips and tilted his head to the side. 'Sounds like Alfie. That dog would hump a stone.'

'He probably did; a stone wouldn't tell him off.' I laughed, then sobered again. 'May he rest in peace. Phil too. Neither of them deserved the endings they had.'

Chihuahua Man nodded and picked up his little dog. As he held him close, I realised that man and dog both wore matching blue hand-knitted jumpers.

'They didn't.' His smile was wry and a little sad. I tried not to breath out too hard. Maybe . . .

'I don't think anyone would have a problem if you join us.'

'Okay,' I said, following them back to the bar Klaus and I had just left. 'Nice place.'

Green Hair nodded. 'They're dog-friendly, and the food and cocktails are pretty good. We haven't booked anywhere, but they should be able to accommodate us.'

Chihuahua Man glanced over his shoulder at the middle-aged couple lagging behind. The woman was about fifty, slim, with silver-blonde hair cut into a neat bob. The man might have been a few years older, although there didn't seem to be much grey in his thinning hair. He was average height, but overweight.

'Don't worry,' Green Hair said. 'They'll follow wherever we go.'

The heavy man's face was beginning to turn red, while the woman's cool expression didn't change.

'Looks like trouble in the C-suite,' Chihuahua Man muttered.

'As long as they bring the credit cards, do you care?' Mr Mastiff replied.

'You'll care if things go badly enough to hit the bottom line,' Green Hair said.

'Is that likely?' I asked.

The three of them shook their heads, but I wasn't sure I believed them.

The older man swaggered forward towards our group and held out his hand to me. 'Jim Clark, CTO.'

'Louise Mallory.' I didn't offer a title. This wasn't a work event. 'My condolences on your loss.'

He harrumphed, but the woman looked more closely at me. 'Have we met?'

'A long time ago,' I said.

She nodded to herself. 'You were part of a consultancy group. Business assurance and transformation, wasn't it? You pitched to us a few years ago but the timing wasn't great and we left everything open.'

'You have an excellent memory, Ms Halder.' I shook her hand. 'Look, I know your company is going through a tough time and I'm not here to do a sales pitch. I hadn't realised who your group was until just now.'

'She knew Phil,' Mr Mastiff explained. 'From the dog park.'

'And I liked him. But if you'd rather I go, that's fine too.'

Tabitha Halder frowned. For a moment, I thought she'd turn me down. But then she nodded. 'Any friend of Phil's . . .'

Tamping down a feeling of victory, I followed them into the bar.

As Jim and Tabitha went to the bar to buy the first round of drinks, the group eased into several smaller circles. Green Hair grinned at Mr Mastiff. 'Bet you he puts that on the company card.'

'No chance. He'll put it on Tabby's.' The two of them watched the senior managers at the bar. Jim patted his pockets and gave the woman an embarrassed shrug. We didn't need to see her eye-roll.

'Easy money.' Green Hair held out her hand.

Mr Mastiff explained. 'Jim's all right, mostly. Generous when other people are footing the bill, but when it's his turn, he's got short arms and deep pockets.' He demonstrated, looking like a short, bald T-Rex. His mastiff gave him a strange look.

'I have clients like that,' I said. 'Some have financial issues, but most are just congenitally tight.'

Mr Mastiff laughed. 'He had a bad divorce, but he was pretty bad even before that.'

'Okay, here's *my* prediction. Tabby'll make an excuse and leave early. Jim'll stay out, probably flirting with any-thing in a skirt, and won't pay for a single drink all night, unless he's pressed into it.'

'Or if he's trying to impress someone.'

I smiled, amazed at how much information they were willing to share with a complete stranger. 'What's the dynamic between them?'

'They were the original founders,' Green Hair said. 'With Phil. Jim's a techie at heart. Probably used to code in his pants until 4 a.m., then eat leftover pizza for breakfast.'

That was an image I didn't need.

She continued, 'He thinks he's a people person, but he's not. That's all Tabby; she kept the staff happy, and Phil worked with the clients and investors.'

Interesting.

'He's not that bad, Kaz,' Mr Mastiff said, turning to me. 'It's not unusual. You get someone with a good idea, they find a few people who can help make it real. At the beginning they all pitch in. Then their skills do 'em in. The CTO is usually the first to go. The guy that can code isn't always good at getting the best out of people.'

'No, Trudy.' Green Hair pulled her whippet's nose away from Mr Mastiff's crotch before returning her attention to us. 'Can't say there wasn't some friction. Phil was really good with people. He was the one bringing in new business and keeping the existing clients happy. Tabby sorts out the operations side of things. Jim, well. He likes swanning around with a grand title, and he like the toys. He likes to play.'

People were congregating around Jim and Tabby as they returned with trays of wine and beer. Mr Mastiff took a bottle of beer while Green Hair grabbed a bottle of Vermentino and a pair of glasses as Tabby passed. She poured one for me and one for herself.

'So, Jim was the odd man out,' I prompted.

'And about to be the odder man out,' Green Hair admitted once her bosses had moved far enough away. 'Rumour had it that Phil 'n' Tabs were looking to put him out to pasture and replace him with a guy who understood what it really meant to be a CTO.'

'What does that mean?' I knew what it meant to me, as a CEO. My firm was relatively non-hierarchical, but I always made a point of finding out what people on all levels were thinking.

'Someone who knows how to lead,' Chihuahua Man said.

'Someone who's not in it just for the title and the perks.'

That was fair, but I felt a strange need to defend Jim. 'Sometimes it's hard to take a step back from the company you helped build, even if it's for the good of the organisation . . .' I frowned, realising I wasn't defending him, I was defending myself.

Focus, Louise!

'What was the dynamic between Phil and Tabby?'

Mr Mastiff raised his empty beer bottle and handed Green Hair his dog's lead. He made his apologies and headed round the bar to the gents'. At my feet, Klaus was pulling me towards a pretty collie, of the Lassie variety, not a border. Usually, he didn't care much for big, fluffy dogs, but he made an exception for collies.

'Pandora's a flirt,' Green Hair said, pointing at the collie. 'Every male dog who sees her falls in love with her, and she knows it.' Pandora gave Klaus a coy look over her shoulder, wiggling her fluffy tail.

I took the hint: Green Hair didn't want to discuss the dynamic. 'Klaus clearly isn't immune.' My little dachshund was doing his 'I'm cute, you must love me' dance for her. 'She doesn't look too immune to him either.'

'Of course she isn't,' Green Hair laughed. She topped up her glass and mine. 'Well, look. It was nice speaking with you, but I really should mingle.' She saluted me with her now-full glass and, holding the leads of both whippet and mastiff, sashayed over towards a group of men, no less flirty than Pandora the collie.

Figuring I'd learned more than I'd expected and unwilling to overstay our welcome, I coaxed Klaus away from his new friends, stopped to thank Tabitha and Jim for their hospitality and headed towards the DLR.

As I rattled towards home on the train, I began to sort through all the new information I'd gathered.

It was starting to look like Jim Clark had a motive to kill Phil. But did he have the opportunity or the spine?

And what about Tabby? Or someone from the team who might have been on the receiving end of a decision that hadn't gone the way they'd hoped?

One thing was for sure: they'd given me a lot to think about.

26

IRINA

The intercom buzzed from the front door. Hamish raised his head from his mat and nudged Irina. She dutifully hit the buttons on her phone to let the visitor into the complex and then the building. Pouring herself another glass of wine, she left the door ajar.

Within moments, it opened all the way. 'You let me in without even asking who I was,' Andy said. 'I could have been anyone.'

She shrugged, not looking up from her laptop. 'You were invited and said you'd be here in twenty. It's now been twenty-one minutes. You're late.'

'For what?' He walked over to her, taking off his jacket but draping it over his arm rather than the back of a chair. 'A midnight booty call?'

'It's 10.21,' Irina corrected. 'Nowhere near midnight.'

Andy raised a blond eyebrow. 'You're angry with me for being *one minute late*?' He turned away. 'If you want an argument, find someone else. I'm out of here.'

Irina didn't look up from her laptop. 'Stay.' When he started moving back down the hallway towards the door, she added, 'Please.'

'Irina, one second you're just about chasing me down, the next you're colder than a witch's tit.' He sighed, turning to face her and leaning against the wall. 'Why? Because I asked you to not put yourself in danger?'

'Nice phrase.' She closed the laptop and swivelled in her seat to look at him. 'I want you to do your job. So far, we're the ones who found your dead body. We found his phone. We've also solved a few local crimes when the police seemingly couldn't be bothered.' She held up a hand. 'Yes, I know the Met is short-staffed. But this is basic stuff.'

'So you summoned me?' His tone moved quickly from incredulous to angry. 'Just so you know, we need to prioritise—'

'What? What trumps a murder? Can you at least let me know if you have any suspects? I don't need to know who. Just let me know that you're doing *something*.'

Andy's silence only stoked her fury. His own was becoming evident from the angry flush on his cheeks.

She took a breath, kept her voice steady. 'Andy, we have people working together to keep our park and our dogs safe. As we always have. We keep each other abreast of what's happening, whether it's a big crime or a small one. You should be encouraging us, not trying to stop us.

Can't you understand? We have one dead body, of a man we knew. We don't want another.'

Irina paused for a long gulp of wine. 'And on top of that, some bastard is trying to poison our dogs.'

'Poison?' Andy said, the tension falling from his shoulders, only to increase in Irina's.

'Yes, poison,' she snapped. 'I messaged you about that.' His expression seemed to indicate that she hadn't. 'Pay attention, will you? There was a Staffie that was poisoned the other day. And according to Gav, there were a string of similar incidents around here a few years ago. He and Lou went to see the old woman—'

'Wait – who's Gav?'

'I don't know. Some old guy from the park. He has an Affenpinscher.'

'What the f— hell is an Affenpinscher?'

'A monkey dog. Little black thing with a kind of squooshed-in face. Hold on, I have a picture.' She grabbed her phone and scrolled through the chat, until she found the one she was looking for. In it, Klaus and Hamish were trying to play with Violet. Which meant that both were doing their charming best while Violet glared at them, her dark eyes half hidden below a wild black fringe. 'There,' she said, handing Andy her phone. 'Violet is the one with the purple collar.'

'Jesus, that's one scary-looking little . . . err . . . dog.' He frowned and enlarged the image, his face paling. Clearing his throat, he pointed to a man sitting on a bench in the background. 'Who's that?'

Irina frowned. 'Pay attention, will you? That's Gav.'

Andy slowly put the phone on the table. Each movement

was precise, as if he was trying to control himself. 'Irina, that's Gavin MacAdams.'

'Look, I remember dogs' names. It's a big thing when I remember their humans' *first* names. You expect me to know their surnames too?'

Andy sighed. 'Irina, Gavin MacAdams was a big name a couple of decades ago. In organised crime. We couldn't send him down for mob activities, but we did get him for beating the piss out of a rival.'

Irina laughed. 'Prison? Gav? You're telling me that *Gav* is a *gangster*?'

'I don't know what he is now, but I know what he was. And that sort of person rarely leaves their past behind. Especially if they stay in the same neighbourhood.' He picked up the phone and looked at the photo again. 'Gavin MacAdams. Of all people. Jesus.'

Irina looked at him hard. 'He didn't kill Phil Creasy.'

'I didn't say he did.' One corner of Andy's mouth twitched, and Irina frowned.

'What?' she snapped.

'I would have thought Gavin MacAdams would have a Dobermann pinscher, not a – what did you call that? An Afflen pincher?'

'Affenpinscher,' Irina corrected. 'As I heard it, he wanted a Dobie. But his daughter made a mistake and bought him the wrong type of pinscher.'

'Intentionally?' he asked, not trying to hide his smirk.

'I don't know. You're the cop. You ask her. But you should know that while Violet – Gav's dog – is little, she's *mean.*'

'Sure,' he grinned. 'Sure.'

Irina shrugged. If Andy wanted to find out the hard way, that was up to him.

Her phone pinged and she glanced at the sender's name, feeling what little good humour she had dissipate without trace.

27

GAV

Partridge Bark

Meg (Tyrion's Mum)

I just heard from **@Sophie** that **@Tim** was beaten up. He was taken to the Royal London in Whitechapel. She was in pieces (I'd be too). She's got a work deadline pending so I'll help out with Loki when I can until Tim's back on his feet.

Louise (Klaus's Mum)

Oh no! What happened?

Meg (Tyrion's Mum)

She didn't know – just got the call that someone found him unconscious by the market square around 11 pm and that he'd been taken to hospital.

How's he doing?

Meg (Tyrion's Mum)

Not good. Who would do something like that to Tim?

There were a fair number of people who might have done it, Gav conceded. Husbands and boyfriends, mostly. Maybe an ex or two. Or whoever had sent the kids after him on Sunday. It couldn't be a coincidence that a couple of days after offering to help Gav find out about the street kids, Tim ended up in hospital. Could he have found something so quickly?

And was this Gav's fault?

Maybe, maybe not, he decided. That buffoon could have got into trouble all on his own, but still . . . Gav didn't believe in coincidences.

He popped open a beer. Violet's growl was low, a gentle reminder, not that he needed it.

'Don't do it,' Doris warned from the front room. 'She's nasty when she has beer.'

'She's nasty when she doesn't,' Gav pointed out. It was only a couple of drops anyway. Enough to get Violet off his case but not enough for Doris to get on it. Violet had hated his wife at first sight and while an uneasy truce had formed in the house, there was still no love lost between his wife and his dog.

Gav splashed a few drops into Violet's water bowl then went to the picture window at the front of the house, staring out at the street. It was already late and the cars that passed were anonymous in the dark. He didn't care about them anyway. Barely even noticed the reflection of the old man staring back at him from the glass.

What seemed like not that long ago, the skyline had been flatter and the world simpler. There'd been rules, even if they weren't the same as the *laws*. For a while that had seemed to change, but now one thing was clear: someone was sending a message to Gav. That he wasn't safe and that his friends weren't safe. Not his old gang, maybe, at least not as far as he knew: his new one. The dog one. The Pack.

He glanced back, watching Violet lap at the beer. She'd be fourteen in December. A few drops wouldn't kill her.

Not like asking the wrong questions would.

Maybe it *was* a message to him; to stop him asking questions. But whoever had thought that would work, didn't know Gav. Being warned off something only made him more determined.

He finished his beer in a couple of gulps and crushed the can in his hand.

When he found out who was behind this, they would have him to deal with.

28

THE PACK

Partridge Bark

**Ella (Bark Vader and
Jimmy Chew's Mum)**

> OMG, we just heard a
> thud and a cry. I think an
> SUV might have hit a dog!

Meg (Tyrion's Mum)

> Oh no! Which one?

Paul (Bark Vader and Jimmy Chew's Dad)

I heard it too, but can't see anyone from the balcony. Did someone further down the road see anything?

Yaz (Hercules's Mum)

I saw a black SUV screaming around the corner. I got a photo of the reg plates.

Irina (Hamish's Mum)

Send me the photo, Yaz, and I'll make sure it gets to the right place.
Bat light, baaaaby.

Fiona (Nala's Mum)

Bet you either the car or the reg plates were stolen. Anyone get a pic of the driver?

Yaz (Hercules's Mum)

No – too dark and they were moving too fast. I'm sure the police can get something off CCTV when the joyriders dump the car. Which they'll probably do.

Irina (Hamish's Mum)

There's no CCTV in that part of the park.

Claire (Tank's Mum)

I'll go check.

Indy (Banjo's Mum)

We don't need CCTV. We ARE CCTV – Canine 'Connaissance TV!

Louise (Klaus's Mum)

Anything about the dog?

Claire (Tank's Mum)

I didn't recognise him. No
blood, but he's limping.
Probably just clipped,
but his dad is taking him
to the vet, just in case.
I guess it's just another
reminder to be careful out
there. As if we needed
it . . .

Friday

29

ANDY

Irina Ivanova

Fancy an early/pre-work run?

It was Friday and he'd been on lates. He knew that spending more time with Irina was a mistake, even if Williams hadn't kept reminding him. The probability of her being involved in Phil Creasy's death was close to zero; as far as he could tell – and he did believe her – she had no motive and no opportunity. Her alibi for Saturday night was rock solid, complete with drunken pictures from someone else's party.

Still, even without Williams's snarky comments, Grieves's subtle threat to take him off the case, or the spectre of some future defence lawyer calling her testimony into question due to any association with him, he was prepared to put her off.

Sure, he was attracted to her, but Jesus, she was prickly. She was hard work, and he wasn't interested in that; it'd taken him years to recover from his last relationship. That said, the fact that her ridiculous little dog smelled of watermelon told him that she had a soft side and a good sense of humour.

It was as if she was trying hard to be something that only existed in her own mind and something else kept trying to break through. It was the something else that intrigued Andy. Even as he was about to text her, telling her that it wasn't appropriate for them to meet, his fingers wouldn't comply, typing out a short message agreeing to a run.

They met at the marina, with Hamish on a lead cinched tight around Irina's waist. 'We can't run that fast,' she said by way of greeting. 'Hamish has short legs.'

Andy looked at the dog, catching the side-eye the Scottie gave his owner. If he didn't know better, he'd swear the dog's expression read *Don't blame me if you're out of shape.*

'Fine.' He smiled. 'We can go at Hamish's pace.'

'Great,' she said, her tone flat, and the look she gave her dog was just as meaningful: *Don't let me down.*

Hamish clearly didn't understand that one. He set off at a brisk trot, pulling Irina with him, who let out a string of harsh Russian syllables that would probably make Williams's rugby mates blush. They ran along the

Thames, passing one pub after another, until they reached the Tower of London. Andy didn't force a conversation, enjoying the silence, but noting that while Hamish seemed comfortable enough with the pace, Irina was wheezing. 'Do you want to slow down?'

'I'm fine,' she snapped, but Andy slowed anyway. They made it back to Limehouse, detouring to the Yurt for a cup of coffee. Irina sank onto a bench outside, panting. She held out her phone. 'My round. But you get it.'

He gave her an arch look. 'I don't know your passcode.'

'As long as the screen's live, you're fine,' she said, leaning back and closing her eyes. 'Just make sure you get water for Hamish while you're at it.'

He opened his mouth to lecture her, but shrugged instead and added it to a to-do list for another time. It was about trust, wasn't it? She trusted him with her phone. That was a big thing.

He queued up at the counter and was looking at the menu board when the first message pinged onto her phone.

As a rule, Andy didn't believe in looking at other people's messages. And especially not those of someone who intrigued him the way Irina did. It was bad form and not the best way to start a relationship, if that was the way things were going.

And he hoped they were.

The message was from someone called 'As Is', saying that he (?) was awake and bored. Not up for a dog walk, maybe, but certainly company. Something about the phrasing made Andy's teeth itch.

Another message appeared.

Louise (Klaus's Mum)

> Saw Sophie this morning.
> She said that Tim Aziz has
> a concussion, broken arm
> and cracked ribs. No idea
> who did it or why. She
> hopes he'll be discharged
> soon. Do you think it was
> because he was asking
> questions about Phil?

'Bloody hell,' Andy muttered. 'Who the devil is Tim and what have you got yourself into now?' He stared at the name again. Aziz. As in 'As Is'? Was Irina the sort of person to think that sort of play on the guy's name was clever? Jesus, what did she call *him*?

Before he could check, a second penny dropped. The dog people were still actively looking into Creasy's murder.

He was beyond furious. A man was dead. Didn't Irina know the risks of getting involved? She had to, and yet she was still doing it.

Before he realised what he was doing, he opened the group chat. And began to type.

30

LOUISE

Partridge Bark

Sophie (Loki's Mum)

Thanks for everyone's well wishes. Tim's doing OK — the doctors said the broken bones and concussion could have been worse. The police are coming to speak with him later today.

'Good,' I muttered to myself, wondering who he'd spoken to before the incident. Turning my attention back to the tiles on my screen showing my colleagues' faces, I said,

'Look, we've had no news from Gen. We'll proceed according to plan: we continue the handover to their team, we document what we've done and our recommendations for the next steps. I know it's already under way. Send Babs and me a copy of the file once you're finished with it. I think Sales can vouch that we have enough opportunities in the pipeline that no one will be on the bench long.'

Babs nodded and took her cue to transition the call into a discussion of the trends our consultants were seeing across the client sites, brainstorming how to use our resources best to get ahead of the curve. The meeting, as always, was well run, and some of the ideas put forward – from all levels of the organisation – were innovative.

The team interacted well with each other. I shifted my focus from Babs to Mandy, who was supposed to still be on leave. On the screen, she didn't look as bad as I'd expected, but filters could hide a lot. I wrote a note to myself to call her after the meeting ended.

But my phone rang as soon as the meeting was over, and Babs didn't bother with pleasantries. 'Have you spoken to Mandy?'

Grateful that she couldn't see my guilty blush, I admitted that it was still on my to-do list.

'Right. So, I did. I'd thought the boyfriend situation was a row. Maybe even a break-up.'

I got the feeling that whatever it was, was worse. 'Please tell me her boyfriend wasn't beaten up … And please, *please* tell me his name isn't Tim Aziz.'

'Tim who? Wait, the man your friend's banging? No. It's worse.' Babs inhaled sharply. 'The boyfriend's dead.'

I tried to calm my heart rate. 'Was he ill?'

'I don't think so. Lou, from what I gathered it was sudden.'

'Oh God. Was it suicide?'

'No. At least, I don't think so. She didn't want to talk about it.'

A sudden death, not illness, not suicide . . .

Grasping at straws, I asked, 'Did she tell you his name?'

'No.'

My stomach turned. I looked around and lowered my voice, although the only one who could possibly have heard me was Klaus. 'You think her boyfriend might be *Phil Creasy*?'

'I don't know, Lou. There was nothing on social media that I could find, but who knows? She's not talking to me. Maybe she'll talk to you.'

Mandy hadn't been at Fidelio's drinks do last night, but that didn't mean anything. Maybe she hadn't known about it or hadn't wanted to go. That was, if she and Phil had even been involved.

I didn't know why I was shocked by the idea. Grace had moved on from the relationship, why couldn't Phil? Mandy was smart, successful and attractive. And while she didn't have a cockapoo, she had a corgi, Amelia, who was one of Klaus's favourites.

And to be honest, I could see Phil and Mandy together a lot more easily than I could see Grace with Macho Mike.

31

LOUISE

Mandy Barker

> Hey Mandy, I thought you were on leave this week. How are you doing?

My brain will implode with nothing to do.

> I get that. Look, if you don't have plans, let me take you out for lunch later.

Okayyy. Have I done something wrong?

> Not at all. I'm offering as a friend, not your boss.

> Ah, OK, thanks. I'm at home, so whatever works for you, Lou.

> Great. Say, noon? I'll come up to you, there's a nice pub nearby isn't there?

Lunch arranged, I remained at my desk for a few minutes, sorting through my to-do list. Babs hadn't yet sent me any information on Fidelio, and I didn't want to push her; there was enough on her plate, and I had a bit more to go on now. So I killed the rest of the morning finding out what I could about Phil's two business partners, James Clark and Tabitha Halder. I printed out their corporate photographs and added them to the Blu-Tacked collection on my wall, next to photographs of Grace and Mike.

I hesitated only a moment before printing Mandy's photograph as well, although I left it on a side table, just in case I was wrong.

It was a sunny day and a nice walk north. Theories danced around my mind as I made my way towards Victoria Park. Walking along the canals, you could almost forget you were in London. Wildflowers were in bloom, and the narrowboats moored along the path were well kept. They were all different colours, shapes and sizes, and most were decorated with interesting sculptures and plants.

As I walked I turned things over in my mind. Had Phil been dating Mandy? Was there a connection between his murder and the poisonings? What, if any, was the gangs' involvement in that, or in the assault on Tim Aziz? Or the attack on Gav? London could be dangerous, same as any city, but it seemed that an awful lot was happening to our dog community within a small amount of time.

Klaus and I left the canal and wound our way through the small streets. This close to Victoria Park, the off-licences, greasy spoons and betting shops were starting to give way to gastropubs and boutiques. We stopped in a pet shop and I bought a small bag of dog treats for Klaus and Amelia, Mandy's dog.

I paused at a zebra crossing, listening as well as looking. As much as I'd been spooked by the near-miss yesterday, it was the only thing I felt safe enough to rule out as intentional. Those lunatic drivers would take out anyone.

Klaus's bark shook me out of my reverie. Two women were walking towards the pet shop, both comfortably attired in loungewear. The first woman held the lead of a tan-coloured Pomeranian with a blue halter half-camouflaged in its long fur. Her friend gripped the lead of a mostly white Boston terrier with a clenched fist.

'Sorry,' I called out in advance, gesturing towards Klaus. 'He's friendly, but can be barky.'

'That's okay,' the woman with the Pom said. 'Mine's barky and not so friendly.'

In fact, from the sounds that erupted from the Pomeranian, the death-grip should have been on his lead, not the terrier's. That was the thing about Pomeranians: they looked sweet, and often were, but could be seriously underestimated.

'Little man syndrome,' the terrier's mum said, looking pained. 'We'll just cross to the other side of the road.' She gave the fluffy Pom a dour look and added, 'Again.'

The Pom didn't seem to care, straining towards Klaus. My dachshund responded accordingly, his barks changing in tone from 'Hi, I don't know you, wanna be friends?' to 'You barkin' at me? YOU barkin' at ME?'

'Stop that, will you?' I said to him. The Pom's owner muttered an apology and picked up the little barking fiend. As soon as they turned a corner, Klaus settled down, his long tail wagging as if that had been great fun. 'That wasn't as cute as you thought it was. Jerk.'

Within another few minutes, we turned a corner ourselves, arriving opposite the blue-grey-painted Morgan Arms. A quick glance around confirmed that Mandy hadn't yet arrived so we sat at a table outside, ordered a few nibbles and a bottle of Sauvignon Blanc from the waitress. Our company didn't have a culture of day-drinking, even on a Friday, and I wanted to send a clear signal that this wasn't an official conversation. She came back quickly with the wine, two glasses and a bowl of water for Klaus.

I answered emails on my phone until I heard Mandy approach. Or rather, until Klaus saw Mandy and Amelia and barked a greeting. This time the greeting was returned, and in moments the two dogs were circling each other, sniffing and playing.

Grateful for Babs's warning, I managed to force a smile and a cheerful tone. 'You know he's half in love with Amelia. It's good to see you, Mandy.'

Mandy was one of those people who was always well presented. In the days when we'd had a dedicated office space, she'd wear sleek dresses to work, with simple but elegant heels, or skirts paired with smart jackets. Her dark hair had never – to my knowledge – dared be out of place.

But today she was wearing cut-off shorts and a top that looked frayed around the edges. There was no sign of make-up on her pale face, and her hair was scraped back from her forehead in a puffy headband, not unlike the one I wore to wash my face.

I poured the wine and slid a glass across the table.

Mandy looked at it, her face losing what little colour it had. 'It's a bad conversation, isn't it?'

'No, no. Babs said you were having a hard time, and to be honest, Mandy, you look a bit rough. Thought you might need to talk. Off the record.'

She hesitated, as if she was considering turning and walking away. Which would have been her right.

I continued, 'This isn't an official meeting. No HR notes needed because, frankly, you're doing a bang-up job. Especially in light of a difficult client. I can order you something else, if you'd prefer?'

Mandy's lips twitched and she eased onto the bench. 'Tony isn't that bad, if you know how to deal with him.'

Her fingers circled the stem of the wine glass, rotating it on the wooden table.

'Relax, I don't bite.' I smiled. 'Usually. Although Moany Tony might disagree.'

The twirling stopped. 'So, this really isn't about work?'

I took a deep breath. 'Babs said that you lost your partner.' I didn't know the right words to say, even if they existed. 'I've had break-ups, but this is something quite different, and I cannot imagine what you're going through. Whatever it is, whatever you need, I'm here to help.'

Mandy stared at her glass for a moment. I gave a discreet yank on Klaus's lead as he started trying to hump Amelia and slipped a couple of treats under the table to distract them.

'It's so hard. It's just ...' Her big grey eyes welled with tears and, half in panic, I pushed the plate of nibbles that the waitress had just brought in front of her. That was one thing I struggled with: other people's tears. Couldn't handle them.

'Why don't you tell me about him, about what happened.'

Klaus was bouncing against my shins again, so I brought him onto my lap. Stroking his soft fur, I added, 'And – I'm sorry for asking this, I should know – what was his name again?'

'Oh.' Mandy gave Amelia a watery smile. 'Philip,' she said, and if she saw me pale, she didn't comment on it. 'His name was Philip, and he was a wonderful man.'

32

IRINA

'What the hell do you think you're doing?' Irina thundered, not caring who else heard. She strode to where Andy sat at a table inside, scrolling through her phone, her life. She tried to snatch it out of his hand.

'Irina!' He didn't look surprised, or shocked. He looked offended. Bloody *offended*? How *dare* he! 'I told you and your friends to leave the detecting to the detectives.' He stood and held up the phone out of her reach, as if it were proof of a crime. 'So now one of your friends is in *hospital*? What's it going to take for you to see sense?'

'See sense? You've bloody broken into *my phone*!' She grabbed it, glaring at him. 'Law and order, my arse. Get out. *Now.*'

'I didn't break into your phone – you gave me the damn thing!'

'To buy coffee, not to violate my privacy!'

He was moving slowly, saying words that didn't penetrate her red haze of rage. She pushed him through the open door, turned her back and stomped over to the counter.

'Espresso,' she snarled at the barista. 'To go.'

The barista kept his face blank and his questions to himself, giving her time to seethe while he made her coffee.

How dare he!

Fuming, she looked at her phone. The screen showed the last Partridge Bark message about Tim.

At least that was good news.

'I know what people think about Tim,' she said to Hamish, who was taking advantage of her inattention to scavenge a piece of croissant from the floor. 'But he's really not that bad.'

Hamish chewed quickly, swallowed and looked up at his mistress, ears moving like black, fluffy bullshit-detecting radar dishes. She clarified, 'Okay, so he's in love with himself, but that doesn't mean he deserved to have the crap kicked out of him.'

The Scottie tilted his head to the side; as much of an answer as he could provide, while his eyes scanned the floor for more treats.

'Don't roll your eyes at me,' she scolded. 'And don't judge me.'

Hamish grunted and lay down, resting his head on his paws.

Irina paid for her coffee, wondering if Andy had found the messages from Tim on her phone. She sort of hoped he had – just desserts for looking through it in the first place. She'd been about to change his alias in her phone from As Is to As Was when Andy had to go and ruin things. There was no point now in not responding to his earlier message.

As Is

> Sorry to hear about the attack. You OK?

Glory of a headache, and enough bruises to make a boxer jealous.

> Pretty.

Going for the rough-and-tumble look. Might not be walking Loki for another couple of days though …

Irina had to laugh. He was beaten up badly enough to land him in hospital and he was still trying to schedule his next booty call.

As Is

> Take your time – there are other people who can

240

walk Loki. Who did this to you?

Damned if I know. Big guys, hoodies, you can guess the rest.

What did you say to piss them off?

So that's the funny thing. I don't know. They came out of nowhere and – boom.

Irina frowned. 'You hear about these random attacks, Hammy, but you never expect it to happen to someone you know.' She sent off one last message and headed home to drop off Hamish and get dressed for work.

When she was ready to leave, he gave her a sad look as she moved towards the door. 'Don't worry, Hamish. I'll be back in a couple of hours. And then we'll do something fun. I promise.'

33

LOUISE

Irina (Hamish's Mum)

Call me when you get this.

I ignored the message. Counted my breaths while I tried to process Mandy's words. The possibility had been there at the back of my mind all morning, but now, hearing her say his name felt like a sucker punch to my belly.

Lead in to the big questions ... Slowly.

'I'm so sorry for your loss, Mandy. How long had you and Philip been seeing each other?'

Mandy brushed a stray tear away with the back of her hand. 'Only a few months. Since March.'

March. Three months. That wasn't a lot of time, but even so, the relationship had clearly meant a lot to Mandy.

'Wow. It must have been a terrible shock. When did it happen?'

There was still a chance that it wasn't him. Wasn't there?

When had I gone from hoping that her dead boyfriend was Phil Creasy to hoping it wasn't?

'Do you know what it's like, Lou, to see a person alive and well, and then to be told he's dead only a few hours later?'

I couldn't imagine it and told her so. 'What happened, if you don't mind me asking?'

Mandy sniffed and fumbled in her bag. I reached into a pocket and brought out a small packet of tissues.

'Thank you.'

'Welcome,' I said, and tried to lighten the mood. 'Careful, though – Klaus likes to eat tissues. He may try to mug you for them.' Klaus gave me a side-on look, as if he was offended that I'd shared his dark secret.

Mandy gave me another watery smile, accepted the tissue and blew her nose. If she noticed Klaus's interested look, she ignored it.

'We'd had dinner together Saturday evening, but Philip said he had work to do and couldn't stay over. Said that he'd call me tomorrow.' Her tears flowed faster now, running unchecked down her face. 'But he didn't, of course.'

'Of course,' I echoed. 'So, you weren't there when it happened?'

'No,' she bawled. Amelia pawed her knee, offering comfort. Klaus, after a quick glance at me, bounced onto her other knee. She put her hands on both dogs' heads, not seeming to notice when Klaus nibbled at the corner of the tissue still in her hand.

Composing herself as best she could, Mandy continued, 'I only found out later. The police called to let me know …' The sentence ended in a hiccup. The tissue dropped from her hand.

Don't look down. Don't look down …

Keeping my eyes on hers, I shook my head. 'What a terrible way to find out.'

She sniffed.

'Did they … Were they able to tell you what happened?'

'It took them a while … The body … Philip's body …'

Feeling sick, I reached for my glass, then pushed it away. 'That bad?'

She nodded. 'They found him pretty quick. I mean, people called the police, you know.'

'Yes?'

'But the police didn't contact me until Monday. It wasn't like him not to call on Sunday when he said he would. And my calls to him went to voicemail. I just knew something was wrong. I tried to work Monday morning, really I did. But I couldn't concentrate, so I asked Babs if I could take the day off.'

I nodded sympathetically, motioning her to continue.

'I just knew it!' Mandy's sobs broke out again, and she covered them with the back of her hand. I pushed the packet of tissues back towards her. She pulled one out and blew her nose with a loud honk.

Klaus had edged next to her, waiting for this one to fall. I gently tugged his lead, but he wasn't moving.

The waitress, passing by, paused and glanced down. Shot another look at the dogs, then at Mandy. I thanked her and waved her away as discreetly as I could.

'Sorry, so it took them a day to contact you?'

'Yes. They phoned Monday night.'

'Because of your missed calls?'

'No. They hadn't found his phone. They spoke to his neighbour and she told them about me. I'd met her a couple of times, you see. She didn't know my surname, but they were able to find my business card on his desk.'

They hadn't found the phone, because someone had thrown it into the park, under a bush?

'Good thing you gave him your card,' I said. Trying for levity, I added, 'I'll make sure we don't stop using them.'

She gave me a weak smile. 'When I gave it to him, I'd written my personal mobile on the back.' She blushed. 'With a big heart next to it.'

'Did the police tell you what happened to him?'

She nodded. Sniffed again. Pulled another tissue from the packet. None of the used ones were on the table, and I had to work to keep myself from looking down.

'They said it was a hit-and-run.'

I tried to process this. Someone had hit him, then thrown his body over the fence? That fence was fairly high – it'd be quite a feat for only one person. Were we looking for two people? Or more? It was beginning to sound more like a gang, but why would they leave his phone under the bushes in the dog park? And surely they'd have shown up on CCTV *somewhere*.

It made no sense.

'Poor Phil,' I said.

'Philip,' she corrected. 'He hates being called Phil.' She corrected herself with a little wince. '*Hated* being called Phil.'

'Ahh, sorry.' I leaned forward, resting a forearm next to the untouched plate of food. 'Mandy, can I ask what Philip's surname was? It wasn't Creasy, was it?'

'Creasy?' she echoed, surprised. 'Like the man who was found in Partridge Park? God no. His surname is – was – Saunders. Philip Saunders.'

Damn.

34

LOUISE

Irina (Hamish's Mum)

Lou? Where are you? Call me back when you get this.

Philip Saunders, not Phil Creasy.

I ignored my phone; Irina could wait.

'That's horrible,' I murmured, shocked at the coincidence. Two relatively young men named Philip, both killed on the same day. Two deaths that should not have happened. I was grateful that Mandy's Philip wasn't the man I'd found in the park, but I had the awful feeling that there could be another woman out there who'd had to find out what happened to her man on a news report asking for more information.

Had she already told the police whatever she knew? With access to more information, did they already have a suspect?

Was that what Irina was texting to tell me?

'Do the police know who did it?' The question sounded flat, even to me.

'Not yet. Not as far as I know at least.' Mandy shifted Amelia's lead to her right wrist, gently pulling her corgi away from the road. She reached for another tissue and blew her nose again. 'But I'm not officially his next of kin. That's still his ex-wife.'

'But they're looking for the car, right?'

'Yes. They think it was an accident. That the driver wasn't paying attention and got spooked. Kept driving out of fear instead of doing the right thing and stopping, getting Philip help.' Her voice had hardened.

'He was a good man, Lou. A genuinely good guy. What right did that stupid driver have to kill him?'

'Are they *sure* it was an accident?' I reached for a now cold mozzarella stick, more for something to do with my hands than out of hunger.

She blinked. 'Of course it was an accident. Why would anyone want to kill Philip?' She straightened her back. 'Whatever would they hope to gain?'

At the end of the lunch, the wine gone, the food mostly untouched, the pack of tissues empty and Mandy in a slightly better state, I dared to look at the ground.

Klaus was sitting next to Amelia. There were little white flakes of tissue, like paper snow, scattered around them, but not as much as there should have been.

The little furry monsters gave me near-identical smug looks.

They'd eaten the tissues.

One pale hand dropped beneath the table as Mandy slipped both dogs pieces of fish. They didn't dither, probably figuring they were being rewarded for tidying up after her.

Between the tissues and the whitebait, Klaus would have a digestive issue on the walk home, but I wasn't inclined to stop Mandy.

My phone buzzed with a third message from Irina:

Irina (Hamish's Mum)

Bloody stupid imbecile man betrayed me. You're right to stay single.

'Work?' Mandy asked, half hopefully.

'No. A friend of mine who's had a row with a guy she fancies.'

Mandy's face turned ashen. 'Well tell her that life is too short, too precious to hold a grudge over a little fight. It just isn't worth it.'

'Yeah, and I'm sure any rational person would agree.' I smiled and shook my head. 'My friend isn't the most rational at the best of times, but I'll remind her when I see her.'

Hoping that Irina hadn't burned bridges with our only link to the police, I waved the waitress over and asked her to pack up the leftovers for Mandy and to bring the bill. She gave the dogs a side-eye and I looked at them under the table again.

'You two are completely disgusting,' I told them.

Mandy frowned and glanced down at Klaus and Amelia. 'Why? What did they do?'

Who knew, maybe she'd see the funny side of it. 'Remember how I said that Klaus likes tissues?'

She blinked owlishly at me and I pointed under the table.

She gagged as she stared at my little innocent-looking sausage dog, while her pretty corgi preened, licking her front paw.

We parted company outside the pub with a warm hug and well wishes. I slipped my phone out of my pocket as Klaus and I turned the first corner. Popped in my earbuds and phoned Irina. 'What did you do?'

'Read the message, Lou. HE betrayed ME.'

With Irina, everything had to be about Irina. An unfortunate trait which had earned her the nickname 'Tsarina'.

'Okay . . .'

'He looked at my phone, Lou! He *broke into* my phone!' Her voice rose with each word, ending on a near-shriek.

'Why? I mean, how? You're in the office. He's a cop. You have a password on the phone, don't you?'

'Of course I have a password,' she howled. 'Do you think I'm *bloody stupid*?'

We paused under a plane tree that Klaus immediately weed on, before proceeding to walk in a circle around the black tarmac beneath the tree, until he found the perfect spot. I pulled out a green bag from the dispenser I kept clipped to his lead. 'So? How'd he get in if you have a password? It's not "Hamish", is it?'

I picked up Klaus's poo as Irina launched into an expletive-laced tirade. When she paused, I asked, 'So if he doesn't know the password and doesn't have the tech skills to properly break in, how'd it happen? Maybe he was just looking at the phone?'

'He 100 per cent was not!'

I tied the green bag closed, trying not to laugh, then I gave in and started to giggle.

'It's not funny!'

'No, Irina, it's not.' The serious façade broke completely and, still laughing, I added, 'It's hilarious.'

I imagined her squaring her shoulders, eyes red and nose expelling puffs of fire. 'How so? We have one friend dead. Another in hospital. And the police are breaking into my PHONE!'

'One policeman. Not all of them.'

'Seriously, Lou. Don't they have anything better to do?'

'I don't know. I'd have thought you'd be keeping him too busy to infiltrate your phone.'

'Jesus. You're supposed to be on my side!'

'Of course I'm on your side. Why do you think he did it?'

A strident patter of high heels on pavement echoed from the phone.

'Where are you now?'

'Walking Hamish. Even my dog betrayed me. He didn't stop Andy!'

Poor Hamish wasn't going to win this one. And neither was I.

'Don't blame poor Hamish. What did Andy see?' Part of me held my breath, half hoping he'd seen a spicy text from Tim.

'I don't know all of it, but he gave me an earful about the work we were doing about Phil.'

'About Phil? Good. I mean, it could have been worse.' I lobbed the poo bag into a nearby bin and encouraged Klaus to start walking south. 'Did he share any insights he might have?'

'He did not! He gave me grief. "Leave detecting to the detectives".' Irina's voice had dropped to a reasonable facsimile of Andy's baritone. 'And *then* he started going on about Tim!'

If he'd found out about Tim already, that was good detective work ... But he didn't seem the type to have a jealous fit. Certainly not over a woman he'd met less than a week ago and who was part of a case he was working on.

That said, if he had, I'd have paid good money to see it.

'So, what'd you tell him?' Maybe it was the wine, but I couldn't keep from laughing. 'Please tell me you didn't go into gory details.'

After a few moments of silent fuming on the other end of the phone, Irina hissed, 'That's not funny, Lou.'

It was time to put things into perspective. 'Look, you met him less than a week ago. If he's asking about Tim, all you need to say is that he's a guy you used to date. As Was, not As Is. Unless you want Andy out of your life, in which case tell him you've never had anyone better.'

I held up one finger, even while knowing she couldn't see it. 'That said, I hope you don't do that. I like him for you. He seems like a good guy, who might not scare easily.'

And – as far as I knew – he wasn't 'dating' half the neighbourhood.

'He betrayed me. What part of that did you fail to understand?'

'Look, whatever your password is, change it,' I said, trying to take the situation seriously. 'I doubt he infiltrated any of your banking or social media apps, but check those passwords too. And then calm down and tell me what he said. In full.'

35

GAV

Gav sat at his usual table at the George, nursing a pint and staring out of the window.

'Whatcha hoping to see, Gav?' Mo asked, standing in front of him, a pint in each hand. ''Cos if it's Christina Aguilera, I got dibs.'

Gav glared at the sleeping creature at his feet. Violet usually gave him a warning when someone arrived. He hoped she wasn't ill.

'Don't worry. Violent likes me,' Mo said. 'We're mates now.'

Gav wasn't sure if Mo's slip on Violet's name was intentional or not, but let it go.

Mo placed a pint in front of him. 'Not like you to be day-drinking, Gav.'

Gav shrugged, but accepted the drink with a simple 'ta'. He was aware that Mo was studying his face. Let him. What would he see? An old man looking out of the window at the market square? Big deal.

Mo took a drink from his lager top.

'Ain'cha supposed to be working?' Gav grumbled.

'Got staff, don't I?'

'That idiot Zed?'

Mo struggled to look offended, but his broad face was too good-natured. 'Hey, I'll have you know that that idiot is my nephew. And he's a good kid. Studying to go to college.'

'Fair 'nuff.' Gav didn't care and tuned out Mo's constant chatter until something his mate said caught his attention.

'Saw the kid arrive back earlier.'

'What kid?' Gav asked.

'The one what got beaten up in the square last night. With the white Jack Russell dog.'

Gav schooled his features to show nothing. 'You know anything 'bout it?'

'The dog?' Mo's smile faltered. 'I heard it was him against three guys in hoodies.'

'The same kids what hang out in front of your place?'

Mo seemed to consider that for a moment. 'No. Don't think so. These guys, they were big. The kids that hang out in front of the News, they're ... well, kids. Scrawny little buggers who think they're tough. Big difference.'

Gav grunted. That didn't rule either set of thugs out of being the ones who tried to knock seven bells out of him, although he didn't want to go there. Not today. 'You seen him today? The kid?'

'Yeah.'

Inhale. Exhale. Inhale. Exhale.

'And?'

'An' what, Gav?'

Mo's playin' with you, mate.

Gav took a sip from the fresh pint and waited. It didn't take long.

'Oh, you mean the pretty boy? Came back with his girl a coupla hours ago. In a cab, so I'm guessing he's still hurtin' a bit.'

Give a bit to get a bit.

'Heard he had a concussion. Maybe broke a rib or two.'

Mo's lower lip jutted out a little. 'I dunno. Mebbe.'

'You're the one what seen him.'

'Saw the girlfriend help him out of the car and across the square. Someone musta been watching the dog. Little ba— thing wasn't with them.'

Gav didn't miss the slip. 'You're friends with Violet, but not with the kid's dog?'

It was Mo's turn to stare out of the window. 'Got no issue with the dog.'

'But with the kid?' Gav's brows raised. 'You gotta problem with the *pretty boy*?'

Mo's brow lowered, and for a moment his usual amiable expression darkened.

Gav leaned forward, hands on the table. 'Awright. Wha'd he do?'

'To me? Nuffin.'

That was too precise. Something had happened, Gav'd bet money on it. 'But to someone you know? A girl? A woman?'

Mo drained his glass and stood up. 'I don't know nuffin'.' He brushed his hands against the front of his trousers. 'Gotta get back to work, 'fore Zed gets hisself into trouble. Good to see you, though, Gav.'

Gav remained seated, thoughts scrolling through his mind. Mo knew something but wasn't talking. The kids who'd gone for him weren't the ones who'd put the pretty boy in hospital.

How many bloody gangs were there these days?

Gav leaned over and put one hand on Violet's back. She looked up at him from the corner of her eye for a moment, then closed it and resumed her snoring. Whatever threat there was didn't seem to concern her, and that was the way it should be.

The way Gav would risk anything to maintain.

He stayed sitting at the table, watching the market traders do their business. Watched people come and go. Women with kids, builders, people with dogs, the lot.

Finally, he saw Pretty Boy's girl take his Jack Russell out for a walk. Gav stood up.

He was taking a chance, but he hadn't seen anyone else enter the flat and he needed to know what had happened. Needed to know whatever the kid had learned. And whether it was what'd landed him in hospital.

Because, Gav was certain, it was all connected.

36

LOUISE

Partridge Bark

> A couple of days in and our patrols are already yielding results! Shall we meet for a drink later and share information? Maybe coordinate next steps?

Claire (Tank's Mum)

> Sorry, I have a date ... and a deadline. But let me know what happens — I'll be on my patrol before the date.

Meg (Tyrion's Mum)

No rest for the wicked when you work on *The Chronicle*? 😉
How about we meet at the Hound around 7? Easy for me to say though as Tyrion and I aren't on the poop patrol rota. C'mon, guys – haven't you heard a dachshund bark?

We'd also been left off the evening rota, but I wasn't about to complain. Nor was Klaus, who'd already had enough of walking and kept bouncing his paws off the back of my legs.

'Tired, are you?'

Another bounce.

'Okay.' I picked him up and draped him over my left shoulder. Rested my cheek against his soft fur for a moment. Reminded myself that this was what I was working for. To keep my dog, myself and my friends safe.

I called the Hound to book the back room and then phoned Babs.

'Afternoon, lovely,' she answered the phone. 'How was your chat with Mandy?'

'Productive. The good news is that her boyfriend wasn't the man I found in the park. The bad news was that it was still a fatal hit-and-run.'

'How is she?'

'Not good. I'm inclined to offer her a second week of paid leave, even though we both know she'll turn it down.'

'If she doesn't, Moany Tony will have kittens. Not sure he knows how to get anything done without her.'

'And yet, has he agreed to sign the contract for the next phase?'

'Nope. But he called earlier. Asked if there's a chance you could go down to see him. Say, at 3:30?'

'In person? He's actually summoning *me* to his office at 3:30 on a Friday afternoon?'

'Looks that way.'

I looked at my watch. It was 2:45. The lunch with Mandy had taken longer than I'd expected, but if Tony wanted to discuss the contract in person, that was fine with me. 'Okay, tell him I can make it there, but I'm on the far side of business casual. I don't have time to change clothes or to drop Klaus off at home. If he wants to see me face to face, Moany Tony will have to deal with that.'

At least I'd put on a bit of make-up for the morning call and had touched it up before meeting Mandy.

'That's fine. I'll let him know. And Samuel is on site at Gen today. I'm sure he'd love to watch Klaus. Throw in a coffee and that boy'll sing your praises for the next century.'

I rang off and looked at Klaus. 'Looks like we're going to get our step count in today, my love.'

Samuel Osman was waiting for me at the Brera coffee shop in the shadow of the iconic Canary Wharf Tower. He was twenty-five, smart, ambitious and had an emotional IQ off the charts. One day he'd be a force to be reckoned with, but now he was like a high-energy kid in a sweet shop, wanting to know everything yesterday.

'Hey, Wizard of Os!' I called out.

Samuel stood up and waved with his entire body, a smartly dressed scarecrow with a charming smile. Only it wasn't me he greeted.

'KLAUS!' He moved past me and got onto one knee to greet my dog.

'Isn't it the rule to greet the boss first?' I asked.

'Yes,' Samuel said, allowing Klaus to lick his face. Klaus had French-kissed most of my friends and about half my employees. It was something we'd all gotten used to. 'And the boss's boss is her dog.'

'Insubordination is a terrible thing.' I laughed and handed over Klaus's lead. 'Anything I need to know about?'

'You read the week's status reports?' he asked.

'Yes, and I was on the call this morning. But what about Tony's mood?'

'Arsey,' he replied as if I'd asked him whether the Pope was Catholic. 'He's smarming around as if he's the cat that got the cream. Not sure why, but keep your eyes open, Lou.'

Interesting.

Samuel handed me a tote bag. 'They're Michelle's. Might not be a perfect fit, but better than what you're wearing.' Inside the bag were a neatly folded white blouse and blue blazer. 'Figured you wouldn't have time to buy something but might have enough to change in the loos. You'll have to make do with the Friday casual look, though. She said you won't fit her shoes or her spare trousers.'

'Fantastic, please thank her for me.'

Samuel shrugged this off. 'Everyone knows she keeps a change of clothes in the office in case she has pasta for lunch and a meeting in the afternoon.' He grinned, an open, easy smile. 'By the way, when you're changing, maybe see if you can get some of the pawprints off your jeans. The rips are trendy, the dirt isn't.'

After instructing Klaus to behave for Samuel, I strode into Cabot Place, detouring to change my top before heading towards the lobby of Canary Wharf Tower. A well-dressed, well-coiffed man at reception took my name, gave me a badge and directed me to the appropriate lift.

I walked past a pair of men wearing 'business casual' attire designed by Armani and Brunello Cucinelli. Spotting my 'dog-park chic', complete with borrowed top and jacket, they seemed careful to not meet my eyes.

Suppressing a grin, I nodded as I passed them and headed towards the lift that would take me to Gen's offices. Smiled at the smartly dressed people in the lift that edged away from me, as though my look was contagious.

My ears popped as it soared upwards, and I breezed out on Gen Tech's floor.

The receptionist was familiar, as was the corporate dance. I approached her desk.

Don't call him Moany Tony. Don't call him Moany Tony.

'Hi, I'm Louise Mallory, here to see Tony Frater. Would you please let him know I'm here?'

'Of course. Would you mind taking a seat,' she said. 'And I'll let his assistant know you're waiting.'

Instead of picking a chair, I meandered over to the long windows and their view over Canary Wharf. Looking down I imagined I could see Samuel with Klaus below. Mostly for something to do, I got out my phone and texted Jake to see how Luther was.

Jake (Luther's Dad)

He's OK thx. Need to ask a favour.

Sure. Go ahead.

I need to go away for the weekend. It's a sudden thing and leaving tomorrow a.m. Can you watch Luther or suggest someone who can? I don't want to leave him with a stranger right now.

Part of me wanted to ask more. Where was he going? Was it with someone special? But I knew I didn't have the right, or the time, to ask.

263

The receptionist called me over, and I followed one of Tony's acolytes past one open door after another until we reached a harried redhead guarding the gates to the Finance department and Moany Tony's Den of Penny-Pinching Perversity.

Unlike the others, his door was firmly closed, the shades on the windows drawn. The little troll kept his office like a cave.

'Afternoon, Tony,' I said, pushing open the door.

He looked up, blinking as if I'd surprised him. 'Oh, Louise. Come in, come in.'

Tony Frater was not a tall man, and while I hadn't expected him to stand up and underline that point, I had expected a courteous 'Have a seat'. Knowing better than to wait for it, I closed the door behind me and sat in the visitor's chair opposite his desk. It was almost a minute before his hooded eyes left the screen and alighted on me.

'Glad to see you again. A bit short notice, though. I hope you don't mind my casual attire,' I added.

Go ahead. You called this meeting. I dare you to give me grief for showing up casually. I dare you.

He grinned in return and leaned back, the chair creaking with his weight. 'Not at all. We do dress-down Fridays here too.'

'Thanks for setting up this meeting. Can I assume you'd like to sign the extension in person?' I asked.

'Ah.' Tony leaned back further, to the point where I began to worry about his safety. One sudden sneeze and he'd catapult himself out the window.

I held my tongue and waited for his return volley.

'I heard you were out with Fidelio yesterday.'

I raised an eyebrow. 'Yes?'

'Are you pitching for their business?' he asked. He righted the chair, only to start swivelling it from left to right in what was meant to be a light-hearted manner.

'I had a couple of drinks with them,' I confirmed. 'But so what?'

'They're not a good investment,' he said.

'Investment?'

Tony shook his head, jowls wobbling. 'You're not dim, Louise. Don't act it. Fidelio is having problems, serious problems. You'd be throwing time and resources away with them.'

'Well, we'd get paid for it of course, but I'm sure you know that's exactly the sort of company we work with. We built our business model on turning around failing portfolios. And failing companies. But that can't really be why you brought me here today.'

He seemed to have the bit between his teeth. 'Fidelio is a waste of time.'

'So you said,' I replied. 'But as far as I know, they aren't one of your competitors, so I'm not sure why you're trying to warn us off.' I crossed one leg over the other. 'If you're worried about us diverting staff from Gen to Fidelio, the best way to prevent that is to sign the contract for the next phase.'

He frowned as if he didn't believe me. Leaning forward, he rested his forearms on the desk. 'Let me give you a bit of insider advice, Louise.'

'Go ahead.'

'Fidelio is having problems.'

The conversation was getting repetitive, and I was beginning to feel as if I'd wasted my time coming here. 'The CEO is dead. I know.'

Tony shook his head. 'Not just that, although it makes things trickier for them.'

His pale blue eyes, without a soul behind them, locked on mine. 'A coup had been in the works for months. Jim Clark, their CTO, had been clashing with Creasy. And he'd been going behind Creasy's back to the Angels.'

'The Angels? He went behind the CEO's back and went straight to the investors? On what grounds?' It was bad form and rarely worked. 'I'd heard they got along.'

Moany Tony laughed, a strange braying sound that lacked any humour. 'What? That they were friends?' He wiped an eye. 'Yeah, yeah, keep telling yourself that, Louise.'

His laughter subsided and he continued. 'The story is that they met at some sort of entrepreneurs' meet-up.' He waved his hand, dismissing it. 'Philip turned a blind eye to Clark's manoeuvring. For a while, at least. Not sure why, because Clark had outlasted his usefulness. He was no longer a value-add. His team were happy enough to have a drink with him, but would they stand behind him? No chance.'

Not too unlike my own observations.

'Creasy should have replaced Clark years ago, but it seems he only recently found the *cojones* to do it. Rumour has it that he started contacting the Angels himself, letting them know of his intention to replace *Jim* ...' Tony smiled a shark's smile '. . . with a CTO who could bring the company forward.'

'Do you know who he intended to replace Jim Clark with?'

Tony touched the side of his nose with one finger. 'Insider knowledge.'

'Fine,' I said, feigning disinterest. 'What about Tabitha Halder? Where does she stand in this?'

Tony shrugged. 'She's a good people person; I'd hire her. But she's not CEO material and she has her hands full keeping people in line.' He smirked. 'Including Jim. And we know how he likes his lines.'

I didn't, but I also didn't care. Tony was going to great pains to make it clear that Jim Clark had a motive to kill Phil, but he also had his own agenda, not least of which was trying to make sure I didn't divert my team to another contract.

'Interesting gossip,' I said, reaching into the canvas tote that Samuel had given me. 'If you have some concrete information, I'd suggest you speak with the Met Police.'

His face deflated like a popped balloon; I hadn't realised he enjoyed gossip this much. 'As much as I'd like to speculate with you on the factors leading up to Philip Creasy's murder, I don't want to waste your time, Tony.'

In the bag, my fingers brushed aside the crumpled blouse I'd been wearing earlier and closed around a neat brown envelope.

'Especially as you invited me here to sign the new contracts.' I smiled, as I pulled out the two crisp copies.

37

LOUISE

Partridge Bark

Indy (Banjo's Mum)

Hey guys, Banjo is
scratching his ears – like a
lot. Any thoughts? Advice?

Fiona (Nala's Mum)

Check with the vet –
they should advise if it's
serious or not.
@Louise – Running late at
work, but will see you at
the Hound?

> Yep, no prob. See you there.

Mandy had given me a lot to think about, as had Tony, whether intentionally or not.

I phoned Babs. 'Hello, lovely,' she answered. 'How was the meeting?'

'Promise me one thing, Babs . . . If you have a problem with me, let's talk first.' I realised as soon as I'd spoken that the tone was wrong. I knew I couldn't take the words back. Just hoped they hadn't caused as much offence as, well, they probably did.

There was a long pause at her end. When she spoke, her voice was confused. 'Of course. Whatever Tony said, he was talking out of his arse. Or trying to get you to acquiesce to a bad deal. You didn't, did you?'

I had to laugh. 'No. He signed the papers we gave him. Thanks for providing those, by the way. And giving the team the heads-up that I was stopping by.'

'Michelle's jacket fit?'

'Yes.'

There was another silence, this time more awkward. 'Lou, look. You know I think the world of you.'

'I know, Babs.'

'And you know I'd love to move up . . .'

'Yes . . .' This time I spoke with less exuberance.

'So let me be clear: I like you. I respect you. And I still have a lot to learn from you. I'm not going to make a move on your company or your seat. It's not my style.'

I didn't miss her slight emphasis on 'you' and 'your'. 'I know that, thanks, Babs. You know how grateful I am to have you.'

'Good. So what brought this on?'

'Moany mentioned that Jim Clark, the CTO of Fidelio, had been mounting a coup against the CEO, Phil Creasy.'

'And thus had motive,' she said. Then cursed. 'Oh, Lou, I'm sorry!'

'For what?'

'I meant to tell you, but with everything going on, I forgot!'

'What is it?'

'We did a bit of digging on Fidelio. Seems they've had a few financial bumps.'

'What sort of bumps?'

'The sort that are common enough but still landed them in a heap of trouble. Sales made too many promises. Ops couldn't keep up. They don't have the people to deliver on their commitments. Not unusual, but they also don't have the money to recruit more staff. And, for whatever reason, the Angels aren't offering up more dosh.'

Because of Jim Clark?

'Thanks, Babs. Anything else?'

'No, that's it. Sorry, Lou. I meant to tell you earlier.'

'That's okay.' Even if she had, I'm not sure the meeting with Tony would have gone any differently. 'Listen, could you do me another favour, if you have the time? Doesn't have to be today.'

'Sure. What is it?'

I took a deep breath. 'I don't trust Jim Clark. How would I go about checking his finances?'

'Checking his finances?' Babs echoed.

'Yes. Maybe Fidelio's as well.'

'What are you up to? And do I need to be worried about someone knocking on my door?'

'No, no. Hey, look, forget I said anything. I don't want you to do anything illegal.'

'As if I would,' Babs snorted. There was silence at the other end of the line. Then she sighed. 'Okay, leave it with me.'

'Are you sure?'

'No. But whatever I find will only be through public channels,' Babs said. 'For both of them.'

'Good. And please, don't stay late on it or look at it over the weekend. You've been working like a Trojan, and you need to go and let your hair down.' I was babbling again, unsure how to stop. 'It'll keep.'

'Are you sure?'

'Absolutely,' I lied. That was the thing they always said on the detective shows: follow the money. And if Jim's came up clean, I wanted to know whether he could have authorised a payment from a corporate account for a hitman to bump off his boss.

38

LOUISE

Babs

> Thanks again for all your help this week. Have a good weekend.

You too, lovely. And try not to get into any trouble.

Klaus and I walked home along the river and canals. We stopped at the flat only long enough for me to feed Klaus, eat a safety sandwich and pick up my 'brainstorming supplies' – a container of Sharpies and Post-its, both of every imaginable colour.

The King's Hound was a relatively old building,

predating the modern new builds and 1960s council flats that surrounded it. Its architecture was simple. On one side, the pub looked 'finished' with flower baskets sprouting fuchsias and begonias, while on the other it looked foreshortened, giving the impression that it had only partially survived the Blitz.

The Hound didn't seem to care, leaning into its mismatched history. Klaus pulled me towards the front door and past potted plants and lemon trees. The main door was open, letting in the evening air, so he didn't even pause as he strutted his way inside.

After-work service was already in full swing. Some people were eating, most were drinking. There were a few dogs in the main room, and Klaus didn't miss the opportunity to greet old friends and sniff the butts of new ones, greeting all with the same cocky bark on the way to the bar.

'If he was tall enough or old enough, he'd probably order a dirty Martini,' the bartender said with a tired smile. 'Shaken, not stirred.'

'Yeah. His name is Bone. Klaus Bone, Double-0 Dachshund and general hound about ... well ... the Hound.' I had to smile. 'But no dirty Martini for him, thanks. He'll have to make do with a bowl of water. Neat. And a glass of the Provence rosé for me.'

'Will do.'

'Actually, can you make it a bottle, Sheri? We'll be in the back room for a while and I suspect the others might need a drink.'

The side of Sheri's mouth quirked. 'You're not the first

to think that. There's already a bottle of Shiraz, one of Sauv Blanc and a bucket of lager in there. I don't want to know what you'll be doing, but keep it legal, will you?'

'I can't comment on that, of course.'

'Of course.'

'And you know,' I leaned forward and assumed a serious look, 'if we do skate around the edges, at least we now have Irina as our secret weapon.'

Sheri stood back and blinked. 'In case you need a lawyer?'

'Nope. In case we need a contact in the force.'

'Full contact?' she asked over her shoulder, shovelling ice into a silver bucket.

'It's a safe bet.'

'Well, good on her.' Sheri put the bucket on a tray, buried the rosé in the ice and added a few glasses. 'I don't want to know details. But if you need me to carry this in, I promise not to take notes.'

'Thank you. You're welcome to join us.'

'Grateful for the invite, but I'm working.'

'I completely understand.'

She offered another tired smile as she placed the tray on the counter in front of me. 'At least Meg ordered nibbles to soak up some of the booze.'

'Gotta love Meg.'

'Yep. You've gotta.' Sheri paused, her hands still on the tray. 'Like I said, I don't know what you're all doing in there – and don't tell me, because I really don't want to know . . .'

She left the thought dangling and I prompted her. 'But?'

'But if you're going after whoever's poisoning the dogs, when you get him, kick him in the nuts for me.'

I'd been in far too many pubs' back rooms since moving from Connecticut to the UK. Some visits had been for corporate functions, but most had been for friends' parties. The Hound's back room was surprisingly elegant. The wallpaper was dark teal and flocked, which made it look old-fashioned, yet cosy. The framed prints on the walls showed a stylised London through the ages, focusing on sport, in an Art-Deco sort of way. The most recent depicted the 2012 Olympics. I hadn't moved east then but given the pub's proximity to the arenas in Stratford and North Greenwich, it had probably been heaving during that summer.

I pushed open the door, allowing Klaus to enter first. There were the usual yaps and barks while he greeted the others. I unclipped him from his lead and smiled as he ran over to Hercules.

Herc stood up suddenly, toppling a nearby chair, then sank back to the ground, edging forward at Klaus height to greet his friend. Tyrion scrambled from Meg's lap to join the fray.

Someone had pushed the tables together into one long stretch. The pub's nibbles – boneless chicken wings, chips and deep-fried halloumi – were interspersed with supermarket tubs of chocolates. A water jug sat, neglected, in the centre, a few slices of lemon swimming in it.

Despite the smorgasbord, only three people sat around the table so far: Yaz, Meg and Dr Cooper. His initial smile widened when he saw the tipple Sheri carried. 'Great minds think alike,' he said.

'I hadn't realised you'd be here,' I said. I hadn't meant for my tone to be as brusque as it sounded, and while he seemed not to notice, Meg blushed.

'I took Tyrion in for his annual exam today and told Dr Cooper that we were meeting tonight. I hope that's okay?'

'Ben,' Dr Cooper corrected. 'We're out of hours. Did you get to your event in time yesterday, Louise?'

'It was more of a catch-up than an event, but thank you for asking.'

Yaz's canny eyes followed the exchange, and I knew there'd be questions to answer later.

'Glad you could join us tonight, Ben,' I said. 'Welcome.'

'Thank you.' His smile turned self-conscious. 'While I don't know how much I can help, I don't like to hear about dead bodies turning up on my patch either.'

He stood up and followed me to a chair on the far side of the room. Put a hand on my arm, drawing me aside. He kept his voice low, although if he thought Yaz wouldn't hear every word, he was dreaming. 'And I need to apologise.'

'To me?' I asked, placing the container of supplies on the table. 'For what?'

'Not for asking you for a drink. I won't apologise for that. And I'm not going to pretend I'm not attracted to you. But I came on too strong, and I think I scared you off. For that, I am very sorry.' He was standing so close

I could smell nothing but expensive cologne. I stared at his hand on my arm until he released me. 'Please forgive me.'

I considered. Any of the dogs that accompanied their humans tonight would know each other, but given the number of them that would be off-lead in a small room – and the treats that Meg (and possibly others) would be handing out – it probably wasn't a bad thing to have a vet on standby.

'Sure,' I said, taking a step backwards, careful not to tread on Klaus's tail. 'It's not a problem. Please stay if you want to.'

'Thank you.'

'Good, then sit down, will you?' Yaz reached across the table to grab a couple of chips, tossing one to Hercules.

I waited until Dr Cooper had taken his seat beside Meg, then turned and pulled one of the prints from the wall, giving me a blank area to work with.

Ejiro arrived next, looking smart in his City suit. He didn't manage to get to his seat beside Yaz before Hercules bounded over, almost tackling him. Then Paul and Ella arrived with a bottle of Pinot Noir and a second bucket of beer.

'Sorry, guys,' Ella said, looking around. 'We left the boys at home.'

Paul grabbed a bottle from the bucket and added, 'Figured that if we brought Vader and Jim, it'd be carnage.'

'Good call.' Ejiro clinked his beer against Paul's.

Fiona and Nala arrived just ahead of Irina and Hamish. Klaus, delighted to have all his friends in one place, was running around the table like a lunatic. 'Close the door, Irina,' I said, 'and you can take Hamish off his lead.'

'The hounds aren't the only ones unleashed,' Yaz murmured.

'WHO LET THE DOGS OUT?' Fiona belted, then pointed to us. 'Who? You? You?'

'Clearly someone started on the sauce early,' Yaz observed.

Fiona flushed and looked down, suddenly intent on unclipping Nala. 'Sorry. Friday work drinks earlier. In my defence, it sounds like a doggy rave in here.'

She wasn't wrong. Once everyone had settled in, I cleared my throat.

'Hey, everyone, thanks for coming,' I began. 'Especially as it's a last-minute thing on a Friday night.'

'If you can make sense of murder, then more power to you,' Irina muttered.

I ignored her. 'A lot has been happening in a short amount of time. We're all looking at different angles, but if we share that info, we might have a clearer picture of what's going on. And what we can do about it.'

People were either nodding or checking to see why the dogs had gone quiet. A quick glance confirmed it: Meg was feeding them treats under the table.

'As I see it, we've got two issues at the moment,' I continued. 'Phil Creasy's murder and subsequent dumping of his body in Partridge Park.' I scribbled on a blue Post-it and stuck it to the wall. 'And the dogs that are being poisoned.' This was duly displayed on a green Post-it. 'Not sure whether they're connected or not, but let's get everything up on the wall and then we can pare it down as we rule things out.' I looked over my shoulder at everyone and grinned. 'And I'm sorry for going all work-like on you. This'll tell you how my brain works,' I joked.

'Add one more, Lou,' Yaz said. 'For the drug dealers. Might be involved, might not, but we can't rule them out yet.'

That went on an orange Post-it.

'What about the attack on Tim Aziz?' Irina asked.

My Sharpie poised over a yellow Post-it. 'What do we know about that?'

'We know he was beaten badly enough to be taken to hospital,' Meg offered.

'He's out now,' said a gruff voice. We turned to see Gav leaning against the wall beside the door. Violet was tucked under his arm, seemingly content to stay out of the canine melee on the ground. 'He says he saw three guys in hoodies, but not much beyond that.'

'Can he identify them?' Irina asked.

Fi paused, halfway through pouring a glass of wine. 'Is Tim okay?'

'He doesn't remember anything else,' Gav said, easing into a seat in the far corner. 'Head's dinked. Ribs are fractured. But the doctors say he'll be all right.'

'You think it was the same guys who murdered Phil?' Yaz said, pointing a halloumi stick at the Post-it in my hand. 'I think we can rule out a connection between Tim and the dog poisoning, but what about the drug dealers? Gangs?'

Gav shrugged. 'He doesn't know.'

I wasn't sure if anyone else noticed the tension leave Irina's shoulders. I'd hoped that her budding romance with DC Andy might have put a stop to the Tim thing, but with them rowing this early in the relationship, he might not outlast the investigation.

Hell, he might not outlast the night. Poor Andy.

'What do we think? Connections to anything else?' I asked, focusing myself and leaning back against the wall.

'Yes,' Fi said. 'But I'm damned if I know what. As far as I know, Tim wasn't involved in the patrols. Wasn't really even asking around about the poisonings. He was just being ... Tim.'

Almost everyone looked away, at their glasses, the ceiling, the dogs. Everyone knew what Fi meant.

'Come on, people. There has to be something,' Irina said.

Across the table Gav kept his eyes lowered, more focused on stroking Violet's head than usual. Something smelled wrong. 'Gav?'

His eyes met mine and it looked as though a blister had burst. 'Spoke to him yesterday,' he said. His voice lacked its usual bolshy confidence and I nodded, encouraging him.

'I had a few issues with some of the locals, day Phil's body was found,' he said. 'I'd been out for a Ruby with Doris. Went to the pub t'see the boys after. Had a sherbet or two. Asked a few questions.'

The Cockney slang would have stumped me when I'd first moved to London. In short, he'd had a curry with his wife, then beers with the lads.

More surprising was that he'd had issues with locals. Gav had that sort of swagger about him, wonky hip or not, that warned people not to mess with him. I tried to catch his eye; he hadn't mentioned this when we'd gone to see Ivy. Why?

'As you do,' Yaz murmured, giving me a subtle gesture to hold my questions and allow Gav to speak.

'As you do,' he echoed. 'But on the way home, a gang of kids wanted to speak to me.'

'"Speak".' Yaz rolled her eyes.

'Same ones who wanted to "speak" to Tim?' Irina asked.

'Dunno. I don't think so.'

'Why?'

He looked uncomfortable. Glanced at his empty glass and at the wine and beer on the table. I suspected he might have preferred something stronger. Dr Cooper grabbed the Shiraz and poured a healthy measure into Gav's glass.

'Look, he heard I was attacked. Offered to ask around. I said I was fine. I *was* fine. But he kept askin'. I shoulda told him to sod off, but instead – and I don't know why – I let him go ahead.'

'You look fine,' Irina said. Her voice was accusatory, and I could have kicked her.

'Yeah. I can take care of myself.'

'Sure you can. You're the big Gavin MacAdams, aren't you?' she said. 'Tough man about town.'

'Irina, stop it.' I didn't know what she was talking about, and I didn't really care. Whatever it was, wasn't relevant. I held up a hand. 'Gav is okay and Tim will be too. We're here to find out what's going on with the spikes in crime. We're here to make our neighbourhood safe, not to snipe at each other.'

Her gaze narrowed, but I held it until she nodded.

'Gav, is there any more you can tell us?' I asked. 'About Tim, or anything else?'

He shook his head. 'A mate of mine reckons it's different groups what attacked Tim and me. Not sure who, but I'm trying to find out.'

'That's it? You trust this guy?'

'With my life.' Gav put Violet on the floor, watching while she tolerated sniffs from Hercules and Hamish. 'I hear anything, an' you'll know.'

'Thank you,' I said. I took a deep breath and relayed what I'd learned about Phil, from his ex and his employees.

'I feel like crap that I didn't follow up with him. After . . .' Yaz said, but everyone around the table nodded.

'We've let Phil down once before,' I said. 'We won't do it again.'

'He's dead,' Irina drawled. 'I'm pretty sure he won't care.'

When I glared at her, she shrugged. 'Just saying.'

One moment, she was part of the group, the next, she wasn't. She seemed more erratic than usual, but the only way to deal with it was to ignore her.

'Whether or not he cares, *I* care. So, I asked around. There might be possible motives within his company. He set up the firm with two acquaintances he met at an entrepreneurs' networking meet-up.' I stuck the photographs of

Jim and Tabby on the wall. 'Tabitha Halder is the COO, and as far as I can tell, both competent and well respected in the company. Jim Clark is the CTO.'

'Which means?' Gav asked.

'Tabitha is in charge of operations. Jim's forte is technology, although the impression I got was that he was less strong when it came to running the technical teams. Both could have motives. With Phil gone, Tabby would be the likely heir apparent to run the firm, assuming the investors don't parachute someone in above her.'

'And the tech guy?'

'Rumour has it that Phil was working with the investors to replace him. We know that Jim knew something was up: he'd also engaged with the Angels – the investors – himself to try to oust Phil.'

Ejiro cleared his throat. 'If you let me know who the investors are, I can ask around. See if anyone has any insights into this.'

'Forgive me, I know I'm new around this table,' Dr Cooper interjected. Once all eyes in the room were on him, he continued. 'And I know that Mr Creasy was your friend, but I've got more of a vested interest in the living. What's the connection to who's poisoning the dogs?' He gestured at the wall with one manicured hand. '*Is* there a concrete connection? And is anyone liaising with the local police?'

Heads swivelled towards Irina, who flushed and sank lower in her chair. 'Yeah, I guess so.'

Dr Cooper looked at Meg and I guessed that she'd fill him in on Irina's liaison with DC Andy. Whatever part of that liaison remained.

'Are they telling us anything? The police, I mean.'

'No,' Irina admitted. 'So far the information has flowed in one direction only.'

Dr Cooper nodded, trying not to show the same disappointment we all felt.

'Okay,' I said, refocusing everyone's attention. 'Back to your first question, Dr Cooper, we don't know what connection might exist. Yet.'

'As she already said,' Irina muttered, glaring at him. 'If you'd been listening.'

If anyone heard her, no one responded. 'But the real question is, who benefits? From Phil's death, I mean. And/or from the poisonings,' I continued.

Meg raised one hand, keeping the other under the table, where the number of dogs surrounding her had increased.

'The gangs,' she said. 'Maybe Phil saw something, so they had to get rid of him. That'd also tie in with why Gav and Tim were attacked when they started asking questions.'

'Which gang?' Gav asked. 'There's more'n one around here. Specially these days.'

I wrote Meg's theory on a larger Post-it, but left it stuck on the pad in front of me. 'That's good, but before we jump to conclusions, let's make sure we put up all the information we have on any of the crimes.'

'We gonna share this with the police?' Paul asked, slanting a glance at Irina.

'Someone else can,' she muttered.

'I'm interested in knowing more about Phil's business partners. Does anyone know where to find them?' Ejiro asked.

I added two more Post-its from my pile, with address information on both. Tabby lived in West London, while Jim was in one of the new-build flats near Vauxhall. 'Amazing how easy it was to find that on the internet,' I said, trying to keep my voice even. Irina was usually my go-to for finding info online, but this time around she'd been unavailable. Or unforthcoming.

'What do we know about them?'

'Tabby seems to keep herself to herself. If anyone else can find out more, I'd be grateful.' I kept my eyes away from Irina.

'And Jim?'

'Jim's divorced. Lost the family home to the ex-wife, so he bought a bachelor pad near the Thames. He's tight but fancies himself as a *bon vivant* and a ladies' man.'

'We can honeytrap him!' Yaz chirped up. Ejiro's brow lowered and she added, 'Well, someone could. Clearly not me.'

'I don't think we need to go full honeytrap, but if someone can bring themselves to flirt with him, we might learn a bit more.' I shrugged. 'I'd do it myself, but he already saw me out with the Fidelio group the other night, and I think even he might smell a rat.'

Although, I did have a long, blonde-ish wig from last Halloween. Would he look that close? How much had he even noticed me? I could . . .

'I'll do it,' Meg and Claire both said.

I looked between them. 'Jim Clark is fifty-three. Having seen him in action on Thursday, I'd say he's after more of a thirtysomething than a twentysomething. Let Claire have a shot at it, Meg. Our local journalist should be able to get whatever answers we need. Without compromising herself.'

'Unless she wants to,' Yaz pointed out.

Everyone stared at her, and she shrugged. 'What? Fifty-three isn't that old. I'm picturing silver fox . . .'

'Put your glasses on and look at the photo on the wall, Yaz,' Irina said.

Yaz squinted at it. 'Oh. Yeah, no. I'm out.'

Avoiding Paul's glance, Ella added, 'I'll go with Claire. Two women out for drinks together will look less obvious than one lone woman.'

'Good point. Thanks Ella.'

Irina expelled a massive sigh. 'I'm sure he's got regular haunts. Everyone does. I'll go online and see what I can find out and text you.'

'Good,' I said. 'Now then, what do we think about the poisonings? Who benefits?'

Three hours later, multiple sets of bleary eyes stared back at me from around the table, and not just due to the vast quantities of wine, beer and gin that had been consumed. The only thing that linked all the strands together was Meg's theory about the gangs, but that didn't mean that we'd unearthed the connection yet.

In the interim, we'd follow the leads we had.

We brought the empties to Sheri at the bar and trudged out the door of the Hound, separating into small groups as we headed towards our respective homes. Irina fell into step beside me, just behind Meg and Claire. 'I'm surprised that your new neighbour didn't show up.'

That was typical Irina, trying to deflect attention away from any conversation she didn't want to have. I was too tired to accommodate that. 'He texted earlier that he couldn't make it. Are you still on the outs with DC Andy?'

'Why?'

'Because you're in an unusually ratty mood.'

It was dark, but the streetlamps caught the sardonic lift of her brow. 'You want details? Oh wait. You know them.'

'Because he looked at your phone? Jesus, Irina. It had to be an easy enough password for him to break into it. What did you do, use Sargie?'

An angry red flush suffused her face, visible even in the dim light. 'What are you talking about?'

'Every time you get drunk, you talk about your old dog. Anyone with half a brain would try that once they realised that you didn't use Hamish or *Mischka* for your password.'

She muttered a string of profanities.

'What?' I asked, and then an idea came to me, one that I knew she'd never admit to. It was rare for Irina to pay for a round, but on those occasions, she did make a point of not going to the bar herself. She'd hand me her phone with a big sigh. I'd bet that she did the same with Andy and then was surprised when he had a look around.

'You're an idiot,' I told her. Her glare confirmed that I was right. 'Look. Change your password, if it makes you feel better. I genuinely don't care if you're banging him,

Tim or some guy you met online. But remember, Andy's our cop on the case. Try not to screw this up for all of us.'

'Tim? What's he got to do with this?'

FFS.

'Sorry, Irina, I hadn't realised that you regularly entertained another guy who happens to have a Jack Russell that looks just like Loki.'

Her pace slowed, but her voice became frostier by the second. 'What do you mean?'

'Do you want me to draw you a picture?' I gestured to the canvas bag carrying my box of brainstorming supplies. 'I can do, if you'd like?'

Hamish strained at the lead, trying to chivvy her along. She ignored him. 'Don't be difficult. The poor man was in hospital.'

Claire and Meg slowed down. Claire looked over her shoulder. 'You both okay?'

'Yeah.'

We walked on in an awkward silence, past a closed barber's shop, a greasy spoon with a poster for an upcoming funfair hanging in the window and a wings place that smelled far too good after a few glasses of wine. Klaus was already pulling towards it.

I stopped and looked at Irina. 'Look, you're both consenting adults. I don't care what you two get up to as long as I don't have to flat-out lie to anyone. But I like Andy. Give the guy a chance, or just cut him loose. Your call.'

Klaus paused, his front paws planted in the direction of the wings place. He turned his head, giving me the side-eye, and I reconsidered my last words, adding, 'Though maybe wait until after we figure out who killed Phil, if you don't mind.'

Just then, the sounds of squealing tyres and a revving engine seemed to ricochet off the buildings. A blue car appeared almost out of nowhere, looking to break the speed of sound. I muttered a curse and scooped Klaus up.

The car skidded towards us, mounting the pavement.

People were shouting, pushing to get further back. With Klaus still in my arms, I leapt over a low brick wall into someone's front garden, not caring about the bushes scratching my legs. The car swerved a couple of times – as if the driver was trying to get it back under control – and then it was gone.

I lowered Klaus to the ground and, forcing a smile, held my shaking hands over my head. 'Touchdown!'

Several pairs of eyes stared at me, confused.

'How much have you had to drink?' Irina asked.

'Enough to know that Klaus isn't a ball,' I said. 'But that was the second near miss of the week and the second time I made it safely into the endzone. Touchdown.' Claire blinked and I cleared my throat. 'Never mind. It's an American football thing.'

'Second time in a week?' Claire latched on. 'Do you think . . .'

'Bah,' Irina answered. 'They get close all the time. It's no big deal.'

'It is a big deal if they get one of us, and this one looked like he was swerving right towards Lou,' Meg said. 'Did anyone get a look at the driver? I think he might have been wearing a cap . . .'

'Hell, it's so dark, I didn't even see what type of car it was, let alone check out the reg plates.'

'Pity Yaz was walking in the other direction. She'd have got a video of it.'

I stepped back over the wall, and only when my friends' backs were turned did I allow myself to take a deep breath, wondering whether it really was a coincidence.

Saturday

39

LOUISE

Irina (Hamish's Mum)

Tabitha plays tennis at a
club near her home on
Saturdays. I'll send you
the link.
And Hamish had
diarrhoea three times last
night.

> Too many treats? Meg
> doesn't cut hers in half.

IDK. I'm staying close
to home today so I can

watch him. He's not himself today.

> Check with Meg. Maybe there was chicken in her treats?

She wouldn't. Everyone knows Hamish's allergic. I gave him Enterosgel, but he's not drinking water and I'm worried he'll dehydrate.

> Look, keep an eye on it, but don't panic. He gets this all the time. If it doesn't get better, call the vet.

Yeah …

I didn't know if it was my little talk or the near miss with the car, but Irina was now going out of her way to be helpful. And that she'd messaged me, rather than the Pack, was as much of an apology as she was likely to offer.

As worried as I was about the second close call with a boy racer in a week – and I was still shaking from that – I was even more worried about Hamish. To be fair, he was

a legend when it came to scavenging. And in this neighbourhood, where chicken bones regularly decorated the
ground, the only question was whether Hamish preferred
the ones with an added helping of hot sauce or not.

The Enterosgel would help, and he'd probably pass
whatever was messing with his tummy by lunchtime and
be back to normal during the afternoon.

I asked Irina to let me know if there was anything I
could do; a message she ignored, so I opted to give her a
bit of space. The offer was on the table, and she knew how
to find me if she wanted to.

Partridge Bark

Tabby plays at the
Oakwood Tennis Club
in West London. I don't
suppose anyone knows
how to play?

Fiona (Nala's Mum)

I already volunteered to
join Jim detail tonight,
but I have a friend who
plays there. Let me make
a call. If anyone plays, she
can probably get them in.
What about you, Lou? I

think I've seen a racquet in your flat.

That racquet is hooked up to a battery, for zapping flies. But if no one else can do it, I'll blag my way through.

Indy (Banjo's Mum)

I can play. @**Fiona**, is your friend any good? I've been looking for a tennis partner.
@**Louise**, can you call me and let me know what sort of questions I need this Tabby to answer?

I took Klaus for a brief walk then recreated the Post-it wall from last night in my spare bedroom/home office, hoping for a sudden inspiration. The only leads we had still felt far too tenuous.

Indy hadn't been at the pub last night, so I brought her up to speed on where we were at, then rummaged in my wardrobe for my Halloween wig. Just in case. Because if Irina couldn't give us a list of Jim's local haunts we might need to spread out a bit more. One of us in each, keeping in contact via WhatsApp until the man arrived.

Assuming he didn't have plans in another part of town.

I found the wig and set it on my head. The long nylon hair was matted, and I looked like a Gorgon.

Klaus stared at it in fascination. 'It's not a toy,' I pointed out.

He edged closer, put a paw on my leg and reached up, giving one long tendril a tentative sniff. 'Nope, not for you.' I lifted it out of his reach and after a few minutes with a brush, it looked better.

With a short skirt and my black top, surely Jim Clark wouldn't recognise me.

Klaus stared at me, again with the side-eye. *What'cha thinkin', Mum?*

'People see what they want to, Klaus. Surely he wouldn't connect a woman with long blonde hair and her sausage dog to a woman with long dark hair and . . . her sausage dog?'

Klaus blinked, unconvinced.

My phone buzzed with a message from Jake, letting me know that – assuming it was still fine – he'd drop Luther off around 4 to 4:30 p.m. And apologising for the later time; his flight out of London City Airport had been delayed. He expected to be back on Sunday evening.

Damn. I'd forgotten about that. I put the wig away. It was one thing to take Klaus out on a surveillance op. It was another to take Klaus and his recently poisoned friend Luther.

Jake hadn't mentioned where he was going, or why. In

fact, he'd been pretty good at not mentioning anything about himself.

But he was attractive, interesting and we seemed to get along. Who knew . . .

The phone vibrated twice.

I opened Jake's message first – a simple thank you and a promise that drinks would be on him when he returned.

Irina's message was just as brief: the names and addresses of three bars, local to Jim Clark's flat in Vauxhall, that had regularly featured on his social media. There was no word about Hamish. I wasn't sure if that was a good sign or not.

Impassioned barking erupted from my balcony. Klaus was standing outside, paws firmly planted and tail wagging. Stepping closer, I heard a few other dogs. Across the canal, Luther was giving it his best, but there was no sign of Hamish and the curtains in Irina's flat were closed. I messaged her, asking how he was doing.

As the dog chorus hit a crescendo, Jake appeared behind his hound. He waved and mouthed a thank you. I smiled, toasted him with my empty coffee cup.

'Maybe she made up with Andy,' I murmured to Klaus, not believing myself as a sick feeling grew in my belly.

Irina (Hamish's Mum)

I sent the info you asked for. Hamish just pooed

blood on my carpet. I need to take him to the vet. Can't get through on their lines – do you have Dr Cooper's number?

Blood? Oh hell. Meg might have his number, but they're only around the corner. Go down there and I'll try calling ahead.

Thank you.

NP. Let me know how it goes.

I looked up the number and called. The line was busy.

If anyone knew how to handle upset tummies in hounds or humans, it was Irina.

I redialled. Still busy.

Irina did her research, knew what to administer and had a cupboard full of boxes and bottles that could easily be a vet's pharmacy display case. I didn't like the sound of blood in Hamish's poop, though.

Redialled. Busy.

Had he just eaten something nasty off the ground? Was it poison, like what had happened to Luther, or just the run-of-the-mill after-effects of scavenging?

Redialled. This time, it was ringing.

What an idiot I was for turning down Cooper's personal number.

'Village Vets,' the receptionist said. 'Can I help you?'

Thank heavens.

'My name is Louise Mallory, I'm calling on behalf of Irina Ivanova and her dog, Hamish.'

'Postcode?'

I gave it to her.

'Problem?'

'He's pooing blood.'

'Do you know what he ate?' Her voice had a hint of polite disinterest that set my teeth on edge.

'No.'

'Okay, I need to put you on hold for a moment.'

An easy-listening version of a song from the 70s assaulted my ear before I could say a word. I tapped my foot. Then opened a browser and checked in with Meg.

Meg (Tyrion's Mum)

> Hey, thanks for coming last night. Any chance any of the treats you gave the dogs had chicken in them?

And have Irina rip my head off? No chance.
I don't take those out

when I know I'm going to see Hamish. I know he's allergic.

You sure?

Absolutely. What's wrong?

Hamish is unwell. I think he might have eaten something ...

I don't think it's because of my treats. And the ones Ben had were lamb. Hamish can eat lamb, right?

Yeah, but do me a favour. Can you text Irina Ben's mobile if you have it?

Sure, I don't think he'd mind. Do you want it too?

It was the last thing I wanted. 'No,' I typed.

As abrasive as Irina could be, she was a good friend, and I loved her crazy little Scottie almost as much as I loved Klaus. But I also knew that Hamish, not unlike Irina, was a walking disaster, in Hamish's case owing to his allergies and his ability to find anything edible (and sometimes inedible) on the street.

'Hi, thanks for waiting,' the receptionist said, taking me off hold.

'Hi, yes, I'm calling about Hamish? Irina Ivanova's dog?'

'Ms Ivanova just walked in with him. We'll be seeing him shortly. What?' There was the muffled sound of a hand over the phone's mic. 'Right. She said she'll call you later. Bye.'

Click.

The surgery was close enough, and the vets had been decent on the few times I'd needed to see them for Klaus, but the receptionist had the bedside manner of Attila the Hun.

That said, knowing Hamish was in safe hands, I could turn back to the other problem at hand. Fiona and Ella were on their way over, to prepare ahead of travelling to Vauxhall. Claire had messaged confirming that she was also on her way and hoping this evening – and the shopping that they'd do if they got there earlier – would be more entertaining than last night's date.

They showed up, similarly dressed in nice jeans (without dirty pawprints on them), pretty blouses and high heels, with matching handbags, but there the similarities ended. Fiona was a tall, red-headed Australian, with an open, easy smile. Ella was petite, French, with sulky full lips and a face more striking than pretty. Like her French bulldog, Claire was stockier, with blonde curls and the sort of infectious laugh that included everyone.

Three very different women, with three very different looks. Once we could pinpoint where Jim was, there was a pretty good chance that he would find at least one of the women attractive enough to chat up.

'Poor Paul,' Fiona grinned.

'Why?' I said, one eye on Irina's empty balcony.

'He's watching the boys tonight,' Ella said, adjusting a scarf around her neck. Her dark eyes glinted with mischief. 'And he's also watching Tank and Nala.'

'He's going to be able to walk four dogs? Paul? *Those* four dogs? By himself?'

'The fool offered. Thought it would be fun.' Claire grinned. 'When I dropped off Tank, he was walking around, calling himself the Dogfather and speaking in a fake Italian accent.'

'Seriously?'

'Totally in over his head,' Ella said. 'He can barely handle Jimmy and Vader on his own. Meg is on call if they run into any trouble.'

'I hope you left them with beer and popcorn. Those hounds will be more entertaining than anything on TV.'

'I've got the dog cam set up. That way I can watch my Jimmy until your Jimmy shows up.'

I hadn't noticed the coincidence until then and laughed along with my friends. 'Has anyone heard from Indy yet?' I asked when our giggles had subsided, trying to get things back on subject.

'My friend's meeting her at 3:30, then they're going over to the club,' Fiona said.

'Does your friend know Tabby?'

'Only by sight.' She held up a finger. 'Got a question: what's the plan if this Jim person is on a date?'

It was a good question. 'As far as I can tell he isn't dating anyone,' I said with more confidence than I had.

'I'm not about to go home with him,' Ella said. 'Obviously. But from what Lou said, he's slimy enough to chat up another woman, even while he's on a date. Let's not worry about that yet.'

Claire was nodding. 'I agree. I'm more worried about what he has to say. Or not say.'

I walked out onto the balcony to gather my thoughts, wishing I could see Hamish sunning himself outside. There was nothing to say he wasn't inside now, being cuddled by Irina. I turned back to my friends. 'If he has something to say, we record it. If he doesn't, no harm, no foul.'

'Illegal recordings aren't admissible,' Claire said.

'Maybe, maybe not. But perhaps they can demonstrate enough cause for the police to search his home. If they haven't already.'

Ella looked at me. 'Have they?'

'I don't know.'

'Tsarina . . . I mean Irina hasn't said?'

As far as I could tell, I was fast becoming the only one not to use that nickname and was holding off as long as I could, simply in fear of slipping and calling her that to her face. Same reason I tried not to call Tony Frater 'Moany Tony'. *At least, not too often,* I admitted to myself.

Regardless, it would have been indiscreet to talk about the problems she and Andy were having, especially in light of Hamish's dodgy tummy, so I gave them the easy answer. 'No.'

Claire's eyes narrowed, sniffing out a story. 'Do you think he's told her?'

'No.'

Ella looked at Claire and Fiona. 'It's not often I get a Saturday night pass. Shall we have a quick one at the Hound before heading over?'

I knew better than to stop them, so I walked them to the door, wished them luck and then messaged Irina again to check on Hamish.

40

INDY

Indy had gone into the day with low expectations. She wasn't part of the Pack's in-crowd. Not because she didn't want to be, but because her rescue dog, Banjo, wasn't interested in other dogs. Humans, yes – but only the ones with treats. Dogs, no. Didn't matter what size or shape, colour or gender, Banjo just didn't care. For the first couple of years after he'd arrived from Romania, they'd done work with trainers. Everyone told her he'd probably become more playful as he developed more confidence, but after a few years, she'd come to accept that he was just asocial.

Which meant that as much as she liked the people in the Pack, she often felt more like an outsider in whatever they were doing, whether it was getting lights put up in the dog park last winter, or finding whoever killed Phil. Last night, instead of heading to the King's Hound to sit in a corner, she'd turned off notifications on her phone and ordered in pizza.

But this morning she'd stared at her messages, not believing her luck. They needed someone to play tennis. Tennis. Of all things.

The one thing she could do. And they needed her.

Maybe she could be a proper part of the Pack after all.

Indy hadn't played professionally since she was a teenager, when an accident on a night out had left her with an elbow injury. Three surgeries later, it was fine for a friendly match, but her chances of playing centre-court at Wimbledon had been shattered. In retrospect, it had bothered her parents more than it had bothered her. She'd pursued a different career, but still played whenever she could, putting Banjo on a hands-free lead and loping along the Thames Path to the tennis courts in Poplar. They weren't the best courts, and her partners weren't the most adept, but she was most herself with a racquet in hand, and there was always a laugh at one of the pubs afterwards. More importantly, it never felt awkward when Banjo lay beyond the baseline, gnawing on an old ball, or under a table, still gnawing the same ball.

Indy had played at Oakwood a few times over the years. She knew they had grass courts as well as clay but not which one Fiona's friend had booked, so she'd prepared for both. She'd left Banjo at home, happily chomping a pizzle treat.

Louise had texted her a picture of Tabitha Halder and a brief bio. Indy had checked with her own sources on the tennis circuit, but all anyone knew of Tabby was that she was a higher-up in some sort of tech company, played a mean game of singles and otherwise kept herself to herself.

She headed west, getting off the Tube at the leafy suburban stop nearest the club. An independent coffee shop across the street was doing good business, its outside tables all accounted for. On either side were clothing boutiques. One had a big name and big price tags. The other didn't have a name Indy recognised but she suspected the garments might be even more out of the price range of normal mortals.

A tall woman with long beach-waved hair sat beneath a plane tree outside the coffee shop. When she saw Indy, she stood up and smiled. Picked up a bright green tennis bag and slung it casually across her chest.

'Hey Indy, I'm Ann.' She pronounced it 'Ayn'; Australian, Indy guessed. Maybe a New Zealander. She knew she should be able to tell the accents apart, but she'd never quite been able to.

'Nice to meet you.' She held out her hand. 'Good job you were able to get a court at short notice.'

'Not a problem. I already had a court, just told my friend she didn't have to embarrass herself on it this week.' Ann laughed.

Indy studied her. Ann, clad in a grey tennis skirt and matching top, had the wingspan of an albatross, but Indy didn't care. She took Ann's comment about her erstwhile tennis partner as a challenge, feeling her competitive spirit flicker to life. This woman thought she was good? That was exactly what Indy wanted. A good game, as much as the opportunity to help the Pack.

What could be better?

41

LOUISE

Partridge Bark

Indy (Banjo's Mum)

At Oakwood. Tabitha is on the next court over. Will try to make contact after the matches.

Claire (Tank's Mum)

We just got off the Tube at Vauxhall. We're pretty early, but as we don't know how early Jim starts, we'll split up now. Ella ... er ... Fiona already pulled some weird guy on the Tube.

Ella (Bark Vader and Jimmy Chew's Mum)

It was Fiona. Not me. But he was kind of cute.

Paul (Bark Vader and Jimmy Chew's Dad)

Excellent. I hope he likes dogs ... There are four here, he's welcome to join us.

Fiona (Nala's Mum)

Not enjoying being Mr Mom @Paul? Left at home with the fur babies while Ella goes out? 😊

I felt like one of the white-coated people in Mission Control the day of a launch. I'd done the best I could to prepare. My team were people I'd trust with my life. Maybe even more – I'd trust them with my *dog*. They were smart. They were motivated. If there was information to be had on either Tabby or Jim, I had no doubt they'd find it.

Everyone was in place, and I had the wig on the table and a back-up plan mapped out. Just in case.

The buzzer for the downstairs door sounded. Klaus's ears perked up and his head tilted to the side. 'Hello?'

'It's me.' Jake's velvet baritone sent a small shiver down my back. It didn't have the same effect on Klaus, who ran into the hallway, barking.

'Come on up,' I said, buzzing him in and joining my hound at the door to the flat. 'I hate to break the news to you, dude, but he's not here to visit you.'

He must have disagreed, increasing the decibels of his barks as the lift dinged.

As I eased the door open, Klaus shot past me into the hallway, barking at Luther, tail wagging. Luther gave Jake a look that said *What? This yappy guy again?* but he allowed his butt to be sniffed and even if he wasn't entirely ready to do the *Hello, little friend* greeting to Klaus, it wasn't far off.

Jake was dressed for travel in jeans, a black T-shirt and a black leather jacket. A grey dog bed was tucked under his arm, and he held a plastic bag for life from Tesco. I led him into the living room and he plunked the dog bed beside Klaus's by the window. On the way back through he spotted a framed picture on the wall.

'Klaus and his friends, Hamish, Tank, Tyrion and Nala, in Greenwich last summer. You wouldn't believe the number of treats that went into getting that one shot.'

'I can only imagine. Let me guess, Hamish is the

Scottie.' He sighed. 'Why do people think it's cute to name a Scottie Hamish or Fergus or Angus?'

'I imagine they're the same people who might call a German dog Niklaus, huh?'

'I guess so.' He acknowledged my point with a half-smile. 'Which one is Tyrion?'

'The dappled dachshund, of course. Meg says there's no better name for her feisty little fiend.'

He grinned. 'She's right.'

'And the pretty cocker spaniel is Nala.'

Luther, after a few half-hearted sniffs around the flat, went to his bed and eased himself down onto it. Klaus pushed out his paws in front of his new friend in a long stretch, his butt in the air. He wiggled it, then hopped his back legs around in a little dance.

'It's his "I'm cute, you must love me" routine,' I explained.

Jake grunted and unpacked his bag on my table. There were four takeaway containers of kibble, the top one still bearing the words *lamb rogan josh* in marker pen, a prescription bottle and an unopened pack of No-Hide rawhide chews. With peanut butter, the lucky dog. There was also a well-loved stuffing-less squirrel and a ball attached to a rope, both sides frayed.

Luther studied us with serious eyes but remained on his bed.

Klaus, his dance having yielded no results, returned to us, watching the squirrel's tail hang off the table with acquisitive eyes.

I pushed it out of sight, while Jake pulled a rumpled piece of paper from his back pocket. He smoothed it out on the table. It was filled with writing that better resembled chicken scratches.

'Dr Hathaway, I presume?' I teased.

His brow lowered. 'What? No, why?'

The joke fell flat and I fought off a blush. 'Your handwriting.'

He handed me a pen from my countertop. 'Then rewrite it if you can't read it.'

Duly chastised, I nodded.

'Luther eats twice a day. He's not fussy on the times. I've portioned up the food, so just dump it into a bowl. If you keep it in the container, he'll eat that too, he doesn't care.' He fished a packet of tablets out of his pocket. 'You need to give him one of these half an hour before he eats. He doesn't need a lot of exercise. He's fine walking, when he isn't feeling too sorry for himself. Just keep him on the lead. He's been known to follow geese.'

'As in, follow their flight path over the water?'

'Into the water, yeah.'

'Fantastic.' My voice had risen half an octave. The canals were pretty, but they were built for transportation. For boats. And while there was the occasional ladder so that a human could get out, if a dog fell in, they wouldn't be able to escape by themselves. And I wasn't sure I'd have the strength to shot-put a Staffie out of the water. Even if it was shallow enough for me to stand in.

'It should only be a day, two at the most. There's more than enough food and you have my number if you have any questions.'

'Yeah, you said. Don't worry – take your time. He'll be fine with us.'

Jake's mouth twitched on one side. 'I know. I just don't like leaving him when he's not well.' He took a deep breath, then expelled it in a rush. 'Thanks again. As I said, drinks on me when I'm back.'

'You're on.'

His smile was tired, but the sparkle in his eyes lit the room. 'The best News-N-Booze has to offer.'

'Now you're talking,' I laughed. I followed him to the front door, surprised that Klaus remained in the living room. Only when the lift closed behind Jake did I shut my door and lean back against it, allowing myself a few moments to daydream.

My phone bleeped from the other room, shaking me from my reverie. It was still too early for Jim Clark, but the girls were having a blast winding up Paul. And our French friend was playing along.

I whiled away the afternoon catching up on some work and watching TV with the dogs. When the phone rang a couple of hours later, I sobered at the name that flashed on the screen. 'Hey Irina. How's Hamish?'

In the background were muffled street sounds; Irina was in a car, and I braced myself before she spoke.

'Not good. We're on our way to the emergency vet.'

'Emergency vet?'

'Village Vets is closed and I can't wait until noon tomorrow when they open.'

I didn't have to think twice. 'I'll meet you there.'

I texted Meg, who had a set of my keys, to pick up

Klaus and Luther. My poor boy followed me to the door, eyes wide, expecting a walk. 'Sorry, my love. You know I don't like leaving you. I don't like leaving Luther either, but I can't take you with me. Don't worry, Meg's on her way over, and you know what that means.'

Klaus tilted his head to the side. Heart melting, I picked up a couple of chew toys and tossed one to Luther, then flung the second further into the living room for Klaus. He bounded after it with an exuberance that hurt my heart, and I slipped out of our flat.

The animal A & E wasn't far away and was located in one of those places that it was faster to get to by public transport than by car. That Irina had opted for a taxi told me just how bad Hamish was.

I sprinted to the DLR and tapped my foot impatiently until the train came, then kept tapping it for the few minutes it took to reach Stratford, where I could connect to the Tube. I raced to the platform – brushing past startled passengers with muttered apologies – and slid through the red carriage doors just before they closed. The sprint at the other end wasn't long, and I stopped at the entrance, panting for breath.

In another life, the building could have been an affluent family's home. The red bricks gave off a warm, reassuring feel; something that I suspected few owners noticed when they had to rush here with a pet emergency.

Inside, the receptionist sat behind a wooden desk. She looked painfully young to be in a job that saw trauma and sadness every day. 'Can I help you?'

'She's with me.'

I looked around, certain I'd heard Irina's voice, but in the sea of people in the waiting room, some with pets on the ground in front of them, some holding them on their laps, some with their fur babies in crates or baskets, it took me a moment to locate her. I'd never seen her look worse. Her eyes were red, her hair straggled around her grey face. Instead of one of the classy ensembles she normally put together, even to go to the dog park, she wore a ratty sweatshirt over ripped leggings and her Gucci trainers.

'Hamish?' I asked, sitting beside her.

'They took him in pretty quickly. The vet is going to purge him.'

'Didn't they do that at Village Vets earlier?'

'No.' Irina slumped lower in her chair. She raked her hair back and resecured it at the back of her neck with a scrunchie that looked like an old-fashioned telephone cord. 'Dr Aspen thought it was only a mild case of diarrhoea. When I pressed her, she told me to bring in samples tomorrow.'

'Okay . . .'

'But she didn't see how much blood came out of him the last time. And I can't wait until they open tomorrow, assuming I even get a Sunday appointment.'

I winced, then jerked my head towards the receptionist. 'What do *they* say?'

'They think it's poison.' Irina's voice wobbled; she was struggling to keep calm.

Air hissed through my teeth. *Not another dog poisoned. Not Hamish.*

I put a hand on her arm, hoping it would help. 'How long has he been in there?'

'Ten, maybe fifteen minutes.'

'Okay. Can I get you a coffee?'

She held up a shaking hand to indicate *No*, and I pressed a small pack of tissues into it, waiting for her to blow her nose. 'He'll be fine, you know. He's young and he's strong.'

'I want to be back there with him.'

It didn't take a genius to realise that they hadn't let her. 'I know you do.'

'He'll be scared without me.'

I put an arm around her and let her rest her head on my shoulder. 'I know that too. But they know what they're doing here.'

Maybe it was a platitude. I didn't know, but I had to believe it was true. So did Irina. So, we sat in silence – in a room full of people who had the same fears for their pets – and counted the minutes until a vet appeared. 'Miss Ivanova? Hamish's mum?'

42

FIONA

Partridge Bark

Indy (Banjo's Mum)

Fi, your friend isn't too bad on the courts. I'd be happy to play with her again. I'm at the bar now — about to make contact with Tabitha. Wish me luck!

I hope you ace it! 😊

Fiona stretched out. She'd have put money on Ann beating Indy, but from the tone of the text, maybe she hadn't.

She kicked off her heels under the table. No one would

notice, and so what if they did? She also put on her glasses, 'cos, you know, girls with glasses are badasses.

And because she couldn't read the book in front of her without them.

That was part of her plan. Look disinterested but keep an eye on things over the top of her novel. If he showed up here he'd spot a single woman for sure, and Fiona had perfected the slow blink to refocus her blue eyes after taking off her glasses. It was the stuff of legend.

She popped a few pieces of Bombay mix into her mouth, grateful that she didn't have to worry about Nala snagging it when she wasn't looking.

The evening crowd was arriving. Most women were dressed as she was, jeans and a smart top. Some wore casual sandals, but most wore heels. A few were dressed for mischief in body-con dresses that showed a bit more body and were a bit less con. Fi didn't know Jim Clark, but if he was as tight as Louise said, he wouldn't want to pay for company. He'd look for a woman who could pay her own way. And maybe his too.

But not on the first encounter. No, he'd want to look flush. Fiona knew the type. Her sister had married a man like that. It had taken something close to a crowbar to get her out of that mess. Pity she hadn't used an actual crowbar on her former brother-in-law . . .

The first man that approached was young, barely out of his teens. He'd be attractive enough once his acne cleared and his voice dropped.

The next was hairier than a bear, with thick brows and fur stretching right down his arms to his fingertips. Fi tried not to grimace. She slept with Nala tucked along one side of her at night. Could she really deal with Paddington on the other? Not a chance. Not with the height of summer still to come and a flat without air conditioning.

The third man, though ... a City type. Quietly confident. Potentially an arse, but that was yet to be determined. Fiona took off her glasses for the slow blink ... and almost missed the middle-aged man strutting into the bar. He was about five foot ten and balding. His shoes were polished, his jeans nice enough. His white linen shirt could have done with an iron. Wrinkled as it was, it accentuated rather than hid the paunch he could rest his beer glass on.

And yet, he swaggered with the arrogance of a man whose bathroom mirror regularly lied to him.

There could be no doubt: Jim Clark had arrived.

43

LOUISE

Partridge Bark

Fiona (Nala's Mum)

He's here.

**Ella (Bark Vader and
Jimmy Chew's Mum)**

On my way.

Claire (Tank's Mum)

Me too – you've saved me
from a trio of blokes livin'
them glory days. Heaven

321

only knows what you
saved Ella from ... 😊

Fiona (Nala's Mum)

Save her?? I'm about to
SINK her. Hey, @Ella –
don't forget to take off
that wedding ring before
you get here!

I followed Irina and the vet towards the consultation room. Irina hadn't told the group that Hamish was ill, and it wasn't my place to. She and I were here for him, and that would be enough.

'Just to let you know,' the vet warned, one hand on the doorknob, 'he's on an IV drip and has been sedated.'

Irina nodded to her as she pushed the door open for us. I tried to brace myself, but nothing could have prepared me for the sight of Hamish lying on a table hooked up to the IV. He looked listless, but his tail gave a small wag on seeing Irina. With a cry torn from her soul, she moved towards him, trying to hold him without messing with the tubes.

'All right,' the vet said, clearing her throat. 'I'm Dr Julie and I've been looking after Hamish. I understand that you gave him activated charcoal when you first spotted the problem. That was smart, but we really needed to get whatever he ate out of his system.'

'I did take him to the vet,' Irina said.

Dr Julie nodded. 'Yes. The standard procedure is to induce vomiting by administering an emetic.' She brushed aside the what-should-have-happened. 'Which he has now had. He's dehydrated, and he's suffering from pancreatitis, which caused the blood in his stool.'

'What's the prognosis?'

She ignored the question. 'I want him to stay on the drip until he's better hydrated and I'd like to keep him overnight for observation. We'll see how he is tomorrow. If all goes well, we can discuss you taking him home then.'

'Tomorrow . . .' Irina echoed, heartbroken. She pressed her lips to the top of his head. 'He's never stayed a single night away from me.'

'We all want Hamish to be well enough to go home with you,' Dr Julie said, caressing the Scottie's face. 'But I'm not going to discharge him until he's ready. Then we can discuss the meds he'll need and the diet that he'll require, at least for the short to medium term.'

It was sensible, and I could see she was trying to give hope without false promises. As much as I wanted Hamish to be home, I understood that she was being responsible.

'Go home, ladies,' the vet said, not unkindly. 'Miss Ivanova, you both need to rest. I'll phone you if anything changes.'

She stood back to allow Irina to whisper to Hamish, and I joined her against the wall. 'Do you think he'll pull through?' I asked bluntly. 'I know you can't make promises and that anything can change, but in your expert opinion, what do you think?'

Dr Julie gave me a sympathetic smile. 'We've seen a lot of poisonings lately. Hamish isn't in great shape right now, but I think he'll pull through. If he's lucky, the pancreatitis will be acute, rather than chronic, but that'll depend on how his body handles it. But no promises. On anything.'

'Thank you for your honesty, and for taking care of Hamish.' I stepped back towards the table, reaching around Irina to caress Hamish's head. 'You get well,' I ordered him. 'I'll wait for you outside, Irina.'

As soon as I got out of the building, I rested one hand against the bricks and gulped in the cool evening air. The vet had been careful not to make promises, but from what she had said, Hamish had a good chance at recovery, for which I was grateful. And to my shame, I was almost as grateful that it wasn't Klaus on that metal table. Needing to hear an update about him, I rang Meg.

'Hey, how's Hamish?' Meg asked. 'I was so scared to hear the news!'

I could hear yapping in the background and breathed a sigh of relief. She had Klaus with her, and he was having a good time with Tyrion. I hoped poor Luther wasn't feeling too persecuted by the little sausages.

'They're keeping him overnight, but we're hoping he'll be better soon.' I took a breath. 'Thanks for taking Klaus and Luther.'

'Didn't take them. I'm at your flat. Didn't feel right to take your hot neighbour's dog when he was unwell.'

I blinked away the vague unease. 'Hot neighbour? You met Jake?'

'Sure. Down at the park this morning. Big guy in jeans

324

and a black T-shirt. Looked like Wolverine with bedroom eyes. Seemed like a nice guy. Any scandal to report, Ms Mallory?'

'No scandal at all. We're friends . . . I think.'

'Well, you must be if he trusts you to keep an eye on his sick dog.'

'Maybe, but thanks for coming round at such short notice. Make yourself at home. Easy on the treats for Klaus, though. I don't want him to start looking like a salami instead of a cocktail sausage.'

'Will do,' Meg said. 'Give Hamish a cuddle for me. Oh, and I saw that you had a box of wine delivered. I put a bottle of Prosecco in the freezer.'

'I have one in the fridge, if you wanted it.'

'I know. I saw it. But I figured that Irina wouldn't want to go home to an empty flat tonight, and Lou, that girl can drink.'

I smiled, grateful for the friends I'd made at the dog park. No, that wasn't right. They were more than friends. They were my Pack. 'Thanks, Meg.'

'Come to think of it, I'm going to put a second bottle in. Looks like things are getting interesting at the very posh Oakwood Tennis Club and in trendy Vauxhall. Or haven't you been checking your messages?'

44

INDY

Tabitha Halder was at the bar, drinking what looked to be carrot juice with a sprig of celery. Revolting. After playing a couple of sets of tennis, surely she deserved something better?

Indy took the seat next to her and ordered a glass of Prosecco. 'Good game?' she asked, although she already knew the answer. Fi's friend was competent but not brilliant on the court, and so Indy'd been able to keep an eye on Tabby on the next court over.

Tabitha rolled her head from one side to the other. 'It was okay. I wasn't playing my best. Damn backhand let me down.'

Indy's drink arrived and she sipped the bubbles delicately.

'Not like yours,' Tabitha continued. 'Your backhand is like a rocket launcher.'

'Yeah,' Indy said, holding the glass between two fingers. 'Thanks. I practise when I can. In fact, I'll rarely say no to more court time. I can give you some pointers, if you like?'

'That would be great, thanks.' Tabitha held out her hand. 'Tabby Halder.'

'I'm Indy,' she said. 'Indira Balasubramanian. Your name sounds familiar. We haven't played each other before, have we?'

'No.' Tabby rolled her eyes and ordered a G & T from the bartender. 'My company's been in the news since the CEO got himself murdered.'

'That's awful. I'm so sorry to hear that.'

Tabby clinked her glass against Indy's. 'Been one of those years,' she laughed, though without humour. 'The CEO's mind was elsewhere, even before he carked it; meant that I had to step up. Our CTO thinks he's more competent than he is. And, to be honest, he causes problems wherever he goes, that I then have to clean up. And with this shark-infested market, I've been busting my gut just to keep the company afloat. Despite the idiots in charge.' She shook it off. 'Sorry, rant over.'

'No worries.' Indy offered Tabby a nearby dish of unsalted peanuts. 'What do you think happened? To your CEO?' She leaned in. 'D'you *really* think he was *murdered*?'

Indy crunched on another peanut, watching Tabby. She didn't wait for an answer before following up with, 'Who do you think did it?'

Tabby exhaled loudly. 'The million-dollar question. Phil was genuinely a good man. And he had a sharp business acumen. He could spot an opportunity and go for it. Did he upset other people who weren't as fast? As successful? Sure. But would anybody kill him over it?' She spread her hands, at a loss. 'I honestly couldn't tell you. But whoever did do it, I hope they rot in jail.'

'Because he was a good friend? A good boss?'

'Yeah, that. And because he left me a pile of shit to deal with. Investors who have the jitters, a CTO who should have been jettisoned years ago and a sales team who consistently promise more than we can deliver.' She gestured to the bartender to bring another round.

'You think one of the investors or the CTO could have done it?'

'Asking all these questions, are you a cop or something?'

Indy laughed. 'I'm a paediatrician. A very curious paediatrician.'

Tabby relaxed a fraction. 'We're all curious, but there's still the fallout to deal with.' The bartender put two sweating glasses in front of them, and Tabby took a gulp of her G & T. 'But to answer your question, I don't know. I wouldn't have thought the investors would have anything to gain by getting rid of Phil – he was an asset. But Jim? Could he benefit? I suppose he might. He's a deadweight, but he's just dim enough to believe the investors would choose him over me.'

'Will they?'

'No chance. They'll probably parachute a CEO in above us both. So, no one wins.'

'No.' Indy sighed. 'Especially not Phil.'

45

CLAIRE

Jim Clark returned to the table with a bottle of wine and four glasses. 'One for Frisky Fiona,' he said, carefully placing a glass in front of Fi. 'One for Coy Claire. One for Ooh La La Ella and one for yours truly.' He unscrewed the bottle and poured, not noticing the eyeroll that passed between the women. The nicknames had been cringey the first time he'd used them, but now they were bordering on offensive. 'I hope you're okay with Sauvignon Blanc. It's from New Zealand's Marlborough region. It's the only white wine my ex'd drink.' From his tone it was hard to tell if that was a good thing, but while the company was sour, the wine was light and crisp.

'Fantastic,' Ella said, looking up from her phone.

At this rate, Claire was pretty sure that she'd win the bet she had going with Fiona: Ella would have her wedding ring back on her finger within the hour. One hundred per cent.

'Your ex had good taste,' Fi said, then lowered her voice and muttered to Claire, 'in wine, and for dumping the fool.'

So far, they'd learned about the ex-wife, the daughter Jim bragged about, but who sounded deranged and the mother. Far too much about the mother. Claire felt bad for any woman desperate enough to become Wife Number Two.

One thing was for certain, it wasn't about to be her.

The evening had already gone on far too long. She leaned forward, twisting a lock of hair around her finger and doing her best to be charming. 'So, Jim. You said you're an entrepreneur with some kind of financial firm? There are a couple of those in the news right now. What do you think about the scandal with that CEO getting killed? Who do you think did it?'

'He was my boss,' Jim said and leaned back, ignoring the chair's squeal of protest. 'Or at least my old one. Not sure who did it, but to be honest, he was bored, already on the way out.'

'Way out?' Claire prompted, leaning forward. 'He was sick?'

'Maybe, I don't know. The last six months, maybe more, he was distant. Distracted. Made some big mistakes that I – and my team – had to fix.'

'Someone killed a *sick* man?' Ella asked, shocked. 'I don't know why that makes it so much worse.'

'I don't know that he was sick,' Jim hedged. 'Just that he wasn't firing on all cylinders anymore.'

'Alfie?' Ella mouthed.

'What sort of mistakes?' Claire asked.

'Why do you think he was distracted?' Ella paused, palming her wedding band from her pocket.

'He was making stupid mistakes. Overpromising things to the investors. Good thing that my team are able to deliver.'

'Uh-huh,' Claire sighed.

'Why was he distracted?' Ella repeated.

'Couldn't tell you. But over the last six months, he'd be on the phone all day, talking differently than he did when dealing with company issues.' Jim didn't wait for the women to ask more. 'He was angry. Didn't raise his voice, that wasn't Phil, right? But you could tell.'

'Do you know who he was speaking with?'

'No. It didn't look like it was company business, so I didn't ask. Why do you want to know?'

Realising that Jim had told them all he could, Claire smiled and slid a business card across the table at him. Her fingers held it in place, in case he thought she was offering him her number. 'I'm a journalist.'

Sunday

46

LOUISE

Partridge Bark

Indy (Banjo's Mum)

I don't think she was involved. Seems resentful that he's gone as he was her ally in getting rid of the CTO, who she called a deadweight. She thinks the investors have an interim CEO in mind, and are focused on 'stabilising' the situation. After a G&T or three, she was pretty open about it. Like I said, I don't think she's involved.

Fiona (Nala's Mum)

Not sure how involved Jim is either. He's more interested in tooting his own horn, and as much as he (or his mum) might like the CEO title, he doesn't seem interested in the responsibility.

Claire (Tank's Mum)

I agree. Even if he'd realised he was at risk of losing his job — and he's arrogant enough to think he'd be fine — I can't see it. He's too squeamish to kill someone himself. Too tight to hire a hitman. And too stupid to keep his mouth closed. He would have blurted it out or bragged about it ... to Ella. In a weak moment ... 😊

Ella (Bark Vader and Jimmy Chew's Mum)

Or his mum could have arranged it for him?

What's all this about his mum?

Claire (Tank's Mum)

He's a bit of a mummy's boy, is all. But he did say that Phil had been distracted for the last 6 months. Maybe since Alfie died? I'd be in pieces if I lost Tank.

Ella (Bark Vader and Jimmy Chew's Mum)

And he was arguing with someone on the phone – Jim thought it wasn't work. Which makes sense – he and Grace broke up around Christmas, yes?

> Yeah, but from what I understand they broke up because he was remote and she moved on pretty quickly. I don't know if he'd still keep calling, being angry at her.

Fiona (Nala's Mum)

No? How long did your ex keep calling after you turfed him out?

Fiona was right, but I wasn't convinced. I'd got the sense that Phil's break with Grace had been pretty amicable. So who would he be angry with?

Meg had spent the night on the sofabed in my spare bedroom/home office, presumably with Tyrion. We'd left Irina where she'd fallen asleep on the sofa, throwing a blanket over her and turning off the lights.

I'd expected Klaus to sleep with me as usual, but he hadn't even come to the bedroom. He'd probably stayed with Meg and Tyrion – hoping there'd be more treats throughout the night – or cuddled next to Luther.

Feeling ropey and stressed in equal measure, I fumbled my way to the kitchen and put the kettle on. Unlike Klaus's rapid staccato, Luther's steps were measured as he padded over to greet me.

I handed him a treat and opened the balcony door to let in some fresh air. In the living room, two empty pizza boxes sat open on the table and the mystery of where the sausage dogs had slept was quickly solved: Klaus lay snuggled in the nook between Irina's head and shoulder and Tyrion was wedged behind her knees. Luther nudged my hand until I massaged his ears.

'When did you all become emotional support dogs?' I asked them.

'All dogs are emotional support dogs,' Meg said from behind me. She wore a Harry Potter T-shirt and black leggings that must have doubled up as pyjamas. 'The problem is that not everyone realises this and some people train it out of them.'

She wasn't wrong.

'Question for you, Meg. Do you know who Phil might have been angry with over the last few months?'

'The world?'

When I didn't answer, she yawned and rubbed a fist in her eye, like a child. 'I don't know, Lou. If you want, I can call the charity he worked with and see if they know anything. They're closed today but should be open tomorrow.'

'Good idea. That'd be great, thanks.'

Klaus gave me a serious stare, as if debating the relative merits of getting up (and possibly being fed), as opposed to staying cosy on the couch. He rested his long snout on Irina's collarbone as he decided. Tyrion didn't dither, pattering down Klaus's sofa ramp and pawing at Meg's leg.

Luther farted.

'No call last night, then?' Meg asked, pretending she

hadn't heard it. 'If I'd drunk as much as Irina did, I might not hear a bomb going off outside the window.'

'Good point.' I picked up Irina's phone from where it lay on the coffee table. The screen was locked, but the only missed calls it displayed were from DC Andy.

'Any news?'

'Not sure,' I said, wondering if he'd called Irina with news on the case, or if it was personal. 'But there's nothing from the vet.'

Shuffling back over to the kitchen, I poured dachshund kibble into two bowls and emptied one of Jake's containers into a third for Luther, setting all three on the floor. Compared to Klaus's food, Luther's looked like golf balls, but that wouldn't stop the sausages from marauding.

Straightening and stretching, I asked, 'How are you feeling?'

'I switched to water the same time you did,' Meg replied. 'Do you think Irina noticed?'

'I don't think she cared.'

Luther gave a low growl when Tyrion came too close to his breakfast, but otherwise the dogs ate more or less without incident, Klaus and Tyrion doing a strange dance as they tried to eat each other's food. I spooned coffee grounds into a large cafetière and added the boiling water.

The companionable silence was suddenly split by the tinny sounds of Russian house music erupting from Irina's mobile. She sat bolt upright and, without blinking, lunged for the phone.

'*Da*,' she said. 'Yes?'

Meg and I looked at one another and silently moved

closer to the living room. Irina nodded once or twice, and then her shoulders sagged, as if the bones had melted away. 'Thank you,' she whispered, and rang off.

'What is it?' we asked.

'That was the vet.' Irina looked at me, blinking away tears. 'They've asked that I come to pick up Hamish.' She buried her head in her hands and began to sob.

'Irina . . .' I moved forward, putting a hand on her arm. I could barely get the words out. 'Hamish? Is he . . .?'

She threw off my hand and wiped her nose on her sleeve, the weeping stopping as quickly as it had begun. 'He'll be fine. Get off me, I need to get changed and get over there.' She stood up and looked around. 'Where are my shoes?'

'Hallway. By the door.'

We listened to her shuffling around as she grabbed her things, then the door slammed. I turned back towards Meg, who was pouring two cups of coffee. 'Looks like the Tsarina is back to normal,' she said.

'And may heaven help whoever poisoned Hamish,' I replied. 'Because when she gets her hands on them, our Russian lunatic will rip their jugulars out.'

47

LOUISE

Irina (Hamish's Mum)

> I have Hamish. We're on our way home.

> Good. Is he OK? Are you?

The doorbell rang.

I glanced at the old-fashioned clock on the sideboard beside my desk – 9:30. Irina had made good time picking up Hamish. Klaus flew down the ramp from the sofa and raced to the door, barking happily.

'Come in, the door's open,' I called.

The sound of nails on hardwood floors was slower than the frantic patter that Hamish usually made, desperate as he always was to come in to play with Klaus. I peered into the hallway, but instead of Irina's topknot and Hamish's black fur, the new canine arrival was honey coloured and pretty, the human taller and red-haired. Fiona unclipped Nala and allowed her to enter first. 'I snuck in behind a couple of your neighbours,' she said.

Tyrion and Luther came to investigate.

'Didn't know you were running a doggy day care business. Do you have room for one more?' This morning Fiona wore no make-up, and her red hair was pulled back in a ponytail, a very different look from the day before. She slid her sunglasses onto the top of her head and put a bag of pastries on the table, giving the graveyard of empty Prosecco bottles on the side a dim look. 'I see you cater to the needs of their humans as well.'

'Tsarina was over last night,' Meg said from the sofa.

Fi looked back at the empties. 'Yeah, I saw your text. Hamish at the emergency vet . . . Jeez. What'd he eat this time?' She reached over the bottles and grabbed a mug from the cupboard. 'I'd have thought Irina'd have drunk more.'

'She was worried about Hamish,' I told her. 'The vet thinks it was poison.'

'Oh hell.' She paused with the cafetière hovering above the mug. 'Is he going to be okay?'

'I think so. She went to pick him up about an hour ago.'

Fi uttered another curse and watched Luther and Nala circle each other, sniffing. Nala cocked her head to the side and rolled onto her back. 'Nala, you tart.' Fi shook her head. 'Who's the other dog?'

343

'My neighbour's. Luther's staying with me for a bit. Sit down and tell me about last night. I really wanted to be there with you ...'

'No, Lou,' she said, sinking onto the sofa beside Tyrion. 'Trust me, you wouldn't have enjoyed it. What a pompous bore. So, Hamish?'

'I don't know much more than that. They took blood and all sorts of other samples for tests. Irina might have got the results while she was there. You'll have to ask her. Tell me about your evening with Jim Clark. He seriously had no idea the investors were going to replace him?'

'No. If anything, he thought Phil and the Angels were going to replace Tabby, not him. Because he goes for drinks with the team, he thinks he's one of them, and pretty much invulnerable. When Claire asked him what would happen if he left, he laughed and said the entire tech team – the backbone of the company – would walk with him.'

'That wasn't the impression I got,' Meg said. 'I have a ... sort of a friend who works there.'

Fi laughed. 'Of course it isn't true, it's all in his head. And maybe his mother's. She called while we were having drinks. He answered it 'Hello, Mummy'. I mean, seriously? A man in his fifties?'

'Did he have any idea who might have had a problem with Phil?'

'They were having financial issues. Good sales books but growing pains. Problem with those sort of growing pains, though, is that you need more money to pay for more kit, more developers. If you don't have the dosh, you need to find someone who does. And the problem with *that* is that the investors get a bigger chunk of the company shares.'

Luther padded up to her and sniffed her hand. 'Don't worry, gorgeous, I smell of Nala,' she said, sniffed her hand too. 'And a bagel with smoked salmon. Which I'm not sharing.' She mitigated that with a scratch behind Luther's ears. Her pretty cocker spaniel was right behind him, pawing for attention.

'Nala was sulking earlier because I took her away from Paul's doggy rave last night, but I think she might forgive me.' Fi looked at me from under long lashes. 'I guess she's not the only one who's sweet on the new additions to the neighbourhood.'

I ignored her and pulled a pastry from the bag. 'So, who gains from Phil's death, then? Tabby doesn't. Jim doesn't. An investor? Was he blocking them from investing more?'

'Jim didn't think so. I mean, he wasn't happy about his shares being watered down, but understood that with more investment they could hire more people and grow his kingdom. I mean, grow the company.'

Meg joined me at the counter, lured by the bag of Nest pastries. 'That would have made the company more lucrative and his shares worth more, even if he had fewer of them.'

'Huh,' I said.

'Huh,' Fi echoed.

'What was all that about Ella?' Meg asked, her mouth full. 'All those texts last night?'

Fi flicked a hand. 'Just winding Paul up. Meggie, you have cinnamon bun crumbs on your chin.'

Meg wiped them off. 'I still don't see who wins here. Either from Phil's death, or from poisoning the dogs.'

Something Irina had said yesterday fluttered at the edge of my mind. I couldn't put my finger on it, though. Just then my phone rang; it wasn't the caller I'd expected, but the conversation, however brief, was intriguing.

48

IRINA

Louise (Klaus's Mum)

Grace says she has something for me but won't tell me what. I'm going to head over to meet her now.

Don't go alone.

I'm not. I'm taking Klaus and Luther.

Luther is recovering from his own ordeal. And as much as he thinks otherwise, Klaus isn't exactly Cujo.

Don't tell him that. I'll be fine. We'll be fine. And we'll stop by afterwards.

You don't need to. Andy is coming over.

Oh good, things are back on. Enjoy! 😊

Irina put down the phone. There was no need to explain herself to Lou, even if she'd asked. It wasn't as if she'd forgiven Andy for breaking into her phone, but she was tired, scared and hungover and she didn't want to be by herself.

And it wasn't like she could call Tim. He had his own problems.

She looked at her watch. Another hour until Andy was off duty. That was fine. She needed to have a shower anyway. Instead, she found herself opening her laptop and typing in a URL. The familiar Village Vets website came up, offering free cat neutering as well as vaccines, pet passports (even though the UK had already left the EU and didn't issue passports as such anymore) and a nifty loyalty scheme.

They branded themselves as high-quality, low-cost neighbourhood vets. The first two points, in Irina's opinion, were factually incorrect. She knew Claire had spent a small fortune with them to sort out a respiratory issue that Tank didn't even have. She also knew that Paul had taken Jimmy and Vader to another vet when they were neutered, saying he was terrified they'd lop off the wrong bits.

And Dr Aspen's incompetence had come close to killing Hamish.

She clicked on the Meet the Team tab.

There were at least half a dozen receptionists' names listed, although Irina had only ever seen a middle-aged woman with a chip on her shoulder the size of Siberia, a chubby woman who seemed incapable of speaking or smiling and a young woman who took fifteen minutes to figure out the till every time she had to use it.

The vets all had a handful of letters after their names. Irina jotted each set down, looking up what they stood for. She made a note to herself to check the registers to make sure they really had those qualifications.

Village Vets seemed to pride itself on being family run, but as far as Irina could tell, the only people who appeared to be related were Dr Caroline Aspen – who doubled as the practice manager – and Tilly Aspen-Whitley who, based on the photographs posted, was probably Caroline's daughter.

Of the five remaining vets listed on the site, Irina knew three had left. She jotted a note to herself to find out where they had gone and why. And there were also a few she'd seen in the practice once or twice who weren't on there – a Dr Mak from South Africa and Dr Weronika, from Poland. Which could mean that the website hadn't been updated, or that they hadn't stayed very long. Irina made another note to herself to find out their surnames.

The last two remaining were Benjamin Cooper and Chetan Singh. Four vets wasn't a bad number; some clinics only had one. And they weren't open seven days a week and with the same hours that Village Vets had. Though presumably they did keep tighter controls on the number of pets that were registered with them.

With Dr Aspen now functioning more as a practice manager and her daughter more a full-time mum than practising vet these days – she'd once bragged to Irina that she only stepped inside to drop off or pick up the kids if her mum was watching them – that left two vets. And both were locums, brought in as needed, but possibly working across several other practices.

Irina clicked into the misspelled section advertising vacancies, not surprised at how long the list was.

She opened a new browser and searched for recent Village Vets reviews.

Village Vets

A friendly and knowledgeable vet. Easy to get an appointment when my mastiff ate my car keys.

Andresz, 1 February ★★★★★

The only nice thing I can say about them is that it's easy to get an appointment. Probably because anyone with

---

a brain would have already found a better vet. My wife and I came in separately with our two dogs, one who passed kennel cough to the other. Two different diagnoses, two different treatments. Neither worked. We had to take our dogs to the emergency vet in Wanstead. Kennel cough. You'd think Village Vets would know how to treat it?

Paul, 3 March ★

DO NOT USE THESE VETS! They told me my dog had parvo. It wasn't parvo. It was poison. I paid ££££ for tests that I'm pretty sure they didn't do. They wouldn't let me see him until after he was DEAD! And they couldn't even apologise.

Phil, 15 March ★

My dog got a foxtail stuck between his toes. We went to Village Vets. They told me there was nothing wrong, but suggested that I switch his food. WTF? We had to go to another vet who removed the foxtail and gave Harley antibiotics for the infection.

Alison, 12 May ★

Don't use these people. I paid for the full vaccine package, only to learn – one week before travelling abroad – that they hadn't bothered to give my dog the rabies jab. And I'd even mentioned to the vet at my dog's last check-up that we'd be travelling abroad!

Three weeks between getting the jab and being able to travel means no holiday, and a small fortune written off. Pretty sure that's negligence. The battleaxe on reception wouldn't let me talk to the practice manager – and couldn't be bothered to say 'I'm sorry' for the cock-up.

Michelle, 15 July ★

The list went on and on and on. For every five-star rating, there were at least four or five one-star reviews, painting a picture of arrogant neglect.

'What the hell?' Irina muttered, looking at the dog bed beside her. Hamish lifted his head and blinked groggily. He groaned and curled into a tighter ball, breaking Irina's heart all over again and filling her veins with a righteous fire. 'These are the people we trust with our dogs' health. Who can you rely on, if not your local vet?'

She began to type, following one false trail and then another, until things became clearer. 'They're a stand-alone shop, owned and operated by Dr Caroline Aspen. The idiot who didn't know enough to purge a dog that ate something dodgy.' She fumed to herself. 'Now, I'm all for being your own boss, Hamish, but these guys have no head office to be accountable to. OFSTED keeps an eye on schools to make sure they're doing what they need to for the kids. The CQC does the same with the NHS. But who audits the vets? DEFRA?'

Hamish's tail twitched, but he didn't have an answer for her.

Irina looked at the reviewers' names again, creating a spreadsheet of owners' names, dogs' names (if they were mentioned), star rating and condition. Some of the names (either dog or human) were familiar, or at least they became so with the added context provided by the descriptions. She had no doubt that the Phil who'd left a review in March was Phil Creasy and that the two dogs belonging to Paul were their own Vader and Jimmy.

It didn't help that while she knew most of the local dogs' names, she didn't know the names of many of their humans. And that there were often many dogs with the same name. She knew of at least four Lokis, three Paddys, a few Nalas, a couple of Montys and more Franks than she wanted to count, most of whom were dachshunds.

With her spreadsheet complete, she scanned through the Pack chat, confirming what she could and finding phone numbers for people she didn't already have in her contacts.

'Right,' Irina said to Hamish, picking up her phone. 'I don't care how close they are, we're finding you a new vet.'

49

LOUISE

Meg (Tyrion's Mum)

> Fi and I still aren't happy that you're going by yourself, but let us know when you're done. Fi's off for a lunch date – who she swears isn't Jim Clark – but I'm just going to take Tyrion to the park.

> We're meeting Grace, not some serial killer. We'll be fine.

> Lou!

Fine, fine. You and Irina can stop giving me grief. I'll text you both on the way back.

Text me first.

For two dogs of such different sizes and temperaments, Luther and Klaus walked surprisingly well together. Mostly moving in the same direction and courteously waiting when one needed to stop to bark at ducks (Luther), chase pigeons (Klaus) or wee on litter (also Klaus).

I was reminded of the statue of Boudicca by Westminster Bridge – with the horses pulling in different directions – and breathed a sigh of relief. Klaus stopped again, pulling us towards a pair of discarded jeans and delicately raising a leg.

On the plus side, there was no sign of the jeans' former occupant, *en déshabille*, returning to claim his now-stained trousers. 'Come on, Klaus. I don't want to be late.'

He didn't seem to care, but with a now empty tank, was happy enough to continue along the towpath.

Grace was waiting for me at the pub near the Three Mills Park, a cup of coffee on the table in front of her and her face shaded from the sun by a broad-brimmed hat. Daphne, sitting on the floor beside her, dropped her chew to bark at the new intruders in her space.

'Chill, Daph,' I said, passing Klaus's lead to my other hand. 'You know Klaus and me. And this is Luther.'

'Cue the dance.' Grace smiled as the dogs circled each other to get in some good butt sniffs. The dance was more complicated with three dogs than with two, especially when two were male, but Daphne didn't seem fazed, easily dancing around the two boys on their leads.

'How are you doing, Louise? Whose is this beautiful boy?' She bent to stroke Luther's head as he passed by. 'Yours?'

'A friend's. What's with all the hush-hush? Don't tell me, Mike's decided he's not a dog person and you need to rehome Daphne?' I leaned down and ruffled the cocka-poo's fur. 'No problem. I'll take her.'

'No chance.' Grace laughed. 'Mike would rehome me before even thinking about sending Daphne away. She's definitely a daddy's girl. Get yourself something to eat and drink. I'm not one for the Sunday lunch here, but the pizza is very good. Then I'll show you what I found.'

I did as she asked, taking the boys inside with me, but allowing the bartender to carry my Diet Coke outside. I thanked her and sat down opposite Grace. 'So?'

She took a deep breath. 'Phil was cutting edge in so many ways. His ideas turned into companies. Those companies were then bought out by bigger companies, giving him the resources to come up with new ideas ... rinse and repeat.' There was a catch in her voice as she spoke; even though she might be very happy with Macho Mike, she wasn't trying to hide the fact that she was still in mourning for Phil.

'Do you think that was it? A disagreement with one of his business partners?'

'I honestly don't know. He seemed to get on with all of them. With everyone. You know Phil, he could have a conversation with a lamp post and make it feel special.' Grace paused, pursing her lips. A few moments later she shook off the memories. 'I wouldn't have thought *anyone* would want to harm him, but obviously someone did. I don't know why, I can't imagine any possible reason for it. But maybe there's something in here that can help.'

She reached into her backpack and pulled out a black leather book. She held it in her hands briefly before pushing it across the table to me.

'Ahead of his time in so many ways,' she said, nodding at it. 'And yet, so behind it in others. Phil was old-school when it came to managing his personal diary.'

'Ah.' My fingers traced the gold lettering on the cover; Phil's initials and the year. 'How did you get it?'

'Your questions got me thinking. I still have a key to the flat. I was pretty sure the police would have taken his laptop – and they had. But for some reason – maybe they overlooked it – they left his diary.'

'Aha.'

'Yeah. Aha,' she echoed.

'And you found something in it?'

She took hold of the diary and began to leaf through the pages. I caught glimpses of Phil's neat writing, in pencil so that it could be erased if something changed. Saw doctors' appointments. Meetings. Birthdays.

What had Grace found? Had Phil been seeing someone? Was that who had killed him?

She wouldn't be rushed, pausing on one page and then

another until she found what she was looking for. She turned the book round and pointed to the entry in question with a manicured red nail. 'Here.'

I looked at it and blinked.

'Why would someone have an appointment with a vet when they didn't have a pet?'

'Grace,' I sighed, disappointed. 'I don't know. You said he was doing work with dog charities. Maybe he was working with them on something. They're big in the neighbourhood.'

She shook her head. 'Not them. He'd have worked with Satan before working with Village Vets.' She pointed to the name in the book. 'Especially that one.'

50

IRINA

The doorbell buzzed, interrupting Irina's train of thought. There were a fair number of veterinary clinics in the area. Every one she'd contacted had told her the same thing: they were operating at capacity, given the huge increase in pets since the pandemic. Quite frankly, the number of vets required to care for them all hadn't yet caught up.

'Yeah, and what about everyone who's moved out of London?' Irina grumbled to herself, stabbing the button on her phone to let Andy through the main gate.

She hit it a second time, allowing him into the building, and unlocked her door. 'Damn man had better have coffee with him,' she growled, looking around for Hamish.

Hamish wasn't on his bed, or hers for that matter. The balcony, empty of furniture, was also empty of dog. It wasn't a large flat. He couldn't be far. 'Hamish,' she called out. 'Hamish?'

She hadn't seen him move from his bed. He'd been there a few minutes ago. She dropped to her knees and edged around her coffee table. In the corner, under the sofa, her poor boy was huddled like a shaggy black rag doll.

'Oh my God.' She reached for him, pulling him out and into her arms. Buried her nose into his soft fur, the scent of watermelon shampoo almost overpowered by the antiseptic from the animal hospital. 'You'll be fine, *Mischka*. I promise . . .'

There was a soft knock at the door. Still holding Hamish, she unlocked and opened it. Andy stood in the hall with a couple of takeaway coffees in one hand, a large bouquet in the other and a laptop bag slung across his chest.

'The flowers are dog-friendly,' he said by way of greeting. 'I checked.'

Irina nodded, holding herself still as she felt her mighty walls of self-control crumble.

Hating herself even as she did so, she took a step back and, for the second time in a day, burst into tears.

Andy put the flowers on the table and gathered her close. In that moment, she didn't care about seeming vulnerable. Didn't care about crossing any lines. Didn't care that he'd betrayed her by abusing her trust. He was here now.

And maybe that was all that mattered.

51

LOUISE

Meg (Tyrion's Mum)

> Big reveal: Grace had
> Phil's diary that had an
> appointment in it with Dr
> Cooper for last Saturday.

Ben? Seriously? He's a
vet, FFS. You saw how
much he loves dogs. I
get that Phil was upset
when his dog died. I
TOTALLY get that. I'd be
a wreck if it were Tyrion.
WILL be a wreck when he

passes — and I hope it's many years from now.

Me too — many, many, many years from now.

Thanks — you too. But my point is that while I even get that Phil might blame a vet for not being able to save Alfie, wouldn't that make Phil a likelier suspect to kill Ben? Not the other way around?

I guess, I don't know. Heading home now.

It was a good point. And as much as Phil might have been upset, I didn't see him taking anger to the point of *killing* anyone. But what about Ben Cooper? Had they fought? Had things got out of hand, resulting in Phil's accidental death?

I hadn't gotten that close to Phil's body, but it hadn't looked to me like he'd been in any sort of altercation.

And I couldn't see Ben Cooper, a man who'd dedicated his life to working with animals, engaging in any sort of fisticuffs. Certainly not if there was any risk of hurting himself, or staining his bespoke, monogrammed shirts.

Another dead end. The latest in a series of dead bloody ends.

Reining in Luther and Klaus, I looked up at the sky. 'I'm sorry, Phil. I'm doing my best. We won't give up, but holy crap. Whoever did this to you is doing a cracking job of covering their tracks.'

The dogs gave me identical flat looks. Not the 'let's go!' followed by yanks on their leads, but 'pull yourself together, woman' gaze.

We couldn't let Phil down. Because Phil now represented everyone with a dog, with a pet, in East London. It was no longer only about finding justice for him. It was about finding justice for all of us.

It was about taking back our neighbourhood and making it safe.

The dogs were right. It was only a setback, far from game over. And I had an idea ...

52

IRINA

The sound of a ridiculously happy ringtone erupted from Andy's phone. He had the grace to blush, flicked the phone to silent and walked to the bedroom to take the call. Their argument wasn't over. He'd overstepped the line and wouldn't apologise for it, but he'd come over when she'd asked and that was as good a start to a detente as any.

Once Irina had calmed down, she'd told him what had happened to Hamish. And what the Pack had managed to piece together. But any quid pro quo had fallen flat; he hadn't shared, well, anything. But he hadn't been angry enough to leave, so that was good, right?

Instead he'd set up his laptop on her dining room table and even though his shift was technically over, proceeded to work from her flat, taking calls from the bedroom.

Did she feel guilty earwigging? No, she did not. And, to

be fair, most of them had to do with other cases. But this one made her ears prick up.

'No, Louise. I don't know why Dr Cooper told you that he didn't know Phil Creasy, but I don't think it's relevant.' He paused and Irina could almost see him roll his eyes. 'No. You know I can't tell you whether we have any suspects . . . Yes, I can confirm that the vets have been cleared. Jesus Christ. It's like anything else. Someone dies and their family blame the doctor. Doesn't mean the doctor killed them.'

It was a small flat and his voice carrying into the dining area was crystal-clear. Irina saw he'd left his laptop on the table; the case management system had been open just before the call so that he could record what she'd been telling him.

'Yeah, Louise, I know it has to do with perspective. But if what you're saying is true, it'd mean that your friend would have killed the vet. Is that something you think he'd have been capable of?'

Irina leaned forward, wondering if he'd locked the screen.

She couldn't believe her luck. He hadn't.

'No, Louise. There were no visible defensive wounds.'

She didn't think twice. He'd perved into her phone. She had the moral right.

'Let me stop you there, Louise,' Andy said from the other room. 'I repeat: Dr Cooper is not a suspect in the case. And no, I cannot tell you who is.' He sighed. 'Both. Cannot and will not.'

Irina's eyes scanned over the information on the screen.

Just what she and the others in the Pack had told him. But there must be more, a list of suspects or something . . . If there was, she couldn't see it. From what she could see, the Pack had got a lot further with the case than the mighty Met Police.

'No, Louise.' Andy sighed again. 'I'm sorry. I know he was your friend. I know this is important to you. But this is an ongoing investigation. An ongoing *police* investigation.'

Irina heard his footsteps approaching and froze, poised to lunge back towards her own chair. The steps retreated; Andy must be pacing.

She quickly clicked to open an attachment. Scrolled through it. It looked like a load of gibberish. She returned to the executive summary at the top and frowned.

It was a report confirming that Phil had a high dose of diazepam in his body at the time of his death and that it had been taken within the previous two hours. Which could maybe imply an overdose?

'Look, Louise. Please listen to me. It's admirable that you want to find your friend's killer, but the key word here is *killer*. He was murdered, and right now you and your friends, including Irina, are putting yourselves in danger. Please be sensible. Be the sensible one. Call off your hounds and leave this to us.'

Be the sensible one? The implication that she wasn't sensible. Irina flicked a two-fingered salute in Andy's general direction and reset the screen to where it had been when he'd left it. She walked past the bedroom to the bathroom, the floor creaking. Andy opened the door, like he was checking to see if she had her ear against it. Not that she needed to, with the acoustics in this flat. Instead she waved in a way she hoped looked natural. In return he rolled his eyes and mouthed 'Miss Marple', before closing the door again.

'Okay, okay, stop, Louise. Look, I'm not supposed to tell you this, but yes, we spoke to his business partners. And the investors. There was no sign of any motive, let alone actual foul play. And your Dr Cooper? We know Mr Creasy went to see him the day before you found him. We know there was a confrontation at the surgery, but we also know – and this is supported by witness accounts – that he left there very much alive. Went for a drink at the Bells afterwards, as a matter of fact. Sank a pint or two. No. I cannot tell you who he drank with. Can't. Won't. Doesn't matter. This is a Met Police investigation, not a dog park lark. I won't ask you again: please, *please*, leave this to us.'

Irina opened the medicine chest and scanned the labels on the prescription bottles one by one until she found what she was looking for. And softly swore.

53

LOUISE

Partridge Bark

> Does anyone know who Phil had a drink with last Saturday? Someone saw him drinking at the Bells before he died. If not, I'll stop by and ask them. Because I'm getting the feeling that whoever had that drink with Phil might have been the last person to see him alive.

Yaz (Hercules's Mum)

Phil drank at the Bells?
Voluntarily?

So it would seem.

Yaz (Hercules's Mum)

Huh. Maybe he saw
something there — it's
not as dodgy as the
George (soz Gav!) — or
pissed someone off
bad enough that they
killed him. Maybe we've
been making this too
complicated?

It was possible. Anything was possible. But there was only one way to find out and the Bells wasn't that far.

'Come on, boys,' I told the dogs. 'We're making a slight detour.'

We moved from one canal path to another. Jake had warned me that Luther liked ducks. What he hadn't mentioned was just how obsessive his dog was about them. And maintaining constant vigilance over a forty-pound Staffie determined to follow them into the canal was proving to be a serious workout.

We approached the pub from the back. Klaus perked up, pulling me through the sad-looking beer garden and stopping short of the door.

He gave me the side-eye. *You sure you want to go in there, Mum?*

I wasn't sure I did, but I didn't have a choice. I pushed through the doors.

The Bells was an old pub and wore every year like a new burden. On the street, the brick façade mostly held up; on the canal side, even the whitewash was trying to flee. Inside wasn't much better and enough paint had chipped to make the walls look like some sort of abstract artwork. The fruit machines outnumbered punters at about two to one and the bunting over the bar wore enough dust to make me wonder if it'd been put up for QE2's coronation.

Yaz was right; it wasn't the sort of pub I could see Phil going to. At least not voluntarily.

In fact, it wasn't the sort of pub I could see most of the Pack going to, with the exception, maybe, of Gav. No wonder Annabel had been in such a state about trying to get it redeveloped when I'd seen her at the Hound.

Ignoring the slight sucking of the wood floors, I walked the dogs to the bar and the grizzled bartender behind it, hoping they wouldn't lick anything that could harm them.

'Afternoon,' I said cheerfully, dialling up my best American accent. 'Can I get a glass of white wine, Sauvignon if you have it. Anything dry, if you don't.'

Up close, with iron-grey hair exploding around his head, the bartender resembled a budget version of that Brexiteer pub mogul. He grunted and pulled a green bottle from a fridge under the counter. From the number of bottles in there, it seemed that alcopops were far more popular than the vino. I braced myself and wasn't disappointed: the wine had gone off and was cruising around Via Vinegar.

I forced it down and hazarded a smile. I knew I wasn't the sort of client the pub usually had, but leaned in anyway. 'A friend of mine was here last Saturday. I was wondering if you might remember them?'

'She look the same sort as you?'

I looked down at myself. My T-shirt had a picture on it of a dachshund holding a glass of wine, along with the slogan 'Stop and sniff the rosé'. Nice jeans but with pawprints on the knees. A delicate gold chain circled my left ankle, only just visible above my rather well-loved muddy trainers. Phil's weekend look had to be more upscale than mine.

I cleared my throat. 'No. My friend's a man. Early thirties. He was dressed in jeans and a blue-and-white checked shirt?' Assuming of course that he hadn't gone home to change clothes between leaving the pub and ending up dead in Partridge Park.

I scrolled through my photo feed. While there were plenty of old pics of Klaus and Alfie, there wasn't one of Phil. So, I brought up the picture from the BBC article and showed it to the bartender.

'American,' the barman said, not bothering to look at it before glancing away.

'Nope. That's just me. My friend was English.'

'Rozzers was already here asking 'bout him,' he said, thrusting the card machine at me for payment.

'O'course they was. He were found dead in the park, like,' a young woman sitting along the bar guffawed, readjusting the strap of her vest top. An old man, further along, made a point of ignoring us, staring out the window at the cars passing along the high street.

Luther started to growl, and I pulled him closer.

'Yeah, that's the guy. Before he was found dead, he was drinking here. Do you remember him? Anything that might have happened with him that night?'

'If you're asking if he got killed in here, he didn't.' The barman scowled at me.

'Okay. Did he have an argument with anyone? A disagreement, maybe?'

'Why d'you want to know?'

'I'm the one who found him. I feel like I owe him, and let's face it, the rozzers are crap at doing anything round here,' I said, the Cockney word sounding ridiculous with my Connecticut accent.

I looked at the three people around me and decided to ramp up the charm. I gave them a smile and ratcheted up my accent until it sounded almost Texan. 'I don't have a warrant card. But I have one dead friend and two that've been attacked. Can y'all help me? I just want to know who he was with that night.'

There was silence and I could almost see the East End wall slam down. It was a them-or-us sort of thing, I knew. Gav would have been far better at this than me. He was one of them, but he hadn't answered my last text, so it was up to me. And all I could do was my best.

Silently offering him an apology, I proceeded. 'Like

I said, since Phil died, two more of my friends have been attacked. You might know one of them. Gav. Gav MacAdams?'

The barman paused and exchanged a glance with the old man on the stool.

'Sounds like you're the dangerous one to know, love,' he sniggered. 'You sure you ain't the killer?'

I ignored him and continued, 'You do know Gav, don't you?'

'Everyone knows Gav,' the young woman replied, again fidgeting with the strap of her top.

'You know that he was attacked in the market square last Sunday? The day after my friend was drinking here?'

'Look, wha'cha getting at?' the barman said, plonking a tea towel down between us like some sort of terrycloth line in the sand. 'You come in here, talking shite about two people. None of it's to do wi' the Bells. Your man, he left here alone an' alive. Gav, he drinks at the George. We don't know nuffin about what happened to him. To either o' them. And we don't want any problems here.'

The other two nodded. I had a feeling that if Luther wasn't sitting quietly at my feet, they might have asked me to leave.

Standing, I turned and met their eyes, one by one. By the time I reached the young woman, Klaus was pawing at my leg, asking to be picked up.

I leaned down and gave the command, catching him neatly as he leapt into my arms. With his head tucked under my chin, I tried one last time.

'Okay, that's fair. I don't want any problems either. I

just want whatever's happening to stop. I was friends with Phil, the dead guy. And Gav, who was attacked.' I took a deep breath and locked eyes with the barman once more. 'What wouldn't you do if they were *your* friends?'

54

GAV

Partridge Bark

Meg (Tyrion's Mum)

@**Irina** – How's Hamish
doing?
@**Lou**, I don't know
anyone at the Bells. But if
you go there, good luck.

Terrible business about the poisoned dog, Gav thought.
He glanced down at Violet trotting beside him as usual.
Thank God he'd trained her to never eat from the ground,
never take food from anyone but him.

No, he wasn't worried about Violet – she'd tear the head
off anyone who tried to come near her – but the other

dogs ... the Scottie, the Staffie, the others. They didn't deserve it.

At least they're alive.

He shook his head and crossed the market square, nodding at familiar faces as he passed. So, the little firecracker was at the Bells. Good luck to her indeed; the people there wouldn't tell her anything. She wore 'outsider' like a badge. Maybe he'd go round later, have a chat with them. He wasn't part of their circle, but maybe they'd talk to him.

Or maybe one of the lads at the George would know.

In the meantime, the sun was high and the market was busy, loud.

So loud that he almost didn't hear Violet's low growl.

He saw them moving fast, coming from the fried chicken place on the corner. Five of them, hoods up, but young, maybe late teens, two of them women. One of them deliberately dropped a box of half-eaten wings on the ground.

'Jesus,' Gav said, edging Violet behind him with his foot. Cursing himself for not being better prepared. He had no knife, nothing to defend himself with. He wasn't even wearing his usual jacket; he'd ventured out in shirt-sleeves thanks to the warm weather.

And as they got closer, he could see that at least two of them had knives.

Gav lunged towards a stall, grabbed a school blazer from a rack and quickly wrapped it around his left arm. It was too much to hope that the polyester would deflect a blade, but the extra padding would be useful.

The vendor looked like he wanted to protest, until he followed Gav's gaze towards the thugs. Then he shrunk back, muttering to himself. A wave of silent energy swept through the market, customers flinching, looking down, moving away. Vendors glancing uncomfortably at one another, on edge.

Gav braced himself, wishing there was someone who would take hold of Violet.

'Heard you was askin' about us,' the first kid said as he drew near. It was Skinny Boy, doing the cobra thing with his head again.

Gav tried to maintain a loose posture. *No threat here, guv.*

But there was. And if they were brazen enough to attack during the day, with witnesses, that wasn't good.

One of the kids with a knife held it like he knew what he was doing.

Gav knew what he was doing too. As the kid lunged forward, he deflected the blow with his jacket-padded arm. Retaliated with a punch. The kid's head snapped back and the rest of them pressed forward.

Gav fought hard. Amid the confusion, he heard Violet barking, growling. Snarling.

Then the low thud of an impact, and her cries.

They'd kicked her.

They kicked a tiny old dog.

They kicked *Violet*.

Fury ripped through him, and now he fought with a hot, red rage. He didn't notice when another person slipped in, quickly picking up Violet.

Didn't notice the small woman, using her body to cradle his dog, kicking at the kids.

Didn't notice the crack as one of his ribs broke.

Didn't hear another shout, louder, deeper.

One by one, the kids backed off, still shouting, still cursing.

Gav sank to one knee, his padded arm clutched over his ribs, his eyes searching. 'Violet?' he rasped.

'I have her,' a winded voice replied.

He blinked the speaker into focus. A small, freckled woman. Late twenties, maybe. In a T-shirt with a dragon on it and with purple at the ends of her dark hair.

He didn't fully register who she was until he saw the sling criss-crossing her chest. Meg.

Holy crap.

Little Meg had defended him? With her sausage dog in that bag?

But the black nose peeping out wasn't Tyrion's. It was attached to enormous black eyes that were dulled with pain and fur that shone with blood. One paw reached towards him, and Gav breathed a sigh of relief. *She's alive.*

'I've been working out,' Meg said with a lopsided grin. 'Kickboxing.' She carefully pulled the sling from around her body and gently handed it to Gav.

'Thank you. Tyrion?'

She waved towards another woman he recognised, the pretty boy's girlfriend, Sophie, who stroked the dappled brown fur of Meg's dachshund while her Jack Russell sat at her feet. Sophie stepped forward. 'Take her to the vet,

THE DOG PARK DETECTIVES

Gav. Meg and me, we saw what happened here. Hell, half
the market saw what happened.'

'The kids?'

She gestured behind him. Turning painfully, he saw that
the five kids were being restrained by three big men. 'Me
and my brothers have got this. We'll make a statement to
the cops.' She rolled her eyes. 'When they arrive.'

Gav nodded and tried to stand. Hissed air through his
teeth and returned to one knee, still cradling Violet.

'Do you want me to take her to the vet, while you go to
A & E? You might have broken something,' Meg offered.

'No,' Gav said, allowing Violet to lick his face, his
hands smoothing down her fur. She must be hating the
bag, hating being confined, but he was grateful to Meg,
grateful to Sophie and her brothers for their help. He kept
stroking her fur, murmuring to her, terrified of what he'd
see if he took her out of the sling. 'I need to stay with her.
I can go to A & E once she's seen to. Then I'm gonna kill
those little bastards.'

55

LOUISE

Partridge Bark

Meg (Tyrion's Mum)

Gav and Violet were
attacked by a gang of
kids. Violet's hurt and
Gav's taken her to the vet.
Guys, be careful out there!

OMG – is he OK? Is Violet?

Sophie (Loki's Mum)

Don't know yet. My
brothers and a few
vendors kept the kids

in place until the cops
arrived. We're going to
give a statement and the
kids have been arrested.

I put my phone on the bar next to the wine/vinegar and looked at the barman. 'I need to go. My friend Gav? Well, he was just attacked again. Will you help or not?'

The bartender shrugged. 'Got nuffin' to do wi' me.'

The old man beside the woman looked tense but kept watching the cars go by.

I wasn't a fool. I knew I was an outsider. But it couldn't be a coincidence that someone like Gav MacAdams was attacked twice in the span of a week. Not in this neighbourhood.

'Fine.' I put Klaus on the ground and gently coaxed Luther to his feet. Over my shoulder I added, 'So when Gav comes in here asking questions, you can tell *him* that you know nothing. And maybe *he'll* believe you.'

In the States, we'd call it a 'Hail Mary' play. In American football, when the quarterback finds himself in trouble, he throws the ball as hard as he can towards the end zone and prays to God that someone on his team catches it. Gav had a reputation once. Maybe he still did. I didn't know, but this was my last card to play.

Painfully aware that the next person to be assaulted could well be me, I stepped through the door, hearing it close behind us with an off-key clank.

I took a deep breath of fresh air, pulled out my phone and waited.

56

LOUISE

Irina (Hamish's Mum)

> Don't ask me how I know, or what it means – I don't know – but Phil had a trank in his system. Diazepam.

> Common enough sedative, isn't it?

> Yeah. For humans as well as dogs (the vet gave Hamish a prescription for it last year for the fireworks).

Maybe his GP put him on it for stress?

Not at those levels, I don't think. Looks like he had enough to take down an elephant.

So ... You think it was an overdose? Why'd he have a drink at the Bells then go to the park to OD? And then hide his own phone in the bushes in the dog park?

I don't know. Maybe it wasn't an OD. I mean, if it was, I think Andy'd have closed the case already.

The Bells doesn't strike me as the sort of place where someone would get roofied with diazepam. And besides, why would someone drug Phil?

It might be something, it might be nothing. I dropped a text to Grace, asking if she knew whether Phil had a prescription for diazepam, then walked the boys back through the beer garden to the canal path.

'Hey.'

I looked up from my phone and blinked at the young woman from the pub. She was still fidgeting with the strap of her top. 'Gonna walk home. Can't stop you from walkin' wi' me, if you're headin' in the same direction.'

I hadn't asked to walk with her, but understood that she probably needed to cover her back in case someone was watching. The boys and I followed her onto the canal path, heading north again. I glanced at the dogs. Luther was still recovering from being poisoned; Klaus had short legs. Both had walked a lot today; I hoped they'd be okay to walk a little more.

'Information ain't cheap,' the woman pointed out as soon as we were out of sight of the pub.

I had no cash on me, other than the £20 note that I kept in the zipped compartment of my dog-walking bag. For emergencies, or if we stopped by the market on the way home. Those stalls were the last place that still hailed cash as king.

'Information might not be free, but it has to be worth the cost.' And that cost had to be less than twenty quid.

The woman seemed to consider it. In the harsh light of day, she had an unhealthy pallor. Red veins on her nose and cheeks defied her heavy foundation, and that vest that she kept fiddling with looked to be on its last legs.

It began to feel like she might be wasting my time.

'Look, tell me what you know. Then we can decide what it's worth.'

'Not gonna happen.' She shook her head, her lank hair barely moving. 'It don't work like that.'

Bartering would have been easier if I had two tens instead of a twenty. That said, one of the first rules of negotiation was to be okay with walking away from the table.

I stopped and swivelled so that my back was to the sun.

'Wot's yer problem?' she demanded, shielding her eyes from the light.

'I don't like being played.' I took the twenty out of my bag and tucked it into Luther's collar. 'If your information is good, that's yours. If it isn't, well, it'll go towards treats for the dogs. Your call.'

She squinted at me and then at the twenty, considering her options. She jerked her head, a silent assent. 'You know what's across the street from the Bells?'

'A Tesco Express. Lighting shop. Dry-cleaner's. The vet's.'

'Yeah. So sometimes people take their pets to the vet. Then instead o'goin' home, they wait at the pub, wi' a pint.'

'So, my friend was waiting at the Bells last Saturday night? While, say, his dog was at the vet's?'

'Yeah, maybe. I dunno.'

'There's a lot you don't know. The dogs will be grateful for that sack full of treats.'

'He were there,' she said. 'That man you was showing on your phone. The one in the news. Was waiting there with a pint. Came in looking rough.'

'Rough?'

'Rough.' She nodded her head. 'But not like he'd been roughed up. Not bruised. Not pissed. Jus' ... I dunno. Rough.'

Her vocabulary was only slightly better than Klaus's.

'How was he dressed?'

'Jeans. Blue-an'-white checked shirt. Like you said in there. Nice shoes. Too posh for the Bells on a Saturday night.'

'Did he meet anyone?'

'For a while, he sat by the window. Looked across the street. Waitin'. As I said, like the others.'

'The others? Pet owners?'

'Yeah. Kept checkin' his watch. The vet's, it closes at six on Saturdays. He didn't get no call from them. Was after six when he left.'

'How long after six?'

'I dunno. Maybe half an hour. An hour?'

She was right that Village Vets closed at six on a Saturday. Which meant that assuming the vets had a bit of paperwork to finish off at the end of the day – though from what I could see, they did most of that between appointments – they were probably gone by six thirty or maybe seven.

'Was he drinking with someone else? Another person waiting for their pet?' If it was someone from the Pack ... oh God. What if someone from the Pack had done this to Phil? And because of the Pack chat, they'd know exactly what was going on!

The girl took on a coy look. 'Wasn't drinking wi' them, no.'

'Them? So, someone was there with him, but they weren't drinking?'

'Didn't say that.'

'He sat with someone who wasn't drinking?' I repeated, trying to get my head around it. Why go to a pub, even to wait, and not order a drink? Even if it was a coffee or soft drink?

'Didn't say that either.'

I was fast losing patience. 'Then what *are* you saying?'

'Someone came in to see him. Bought a couple o' pints. Took 'em over to him an' sat down.'

'Who was it?'

'I dunno.'

'But not one of the regulars? Someone dressed like Phil? Like me?' I pulled the twenty from Luther's collar. 'Tell me about him.'

She seemed to consider the question. 'I told you. Your friend took a couple o' sips o' that beer. Kept lookin' out the window. When he left, it were sharpish, and he didn't look back.'

I tried not to sigh aloud. 'And what about the guy that bought him that beer?'

'Oh. That weren't no bloke. That were a woman.'

57

IRINA

Partridge Bark

Grace (Daphne's Mum)

As far as I know, Phil was not on diazepam. BUT he was pretty cut up after Alfie died, and then we broke up. It's possible a GP might have prescribed him something. Sorry I can't help more.

Irina glanced at Andy from under her lashes. He was looking at his own phone, frowning. If he'd noticed that she'd used his laptop to view the tox report, he didn't say anything. In fact, it almost looked as if he was trying to ignore her. In her own home.

How the devil was she going to manage to get him to snog her when she couldn't even get him to look up?

She stood and stretched, aware that her top went tight over her chest when she did.

He didn't even glance up.

What is it going to take?

He was the one who'd come over. He was the one who'd made the effort. And yet he was content to work from her dining table without even a hint of conversation. What was she to him, just a key to good broadband?

She slowed as she passed by him, but she couldn't see his screen clearly enough to learn what other info he had on the case. She pretended to rummage around in the kitchen. Irina was the queen of delivery service, but she usually kept cheese and crackers around. She put together a small plate and brought it over to him.

He adjusted the screen as she approached and put his phone face down. Rich, considering how he'd had no issues looking at her private messages.

'Need a break?' she asked.

He gave her a tired smile. 'Thanks. Yeah. Give me another half hour or so, then maybe we can go for a walk? Get some air?'

'Perfect. I have some work to finish up too.' She left the plate at his elbow and retreated to her desk in the corner. If he wasn't willing to share his information, then she didn't need to share the profiles she was building of the primary vets at Village Vets.

<u>Caroline Aspen</u>
- 61, lives in Greenwich with husband Anthony (retired)
- Graduated with honours
- According to Companies House, the sole director for Village Vets

Caroline wasn't on social media, but Irina figured that daughter-dearest might be able to add some insights into Mummy's life.

<u>Tilly Aspen-Whitley</u>
- 32, lives in Greenwich with husband James, a mortgage broker
- Two children at private schools, the elder (son) boarding, the girl living at home
- Current nanny looks like she's from Spain
- Studied veterinary medicine at the University of Nottingham
- According to Insta, currently spending the summer at the family home in the South of France
- Plenty of expensive-looking holidays abroad, many featuring Mummy and Daddy

<u>Chetan Singh</u>
- 39, studied in India. Certified as a vet in the UK in 2015
- Lives in Bow with his wife. Two daughters (aged 10 and 12) both at private schools
- Second house in Whitstable valued at £1.7M
- Insta accounts show travel to Bali, Turks and Caicos and Maldives within the last two years

<u>Benjamin Cooper</u>
- 37, studied vet medicine at the University of Surrey, single
- Lives in a penthouse flat in Canary Wharf, estimated value £1.5M
- Owns a new Mercedes convertible (old one recently stolen - check this)
- Insta account shows multiple trips to Thailand, Bali, and Monaco and the French Riviera, not to mention dinners at London's top restaurants

Who do they think they are? The Real Vets of Hollywood, *only in East London?*

Irina glanced at Andy – who looked intent on his own laptop – and returned to her screen. With Tilly abroad all summer, the practice was operating with only three vets. And two of them locums. And the third only saw patients when she had to.

Irina's fingers danced over her keyboard.

According to Google, the average starting salary for a vet was around £30,500 to £35,500. With more training it could go up to £70k, or even as high as £92K. Getting the numbers for locums was a bit more difficult, but if they were anything like those figures, it would still mean that they were all living well; potentially above their means.

Which might explain why they'd decided to open for a few hours on Sunday afternoons. You couldn't get a GP appointment on a Sunday, but you could get one for your pet at Village Vets, assuming you were okay to pay an emergency appointment surcharge. Only that would stretch the vets pretty thin. And tired people made mistakes.

'Is that how they fund those sorts of lifestyles?' Irina muttered.

'Pardon?' Andy asked, looking up.

'Nothing,' she said, flipping her hand dismissively. 'Just talking to myself.'

But her fingers didn't leave the keyboard. Each search brought with it more questions.

58

LOUISE

Partridge Bark

> It wasn't a man that drank
> with Phil. It was a woman.

Irina (Hamish's Mum)

Dr Aspen?

> Not from the description.
> Younger. Pale. Seems like
> he bolted not long after
> she bought him a beer.

Yaz (Hercules's Mum)

You trust this info? Maybe this mystery woman roofied him??

The girl from the Bells cleared her throat. She hadn't given me the information I'd hoped for, but what she'd said had opened up a few new possibilities. 'Okay,' I decided, handing her the twenty. 'It's yours.'

She smiled, tucking it into a pocket, before turning off the canal path, still heading north.

I felt a tug on Klaus's lead. 'For heaven's sake,' I sighed, allowing him to pull me over to the same discarded pair of jeans that we'd seen on the way up the canal. Klaus sniffed at them from every angle and raised a leg. 'You marked them on the way to meet Grace. Then on the way here. And again now? Who exactly do you think claimed them in the last, like, half hour?'

Luther waited for Klaus to finish, then urinated on the same spot, his amused eyes watching me.

A woman. A *young* woman. That was a twist I hadn't expected.

'Who hated Phil enough to kill him?'

The dogs didn't have an answer, so we turned round and headed for home. Luther lunged for a duck, forcing my attention off the theories just in time to keep the big guy from diving into the canal.

Irina had said there'd been drugs in Phil's system, but

there'd been no visible signs of an overdose. Also no visible signs of a fight. His knuckles hadn't been bruised. *No visible defensive wounds,* Andy'd said.

Phil wasn't a pushover. He wasn't huge, but he was big enough to fight back if there had been some sort of confrontation.

The key word was visible. Had there been bruises I hadn't seen, hidden by his clothes?

The wildcard was the diazepam. If he'd taken too much it would have affected his behaviour and surely someone in the pub would have noticed. Maybe they'd have called 999, or chivvied him out the door. But regardless, who would go to the trouble of getting rid of the body?

It would have taken all three of the people I'd just seen in there to lob Phil over the fence if he'd passed out, or OD'd. And *someone* would have seen that, surely?

Was that why they were being so cagey about it?

Was it why the young woman had given me the story about the woman who'd met with Phil that night?

Something didn't feel right. There was no way an average woman would have been able to get Phil over the fence on her own. And statistically speaking, there just weren't that many female murderers compared to men. Or at least, not if you took out of consideration women who killed in self-defence ...

No. If a woman really was mixed up in this, then she was probably working with someone else.

Jake's words rang in my mind; the killer in his book was the person who'd gotten close to the police investigation. I'd joked that in this case that would mean it must be Irina, but what if I'd got it wrong? What if the killer wasn't trying to get closer to the police's investigation, but to ours? What if he wasn't working alone, but had roped in a woman?

But who? And what hold did he have over her?

Did she like to kill, like some sort of Bonnie to his Clyde?

Or did she just care that much for him?

Muttering to the dogs, I texted Gav and then Irina. And headed faster down the canal.

59

GAV

Gav was sweating. Every breath he took hurt, but nothing ached more than his heart.

'Take a seat, Mr MacAdams,' the receptionist said. 'Hovering over me isn't going to make things go faster.'

'She's in an awful lot of pain,' Meg said, her face earnest as she clutched Tyrion to her chest. Gav no longer saw her open, honest face and classed her as a country oik. Not after the roundhouse kick she'd delivered to that kid's head.

'What happened?' the nurse said, standing behind the middle-aged battleaxe stationed at reception.

'Some little sh— kid kicked her.' Gav lowered his brow in a way he knew intimidated people who didn't know him. And terrified those who did.

The nurse nodded to the receptionist. 'See which appointments can be moved. We'll need to X-ray her and see what, if anything, is broken.'

Gav understood the more frightening words left unspoken – *internal bleeding*.

The nurse retreated through the back door, while the battleaxe did her best to ignore him. He looked at her name tag, memorising it. Joanna Hoey. Well, he'd make sure that Joanna Hoey would understand who she was talking to. He glanced at the mousey woman beside her. The one who hadn't lifted a finger to help. Freya Willis.

'Let's sit down, Gav,' Meg said, her soft hand on his arm. She led him to a row of chairs, whose only occupant was a young man with a wicker carrier on his lap and crazy hair like from a Japanese cartoon.

'Scoot over, Cat Boy,' Gav said.

'My name's Ethan,' Cat Boy said. A slight flush stained his cheeks, but he scooted one chair over so that Gav and Meg could sit together and turned his body towards the wall.

Gav eased himself into the chair, stroking Violet's soft fur. Hope blossoming when she growled at the cat peering out through a hole in the wicker.

Gav acknowledged this with a slight nod, whispering reassurances to Violet – hoping that he wasn't lying to her – and staring at the two surgery doors, wondering which idiot he would need to trust to save her.

'She'll be fine.' Meg's soft voice was calm, her hands moving over her dachshund's body, trying to calm him. Gav knew not everyone liked the vet's. She didn't have to be here. Didn't have to wait with him. But he was glad she was and gave her an abrupt nod.

One of the surgery doors opened. A young man

emerged with a brown-and-gold cocker spaniel sporting a Cone of Shame. He glanced at Gav. 'Stupid dog. Fourth time in two years he gets a foxtail stuck so far in his ear that he needs surgery. Gonna be another £500.'

The battleaxe smiled. 'It's a dangerous operation. We needed to anaesthetise Fabio.'

'Dumbass dog,' the man retorted in a low tone, but this time he went down on one knee to stroke Fabio's head. He leaned in close to whisper to him, 'Lisa's already bought you a present – a snood to keep the bloody foxtails out of your ears. Won't you just hate that?' The words were harsh, but the tone was soft.

Dogs didn't like snoods any more than wearing the cones. Gav figured their mates made fun of them, but he heard the love in the man's voice. Understood it.

'Violet MacAdams?' Dr Singh had emerged from one of the doors and spoke as if he were shouting across a loud, crowded A & E ward, instead of a small surgery with only Cat Boy, Meg and Gav sitting in the waiting room chairs less than a metre away.

Cat Boy looked like he was about to protest, until a glare from Gav set him straight.

'Let's go, darlin'.' Gav stood, cradling Violet. He felt Meg stand and follow behind him into the examination room.

'Only one person at a time,' the battleaxe said.

'Sod off,' Meg replied cheerfully, winking at Dr Singh.

'It's all right,' the vet said and stepped back to allow them to enter. 'Tell me what happened.'

Gav explained, leaving out anything not directly related

to Violet's wounds. The vet didn't need to know about the previous attack on him. He might tell the police, but even that was up for debate; there wouldn't be anything they'd do about it anyway.

'Okay, so first we're going to X-ray her. See what's broken. Check for any internal bleeding. Once we know more, we'll tell you what we can do for her.'

'Do whatever you need to,' Gav said, his voice breaking.

Dr Singh nodded and picked up Violet, walking towards the door behind him. When Gav made to follow, Dr Singh turned. 'I'm afraid you can't come in the back. Either of you.'

'What? She's hurt. She's scared. She needs me with her.'

'I am sorry, but it is our policy.'

'Sod the policy,' Gav growled.

'Best you go home, sir,' Dr Singh said. 'We'll telephone you when we know more.'

Gav looked him square in the eye. He knew what the outcome would be if he went home. 'I'll wait.'

'So will I.' Meg's soft voice held a hint of steel.

Gav returned to his seat next to Cat Boy. He leaned back against a poster warning against canine and feline obesity and sighed. When he felt his phone vibrate in his pocket, he handed it, unlooked at, to Meg.

She adjusted Tyrion in her arms, glanced at the screen and felt her blood run cold.

60

IRINA

Louise (Klaus's Mum)

There might be no CCTV on the side of the park where Phil was found, but what's the chance there might be CCTV outside an East London boozer?

> Possible. Which one? Why?

See if Andy knows whether the CCTV outside the Bells shows the exact time Phil left.

> I'll ask. Exact time? Why?

'Andy?' she drawled.

He looked up from his phone, his pale eyes wary. 'Yeah?'

She wasn't sure what the right protocol was to ask a man she barely knew about a case he'd asked her to stay away from, but she had a feeling that a big clock somewhere was running down and the niceties could go and get stuffed.

'Who was Phil drinking with in the Bells that night?'

'I asked you to leave it,' Andy said, iron in his voice.

'Sure, of course. But you mentioned that he was drinking with someone, and you didn't say who. No CCTV to see who dumped his body, so hey, that was lucky for them. I was just wondering if there'd be CCTV outside a pub.'

'Irina ...' The iron in his voice turned to steel. 'I can't tell you, and I won't tell you. First, because it's sensitive information. Second, because I bloody *asked you to leave it to us*.'

'Yeah,' she continued, undeterred. 'You told me. But you keep forgetting, he was my friend. And in the week since I found him, two more of my friends have been attacked. And my dog was poisoned. What do you expect me to do? Nothing?'

'Exactly.'

Irina looked away. Two minutes ago, the plate on the table had held a few slices of cheese and a handful of crackers. Now, only the crackers remained and Irina hadn't seen Andy eat a thing. 'Hamish?'

Irina's wild gaze landed on him, sitting calmly on his bed in the corner. He was wearing the sort of too-innocent expression that children and dogs get when they know they've done something wrong.

'Hamish ...' She fell to her knees, shaking a finger at him. 'You know you're not supposed to eat cheese! Especially not now, when we've only just come back from the emergency vet!'

Hamish shot past her back, dodging her efforts to catch him. He scurried out of reach under the sofa. From his safe spot, he looked back at her, his dark Scottie eyes half hidden by grizzled old-man eyebrows.

Unrepentant.

'Jesus flippin' Christ, Irina!'

Andy's angry voice startled her enough that she banged her head on the coffee table.

Rubbed it angrily, she crawled out and looked over at him. 'What's your *problem*?'

'What's wrong with you? With all of you?'

He was no longer at the table. He'd moved to her desk while she was chasing Hamish. In one hand he held a half-eaten cracker. In the other, the legal pad she'd been writing on. He held it aloft, waving it around like a semaphore flag.

She sat back down, feeling as unrepentant as Hamish, who was still under the sofa behind her. 'What? That stupid woman almost killed Hamish. If I hadn't given him the Enterosgel, if I hadn't taken him to the emergency vet, he'd be dead. Because of her. Because she couldn't diagnose a poisoning. Couldn't get that crap out of him before he got pancreatitis! Scotties are prone to it. Did you know that?'

Andy's voice lost some of its heat. 'I know schnauzers, cockers and poodles are. I didn't know Scotties as well.'

'Well, you're not a vet, are you? She is. She should *know*!' Irina stood up and dusted her hands off on her legs. What did you think? That I wouldn't look up the reviews? They weren't as bad when I registered Hamish there, obviously, but now, it looks like one horror story after another.'

She snatched the notepad out of his hand and put it back on her desk. 'For heaven's sake, Andy. If you think I'm not going to lay the mother of all negligence claims on Caroline Aspen and her dodgy vet practice, think again!'

Andy's phone buzzed again. He picked it up and glanced at the screen. So, in the middle of an argument, his phone was more important.

She picked the notepad up and slammed it back down on the wooden desk. 'If your phone is so damn important, go. Go now.' She pointed one shaking hand at the door. 'Go and do not come back.'

61

MEG

Louise (Klaus's Mum)

> Are you on drugs? You can't possibly think the VETS had something to do with this?

Are you still with Gav –
how's he doing? How's
Violet?
TBH, I'm not convinced
of anything, but if you are
still at the vet, I need you
to ask them a question …

Gav was a mess. Meg understood it; she'd be in pieces if anything happened to Tyrion. She stroked the soft fur on the dachshund's head and kissed his ever-wet nose. *No purer love existed*, she thought, *than the love of a dog.*

She looked at Louise's text message again, fighting down a wave of nausea. As casually as she could, she stood up and sauntered over to the desk. She kept her eyes on the receptionists and softened her features, knowing how much people underestimated her when she did.

'Must be a tough job, working in a place like this.'

The battleaxe receptionist grunted.

'Just saying, I know what it's like. You need to pick up so many more things than just manning the phones.'

The woman looked at Meg with opaque eyes.

'Do you at least get to do some of the fun stuff?' Meg asked, adjusting Tyrion on her shoulder to avoid him scratching through the material of her blouse. Tyrion hated the vet's. Hated the receptionists. He would march her past the front every time they came close and tremble when they came inside. Usually, it broke Meg's heart, but today there were bigger issues.

'Fun stuff?' the receptionist scoffed.

'Sure. Like stocktakes.'

The battleaxe raised her thick, tattooed eyebrows a degree higher. 'Stocktakes are fun?'

'Well, no,' Meg said. 'They're probably quite dull. But the fun part is when things don't add up. Like, say, if you find out that a phial of acepromazine or, oh, diazepam has gone missing.'

'Diazepam is for humans,' Cat Boy said from behind her.

'Sure. Sure it is,' Meg said. 'But it's also used for dogs. What would you do if a phial or two went missing, Miss ...' Meg leaned closer and read the name on her tag. 'Ms Hoey? Or do you have a system to see who took something out and which animal it was administered to? Do you cross-reference to check that it really was given to that dog, or cat, or whatever? Or if it wasn't?'

'Are you accusing them of stealing drugs?' Cat Boy said, holding the wicker carry-case closer to his chest. Gav also paled, no doubt thinking of Violet in their care. Meg reflected that she probably should have waited until Violet was out of the surgery before asking Louise's questions.

'You accusing one of our people of *taking drugs*?' The battleaxe pulled herself up. 'We're not that sort of business.'

'No, not at all,' Meg said, keeping her eyes on the woman and her senses primed and alert. 'I'm not saying anyone *used* the drugs themselves. I'm just wondering about the possibility of taking them to sedate someone else. Like someone who's been causing problems for the surgery.' She noticed a vague shape that had paused on the other side of the semi-transparent door behind the reception desk. 'Someone like Philip Creasy.'

She smiled and Gav blinked, again seeing that core of steel in the little woman. Meg levelled her gaze at the receptionist. 'You remember him, don't you? His dog died here last December. He came in around a week or two ago, didn't he?'

The battleaxe didn't waste time shooting down the accusation, though her mousey colleague's face had gone from pale to sickly-grey. But a sudden crash from the back drew Meg's attention. She pushed past the two women and through the door after the shadowy shape, catching a fleeting glimpse as it ducked behind some shelves. It was the same size and shape as Dr Ben.

Dr Ben, FFS. She'd *trusted* him! And what? He'd killed Phil? She couldn't believe it, but innocent men didn't run. Not like that.

'Violet!' Gav howled. Meg heard the door she'd just burst through bang against the wall behind her and knew Gav had followed her into Village Vets' inner sanctum.

Holding a terrified Tyrion against her chest, she sprinted past shelves lined with medications, but the figure in the blue scrubs moved faster than she could with Tyrion's long body clinging to her shoulder. He struggled for balance, his claws digging into her skin.

She ignored the pain, evading the boxes that had fallen in her way and following the figure out of the back door and into the car park. Nothing seemed to move, not a man, not a car. 'Damn,' she muttered, slightly out of breath.

She was about to turn around and face the irate battle-axe when she spotted a flash of blue by the canal, moving north.

'Got you,' she said and pulled out her phone, putting Tyrion on the ground so that she could type faster.

62

LOUISE

Partridge Bark

Sophie (Loki's Mum)

My brothers just
finished giving witness
statements.

Sophie (Loki's Mum)

@**Gav** & @**Meg**, they'll
want to talk to you too.
Nice roundhouse kick,
@**Meg** — remind me not to
piss you off!

'Will you stop it with the ducks, Luther?' I braced myself as Jake's Staffie lunged at two Egyptian geese, their normally stoned expressions changing to alarm. They squawked and took flight. Luther, clearly feeling better after sunshine, fresh air and a long walk, came close to yanking my arm from my shoulder in his need to give chase. 'If you drag me into the canal, I will never forgive you.'

My phone vibrated again.

'Stay,' I ordered. 'Both of you.' I switched Klaus's lead to my other hand and pulled out my phone.

Partridge Bark

Meg (Tyrion's Mum)

He bolted. It was Dr Ben, of all people, and he's fast. Running up the canal, heading north. The receptionist – the little one – ran away too. One of the people in the waiting room is running after her. Anyone nearby?

Claire (Tank's Mum)

I see her running down the high street. I'm going after her.

I was right!

It *was* Cooper, and he wasn't working alone.

I looked around for the familiar shape of Ben Cooper. We were still north of the surgery and as occupied as the boys had kept me, I was certain I would have noticed him pass by.

Ben Cooper had to still be ahead of us. I slipped the phone into my pocket and eased the boys into a trot, scanning the area ahead on both sides of the canal.

The leaves were in full season, lush and green. Some parts of the path were overgrown and blackberry brambles clawed at my clothes and arms; I ignored them.

'He's not getting past us,' I promised. The words were barely out of my mouth when I saw a flash of blue on the far side of the canal. Bright blue, like the scrubs the vets wore. 'Damn.'

Our trot became a lope, and the lope became a sprint for the bridge. I was worried that I'd have to carry Klaus, but he was straining against his lead.

The bridge was old, with uneven paving stones that allowed pedestrians (or people towing boats) to get a better foothold when the ground was wet. It was pretty, but dire to run over. The timing had to be precise, or you'd trip.

Pulled by two dogs that thought they were trying out for some Alaskan sled race, I mistimed it. My toe smashed against a protruding brick, and I felt myself soar through the air, powered by the twin engines of Staffie and sausage. I put my hands out to break my fall and the bricks scraped the skin from my palms and knees, even more so as the dogs, their leads still wrapped around my wrists, propelled me forward for another few metres.

While I lay there, winded, there was another scrape of neoprene against flesh, and Luther pulled free, his lead trailing behind him. Klaus gave me a concerned look, as if he was wondering whether he should stay with me or follow his friend, but with his lead still firmly around my wrist, he didn't have a choice.

'Luther! Come back here!'

Only he didn't. He had better prey in his sights. Better even than an Egyptian goose: he had the chance of running down a *vet*.

I scrambled to my feet, grabbed Klaus and sprinted after Luther.

Dr Cooper was rounding a corner, pushing past a blackberry bramble. He couldn't have seen what was on the other side.

While a Staffie at rest resembles a happy land hippo, when running, with their heavy muscles rippling, they are things of beauty.

Luther leapt, catching the vet at the shoulders, the force of the impact knocking Dr Cooper backwards. He landed hard, his head bouncing once against the packed dirt path, then lay still, with twenty kilos of muscled Staffordshire terrier on his chest and his eyes closed.

'Luther, down!' I shouted, not sure if he would obey.

Luther looked at me, his normally amiable features almost scowling. He growled low in his throat, but obeyed, stretching out on top of the vet.

Dr Benjamin Cooper wasn't going anywhere, any-time soon.

I reached them, setting Klaus down. 'Dr Cooper? Ben?'

Nothing, no response. I leaned down, my fingers against his neck. Relieved to find that his pulse was still strong.

I didn't trust him not to try something, and I didn't trust Luther unrestrained either, not with the canal's ducks so close. I slipped his lead back round my wrist and unclipped Klaus, wrapping his orange, hedgehog-festooned lead around Cooper's hands and feet. As I stepped back to view my work, Klaus moved forward, raised one stumpy leg and weed on the vet's shoulder.

'Well done, baby,' I said. Pulling out the phone, I let the Pack know that I'd managed to apprehend Dr Cooper by the old stone bridge, asking whether someone could call the police and telling Irina to let DC Andy know what had happened.

Partridge Bark

DC Andrew Thompson

Stay where you are, Louise. I'm on my way. Claire, keep the receptionist on the high street if you can. Williams isn't far.

'That was fast,' I said, and then did a double-take, confirming that I'd messaged the Pack and not Andy.

When had Irina added him to the chat?

Holy crap, had he been following everything we'd been doing?

'You all right, love?' an older man said from a nearby narrowboat. His shirt was off, baring a less than svelte figure, but his kind eyes were taking in my bleeding hands and knees.

The sounds of sirens cut through the afternoon, and in moments, I could see DC Andy's gangly figure making his way along the canal path.

He skidded to a halt. If he was impressed by my creativity in securing Dr Cooper with a lead, he kept it to himself, pulling a set of handcuffs from his rucksack.

I pulled Luther away to give Andy space to do his job. He checked for a pulse first, and for a moment, I felt panic set in. 'He was alive a few minutes ago.'

'Still is,' Andy said, neatly replacing Klaus's orange hedgehog lead with a pair of steel handcuffs. He handed it back to me. 'I'll take it from here. You might want to take the boys home and clean yourself up.'

I looked down. My palms and knees hadn't looked like that since childhood, but I wasn't about to apologise for it.

Dr Cooper stirred. He moved his head, his eyes slowly blinking us into focus. Klaus growled and I held him closer.

DC Andy stepped forward.

'Dr Benjamin Cooper, I'm arresting you for the murder of Philip Creasy.'

A little part of me unlocked, and with each of his words I felt the stress of the past week ebb away.

'You do not have to say anything. But it may harm your defence if you do not mention when questioned something which you later rely on in court. Anything you do say may be given in evidence . . .'

What he didn't offer Ben Cooper was the right to clean Klaus's wee from his face and shoulder, but I wasn't about to suggest that. Andy hauled the vet to his feet. With one hand on Cooper's bound wrists, he steered him back along the canal.

'Wait.'

Andy turned round and raised a fair brow at me.

'The receptionist?'

'What you and your friends did was dangerous and irresponsible,' he said, not answering my question. 'I cannot condone vigilantism, in any form.'

Abruptly, he turned and walked away. I blinked at the shirtless man, whose bemused gaze followed Andy and Cooper up the ramp to the high street.

'You want to come inside and get yourself cleaned up, miss?' he asked.

'No, I'm fine,' I responded. 'Just happy to see justice being done.'

'For a change,' he grunted, and carried on along the canal.

'For a change,' I echoed, with a smile.

63

ETHAN

'Get her,' the woman with the funky hair screamed, and Ethan didn't think twice; he'd heard enough.

'Watch her!' he told the old man, pushing Marlowe's wicker basket towards him. He followed the skinny receptionist down the road, past the cut-through to the canal. He lengthened his stride, easily passing a stocky blonde woman with crazy curls, barely hanging on to an equally stout pale dog with a squashed-in face, big ears and bigger teeth. Both were wheezing as they ran.

The skinny woman barged into a rubbish bin so that it fell behind her, spilling recycling out into the street. Ethan leapt over it, his fists clenching but his breathing evening out.

She tried it again with one of the council's bins, but it wouldn't budge, losing her time.

Ethan could see he was gaining on her, seeing her

mousey ponytail getting closer and closer. He reached for her, but she was still just that bit too far away.

She neared an intersection, and he knew that if she made it across and he didn't, that would be it. So, he closed his eyes and dug deep for just a little bit more strength, a bit more speed. And leapt again, this time leading with his arms, grabbing her around the waist and landing them both on the hard pavement.

She writhed, digging her nails into his hands, trying to get away, but he gripped her harder.

A pair of black trainers came into view, with two sets of black paws on either side. 'Well done, mate,' someone said with an incongruous French accent.

Ethan looked up, following black trainers to black jeans to a black T-shirt printed with a spoof Star Wars picture of a Stormtrooper with an AT-AT-like dog, which was raising a massive robotic leg to wee on something. The human was short, and very possibly just as hairy as the big black Labrador retrievers on either side of him. 'Nice run, my friend.'

Ethan nodded, afraid to get up, but even more afraid that the receptionist would get away.

'Bloody everlasting hell,' someone wheezed from behind him. Over his shoulder, the stocky woman with the stocky dog had stopped; her hands were on her knees while she caught her breath. Her dog discreetly vomited beside her.

'So, what do we do?' the Frenchman asked.

It was a good question, Ethan thought, still holding the receptionist in place. 'Anyone want to help me with this one?'

'She isn't going anywhere,' the woman said. 'The police are already on their way.'

Which meant that it could be anytime between now and Godot showing up. The man and woman were both focused on their phones, neither making a move to help him up. One of the Labs lay down so that they were eye to eye with him, and Ethan wondered what it would do if he edged backwards away from it.

He sighed and did his best to avoid the doggy breath in front of him, the smell of sweat and fear from below and the barfing bulldog by his feet.

'Can someone check to see if Marlowe – my cat – is okay?' he asked, and held on to the receptionist just a little tighter as a car pulled up to the kerb beside him.

'Weeeelll,' another voice said. 'What do we have here?'

From the ground, the man looked enormous, but in truth, he wasn't that much taller than the guy with the Labs. Just broader. Like a rugby player. And holding a set of handcuffs. With his free hand, he flashed a warrant card. 'Detective Constable Williams,' he said, dropping to one knee beside Ethan. He leaned closer to the woman. 'And you, madam, are under arrest for the murder of Philip Creasy.'

64

LOUISE

Partridge Bark

Claire (Tank's Mum)

Some guy just tackled the receptionist, but Tank and Paul's labs joined in the fun, so we've got to give them some credit or they'll feel left out. I'm off to write this up – and if anyone gives this story to the Beeb or any other news outlet, I'll kick them into next week.

Fiona (Nala's Mum)

Exclusive breaking news from *The Chronicle*? 😉

Claire (Tank's Mum)

Damn straight!

Meg (Tyrion's Mum)

Well done! Dr Chet bandaged up Violet and Gav just took her home. I say we meet at the Hound for a victory drink!

Yaz (Hercules's Mum)

Seconded!

Claire (Tank's Mum)

I'll meet you there as soon as I submit the story. Text me if there are any updates.

I went home, took a shower and did my best to clean up my bloody knees and palms, cursing as the disinfectant burned like hell. I bathed Luther and Klaus while I was at it. Then, with the boys smelling of baby powder and shampoo and me smelling mostly of antibac, we headed out again.

I entered the pub through the side gate, arriving in a small beer garden. My friends were easy enough to find, ranged along the far wall. Meg was sitting next to a young man. She looked tired, but her eyes shone. Across from her, Yaz leaned back, keeping Hercules on a very short lead. Paul had no such decorum; Bark Vader and Jimmy Chew were lounging in the sun by his feet.

'I thought I'd be late,' I said, easing onto an empty chair that had been pulled up to the table.

'Nah, the others are on their way,' Yaz said. 'Cat Boy only just arrived.'

'Ethan,' the young man corrected her. He ran his fingers through hair that looked like it had been styled after some manga character and held out a hand to introduce himself. We both looked at the bandages swathing mine and he offered an embarrassed smile instead.

'Schrödinger here had to take kitty home, so he wouldn't need to worry if the cat in the box was alive or dead.' Yaz lifted a pint glass.

'Marlowe,' Ethan sighed. 'The cat's called Marlowe.'

Paul leaned over and clinked his glass with Ethan's. A cat-loving guy dressed like a manga hero, bonding with a Frenchman who was into dogs and Star Wars. It made a strange kind of sense, if you didn't think about it too hard.

'Ethan was the one who ran down the receptionist from Village Vets. I figured we owe him for that,' Meg said, the tone in her voice offering more than a hint of her interest in him.

'The skinny one, or the one that looks like a rugby prop?'

'But of course, the skinny one,' Paul said. 'And to be fair, she was moving quite fast.'

'Welcome to the Pack, Ethan,' I said. 'Can I get you another drink?'

Ethan looked at Luther and paled.

'Don't worry about him. As far as I know, he only hates vets. Yaz, hang on to their leads for a second?'

I went inside and ordered another round. While Sheri prepared the drinks, I fired off a message to Jake, letting him know Luther was a hero and where to find me when he got back into town. And another to Grace, in case she wanted to stop by for a drink.

Sheri put my glass of Sauvignon Blanc in front of me and glanced at my hands. 'You going to be okay to drink that?'

'I'll be better after I finish it,' I grinned. 'Disinfecting myself from the inside out.'

'Looks rough.'

'You should see the other guy.'

'You were involved with that? The vet that got arrested?' She picked up the tray with the others' drinks and gestured for me to lead the way. 'The next round is on the Hound, Lou.'

'He was supposed to get eight teeth removed,' Meg's new friend was saying as we returned. 'But when I heard what was going on, I couldn't risk it. I registered somewhere else. He'll have them removed next week.'

'Little Meggie's latest stray,' Yaz murmured to me.

'Where's Claire?' I asked.

'You have to ask?' I didn't, and we both spoke at the same time, 'She's at home, writing up the story for *The Chronicle*.'

Irina arrived next, carrying Hamish. She nodded to Sheri and sat down beside me. As soon as she set Hamish down, he lunged for Klaus and in moments they were rolling around the floor by our ankles.

'At least now we know what Andy was doing with your phone that time?'

Irina glared at me. 'I don't know what you are talking about.'

She was either playing stupid, or playing to the crowd. Whichever it was, I was happy to explain to the others. 'Andy added his name to the Pack chat while he had Irina's phone.' I turned back to her. 'Unless it was you who added him?'

Her sour face made it clear that she hadn't.

'Wait,' Yaz said. 'He was in the group? Our group? This whole time?' She lowered her glasses and gave me a stern look. 'You gonna kick him out, or shall I?'

'Look, if he hadn't been in the chat, then I'd still be on the canal path, waiting for the police to arrive. I might not like his methods, but I'm grateful for the results.'

'Keep telling yourself that when he violates your phone, your trust,' Irina said grimly, reaching for my glass and taking a large sip.

One by one, the rest of the Pack filtered in. Ejiro. Fiona and Nala, along with Ella, who reported seeing two cars being towed from the vet's little parking lot: Cooper's Merc and an old Ford. Indy came in with Banjo, tossing him a well-chewed tennis ball but not making an excuse when he ignored the other dogs to lie under the table and gnaw on it some more.

'Right,' Irina said, with another gulp of my wine. 'Anyone want to find out what I learned while Meg and Lou were taking down the bad guys?'

She didn't wait for a response. 'I think Phil knew Dr Cooper had made a mistake when he was treating Alfie. Maybe it was a misdiagnosis, maybe something worse. But I found a woman who wrote a review not long afterwards describing a confrontation between him and a man accusing him of malpractice. I spoke to her, and we're both pretty sure it was Phil.'

I leaned back and tried to flex my fingers, feeling the tightness of the makeshift bandages. 'I think Phil had suspicions that something was off when Alfie died. Maybe he suspected that Alfie's diagnosis was wrong and then kept a watchful eye on the surgery.'

Paul pointed to Luther. 'Maybe he noticed poisonings in the neighbourhood and tracked it back to them? I mean, who else benefits?'

'But no, that can't be right,' Ella disagreed. 'He's a vet, his job is to *save* animals. And if Phil had proof, why wouldn't he go to the police?'

'He didn't have any proof, I suppose,' I said. 'But I'm guessing that he threatened to expose Cooper.'

'Oh my God,' Meg said, her eyes welling up. 'I had no idea, or I'd never have invited him to join our meeting on Thursday. I'm so sorry . . .'

Irina took another big gulp from my glass. 'Whatever the reason, I reckon that when it kicked off, the bitch on reception alerted the other vets and they threw Phil out. But instead of going home, he went across the street to the Bells, waiting for Cooper to leave the surgery. Cooper must have seen him go in there and sent the receptionist over. She dosed Phil with something strong enough to slow him down. Maybe give Cooper enough time to get out. Or call the police. Whatever.'

'She drugged him?' Ethan asked, wide-eyed.

'Looks like it,' I said. 'Maybe it didn't have enough time to take effect, as it didn't slow him down too much. He saw Cooper leaving the surgery and rushed after him. There must have been another tussle. I'm not sure exactly what happened, but Phil ended up dead. Cooper bragged to me about a new Merc he had delivered this week. I wouldn't be surprised if he'd stashed Phil in the old one, and as soon as he dumped the body, he dumped the car too, to get rid of any forensic links to the murder.'

Sheri reappeared, this time carrying a bucket and half a dozen glasses on a tray. Behind her, Gav eased in with Violet in his arms, a Cone of Shame around her neck. Her dazed black eyes moved to each of the dogs around us, almost daring them to make fun of her. She was about a 5 out of 10 on Violet's Demented Scale, which was pretty good going for the day she'd had.

'That was a remarkably fast trip to A & E,' Meg said.

Gav gave her a one-shouldered shrug. 'A mate saw to my ribs. Bruised, not broken. Same with Violet. We were lucky that the kid who kicked her was only wearing trainers and not heavy boots. And that she moves fast for an old girl.'

Violet squinted and leaned closer to Meg, who obligingly gave her a treat. I tried to hide my surprise. Violet had never accepted a treat from me.

'She bit his ankle,' Meg said. 'I'd have her watch my back any day.'

Sheri put down the tray and uncorked a bottle of Bolly. 'I'll be back in a sec with your lager, Gav.'

He nodded, but his attention was on Meg. 'And I'd have you watch mine. Thank you,' Gav said.

'It wasn't just me, Sophie's brothers helped.'

Yaz pointed a finger at me. 'Before I forget, you're gonna need to let Annabel know what happened.'

'Me?' I blinked. 'Why?'

'She thinks you're trying to fix her up with Dr Cooper.' Yaz leaned back in her chair and rested her hand on Herc's head. 'She mentioned it when I saw her on Friday. Though, I'd be careful: when she finds out he's a murderer, she might just murder you.'

'The posh girl's good people,' Gav growled, pouring the champagne. 'She'll laugh. Maybe tell her daddy she had a brush with rough.' He paused, noticing Ethan. 'So, you're running with the dog pack now, Cat Boy?'

'Ethan,' Cat Boy corrected, grinning and raising his glass.

Sophie and her brothers arrived; one of them unclipped

Loki's lead, watching him join the canine scrum. Sophie took a seat on the far side of the Pack, her cool gaze slipping off Irina's.

She definitely knows about Irina, I realised. And yet, she hadn't dumped Tim. And *that* was nothing short of a miracle.

I looked up from the assorted dogs' antics to see DC Andy leaning in the pub doorway, half hidden behind a potted lemon tree. I had no idea how long he'd been standing there, but figured it took a lot of guts to show up after the way Irina had treated him.

'How long have you standing there?' Irina had also spotted him.

'Long enough.'

I pushed a chair back. 'Join us, Andy.'

He looked as though he wasn't sure whether he'd rather walk on hot coals, but the others nodded and ignored Irina when she muttered 'Sneak'. She made a point of looking away from him, her eyes on her phone and a message from As Was with an accompanying dog emoji.

'Any news you can share?' I asked Andy, mortified by my friend's behaviour.

Paul handed him a beer and the detective took a long sip before answering. His eyes met mine.

'We've just put out a statement,' Andy said. 'We've arrested two suspects for the murder of Mr Creasy.'

'Did Cooper say anything about poisoning our animals?' Paul asked.

Andy, about to sit down, paused. 'I'm afraid I can't share any more than that.'

Irina took a deep breath and leaned in towards him.

'There's no evidence that Hamish's falling ill was down to Cooper,' Andy pointed out before she could speak.

'Seems too much of a coincidence for it not to be.' Yaz shook her head. 'Jesus.'

'I'm going to kill him,' Irina growled. 'And I'll make it slow. I'm gonna go after him *legally*. And I'm gonna go after Village Vets, because the others had to know what he was doing. Especially if Phil had lodged complaints. I want that place closed. I want them rotting in jail. With no friends, no family, no money.'

'Whatever you can claw off them, give it to the shelters,' Meg suggested.

Irina nodded. 'Dr Cooper has built a pretty lavish lifestyle off the backs of our dogs. Nice trips around the UK and abroad. Michelin-starred restaurants. Property. All the vets have. There will be a paper trail, and I will find it.'

'To be honest, I'm still trying to get my head around that part. How could that be worth it?' I murmured. I turned to Andy. 'What about the receptionist? Did she confess to drugging Phil?'

Before he could repeat that he wasn't allowed to tell us anything, Yaz spoke. 'Freya Willis has fancied Cooper for ages. Betcha she'd have done anything for him. Maybe even slipping Phil something to slow him down. Give Coop enough time to leave the surgery.'

Irina studied me. 'Maybe she fancied him enough to take out the competition?'

'What do you mean?'

Her laser gaze moved to Andy but she still seemed to be

speaking to me. 'Want to bet that old Ford that Ella saw being towed was blue? A blue Ford, like the one that tried to run you down the other night?'

'Jesus.' I exhaled. 'She actually wanted to kill *me*?'

'You were the one asking questions, Lou. So you became another target.' Yaz pointed her glass at me. 'Or maybe she just didn't like the good doctor's interest in you.'

'But he's creepy!' As soon as the words came out, I realised that I sounded like a five-year-old, but I couldn't stop myself from adding, 'And a murderer!'

'I don't think she saw that side of him,' Meg said. 'She heard him asking about you. Saw you two go out for a drink. Watched him go with us all to the pub the other night.'

'But it was you who invited him!'

Meg shook her head. 'Doesn't matter. She read more into it, when realistically he might only have been trying to find out what we knew about the case. No offence, Louise.'

'Wait a second.' I held up a finger, trying to get my head around the situation. Realising that my hands had begun to shake, I laid them flat on the table. 'You're saying that the car that almost hit me a few days ago . . . the first time. That was her too?'

Irina refilled her glass, nonchalant. 'Wouldn't be surprised.'

'But that was before the trip to the pub. Before I had the drink with him. Almost exactly before . . .'

Irina took a sip. 'Yes?'

'But why would she see me as a threat that early? Had he . . .'

'Known you were the one who found the body?' Meg said. 'I'd bet he knew within a day or two. Paul said something in the chat about you and Irina finding the body, didn't he? Someone could have mentioned it to Cooper. When I saw him, I thought he was just keen on you. Sorry, Lou.'

That was a lot to take in. I gulped down the wine in my glass and refilled it.

'So in the span of a week, you have a vet and his receptionist, two "decent upstanding members of the community", killing a man to protect themselves. Poisoning two dogs – that we know of. And trying to kill me. Christ Almighty.'

'We have no confirmation that they poisoned Luther or Hamish,' Paul said.

'And I don't think Freya or Dr Cooper meant to kill Phil. They . . . their job was to save lives,' Meg continued. 'But they wanted to save themselves more. I agree, I think Freya only wanted to slow Phil down. Maybe Dr Cooper did take a syringe of something with him to protect himself, or maybe he didn't. The coroner might have found an injection site, or not. Maybe it was an overdose, or a reaction or something, but the upshot is that Phil Creasy was dead.'

Andy listened, his expression noncommittal, which more or less told me we were on to something.

'Wouldn't a scalpel have been a better choice?' Fi asked.

'Not for someone whose preferred weapon is poison,' Yaz said. 'A scalpel would leave an open wound, and those things are messy. Blood might get on his nice shirt.'

Cold fear iced down my spine, and I spoke, more to distract myself from the peril I hadn't known I was in. 'He'll plead self-defence, won't he? An accident, not murder.'

Andy took a sip of beer. He might not be able to share any information with us – I understood that; he needed to make sure the case was clean when it got to court – but despite Irina being, well, *Irina* to him, he'd still shown up for us. And that meant a lot.

'He won't get away with it,' Irina said. 'Not if I can help it. Once the criminal trial is over, the civil ones will begin. Dr Cooper might not be dead, but I can promise you, he will be destroyed.'

'What about them kids that attacked me and Violet?' Gav asked. 'And the ones that put her man in hospital?' He pointed his beer in Sophie's direction.

'That's not my case, but I can say that Dr Cooper swears he had nothing to do with the attacks on either you or Mr Aziz.'

'What about the woman? Willis.'

Andy shook his head. 'No. And I believe them. If you want my opinion, though – and it is only an opinion?'

Gav nodded.

'Well, it might have been a case of wrong place, wrong time, but you have a big name, Mr MacAdams. And a bigger reputation around here. Might be that those kids wanted to make a name for themselves by taking you down.'

'Me? I'm just an old man.'

One side of Andy's mouth twitched. 'An old man who was once a legend on this patch. They might be new to the area, but someone would have told them. Maybe pointed you out. And after the first attack, well, they'd be looking for retribution.'

'You arrested them?'

'A couple of uniforms brought them in earlier. As I said, it's not my case, but I hear there were plenty of witnesses, including some of the people around this table,' Andy said.

'And what about the pretty boy? Her man?' Gav pointed to Sophie again.

Interesting that it was Gav who was asking the question and not Sophie herself. Her expression betrayed her interest, but she didn't seem as angry as I would have been if it were my boyfriend who'd been beaten badly enough to require an overnight stay in hospital.

Andy shook his head. 'Sorry. No one's holding their hand up for that one.'

Why wasn't Sophie angry? Pressuring the police to find Tim's attackers? Why didn't she want justice for him? He might not be the best boyfriend, but . . .

I stared at her and blinked in realisation.

Sophie was tall; as tall as Tim. It stood to reason that her brothers would also be tall, if three of them had been able to restrain the five kids. What if . . . What if they knew that Tim was cheating on Sophie? What if they'd decided to take it into their own hands?

Would Tim rat on them?

No, or at least I didn't think he would. Being beaten up by a gang brought a lot more sympathy than being beaten up by your girlfriend's brothers because you were a cheating swine. Or maybe he didn't want to betray

Sophie further by getting her brothers into trouble with the police. Instead, he'd maintain that he hadn't seen who attacked him; too dark to get a good look and all.

It was only speculation, but it felt right.

Andy sipped his beer. 'Not my case,' he reminded us. 'Louise, your phone is buzzing.'

I glanced at the message and smiled.

Jake (Luther's Dad)

> Well done, Luther! Thanks for watching him. Just got home – knackered. Place is too quiet without the brute. Give a shout when you're going to drop him off and I'll open that bottle.

As far as an offer for a date went, it didn't even make it onto the scale, but it would be good to see Jake again. I stood and picked up Klaus. Checked to make sure Luther's lead was still around my wrist. 'Well then, that's us off.'

'So early?'

'Gotta take Luther home to his dad.'

Gav was the first to raise his glass, but the others followed swiftly. 'You're a walking disaster,' he said. 'But you've got brass, girl. And determination. We wouldn't be here without you.'

'You wouldn't, for sure,' Yaz said, but leaned up to kiss his weathered cheek. 'Thought we'd never get you to drink anywhere but the George.'

Ejiro put a hand on his partner's shoulder and said to me, 'Thanks for seeing this through, Lou.' He raised his glass as well.

I nodded and ducked my head, feeling oddly exposed. I gave my friends an awkward smile and picked up the wine glass that had found itself edging towards Irina. 'To all of us,' I countered. 'No. To the Dog Park Detectives.'

'"Dog Park Detectives", huh?' Yaz tried the syllables out and nodded. 'I like it.'

'To the Dog Park Detectives.' Irina raised someone else's glass and gave Andy a rebellious glare. 'Unleashed.'

Acknowledgements

When I came up with the idea for *The Dog Park Detectives*, I wasn't sure if it was brilliant or barking mad, so I called my agent. James Wills is a great agent and a terrific sounding board, but when I finished the pitch he was uncharacteristically silent (at which point I was convinced it was a crappy idea). Then he said, 'It should have been done to death, but for some reason, it hasn't. Write it. Write it now.' And as James's advice is always solid (please don't tell him I said that), I did.

I couldn't be happier when he found a home for the series with Simon & Schuster and the legend that is Katherine Armstrong. Kath is more than just the firm hand on *The Dog Park Detectives*' lead, elevating it to the story you're reading now; she's become a good friend, championing my stories, sharing my love of a good Douro red – and allowing me to spam her with puppy pics! Any mistakes that are in the book are mine alone.

People think that writing is a solitary sport, and if that's true, publishing certainly isn't. I am incredibly grateful to have not only Katherine but the rest of the Simon &

Schuster dream team (my 'Publishing Pack') in my corner. Many, many thanks to Georgie Leighton, Jess Barratt, Rich Vlietstra, Ben Phillips and Amy Fletcher.

So, *how exactly* did the story come about? Well, shortly after my second spy book (*Resistance*) was released, my friend and fellow author Kate Bradley offered excellent advice: 'Always have an idea for something completely different in your back pocket.' Up until that point, I wrote WW2 espionage . . . I wasn't sure what else I *could* write. As I was muttering that aloud, my dachshund gave me the infamous side-eye, and I realised that it was time to write about what I knew, not just what I had fun researching. Kate, for that advice alone, I owe you wine. A lot of wine.

The Dude is a pandemic puppy, and until I brought him home, I had no idea about the community that flourished around the local dog park. Not unlike a school yard (or how I imagine one to be), our park brought together people from just about every walk of life with at least one common interest: our love of dogs. And while I haven't written any of my pack into *The Dog Park Detectives*, they certainly provided inspiration, so a tremendous shout-out (and much love) to the Real Dog Mums of East London, the ever-fabulous Kalpna Chauhan, Claudia Braglia Hernandez, Eser Sarachoglou, Jenna Fong Sing, Jay Ersapah, Opor Ploynita, Chantal Coleman, Petra Losch, Becki Pedley and Imogen Webb. (Apologies if I've accidentally missed anyone out!) And a massive thanks to our friend Dan Gustavina, who minds the Dude when I need time to focus on work.

I must stress that Partridge Park and the *Dog Park*

Detectives Pack are fictional, and set in a fabricated area of East London. With the exception of Klaus, who is shamelessly based on the Dude, and my friend Samuel Osman, who convinced me to use his name, all people, dogs and situations are completely made up.

I am immensely grateful to my MOD Squad Beta Readers, Kelly West, Catie Logan and Gerry Cavanagh. My old team didn't disappoint, cheering me on and rooting out any inconsistencies in the draft.

On the other side of the pond, my brother Stephen has been a rock, and his kids Matthew and Alexandra are ever my shining stars. I am so lucky to be able to call them family. Matthew, I promise: one day we will write that book together!

And let's not forget naming (but never shaming) the rest of my friends who make sure my glass is half full: Sharon Galer, Martina Tromsdorf, Monique Mandalia-Sharma, Steve Carter, Tom Mac, Alison Turner, Aneta Wojcik, Leigh Oliphant, Lisa Rosier and Zara and Brian Ransley.

Last, but never least, my beloved Dude, who inspired this journey and has been with me every little step of the way. I never realised how much I could love the little monster, but every day I love him more.

He and his four-legged friends approve of this story – I hope you do too.

Blake Mara x